CHRISTOPHER BUSH
MURDER AT FENWOLD

CHRISTOPHER BUSH was born Charlie Christmas Bush in Norfolk in 1885. His father was a farm labourer and his mother a milliner. In the early years of his childhood he lived with his aunt and uncle in London before returning to Norfolk aged seven, later winning a scholarship to Thetford Grammar School.

As an adult, Bush worked as a schoolmaster for 27 years, pausing only to fight in World War One, until retiring aged 46 in 1931 to be a full-time novelist. His first novel featuring the eccentric Ludovic Travers was published in 1926, and was followed by 62 additional Travers mysteries. These are all to be republished by Dean Street Press.

Christopher Bush fought again in World War Two, and was elected a member of the prestigious Detection Club. He died in 1973.

By Christopher Bush

CHRISTOPHER BUSH

MURDER AT FENWOLD

With an introduction
by Curtis Evans

DEAN STREET PRESS

To

MRS. ROBERT BARCLAY

of

Broclamont House,
Ballymena

Perhaps you don't believe me; well,

It doesn't really matter.

The world will still go round you see

And little pigs grow fatter.

REED MOORHOUSE.

INTRODUCTION

THAT ONCE vast and mighty legion of bright young (and youngish) British crime writers who began publishing their ingenious tales of mystery and imagination during what is known as the Golden Age of detective fiction (traditionally dated from 1920 to 1939) had greatly diminished by the iconoclastic decade of the Sixties, many of these writers having become casualties of time. Of the 38 authors who during the Golden Age had belonged to the Detection Club, a London-based group which included within its ranks many of the finest writers of detective fiction then plying the craft in the United Kingdom, just over a third remained among the living by the second half of the 1960s, while merely seven—Agatha Christie, Anthony Gilbert, Gladys Mitchell, Margery Allingham, John Dickson Carr, Nicholas Blake and Christopher Bush—were still penning crime fiction.

In 1966--a year that saw the sad demise, at the too young age of 62, of Margery Allingham--an executive with the English book publishing firm Macdonald reflected on the continued popularity of the author who today is the least well known among this tiny but accomplished crime writing cohort: Christopher Bush (1885-1973), whose first of his three score and three series detective novels, *The Plumley Inheritance*, had appeared fully four decades earlier, in 1926. "He has a considerable public, a 'steady Bush public,' a public that has endured through many years," the executive boasted of Bush. "He never presents any problem to his publisher, who knows exactly how many copies of a title may be safely printed for the loyal Bush fans; the number is a healthy one too." Yet in 1968, just a couple of years after the Macdonald editor's affirmation of Bush's notable popular duration as a crime writer, the author, now in his 83rd year, bade farewell to mystery fiction with a final detective novel, *The Case of the Prodigal Daughter*, in which, like in Agatha Christie's *Third Girl* (1966), copious references are made, none too favorably, to youthful sex, drugs and rock and roll. Afterwards, outside of the reprinting in the UK in the early 1970s of a scattering of classic Bush titles from the Golden Age, Bush's books, in contrast with those of Christie, Carr, Allingham and Blake, disappeared from mass circulation in both the UK and the US, becoming fervently sought (and ever more unobtainable) treasures by collectors and connoisseurs of classic crime fiction. Now, in one of the signal developments in vintage mystery publishing, Dean Street Press is reprinting all 63 Christopher Bush detective novels. These will be published over a period of months, beginning with the release of books 1 to 10 in the series.

Few Golden Age British mystery writers had backgrounds as humble yet simultaneously mysterious, dotted with omissions and evasions, as Christopher Bush, who was born Charlie Christmas Bush on the day of the Nativity in 1885 in the Norfolk village of Great Hockham, to Charles Walter Bush and his second wife, Eva Margaret Long. While the father of Christopher Bush's Detection Club colleague and near exact contemporary Henry Wade (the pseudonym of Henry Lancelot Aubrey-Fletcher) was a baronet who lived in an elegant Georgian mansion and claimed extensive ownership of fertile English fields, Christopher's father resided in a cramped cottage and toiled in fields as a farm laborer, a term that in the late Victorian and Edwardian era, his son lamented many years afterward, "had in it something of contempt....There was something almost of serfdom about it."

Charles Walter Bush was a canny though mercurial individual, his only learning, his son recalled, having been "acquired at the Sunday school." A man of parts, Charles was a tenant farmer of three acres, a thatcher, bricklayer and carpenter (fittingly for the father of a detective novelist, coffins were his specialty), a village radical and a most adept poacher. After a flight from Great Hockham, possibly on account of his poaching activities, Charles, a widower with a baby son whom he had left in the care of his mother, resided in London, where he worked for a firm of spice importers. At a dance in the city, Charles met Christopher's mother, Eva Long, a lovely and sweet-natured young milliner and bonnet maker, sweeping her off her feet with a combination of "good looks and a certain plausibility." After their marriage the couple left London to live in a tiny rented cottage in Great Hockham, where Eva over the next eighteen years gave birth to three sons and five daughters and perforce learned the challenging ways of rural domestic economy.

Decades later an octogenarian Christopher Bush, in his memoir *Winter Harvest: A Norfolk Boyhood* (1967), characterized Great Hockham as a rustic rural redoubt where many of the words that fell from the tongues of the native inhabitants "were those of Shakespeare, Milton and the Authorised Version....Still in general use were words that were standard in Chaucer's time, but had since lost a certain respectability." Christopher amusingly recalled as a young boy telling his mother that a respectable neighbor woman had used profanity, explaining that in his hearing she had told her husband, "George, wipe you that shit off that pig's arse, do you'll datty your trousers," to which his mother had responded that although that particular usage of a four-letter word had not really been *swearing*, he was not to give vent to such language himself.

Great Hockham, which in Christopher Bush's youth had a population of about four hundred souls, was composed of a score or so of cottages, three public houses, a post-office, five shops, a couple of forges and a pair of churches, All Saint's and the Primitive Methodist Chapel, where the Bush family rather vocally worshipped. "The village lived by farming, and most of its men were labourers," Christopher recollected. "Most of the children left school as soon as the law permitted: boys to be absorbed somehow into the land and the girls to go into domestic service." There were three large farms and four smaller ones, and, in something of an anomaly, not one but two squires--the original squire, dubbed "Finch" by Christopher, having let the shooting rights at Little Hockham Hall to one "Green," a wealthy international banker, making the latter man a squire by courtesy. Finch owned most of the local houses and farms, in traditional form receiving rents for them personally on Michaelmas; and when Christopher's father fell out with Green, "a red-faced, pompous, blustering man," over a political election, he lost all of the banker's business, much to his mother's distress. Yet against all odds and adversities, Christopher's life greatly diverged from settled norms in Great Hockham, incidentally producing one of the most distinguished detective novelists from the Golden Age of detective fiction.

Although Christopher Bush was born in Great Hockham, he spent his earliest years in London living with his mother's much older sister, Elizabeth, and her husband, a fur dealer by the name of James Streeter, the couple having no children of their own. Almost certainly of illegitimate birth, Eva had been raised by the Long family from her infancy. She once told her youngest daughter how she recalled the Longs being visited, when she was a child, by a "fine lady in a carriage," whom she believed was her birth mother. Or is it possible that the "fine lady in a carriage" was simply an imaginary figment, like the aristocratic fantasies of Philippa Palfrey in P.D. James's *Innocent Blood* (1980), and that Eva's "sister" Elizabeth was in fact her mother?

The Streeters were a comfortably circumstanced couple at the time they took custody of Christopher. Their household included two maids and a governess for the young boy, whose doting but dutiful "Aunt Lizzie" devoted much of her time to the performance of "good works among the East End poor." When Christopher was seven years old, however, drastically straightened financial circumstances compelled the Streeters to return the boy to his birth parents in Great Hockham.

Fortunately the cause of the education of Christopher, who was not only a capable village cricketer but a precocious reader and scholar, was taken up both by his determined and devoted mother and an idealistic local elementary school headmaster. In his teens Christopher secured a scholarship to Norfolk's Thetford Grammar School, one of England's oldest educational institutions, where Thomas Paine had studied a century-and-a-half earlier. He left Thetford in 1904 to take a position as a junior schoolmaster, missing a chance to go to Cambridge University on yet another scholarship. (Later he proclaimed himself thankful for this turn of events, sardonically speculating that had he received a Cambridge degree he "might have become an exceedingly minor don or something as staid and static and respectable as a publisher.") Christopher would teach English in schools for the next twenty-seven years, retiring at the age of 46 in 1931, after he had established a successful career as a detective novelist.

Christopher's romantic relationships proved far rockier than his career path, not to mention every bit as murky as his mother's familial antecedents. In 1911, when Christopher was teaching in Wood Green School, a co-educational institution in Oxfordshire, he wed county council schoolteacher Ella Maria Pinner, a daughter of a baker neighbor of the Bushes in Great Hockham. The two appear never actually to have lived together, however, and in 1914, when Christopher at the age of 29 headed to war in the 16th (Public Schools) Battalion of the Middlesex Regiment, he falsely claimed in his attestation papers, under penalty of two years' imprisonment with hard labor, to be unmarried.

After four years of service in the Great War, including a year-long stint in Egypt, Christopher returned in 1919 to his position at Wood Green School, where he became involved in another romantic relationship, from which he soon desired to extricate himself. (A photo of the future author, taken at this time in Egypt, shows a rather dashing, thin-mustached man in uniform and is signed "Chris," suggesting that he had dispensed with "Charlie" and taken in its place a diminutive drawn from his middle name.) The next year Winifred Chart, a mathematics teacher at Wood Green, gave birth to a son, whom she named Geoffrey Bush. Christopher was the father of Geoffrey, who later in life became a noted English composer, though for reasons best known to himself Christopher never acknowledged his son. (A letter Geoffrey once sent him was returned unopened.) Winifred claimed that she and Christopher had married but separated, but she refused to speak of her purported spouse forever after and she destroyed all of his letters and other mementos, with the exception of a book of poetry that he had written for her during what she termed their engagement.

Christopher's true mate in life, though with her he had no children, was Florence Marjorie Barclay, the daughter of a draper from Ballymena, Northern Ireland, and, like Ella Pinner and Winifred Chart, a schoolteacher. Christopher and Marjorie likely had become romantically involved by 1929, when Christopher dedicated to her his second detective novel, *The Perfect Murder Case*; and they lived together as man and wife from the 1930s until her death in 1968 (after which, probably not coincidentally, Christopher stopped publishing novels). Christopher returned with Marjorie to the vicinity of Great Hockham when his writing career took flight, purchasing two adjoining cottages and commissioning his father and a stepbrother to build an extension consisting of a kitchen, two bedrooms and a new staircase. (The now sprawling structure, which Christopher called "Home Cottage," is now a bed and breakfast grandiloquently dubbed "Home Hall.") After a falling-out with his father, presumably over the conduct of Christopher's personal life, he and Marjorie in 1932 moved to Beckley, Sussex, where they purchased Horsepen, a lovely Tudor plaster and timber-framed house. In 1953 the couple settled at their final home, The Great House, a centuries-old structure (now a boutique hotel) in Lavenham, Suffolk.

From these three houses Christopher maintained a lucrative and critically esteemed career as a novelist, publishing both detective novels as Christopher Bush and, commencing in 1933 with the acclaimed book *Return* (in the UK, *God and the Rabbit*, 1934), regional novels purposefully drawing on his own life experience, under the pen name Michael Home. (During the 1940s he also published espionage novels under the Michael Home pseudonym.) Although his first detective novel, *The Plumley Inheritance*, made a limited impact, with his second, *The Perfect Murder Case*, Christopher struck gold. The latter novel, a big seller in both the UK and the US, was published in the former country by the prestigious Heinemann, soon to become the publisher of the detective novels of Margery Allingham and Carter Dickson (John Dickson Carr), and in the latter country by the Crime Club imprint of Doubleday, Doran, one of the most important publishers of mystery fiction in the United States.

Over the decade of the 1930s Christopher Bush published, in both the UK and the US as well as other countries around the world, some of the finest detective fiction of the Golden Age, prompting the brilliant Thirties crime fiction reviewer, author and Oxford University Press editor Charles Williams to avow: "Mr. Bush writes of as thoroughly enjoyable murders as any I know." (More recently, mystery genre authority B.A. Pike dubbed these novels by Bush, whom he praised as "one of the most reliable and resourceful of true detective writers", "Golden Age baroque, rendered remarkable by some extraordinary flights of fancy.") In 1937 Christopher Bush became, along with Nicholas Blake, E.C.R. Lorac and Newton Gayle (the writing team of Muna Lee and Maurice West Guinness), one of the final authors initiated into the Detection Club before the outbreak of the Second World War and with it the demise of the Golden Age. Afterward he continued publishing a detective novel or more a year, with his final book in 1968 reaching a total of 63, all of them detailing the investigative adventures of lanky and bespectacled gentleman amateur detective Ludovic Travers. Concurring as I do with the encomia of Charles Williams and B.A. Pike, I will end this introduction by thanking Avril MacArthur for providing invaluable biographical information on her great uncle, and simply wishing fans of classic crime fiction good times as they discover (or rediscover), with this latest splendid series of Dean Street Press classic crime fiction reissues, Christopher Bush's Ludovic Travers detective novels. May a new "Bush public" yet arise!

Curtis Evans

Murder at Fenwold (1930)

In his 1946 memoir *Spring Sowing*, Christopher Bush (writing as Michael Home) recalled, seemingly without rancor, the stratified social system of Great Hockham, the Norfolk village of his Victorian boyhood, where "the village was the village, and Hall and Vicarage were Hall and Vicarage, and that was that."

> We did not bless the squire and the parson and their relations or pray to be kept in our proper stations, for those stations were centuries old and we were not even aware of them. Radicals like my father...might rail against squires and parsons in general, and Game Laws and endowments, and despair at the subservience and disunity of the laboring man, and yet tacitly accept the system and their part in it. But the private life of the Hall and Vicarage was as far removed from our own as that of Her Majesty, and Finch [the squire], though a just man and a fair landlord, was never lavish of his presence, so that his public appearances lent a kind of awe to his state. John Pardon [the vicar] was different, though he could unbend with no cheapening of himself or his office. But when we passed the Vicarage and saw tennis-parties in progress on the courts, with the white blouses of the ladies and the blazers of the men, or when we saw the traps or dog-carts and their smart coachmen arriving for some call or garden-party, we even felt in some vague way that the village was being honoured by such things. Tennis and golf were games that conveyed nothing to us, and I doubt if one of us had the faintest idea how they were played.

In the 1890s, however, Great Hockham's ancient ways began to shift with the forces of modernity. The squire, Henry Thomas Partridge (or "Finch" as Bush associatively dubbed him in *Spring Sowing*), began letting the Hall and its shooting rights to an international banker from the City, whom Bush decades later derided (giving him the telling alias of "Green") as "a red-faced, pompous, blustering man unversed in country history and ways." After a series of postwar financial reverses, the Partridges finally took flight from Great Hockham, selling the Hall and Estate in 1930 to a firm of speculators and thereby sundering ties of well over a century's standing between village and Hall.

Better than most British detective novelists of his generation, Christopher Bush knew down to the ground the rural British world that during the first decades of the twentieth century was irrevocably passing, lamentably to him, into the pages of history. Yet Bush wrote comparatively little about country life in his Golden Age detective fiction, choosing instead to treat this subject in his mainstream "Michael Home" novels. Exceptions are the author's mysteries *The Case of the Unfortunate Village* (1932), *The Plumley Inheritance* (1926) and *Murder at Fenwold* (1930). The latter novel, the subject of this introduction, portrays a country house beset by devious murder in Breckland, the gorse-covered region of sandy heath in Norfolk and Suffolk from which Bush had come and about which he wrote with warmth and affection in so many of his Michael Home books.

As the runaway success of the recent British television drama series *Downton Abbey* (2010-2015) indicates, the fascination with the British country house milieu of a century or more ago is hardly confined to a certain strata of traditionalist mystery writers from the Golden Age of detective fiction. To the contrary, it remains much with us today. The continuing popularity of British country house mysteries from the Golden Age of detective fiction attests to this fact as well. Although out-of-print for nearly nine decades, Christopher Bush's *Murder at Fenwold* is a notable example of the country house mystery subgenre that should appeal to fans of vintage crime fiction today.

The focus of events at *Murder in Fenwold* (a frontispiece map is included) are Fenwold Village and Fenwold Hall, the grand home of the recently deceased Cosmo Revere, "the biggest thing in the aristocrats of several counties." A veritable museum filled with fine paintings, calf-bound books and antique furniture that make the "collector's mouth" of Ludovic "Ludo" Travers, Christopher Bush's amateur detective, water (Christopher Bush himself shared Ludo's appetite for such things), the Hall at Fenwold is a vaster and grander mansion than the demure Georgian Hall at Bush's beloved Great

Hockham. Happily there is an ample retinue of servants and dependents at Fenwold to keep a squire's life running smoothly:

> There were, he learned, eleven maids in the house, including the cook....There were four footmen in addition to the butler, in the gardens a dozen men and lads, about the garages and stables a dozen more. Then there were the agent's staff—tradesmen, woodmen, keepers, stewards, and farm workers. Except for two farms let to tenants, the village of Fenwold had moved, lived, and had its being round the person of Cosmo Revere.

Although at his demise Cosmo Revere had reached his seventieth year, he did not expire naturally, suffering instead, it appears, one of the more unique precipitated mortal exits in mystery fiction: death from a falling tree. (It seems that Revere, though elderly, was an enthusiastic amateur woodman.) An American philanthropist meets his quietus by means of a toppled Egyptian statue in S.S. Van Dine's *The Scarab Murder Case* (1930) and the younger son of a decayed English gentry family is killed in the collapse of a cursed ancestral edifice in John Rhode's *The Bloody Tower* (1938), but such diabolically contrived murders are comparatively rare in true detective fiction (even in the Golden Age), compared with those less overtly dramatic fatalities facilitated by gun, dagger, poison, rope and the crime writer's ever-reliable old stand-by, the blunt instrument.

At the time of Cosmo Revere's death, John Franklin happens to be on hand in the Fenwold vicinity with Ludovic Travers visiting Ludo's old childhood friend Geoffrey Wrentham at Hainton Vicarage. Both Franklin and Travers, Bush readers will recall from *The Perfect Murder Case* and *Dead Men Twice*, are affiliated with that "great firm of inquiry, advertising and publicity agents," Durangos Limited (Franklin as head of its detective bureau, Travers, the author of the bestselling *The Economics of a Spendthrift*, as a financial consultant); while Wrentham, a Great War veteran and son of a Breckland country vicar, previously investigated with Travers the bizarre mystery of *The Plumley Inheritance*. After studying the scene of the Cosmo Revere tragedy, Franklin concludes that the great landowner's death was not an accident, as it has been hastily ruled, but rather a most deliberate murder. (The book includes several diagrams to help readers visualize how the foul deed was worked.) At the request of the Estate's lawyers, who share Franklin and Travers's suspicions, Durango's finest travel to Fenwold so that they can surreptitiously investigate matters on behalf of Cosmo Hubert Grant, the American heir to the Estate. The well-born Travers takes the guise of a representative of the firm tasked with settling Estate matters and the more humbly circumstanced Franklin adopts that of Travers's manservant. The masquerade leads to this amusing exchange between the two:

> "Do you know, I think we're getting rather close," said Travers. "What about those duties of yours? Any idea how to carry on?"
> "Just the vaguest," laughed Franklin. "I thought of using all the common sense I had and putting down all the howlers to your eccentricity."
> "A perfectly good sheet anchor!"

Present at Fenwold Hall and its peripheries are Leila Fortresse, Cosmo Revere's bewitching niece and ward, who is of a figuratively Bohemian outlook and a literally Parisian upbringing (three decades ago, at the turn of the century, her mother scandalized both family and Fenwold by running away with her music master); Colonel Warren, a boastful and blustering local official; Captain Leeke, Cosmo Revere's mercurial estate agent; Augustus Haddowe, the newly-installed vicar with a partiality for amateur theatricals; Castleton, the late vicar's son and something of a playboy; and George Carter, a recently-arrived antiques dealer, both ill-tempered in disposition and ill-favored in appearance. Several of the men not unnaturally are attracted to the captivating Leila Fortresse, though the woman-shy Travers and his pal Franklin, who derisively dubs Leila the "Queen of the Vamps," manage to resist her "kittenish" charms. Also on hand at the Hall are the Royces, a married butler and housekeeper who seem to constitute the perfect servant couple. ("Everybody in Fenwold knows their place.")

Although *Murder at Fenwold* is a lightly-written and amusing mystery novel that is representative of a time when death was a game in crime fiction, there are moments when Christopher Bush sounds a doleful and elegiac note for a vanishing England. Locals reflect that Cosmo Revere never really recovered from the Great War, in which his only offspring, his sons Cosmo and Lyonel, valiantly perished; and the widower's hopeful effort after the armistice to install as mistress of the Hall the thoroughly modern Miss Fortresse, with her pronounced taste for noisy jazz bands and raucous rounds of roulette, failed miserably. Not long before the solution of the case is revealed, "Ludo" Travers reflects, with more than a touch of melancholy, on how he will miss Fenwold (murders notwithstanding).

> It would be rather jolly to get back to town and yet the thought of leaving Fenwold brought a feeling that was difficult to analyze. It was not so much the loss of comfort and exalted ease—he could have afforded those any day if his taste demanded them. It was not that. It was the recognition that for all the chilliness and hauteur that had struck him when he first saw it Fenwold Hall was a lovely and lovable place. It was an evocation of the past; of the times when life was stately and men had time to pause and look on beauty. There was a kind of seclusion that brooded over it and harmonized with his own peculiar personality. Admit the truth and call it a feudal survival; admit its immensity—the breadth as it were of the canvas—and even then you had to admit a magnificence and glamour and a strange, holding sort of appeal.

One need not be in a nostalgic frame of mind concerning English country life a century ago to enjoy *Murder at Fenwold*, however. In a May 24, 1930 column in the *New York Evening Post*, Dashiell Hammett, a chronicler of modern American urban crime in his recently published masterwork *The Maltese Falcon* (1930), praised *Murder at Fenwold* (under its American title, *The Death of Cosmo Revere*) as a "cleverly plotted tale of murder...in rural England." In the United Kingdom later that year, on December 6, 1930, the *Spectator*'s crime fiction reviewer concurred, declaring: "It is always a pleasure to read a really complicated detective story and *Murder at Fenwold* fully deserves a place in this category." The appeal of the puzzle, it seems, is both universal and perennial.

CHAPTER I
FRANKLIN TELLS A STORY

"THE THING that puzzles me," said Wrentham, "is why any mysteries are ever left unsolved. What with the official sleuths and the unofficial ones like Franklin here, and the Press and the general body of law-abiding citizens like you and me, Ludo; well, I ask you?"

"It's no use your trying to pull Franklin's leg," said Ludovic Travers, giving his glasses a polish. "He'd be an uncommonly poor sleuth if he couldn't see through you."

Franklin cocked an eye at the pair of them. "Talking shop, *and* if there were any way of proving it, I'd like to bet that ten times more of what we call mysteries never come to light, than there are either solved or unsolved."

"You're thinking of the number of people who've been done in with arsenic and buried with a perfectly sound certificate," suggested Travers.

"Well, that's one class. I don't know if I can think of the lot of 'em at the moment. Still; think it over. All the people with a decent sized skeleton in the family cupboard; all the blackmailing that goes on; the number of people living lives of hermits and the simply colossal number living double lives and never getting found out."

Wrentham freshened up his whisky with a squirt of the siphon. "I suppose you're right. You must have been a trifle suspicious more than once in your life—sort of run up against something and sensed there was a skeleton about somewhere?"

"I expect I did; if I could only think of 'em."

"If I might be allowed to put in a pretty simile," observed Travers; "Franklin must have been rather like that brindled bitch of yours. When she puts up a hare she goes straight on. While she's chasing that she may put up three or four, but she's disciplined enough to know that one job's got to be finished at a time."

"It isn't for me to agree," said Franklin, "but as far as I'm concerned, or used to be concerned, it's perfectly true. Many a time when I was at the Yard I'd be on a case and another trail would cut clean across the one I was following. Of course there'd be no time to go off the main road into the side track but sometimes you'd report to the necessary quarter, and if you heard no more about it you'd wonder what had happened and what it had all really been about."

The three of them were seated at the moment in the smoking-room of Hainton Vicarage. Wrentham, agent of the immense Hainton estate, might have been guessed as the host if only from the fact that his legs were balanced on the mantelpiece. In the subdued light of the lamp his face was the colour of a mellowed, tile roof, and that tooth-brush moustache of his added an expression of austere control which was the last thing in the world that he possessed. In the corner of the settee legs tucked under him, was John Franklin, head of the detective bureau of Durango House, and looking more like a fellow agent or country doctor. A glance at his eyes and the cut of his mouth would tell you that he was a fellow not easily ruffled—perhaps the best of all qualifications for the company he was in. As for Ludovic Travers, he was so embedded in another chair that from a front view he seemed a head on the end of perfectly enormous legs. With the mantelpiece they made a square in the middle of which was the table, so happily adjusted that with the least possible effort a hand might pick up a glass or set it down.

"A thing happened to me once," went on Franklin, "which I shan't forget in a hundred years. It's rather a long story, but if you'd like to hear it—"

"Why not?" began the other two, and then the major, "When Ludo's done interrupting, you get on with it."

"Right-ho!" laughed Franklin. "By the way I'm a pretty poor hand at spinning a yarn and that's no false modesty, but what happened was something like this. It was about three months before I left the Yard; let me see, that'd be a couple of years ago. I was on a case in the neighbourhood of Camden Town and I'd arranged to meet a man—proprietor of a public house as a matter of fact—who'd promised to give me news as to the movements of certain parties I was interested in, and as it wouldn't have done for him to have run any risk of being seen with me, we'd agreed to meet at a spot at the back of an old timber yard; some hell of a place as the major would say, with a disused factory and a filthy canal and miles of alley ways. Of course real detectives aren't expected nowadays to disguise themselves, but that night I'd got on—"

"Not that really charming plus four suit of yours?" broke in Wrentham flippantly.

"Shut up, Geoffrey!" snapped Travers, and the major, after giving Franklin a wink, resumed his lethargy.

"Not being on holiday," went on the story-teller, "I didn't think of that particular camouflage; however, I was looking a pretty tough lad that night and a poisonous night it was, what with a drizzle and fog pockets everywhere. However, my man turned up all right and from what he told me I thought I'd push on a bit further. A few minutes later I knew I was lost; as a matter of fact, though I didn't know it at the time, I'd wandered round in a circle to the back of the factory again. The fog was very thick just there so I backed into a kind of passage not far off a lamp and waited for somebody to roll up and give me my bearings.

"I'd been there about two or three minutes when I heard footsteps, and I was just going to move out sort of casually when they suddenly stopped and something told me to keep doggo. There happened to be a bit of fencing at the side of the opening where I was, so I crouched down behind it, well out of the gleam of the lamp. Then the man, whoever it was, whistled—a furtive sort of whistle—and in a second or two somebody answered away out in the fog. Then the first man whistled again in a different way, listened for a moment and moved along a bit; actually slap bang in front of my piece of fencing. I got a good view of his hefty back, big as the end of a house and I reckoned there was a good six foot of him into the bargain. Then I heard more footsteps and two men came into sight, shuffling up—or cringing up if you like. One was a rat of a man and the other a big negro who looked as if he'd just been kicked out of hell."

Travers drew in his legs and sat up in the chair. "You're not piling it on?" came Wrentham's voice from the depths.

"I'm toning it down," said Franklin. "I'll admit that the conversation isn't every word correct but it's near enough. I've thought about that night a good many times since and I think it's a fairly faithful account. The very first word that was said for instance, made me hold my breath.

"'Well, Peters; you're a punctual little fellow. Who's your blond friend?'

"Mind you, it wasn't the words; they're pretty ordinary. It was the culture in the voice and the purity of the accent. It was the least bit blasé and all the time perfectly charming and—well, musical, and yet it struck me as authoritative. Whoever the man was he was an aristocrat to the finger tips. That of course was Bigback. Ratface had a cockney whine—professional beggar type.

"'He's off the boat, boss. Skipper said he'd better come along as I was carryin' all this dough.'

"'Damn thoughtful of him—and very touching,' said Bigback. 'Well, what the hell are you standing there for? Pass it over, then you can hold hands and be damned to you.'

"I was squinting out of a knot hole and the fog seemed to be a bit thinner. It was something like being in the front of the stalls for a first-class thriller. Ratface looked at the negro and he might as well have looked at the wall for all the answer he got, so he fumbled very laboriously in his breast pocket and finally hauled out a roll of what were probably notes. Then he had another look at the negro; then he made a suggestion. 'What about goin' to a nice quiet little pub, boss, where we can see what we're doin'?'

"I couldn't see for a second or two because Bigback squared his shoulders well into the fence, but it looked to me as if he saw through the game quicker than the other two imagined.

"'No, I don't think so, Peters. Pubs, as you call them, are full of temptations.' Then his voice changed. 'You come across pronto, or I'll cut the guts out of you!'

"He made a step forward and the next moment I heard him rustling the notes. Then he shoved them into his pocket. 'What about the passport?'

"There was silence for a bit then Ratface appealed to the negro. 'He said he was goin' to send it later; didn't he, Bob?'

"Bigback took a step or two towards them. The negro squared up with his fists and Ratface got behind him. The other backed to the fence but well clear of my knot hole.

"'Oh, that's the idea is it? Most ingenious! Well, Peters, you stay here. And you, you bastard, you get back to the office and bring him along here! Tell him if I haven't that passport inside ten minutes I'll carve the guts clean out of him.' Not much Oxford about that as I say it, but except for being a bit more matter of fact the voice was just as delightful.

"Then the fun started. Ratface gave a quick glance down the road into the fog, then squealed out, 'There's somebody comin', boss. Look out! Here's the police!' Bigback turned his head for a moment and the negro was on him like a streak. I can't describe the fight like a broadcast announcer, but the two big 'uns were at it with their fists, grunting and panting and thudding, and Bigback cursing away like hell. There wasn't much Balliol about that torrent of blasphemy he let loose. It absolutely made your blood run cold. And there was Ratface dodging round with a nice little silencer in his hand, trying to pick Bigback out of the scrap-heap, until he got a sideways kick on the kneecap and rolled on the ground groaning like blazes and then spitting like a cat.

"Then Bigback did a perfectly amazing thing and did it quicker than I can describe it. The negro seemed to give a wild swing and just as he ducked it he let fly with his foot and caught him clean in the belly, and as he doubled up and grunted he caught him another kick clean on the point of the chin and the negro just gave a sort of gurgle and sank down. Bigback stood there panting for a moment and just as he went to have a look at him Ratface hit him behind the ear with his lump of lead piping and he went down like a pole-axed bullock. I don't think he'd quite hit the ground when Ratface was going through his pockets. You fellows laugh about the police keeping out of a scrap, but I don't mind telling you it all happened so quickly that I must have had my mouth open and my eyes bulging like marbles. Then, just as I *was* going to get up from my knees, all cramped, Ratface got down, hitched the negro over his shoulder, staggered up and tottered off.

"I was just going to make a bolt after him and then my knee gave way—leg all needles and pins—so I thought I'd have a look at Bigback and see how he was coming along. I could still hear Ratface padding away in the fog and there was I, rubbing my leg and squinting at Bigback at the same time, and when I clapped eyes on him I didn't half have a shock. What do you—well, after what I've told you, what did you expect me to see?"

"Lord knows!" said Travers. "Broken-down Oxford don."

"Don't be a damn fool, Ludo," cut in Wrentham. "You never knew a don who could put up a scrap like that. I know what you saw. Bloke in evening dress—full war-paint, top hat, diamond studs; amateur cracksman, king of the underworld, Raffles—"

"Shut up, Geoffrey! What *did* you see, Franklin?"

"Well, he'd on the filthiest set of dungarees you ever saw on a third-class stoker—and a stubbly beard, about three days' growth. Only his hands—they were all different; white as milk, sort of flat at the nails and manicured absolutely—well, first class. And his face! Most attractive I ever saw. You chaps may laugh, but do you know what I called him?—sort of passed through my mind as soon as I had a look at him? The Marquis! Don't think I'm blowing about it, but the previous night I'd happened to be at the Mansion House and a chap like that was speaking there at a banquet—Spanish fellow, marquis of—well, lord knows what, string of names as long as your arm. That's what this chap Bigback reminded me of. Honestly I can't describe him, but he'd a noble sort of face; magnificent white hair, nose like a Roman general's; made you think of the real old aristocracy—dukes, sedan chairs, wigs, duels and—well, there you are! Ever since then I've called him the Marquis—to myself."

"That was damn queer!"

"Wasn't it? You see I think the atmosphere of the place had a lot to do with it; that perfectly appalling neighbourhood and the unexpectedness and so on. Still, there he was."

"What happened then? Was he dead? "

"Lord no! Just knocked out. His face looked pale enough, like one of those stone crusaders you see on tombs in cathedrals. It was sort of intellectual—and dignified. Oh yes, and he'd got the devil of a gash over his eye where he hit the road when Ratface slugged him behind the ear." He paused for a moment and shook his head. "I'd know that face again wherever I saw it. Absolutely unique sort of face. You could never forget it."

"What did you do then?" asked Travers.

"Well, as I've been telling the story you'd think I'd been there five minutes. As a matter of fact, it all took place in a second or two, because I thought I could still hear Ratface—so I legged it after him for all I was worth. I got about twenty yards or so in the fog, then I couldn't hear a sound. Then I had a minute or two exploring round, but a pretty hopeless job that was, what with the fog and that rabbit warren, so I nipped off back again to attend to his excellency the ambassador. I found the place all right, but when I got to it he wasn't there! I stepped out down the road the way I thought he'd gone and came a cropper over a heap of refuse. That slowed me down a bit and to cut a long story short I spent an hour exploring the neighbourhood, and as it was too late to go where I'd intended I just went home."

"How perfectly extraordinary! And you never heard any more about it?"

"Not a word. I called at divisional headquarters on my way and made a report, but they knew nothing and what's more they never found out anything. And that's the last I've heard about it, in spite of enquiries at all sorts of times from all sorts of people."

"Ever try to fit the pieces together?" asked Travers. Franklin smiled. "*Try* was as far as I got."

Travers nodded. "I suppose anybody with an active imagination could make anything out of an opening like that."

"Mind you, I'm not throwing doubts on Franklin's veracity," put in Wrentham, "but if I ran across a mixture of blaspheming ambassadors and negros I should say as little about 'em as if they'd been pink rats and green elephants." Then he smiled to himself. "Funny thing if you ever ran up against that bloke again one of these days."

"Funnier things than that," remarked Travers.

"Now come, Ludo! Don't get quarrelsome in your cups. It would be a pretty remarkable coincidence."

"Coincidence, I admit; but not remarkable. Even with quite ordinary people like you and me, coincidences are common enough. Franklin's different. He's always more or less on the trail. *Ergo,* it seems to me he'll have jolly hard luck if one of these days his trail doesn't cross that of the interesting bloke he's rather nicely called the ambassador. I could name heaps of criminals who'd never have been hanged if they hadn't been caught in some petty bypath as Franklin called it —men like Brown and Kennedy, for instance, who killed that Essex policeman."

"Perhaps you're right," admitted the major, glancing at the clock. "You and Franklin carry too many guns for me. By the way, I know it's our last night and all that, but how late do you young lads propose sitting up? I've got a job of work to do before we go in the morning. What about your bags? All packed?"

"Everything right and tight," said Franklin. "And how many miles *is* Fenwold, by the way?"

"Just about twenty. Take Ludo about twenty minutes in that fire-engine of his and me best part of an hour in the Morris."

"The fact of the matter is," said Travers, "you want to drive the Isotta. You've been itching to break your neck ever since you clapped eyes on the damn thing."

"And why not?" asked the other airily. "Cause of science and so on. And what about a nightcap?"

"Well, whether you break your neck or not, major," said Franklin, "you've given us a thundering good time. It's the best fortnight I've ever had. You sure you can't join us in a round before coming back?"

"Not a hope. Must go to that show and then there's that conference up north. And before I forget it I want to show you something at Fenwold. Pull up at the church. You'll only have to wait half an hour till I turn up."

"What about giving you a tow?" suggested Franklin.

Wrentham began measuring out the nightcaps. "A moment ago, young fellow, you were proposing votes of thanks and now you're making bad jokes about a perfectly honourable car. Thank God I've never had a thankless child."

"We've only your word for that," retorted Travers.

The others laughed. "Not so bad!" said the major. "Well, here's how. May you come down longer and oftener. You're a damn nuisance, but my wits get rusty if I haven't some poor boobs to keep them sharp on. And what were you saying, Ludo, about my driving your car?"

CHAPTER II
BLOOD AND STATE

(i)

IT WAS an unromantic advertisement for the sale of a hundred thousand or so of second-hand bricks that made Major Wrentham accompany his guests as far as Branford after their fortnight's visit. Leeke—Cosmo Revere's agent—had apparently that quantity to sell; Wrentham had a job for which second-hand bricks were as good as new, and that was that. Moreover, he and Leeke occasionally played together for the Vagrants and knew each other pretty well. As for Travers and Franklin, there was an eighteen-hole course in the little town, and with rooms booked at the "Angel" they proposed putting in a further day or two before returning to town. Wrentham, with the promise of a try-out later, rode with Travers and saw the countryside through the screen and along the sinister radiator of the long Isotta.

Well before Fenwold village they slowed down and waited for Franklin to catch up in the Morris; then Ludo drew up alongside the low, squat church.

"Splendid!" said Wrentham. "Just hang on a minute and I'll get the pew-opener."

He slipped across to the solitary cottage and came back with a key.

"Looks a pretty old building," remarked Franklin as they stepped down to the cool, stone floor.

"No shop!" whispered the other facetiously. "No deductions permitted. However, what about these?" and he waved his hand at the storied urns and tablets that decorated the walls like a mosaic.

Ludo adjusted his glasses and peered round. "A monstrously old family, these Reveres?"

Wrentham lowered his voice to the necessary religious pitch. "The earliest here is about 1500 but they're heaps older than that. I was here a good many years ago and Cosmo Revere himself showed me round." He pointed to an inscription on the grey floor of the aisle.

Cosmoe Revere
of
Fenwolde.
Born 1481, Dyed 1559
Aged 78 yeares.
O howe amyable are thi dwellynges
Thou Lorde of hoostes.

"Weird sort of text," whispered Travers. "Prayer-book obviously. Are they all called Cosmo—the head of the house, I mean?"

"I rather fancy so, but Franklin can check up round the walls."

"I wonder why there isn't a title among 'em," remarked Franklin. "You know that old map of the county you were showing us last night with a huge splash of green for Fenwold Great Park? Surely a family who've owned a place like that for centuries ought to have been ennobled?"

"Quite the reverse. Some very old families—the ffanes of Laxton for instance—always considered they were a sufficient nobility in themselves. Sort of got to be a family tradition; accepting or touting for a title wasn't done. Better be a Revere of Fenwold than a brand new Baron of Breckland."

"I think I rather sympathise," said Travers. "After all, what's it matter. If you have the substance why worry about the rest—the shadows and unsubstantial things?"

"Perhaps you're right. Now then; this is what I wanted you to see. Cosmo Revere didn't mention it when I was here before." He led the way into a vast, square pew-space whose high, carved oak back must have hidden the aristocratic occupants from all gaze but that of the parson perched aloft in the tall pulpit. All round the top of the enclosure went a line of carving, cut deeply and none too artistically.

> "Hye on a tree oure lorde did henge and die
> benethe a tree the laste revere shall lye."

Travers frowned slightly as his eyes ran along the carving for a second time. "An extraordinary problem!" he remarked.

Franklin looked round quickly. "You mean, who did the prophesying?"

Travers smiled. "To tell you the truth I was more or less thinking aloud. But it *is* peculiar."

"The legend explains it pretty well," said Wrentham. "One of these Reveres fell foul of a rustic in the village for killing his deer and strung him up on an oak tree. The story goes he had a brother a wood-carver and a mother a witch, and the brother hacked out this cheerful extract from Old Moore and then legged it for all he was worth."

"And what happened to the witch?" asked Franklin.

"History is silent," replied Wrentham sententiously, and then to Travers, who was feeling the carving with the tips of his fingers, "Oh, it's genuine enough; at least it's in Bloomfield's history—the carving, I mean, not the explanation."

But it was not till they were again in the porch that Travers made his objections. "That carving now. Genuine enough, as you say, but the legend's well out of it."

Wrentham couldn't resist trying to be humorous. "There you are, Franklin; I could see it coming. Lynx-eyed Ludo, the human bradawl."

"Well, isn't it?" retorted the other. "What's the supposed date of that legend? Early sixteenth century—say Henry the Eighth."

"And why not?"

"No reason at all—provided you don't connect it with the carving. If you judge by look and feeling alone, that's very much later. A sixteenth century rustic would have written doggerel, not a perfect couplet in iambic pentameters; and the doggerel would have been in crude sort of fourteen syllabled lines—like:
'High on a tree our blessed Lord did suffer and did die '
and so on. To put it rather more nicely, do witches pronounce their malisons in metre a century in advance of the fashion?"

"Why couldn't it have been later?"

"Ah, that's the problem. How late in English history could a Revere have hanged a man with impunity? Mind you, I may be wrong about the whole thing."

"Why didn't the then owner of Fenwold remove it?" asked Franklin.

"Good!" exclaimed Travers. "Why didn't he?"

"Ask me another," was the reply. "You're a nice pair of detectives. The first problem I put to you two experts this holiday you have the nerve to ask me to solve for you." He seated himself comfortably at the wheel of the Isotta. "Now then; you two lads like to crawl round? It'll take me about a quarter of an hour."

"Which is the Branford road?" asked Franklin.

"You can't go wrong—straight as a die. I turn to the left to the Hall—you'll see the big gates. Tobacco? There's a shop on the village green. And mind you take care of that Morris." There was a sort of grind, a snort, a spurt of dust and the car was gone.

"I think," said Travers, "that if I had to find an epithet for Geoffrey, I should describe him as volatile."

"But an extraordinarily good chap."

"Absolutely. About the best there is. The trouble is he hates the idea of being taken for a brainy person and therefore disguises himself with a persistent sort of flippancy. Yet I know for a definite fact there are few cleverer men at his job than he is."

It was not until they were letting the Morris laze along the shade of the Branford road that he reverted to the subject of the prophecy.

"Anything unusual about that carving, did you think?"

"Well, I don't think I noticed anything."

"It's really the fault of that lumber-room of mine," explained Travers. "As you know by this time, my head's full of the most extraordinary collection of rubbish. The things I'd like to remember, I can't, and everything else I read seems to find an empty spot and stick in it. Have you read anything recently about this Cosmo Revere?"

Franklin thought for a moment, then shook his head.

"It was in a newspaper; this spring if I remember rightly. This particular Revere, who'd now be about seventy and seems the biggest thing in the aristocrats of several counties, had a great admiration for Gladstone. One of the ways he shows it is by his hobby; he fells trees."

"For exercise?"

"Well, I imagine so. Of course heaps of people have done it—I mean cutting down trees on their estates; only what recalled it to me was the awful row there was. A reporter secreted himself in the wood and took a picture of the aristocratic lumberman, and his paper printed it, legend and all. Of course he was perfectly furious. His lawyers threatened legal action and that's all I remember. Perhaps they're still at it."

"He doesn't happen to be the last Revere by any chance?"

"Lord knows! If he is, he probably imagines he's sufficiently above prophecies to afford to disregard them."

"Or else he's passionately fond of the hobby?"

"Quite! Or he might have begun it for sheer cussedness and now, as you say, keeps it up because he likes it. Now what about pulling up and waiting for Geoffrey? We shall probably have to identify his body."

They drew the Morris in on the grass verge and squatted on the low, brick culvert that spanned the tiny river and pulled out their pipes. Ten minutes later in the unseen distance there was the unearthly gurgle of a car. Ten seconds later there came into sight a black spot in a cloud of dust.

(ii)

The gates of the lodge safely behind him, Wrentham treated himself to the thrill to which he had been looking forward. From the main road to the Hall is a long arc of drive—half a mile or so of perfect surface with broad, grass borders and the trees of the avenue well back on each side. The speedometer passed the seventy, crept slowly towards eighty and then, the adventurous moment over, sank to a steady fifty. Then as the long, greyish-white front of the Hall came into sight, he realised that to make a racing track out of a man's private drive was hardly the best of form, and slowed to a decorous forty.

Among the trees of another great avenue that ran from the front of the Hall away to the horizon, deer were browsing. Everything seemed huge, colossal. The park stretched away into an indefinite blue and the Hall itself, with its drab colouring and air of remote coldness, looked down from a slight rise of ground over wide sweeps of tended grass that merged imperceptibly into the grassland of the park itself. But when he left the drive by the right fork through the trees, all this bareness of grandeur was lost. Things became more intimate and homely. There was the red of out-buildings, old walls that enclosed gardens, here and there a cottage and everywhere signs of life. In spite of the sun that beat on it, everything out there on that immense front had seemed statuesque, aloof and even repelling. Here, at the back among the hirelings, life seemed very English, very pleasant and companionable.

A man came from a side gate, pushing a barrow, and Wrentham stopped the car in the shade of a tall, cypress hedge.

"Isn't the estate office here?"

"That's it, sir, on the right. Was you wantin' Captain Leeke?"

"I was, rather."

"He went through the south garden there, sir, a few minutes ago."

Wrentham thanked him and strolled on. The gate from which the gardener had emerged led him to a walled garden where more men were working. A hundred yards of paved walk between fruit trees and flowers brought him to a door set in the fifteen foot wall. He lifted the latch and it swung away, disclosing a stretch of smooth lawn and a cedar beneath which a peacock was stepping. In the background were gigantic yew hedges, and through a clipped doorway he could see a splash of colour. Then he heard the voices.

"I won't stand it any longer, Leila. Don't drive me too far."

"My *dear* man; please don't be tragic. When you look like that you're *too* pathetic."

"I'm glad you think so." The voice was sulky. "When your uncle hears about you and Castleton—"

"Mr. Castleton is a perfectly *charming* man!"

The woman's voice went on but Wrentham moved away. It had certainly been Leeke who was speaking but who the other was he hadn't the faintest idea. Then, while he stood irresolute, the voices began again, nearer than ever.

"You shan't go on like this. I tell you I saw you and Castleton under those trees—"

Then the woman's voice. "I don't care two teeniest damns what you think. Mr. Castleton would make the most adorable husband—"

There was nothing for it but subterfuge. He stepped back quickly, called to an imaginary gardener, "All right, thanks. I'll find my way," paused for a moment and then passed through the clipped arch. On his left, beyond a deep herbaceous border, could be seen the Hall and in front lay more lawns, broken here and there by rose beds. Out of the corner of his eye he could glimpse on his right a man and a woman. Then a dog yapped and he turned his head.

Close by the hedge and facing him stood a woman. She was hatless and with hair cropped short but for two crescents of black that curled from round her ears. His first impression was that she was Spanish—those dark eyes, the dark complexion and the tantalising set of the mouth. Her left hand was thrust into the pocket of her knitted suit and from the fingers of the other hung a cigarette. By her feet was a black spaniel. Half turned towards him, in grey flannels and tweed coat, stood Leeke, and the scowl on his face shifted suddenly as he caught sight of the intruder who stood hesitating on the flagged path.

"Good lord, major! What are you doing here?"

"I say; I'm very sorry," began Wrentham. "They told me I should find you somewhere here—"

"Well, you have, haven't you?" laughed the other and turned to his companion. "I don't think you've met Major Wrentham. This is Miss Forteresse, major."

An extraordinarily attractive woman, thought Wrentham. A bit on the small side, perhaps, but what a figure! Those ear-rings— and those eyes! Ought to have had a couple of peacocks instead of that spaniel.

"Isn't it too gorgeous this morning?"

"It is rather jolly," he replied, "Great morning for a round of golf."

She made an affected moue. "Too strenuous really. Captain Leeke and I were just agreeing how foolish it is to give way to excitement."

What the double meaning was Wrentham didn't know, but he saw the curl of the lip as she flashed a glance at Leeke, and he saw the cloud that came over his face. As for the flagrant temper in his answer, it couldn't very well be missed.

"Would you mind if—er—if we—"

She gave a little ripple; a laugh all exasperation and indifference. "My *dear* man—" and bent to pat the spaniel.

As Wrentham bowed, Leeke took him by the arm and drew him away. The whole proceeding was so theatrical that he was feeling a bit of a fool, and it was not until they were in the walled garden that the other ventured to explain.

"That's Leila Forteresse—Revere's niece. Rather original in a way. Glad you rolled up. Must have been trying for half an hour to get clear."

Wrentham's comment was diplomatic. "I didn't know there was a niece. She been here long?"

"About a year." He changed the conversation just as abruptly. "How's the cricket going?"

"Oh, pretty fair. You're not playing much?"

"Damn sight too busy. Hainton's no joke, but really—you've no idea. And between ourselves Revere's getting a bit of an old woman."

Somehow Wrentham didn't like the turn the conversation was taking. "That reminds me," he said and broached the subject of the bricks. Ten minutes later the deal was concluded. Wrentham pulled out his watch.

"Good lord, major. You're not in all that hurry?"

"Sorry," said Wrentham. "Couple of people waiting for me down the road. Been staying with me and I'm seeing them as far as Branford. What about coming along?"

Leeke shook his head. "I'm expecting Mr. Revere back at any minute."

"Is he away?"

"Went off last night. Some flint grubbing expedition or other. What about a tankard before you go?"

"Sorry. Awfully good of you and all that, but I must be pushing off. Have a peep at the car."

Leeke stood enraptured. "My God! She's a beauty! Somebody left you a fortune, major?"

"'Fraid not. Belongs to a chap who's waiting down the road."

Leeke grunted. "Damned if I know how some of these blokes get their money. I'll never have a car like this unless," he paused perceptibly, "unless some relative I've never heard of prefers me to the dogs' home—or Badger's Brush wins the St. Leger."

"Let's hope for both," said Wrentham, perfectly solemnly. "I suppose I shall have to go all the way back, by the way?"

"Not at all. Keep straight on and the Branford road's only a couple of hundred yards or so. You'll have gone a sort of half circle. Hallo! What's that chap in a hurry for?"

Round the corner by the old stables, panting like a dog, a man came running; a keeper by the look of him and beat to the world. He pointed behind with his arm before he found breath to speak.

"Mr. Revere, sir! In the wood!"

Leeke drew himself up and frowned slightly. "In the wood? What wood?"

"Lammas Wood. He's dead, sir!"

"Dead! What d'you mean 'dead'?"

"A tree's fell on him, sir!"

"Good God!" He grasped the major's arm. "What's the best thing to do?"

Wrentham took command. "What's your name?"

"Westfield, sir."

"Mr. Revere was dead?"

"Dead as a doornail, sir. Knocked down by a tree."

"Can I get this car up there?"

"Yes, sir. Near as nothin'."

He turned to Leeke. "Your car all right?"

Leeke nodded.

"Right-ho then. You phone the police and the doctor and fix up where to meet 'em. I'll push on with this chap and see if I can do anything. Will Captain Leeke know where to come, Westfield?"

Leeke put the question himself. "Where the hut stands?"

"That's it, sir."

In ten seconds the Isotta was skimming along the back road that curved to the village.

CHAPTER III
CLOUDED WITH A DOUBT

(i)

"WESTFIELD," ordered Wrentham, "you get in with those gentlemen and explain all about it."

The other two, considerably mystified, got in, too, and followed in the wake of the Isotta. Half a mile on it swerved to the left down a narrow lane which soon petered out to a track that ran by the side of a wood. Then the track grew even less defined and lost itself in dry meadow-land till a shout from Westfield gave the signal to stop. In the hedge on the left was a gate leading to a path barely visible in the dense undergrowth.

"How far now, Westfield?"

"Two hundred yards into the wood, sir."

"Good! You hop out and open that gate."

Then Wrentham made a brainy suggestion. "I've been thinking about this business. What do you say if I go on alone with the keeper and you two follow on in a couple of minutes? If you come now there's just the possibility you might have to attend the inquest."

Franklin, in spite of a natural desire to see all there was to see, agreed at once. "I take it it's a plain case of accident, but all the same it's a good idea."

After the hot sun that scorched down on the open grassland, the wood had a coolness that was sensuous and yet invigorating. The dew still lay heavy on grass and nettles and every now and then came a whiff of honeysuckle. It seemed a strange thing to be going in search of death in a spot where the hand of man was scarcely to be discerned. But a hundred yards along the path—wider than it had appeared from the distance—was a plain track to the right.

"Hallo!" exclaimed Wrentham. "What's been along here? Aren't those wheel marks?"

"That'd be the hut, sir. Mr. Revere allust had it drawn in where he was goin' to do any fellin'."

"What'd he do that for?"

"He had an oil stove in it, sir, so that he could make himself a drink and change his clothes." Then he lowered his voice. "Here's where he is, sir."

To the right stood the hut on the edge of a circle of fifty good yards' diameter, clear of trees and bare of undergrowth and its dark leaf-mould apparently undisturbed. Almost at the edge of this circle lay a tree—a youngish oak—with branches like the spokes of a broken umbrella and leaves already withered. At the side and almost clear a man lay, sprawled out foolishly; face upwards and body curiously awry. Wrentham moved up gingerly and bent over him. That he was dead there was no possibility of doubt and plainly visible at the back of his forehead was the wound where a bough had struck.

For some moments he stood contemplating the motionless figure. Perhaps in his mind were Ludo's words on death and shadows and unsubstantial things or perhaps he remembered the simple courtesy of the man he had seen so many years before. Even then, as he lay there, there was an indefinite something about Cosmo Revere that seemed unique. The face looked dignified, dispassionate

and even serene. The silver beard—fashion of an earlier generation—was unstained and it seemed as if the bare arms where the
rolled sleeves showed them as far as the elbows, must be those of a
man cast in a cruder mould. The flannel shirt was open at the neck;
the grey flannel trousers were almost unmarked and the leather
belt was in position. The boots were heavy with mould and one had
its lace undone.

He bent and touched the cheek with his fingers. "Dead enough.
Must have been instantaneous, too."

He moved to the stump where the white chips were scattered.
On the ground behind it lay an axe. Ten feet to the right was the butt
of the tree and between it and the stump was a small cross-cut saw.

"Pretty obvious what happened," thought Wrentham. "Bough
hit an obstruction, stump slewed round and before he could get
clear another bough caught him."

He looked up at the sky—then down again. Then he frowned.
For a moment or two he stared at the stump, then at the butt.
Something was puzzling him, as Westfield could see.

"Lost somethin', sir?"

Wrentham pulled himself together with a jerk. "Er—no. Just
looking at the lie of the land. By the way, would you mind keeping
an eye on the cars while those two gentlemen are here? We shan't be
more than a minute or two." As he was speaking they came in sight,
the soft surface of the leaf-mould giving no warning of approach.

"Hadn't we better keep out of the way?" asked Franklin.

"Don't think it matters. Look where you've just trod—you can't
see a sign of a footprint. And come over here a second; there's
something I want you to see. Notice anything up there?"

Both gazed attentively. "Can't say I do," said Franklin.

"Hm! Well, you two have a quick look round." Franklin wondered what he was getting at. "But isn't it an accident?"

"Why not?" replied Wrentham enigmatically. Franklin shrugged
his shoulders. "What's the hut for?"

Wrentham told the pair of them. Franklin nodded casually and
went over. He mounted the short ladder of five steps and tried the
handle of the door. It opened and he stood there peering in.

Wrentham stood idly regarding the sky, then all at once looked round at the scattered chips, picked up one and put it in his pocket. Just then Travers called quietly.

"One minute, Geoffrey! What do you make of this?" On the forehead of the dead man was a stain, a sort of orange smear. "Looks like sand," said Wrentham and bending down, moved the head gently. "Goes right round—and into the wound too." He grunted. "Where on earth did he get that?"

"That's what I wondered. All the soil round here is grey."

"Just a minute," said the other. "Let's look at it fairly and squarely. This soil is sand and dead leaves. But it's earthy sand—dirty silver sand. Not a spot of colour in it. He couldn't have got tawny sand on his face then as he fell."

"There's none on the axe and saw. What about a rabbit burrow? His hand might have come in contact with that and if he drew his hand across his face or dirtied his handkerchief it might account for it."

Five minutes' scouting knocked the bottom out of that. There were plenty of burrows but silver sand, every one of them. Then Wrentham looked at the stain again. "Nothing on the hands, Ludo. I'll see if I can wriggle out his handkerchief," and out the handkerchief came, crumpled but perfectly clean.

"Did it come off the bough that struck him?"

"Same problem," retorted Wrentham "How did it get *there?*"

"How did *what* get there?" asked Franklin, reappearing as if from nowhere.

"We were wondering if this *was* sand," said Travers. "Shouldn't be difficult to find out," and stooping down he gently wiped a few grains on to a sheet of paper and had a good look at it. "I should say it's a hundred to one it's sand."

Then Wrentham made up his mind. He took Travers' arm and motioning Franklin, moved slowly away.

"If you people don't mind I want to suggest something which may sound very ridiculous. The fact of the matter is there are things about this business I don't like the least bit. Franklin here has forgotten more than I shall ever know but this happens to be the one case where I can see things he can't, because they're mixed up with the way I earn my bread and butter. I'm sure Revere wasn't killed by that tree and I'll tell you why later."

Travers looked remarkably serious, even for him. Franklin nodded and said nothing.

"If there *is* anything in what I say, Franklin's likely to have a job on his hands. You two had better get off quick before the authorities come along."

The others didn't seem to grasp it.

"What I mean is, if everybody knows who Franklin is—and they're quite likely to after that Perfect Murder Case—he won't be able to work in the dark. You didn't attract any attention in the village?"

"Didn't see five people all told."

"Good! You take the Isotta and push on to Branford. I shall have to stop here till the others come. Wait for me at the 'Angel' and have lunch if I'm not there at 1.0."

Outside the wood Westfield sat on the bank, steadily regarding the car.

"In case I forget it," said Wrentham and slipped him half a crown. "Nip off back to the wood, will you, and I'll be along in a second. These gentlemen have to go now."

The man touched his hat. "Excuse me, sir, but if you want to get to the road you can go right on. It's a bit rough but you'll strike it, sir, if you keep alongside the wood."

"Splendid!" said Wrentham. "By the way, where's the nearest sand or gravel pit—ordinary yellow sand?"

The man looked surprised. "There ain't none this side the village, sir. This is all for game—kept private. The gravel and sand pit's right in the village."

Five minutes later came the first of the arrivals.

(ii)

With Leeke were two people; one obviously the village policeman and the other a man of mature age whose general bearing, white moustache and florid complexion announced the retired military man. Behind them came two gardeners whom Leeke motioned to remain at a distance.

"Doctor'll be here in a minute," explained Leeke quietly. "Westfield, you slip off to the road in case the doctor doesn't know where to stop, and bring him here."

The military gentleman, looking as out of place as could be with his pearl-grey suit, white spats and grey bowler, glanced at Wrentham suspiciously as much as to say. "What the devil's this fellow doing here?"

"This is Major Wrentham, colonel," explained Leeke. "Colonel Warren, major, is chairman of the local bench and I was lucky enough to run across him and bring him along."

All the same, as Wrentham noted, the words seemed much more formal than enthusiastic. There was even a suspicion of a sneer on his face as he caught Wrentham's eye.

The colonel nodded. "If he was dead, why didn't he wait for the police?"

Leeke explained more fully.

"He couldn't do any good," snapped the other. Wrentham was beginning to feel annoyed. To be talked at in the third person was neither courteous nor necessary.

"If Mr. Revere hadn't been dead," he put in abruptly, "my coming might have made all the difference."

The other glared but made no comment, then turned his back and made for the body. He grunted once or twice like a man wrestling with a problem. The oracle spoke.

"Can't think why a man like Revere should let a tree fall on him. Not much of a tree either." Then to Leeke. "I think we must get him to the Hall as soon as possible. Got a cloth or something?"

Wrentham suddenly felt the blood rush to his face with the surge of anger that came over him. Hadn't this blustering old fool any sense of decency? Any realisation of the presence of death? Then he found himself speaking and his voice sounded to himself unnaturally forced and brusque.

"Excuse me, sir, but hadn't you better let the doctor see him first?"

The colonel opened his mouth, closed it, then opened it again. "He's dead, isn't he? What good can the doctor do?"

"There's no need to brawl. The doctor might say *how* he died."

Leeke was looking decidedly self-conscious. Then the constable put in an obsequious word on the side of authority.

"If he's dead, he *is* dead, sir."

Wrentham shot such a look at him that his eyes fell and at that precise moment the doctor appeared, full of fussiness and apologies. He was a not uncommon specimen of the older school of country practitioner—none too smart in appearance and satisfied with himself and the occasion. "This is a terrible business!"

The colonel nodded heavily. "Most regrettable. Most regrettable! How long's he been dead, Parrett?"

The doctor made his inspection. When he got up from the ground, brushing his knees, he made for the nearest branch that lay with its end sunk in the mould. "I expect this was the end that hit him. Yes—here's the blood," Then he shook his head again—a forced condoling sort of business it seemed to Wrentham. "He undoubtedly tripped over his own bootlace as he was trying to get clear."

Wrentham stood his ground but the others moved over and watched as the doctor illustrated his point. "One thing was fortunate," he added. "Death was instantaneous. And it took place at least twelve hours ago."

Leeke gave a sort of gasp, opened his mouth as if to speak, then rubbed his hands together nervously. "There's a rug in the van, colonel. What about getting him away?"

The little procession passed slowly through the shadows to the path. "No need for you to stay, Turner," said the colonel, and the voice seemed stridency itself after the silence. "Only keep out of the way of the van. We don't want the whole village hanging on our heels."

Damn the fool! thought Wrentham furiously. Probably thinks this was staged for his benefit, and he stepped back a yard or two, wondering what was the best thing to do. Then the doctor's voice broke in.

"Leeke didn't seem to believe he'd been dead for twelve hours."

"H'm! Young fool!" blustered the colonel. "Some cock and bull story he was telling me. To-day's Wednesday. Yesterday, Tuesday, some fellow from the village called to see Revere and Revere went out after dinner—down to those stones of his probably—and didn't come in any more."

"He didn't sleep at the Hall?"

"I don't know," spluttered the other. "Probably didn't know what he was talking about. Fellow's tight half his time. Break his own neck one of these days."

Parrett nodded and the pair moved off. Wrentham followed at a distance. Outside the wood, the van—a motor game-cart by the look of it—was still waiting.

"You coming with me, colonel?" asked the doctor.

"No. I'll go in the van. Must explain things at the Hall. Ladies and so on."

He motioned the men to get in; got in himself and the steps were drawn up. Leeke mounted by the driver and with a grinding of gears the van moved on. Wrentham watched its slow progress to the end of the wood, then, turning his head, became aware of the doctor watching also the disappearing of the incongruous cortège. Their eyes met and Parrett, relieved of the presence of his officious and overwhelming companion, seemed to notice Wrentham for the first time. Apparently too he recognised an equal.

"The last of the Reveres goes home to his fathers." Wrentham hardly knew what to say. There seemed no particular bitterness in the remark; certainly no jocularity or attempt at a cheap smartness.

"Well, he died doing a man's job of work," was all he could find.

"How'd you come to be there?" asked the doctor. Wrentham explained at some length and they strolled back towards the cars.

"He actually *was* the last Revere?"

"Oh yes. Both the sons—splendid fellows—were killed in the war. Guards of course—and both unmarried."

"Who inherits, do you know?"

"I believe there's a nephew in America. He was over here on a visit after the war. I didn't see him myself."

"Isn't there a niece?"

The doctor laughed. "You mean Miss Forteresse. There'll be no more jazz bands at Fenwold Hall—take it from me! You coming my way?"

Wrentham would have liked to say yes but he daren't risk it. And was he to say anything to him or not? Somehow he didn't cotton to the fellow. However, there'd be no harm in taking a risk.

"By the way doctor, I noticed a rather peculiar thing. I expect you saw it too—that stain on the face; sand or something."

"Peculiar! Why peculiar?" The doctor shrivelled back into the professional man.

"Well, I just wondered how it got there. All the sand in that wood seems to be white."

The doctor seemed amused, but he begged the question.

"Sand! My dear chap, that's the only thing there is in this part of the world. If it doesn't rain every week, it's a Sahara." He paused for a moment. "Yellow sand, eh? I certainly wiped a stain off his face."

"And if you'll think it over," went on Wrentham, "isn't it strange that a man of Mr. Revere's experience should die like that?"

"My dear sir! I'm not an old man as old men go, but I've held post-mortems on—let me see—at least four men, experienced timbermen all of them, who've been killed by falling trees. There was one only a year ago in this very parish and in practically the same way."

"You mean?"

"Branch caught an obstruction as the tree fell; tree slewed round and hit him. In Mr. Revere's case he undoubtedly tripped over his own bootlace."

Wrentham nodded in agreement. "All the same it's strange he should go tree-felling at night. You said he'd been dead twelve hours?"

"Why not—if he wanted to?" and he shrugged his shoulders. "Last night was as light as day. That open space in the wood'd be easy enough to see in. Besides, people in these parts take anything a Revere does for granted."

"I wonder where they thought he'd gone to all night?"

"Oh, he spends a lot of time at the dolmens—sort of miniature Stonehenge affair. Got some brand new theory on moonlight."

"Really!" Wrentham raised his eyebrows. "Quite near here, are they?"

"Best part of a mile I should say. Right in the corner of the park as a matter of fact."

"I shall have to have a look at 'em some time. Mr. Revere did a lot of felling?"

"Quite a lot. Not much these last few weeks. He was remarkably able I've been told. You coming with me or—"

"Thanks very much Doctor, but—er—that's my car there."

The doctor smiled and apologised; fussed a further good-bye and left Wrentham to it. Inside the wood again the air seemed to take on a chill and everything to be pervaded by a gloom which the presence of company had made less oppressive. For some moments he stood by the fallen tree, then suddenly that bare circle of earth seemed to strike him with a depression that was almost tangible and he turned back to the open grassland. Half an hour later, he was in Branford.

CHAPTER IV
FELLING AS ONE OF THE FINE ARTS

IT WAS THREE very different people who sat talking after lunch in a corner of the smoking-room at the "Angel." Travers seemed rather worried, Franklin somewhat on edge, and the coolest of the party was—of all people—Geoffrey Wrentham.

"Let's compare notes before I say anything," was his suggestion. "Anything strike you this morning, Ludo?"

Travers smiled ironically. "Only this. Anybody else who'd been watching us would probably have been struck dumb at the way we performed. A couple of minutes' contemplation of a tragedy, another minute's musing on the narrow bounds between life and death and then—a wild burst of activity; one looking for this and another for that."

"Perhaps you're right," said Wrentham. "All the same, supposing you were watching the last moments of a favourite aunt and suddenly saw a bottle labelled 'Arsenic' peeping out from the pillow, wouldn't you feel rather restless?"

"I'll own up," admitted Franklin, "but it was the major here who set me off. No sooner did we get in the wood than he asked us to look at something peculiar. Then he hinted it wasn't an accident. Then it suddenly struck me that a man wouldn't want oil stoves and hot drinks in the middle of a blazing summer, so I went to the hut and had an inspection. You can't blame me. After all it's my job to take hints."

"You mustn't take me too seriously," said Travers. "I just felt in a moralising vein for the moment, that's all. But what *did* you see in the hut?"

"To tell the truth, nothing at all. Just the clothes he changed from, the oil stove and matches, some tins of biscuits and what looked like foods, a big filter jar of water—and that's all. Oh yes, and there were some ropes and tools in the corner; probably what he used for the trees—and a grey shooting hat was on a deal table just inside the door."

"Nothing on the hat?"

"Not a thing. Absolutely spotless. No blood. No sand."

"And nothing else struck you at all."

"Well, after you'd gone we mentioned the extraordinary coincidence in the nature of Mr. Revere's death. And we noticed the size of the tree. From what Westfield was telling us as we came along we were both expecting to see a typical oak. How on earth did a man—an experienced man—come to be killed by a miserable thing like that?"

"It isn't the size, it's the speed it falls at," said Wrentham. "But I think I can put you right there," and he went over the conversation with the doctor. "Not only that," he added, "I've known a very experienced timber feller killed by a very small tree. It's a risky business as anybody who knows will tell you. What about you, Ludo? See anything peculiar?"

"I don't know that I did, except the sand—and we know all about that."

"Right-ho, then. Now I'll tell you what *I* saw. Mind you, I'm not going to claim any credit, because to a man who knows the very first thing about his job, it was as plain as the nose on his face. The point is, do either of you know anything about timber felling?"

"I've only the vaguest idea," admitted Travers.

"Only what I've seen on the movies," laughed Franklin.

"Then here's some paper I got from the lounge, if you'll gather round. Do you know what a fall is? You don't. Well, look here.

"This is a perfectly normal tree, clean out in the open. If it stands reasonably upright, it can be felled in any direction you like. Say we want it to go to the left. Very well then. With the axe we cut what is called a fall, from A—B, just over half-way through. The fibres of

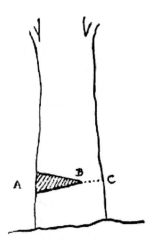

the tree still hold it up. Then with the saw we start from C towards B and as soon as we feel the tree totter, away we move to the right and down she comes to the left, within a foot of where we wanted it. That's of course if there are no obstructions. If the tree hit another as it fell, naturally, there'd be the risk it'd spin right over. That's why you take jolly good care your tree's got an open space to fall in. If it hasn't, you've got to cut off obstructing boughs from other trees or even cut down any small tree that stands in the way.

"Now let's get it perfectly clear. What I've drawn here is a *tree;* something valuable—good timber if you like, that's got to be felled clean. You got that all right? Good! Then we'll have a look at another one. What d'you think of it? Pretty awful specimen, what?"

Franklin smiled. "If it's like its picture, it's all you say it is."

"You can take it from me that it's—well, as drawn. Thick round say, as a pail—a small pail. Timber not worth a cuss! not enough for a decent sized gate-post in the whole length of it. All the same, let's suppose it's got to come down. Say it's in the way of a better tree. How would you get it down?

"I'll tell you. You slosh it down. You start right down to the ground and go at it with an axe or saw, starting at C first and finishing up at A. You don't give a cuss what happens to the timber. It's just like clearing away rubbish. You know it must fall to the right and all you have to do is take ordinary precautions. In other words, don't cut too much at C. Just give her a start, then stand well clear at A and let her have it with the axe or saw." Then he looked at the couple of them in a queer sort of way. "This tree, by the way, is a sort of photograph of the one that's supposed to have killed Revere."

"But you never saw it before it was felled?"

"I know I didn't. But I know it must have stood just like that. The butt lay there for inspection. The stump slopes to the right. If you looked up and saw what I saw, you'd have noticed the clear space where the top spread out and you'd have seen the exact line it took as it fell by the torn twigs of the trees round it."

Franklin nodded. "That's right enough."

"Now let's go on from there," said Wrentham and it was rather comical to watch the earnestness of the effort. "I've told you what any experienced woodman would have done with that tree—and Cosmo Revere *was* a good man at the job. But what did the man who actually felled it do? Let's call him X. X knew a little but not much. He wanted to fell that miserable little tree just as he thought Cosmo Revere would have felled it. But all he knew—all he had seen if you like—was the felling of decent trees. Therefore he treated it as a decent tree. He set a fall in on the right—only a little one or the tree would have split right up—then got to work with the saw on the left. Think of the pressure as soon as he started to saw. Suppose you saw a thickish bit of wood half through and snap the rest off on your knee? What happens? You leave a jagged bit of unsawn wood in the middle. Well, that's what this tree did as soon as he'd sawn for a moment or two. The tree snapped off. Something like this, I imagine.

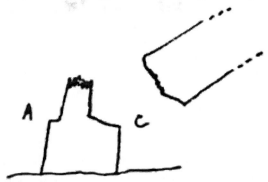

Then of course he was in the devil of a muddle. He'd think to himself, 'Cosmo Revere would never leave a tree like this.' So he started first of all to cut off that jagged piece with the axe; then finished it with the saw, so as to make the stump smooth."

"Good Lord! How do you know that?"

Wrentham pulled out the chip from his pocket. "Here's direct evidence—an actual chip with the jagged top to it. If you look at the stump you'll see the axe marks, and then where he finished up with the saw."

Franklin scratched his head. "Extraordinary! Wish you'd pointed that out while we were there."

Wrentham shook his head. "You couldn't do that sort of thing—not when he was lying there. Silly perhaps, but that's how I felt. However, you can take it definitely from me that Cosmo Revere *didn't* fell that tree. And here's some more evidence.

"Let's suppose he did fell it. At the moment the tree fell he was supposed to be sawing at A. Even if he'd sprinted he couldn't have reached the spot where he fell so as to let the tree deliberately hit him.

"Not only that. Cosmo Revere would certainly have stepped away to the left from A so as to have let the tree fall away from him. How then did he get where he was?

"And another perplexing thing. There may be some mad reason, as I told you the doctor said, why he should fell a miserable specimen of a tree by moonlight; an affair for a man who had good tools and knew his job, of not more than a minute or two. Then why did he go to all the bother of changing? He couldn't have felled a real big one—like that huge fellow next to it—by moonlight. What I mean is he wasn't going on working. Why then did he change?"

"Just a minute," said Travers. "About this moonlight theory. Let's say X killed him, felled the tree and laid the body beside it. Wouldn't X know the doctor'd be sure to state the exact time he was killed? X knew that somebody'd be bound to say 'What the devil did he mean felling trees by moonlight?'"

"I was coming to that," said Wrentham patiently. "X was sure nobody'd go near that wood. I'll bet you a fiver Cosmo Revere used to be away quite a lot without giving notice. If the body had been there another twenty-four hours, everyone'd have said he'd been killed felling a tree in the *morning*"

"You may be right, especially if those woods were particularly private."

"But you heard Westfield say so."

"That's right. So I did. But would you mind doing something. Just what do you think happened—about the murder?"

Wrentham thought for a moment. "Well, X killed Cosmo Revere by a blow on the head, then got his body to the wood. When he killed him or while the body was being removed, some sand got on the dead man's face. X knew all about the tree beforehand. He chose it deliberately because he could fell it and bolt in less than no time. He arrived at the tree, changed the dead man's clothes, felled the tree as I have described, placed the body, put some blood on the handy end of a bough and then hopped it. That's a quick idea of what I think happened."

"About the hat," said Franklin. "If he was killed elsewhere he'd have had his hat on, unless the killing was done indoors."

"That I can't say anything about," admitted Wrentham. "But let me add one last thing. You remember what I was saying about X cutting off the jagged top of the stump? and how he forgot the chips'd be left lying about and the saw and axe marks'd be seen? *He forgot something else*. When the tree snapped off and left the jagged piece on the stump, he forgot the fact that he couldn't really disguise it by cutting it off. There must have been a corresponding hole in the butt where the jagged part was torn out. It was there. Anybody could see it. Now I ask you. Would Cosmo Revere—after what I've already told you, mind you—have done all that ridiculous camouflaging? I'm certain, I tell you. I'd risk all I've got that Cosmo Revere had nothing to do with the felling—or rather the butchering—of that tree."

Travers took off his glasses. "I'm perfectly convinced. But what about a jury?"

"Ah, that's the point. You heard what I was telling you about that priceless old fool in the wood. If Leeke and the doctor had been there alone I'd probably have told them what I've been telling you and they'd have had to take notice. But look here now. What about the three of us going back to the spot so that you can see everything for yourselves? We'll leave the Morris in the top lane and walk the rest. I'll go all over it again and if you agree we'll put the matter before the responsible authorities and they can stew in their own juice."

Franklin hopped up like a shot.

"Just a second," said Travers. "Was there any sand on the clothes in the hut, or on the floor?"

"The clothes I didn't touch but there wasn't any on the floor. I'd swear to that."

"Oh come along!" said Wrentham. "We can argue that out on the way. The great thing is to get back to that wood."

But when a quarter of an hour later they turned the bend of the wood and came in sight of the straight stretch that led towards the track, it was plain that things had been happening. Groups of people were walking away and further off a policeman was turning back new arrivals. The sightseers and morbid ones had evidently heard all about it but had been forestalled by somebody who knew them as well as they knew themselves. Moreover, from the wood came the sound of chopping.

"Extraordinary!" said Wrentham. "Wonder what's up? There's Westfield on duty by the gate. You fellows stop here out of sight and I'll find out what's happening."

Westfield had a lot to relate. According to his story, cut down to the barest essentials, what had happened was this. When the van containing Cosmo Revere's body reached the Hall by the back road, it was met by Royce the butler and the vicar, both of whom seemed very distressed at the terrible event. Westfield's telling was a stolid one, but even from that Wrentham could gather that the scene had developed into a theatrical one. The vicar had expressed the opinion that just as one destroys a bull or a horse that has killed a man, so the tree that had been the cause of a man's death should be done away with, root and branch. Leeke and Colonel Warren had also taken part in the argument and an additional reason for its destruction was brought forward. If left, it might become an object of vulgar curiosity and a resort for sensation-mongers. Leeke had agreed and Colonel Warren had straightway blustered into action. Leeke seemed to have been stampeded into sending forthwith men to clear the site of the tragedy and then to seal up the gate and run barbed wire along it and the hedge. The hut had already been taken away and by this time was doubtless in the Hall yard. All of which of course was pretty disastrous news, and Wrentham reported it at once.

"Won't they get into the hell of a row for doing that?" asked Travers indignantly.

"Not they!" said Franklin. "The whole thing's a closed corporation. Colonel Warren's the big noise. The doctor's got his own theories to back him up. The jury'll be a collection of sheep."

"Infuriating!" snapped Wrentham. "Not a damn one of 'em knows a blasted thing about felling a tree."

"Have another look," suggested Franklin. "We might be able to find something they've left."

Westfield made no bones about passing the major through, but fifty yards down the path he had to step aside. A horse was dragging to the gate the trunk of the tree and behind came two tumbrils with the branches. When they were by he went on quickly. That bare circle of wood was now more bare than ever. Even the stump had been cut off below the ground and the leaf-mould, smoothed over its site, concealed the last trace of the tree that had stood there.

Back at the gate he passed over another half crown to the keeper. As he took it the man looked up and their eyes met. He hesitated for a moment, then, "Could I have a word with you, sir?"

Wrentham lowered his voice. "Confidential you mean?"

"Yes, sir."

"What time do you knock off?"

"Six, sir."

"Can you get to the 'Angel' at Branford by seven? The public bar?"

"Yes, sir. I'll bike it."

"Good enough. I'll be there and fetch you through to my room. Keep a still tongue in your head Westfield."

The man nodded. "Don't you worry about that, sir."

A minute later the three were arguing it out all the way to Branford. An hour later in Travers's room at the Angel it was still going on.

CHAPTER V
TRAVERS GOES TO TOWN

A WOULD-BE wit once remarked in reference to the view afforded by the solid and dignified mass of Durango House side by side with Charing Cross Station, that it always reminded him of a bishop taking a dachshund for exercise. When the great firm of enquiry, advertising and publicity agents built that stupendous headquarters, there were some who wagged their heads and wondered where the money was coming from. That of course, as events move nowadays, was in the dim past of a whole decade ago; since when Durangos have built a good many sub-offices that have cost more money and caused less comment.

One supposes too, that the same beards wagged when from time to time Sir Francis Weston had made his sensational appointments to the control of the new Durango departments. Ludovic Travers for instance, whose *Economics of a Spendthrift, Stockbrokers' Breviary* and weightier text-books gave him in economics much the same position that Wells occupies in social criticism; what must it be costing to have such a man as financial adviser or chancellor of the Durango exchequer? John Franklin too; what would he have to be paid, after the enormous publicity of the Perfect Murder Case? But as far as Francis Weston was concerned there were three things that mattered. He had unrivalled efficiency, magnificent advertising, and by no means least, Durangos had more than once been able to issue bonus shares.

It was eight o'clock that Wednesday evening when Ludovic Travers reached Durango House to find Sir Francis waiting in his private room. As a result of the final deliberations of the late afternoon it was Travers who had been despatched to London. For one thing Franklin couldn't have handled the Isotta and for another he was anxious to stay where the scent seemed warmest.

Sir Francis seemed discreetly amused, perhaps at the incongruity that was presented by Travers—mild, bespectacled, a man of books rather than action—thrust once more into a sensation and this time not of his own seeking.

"You seem to have been having a busy day," was his greeting.

"Well, I wouldn't go so far as that, Sir Francis. Franklin perhaps. He got you all right on the phone?"

"He did, and surprised me pretty considerably—and sent a long list of things he wanted to know."

He waved Travers to a chair. "As a matter of fact I've got some information and ought to have more at any minute. Would you like to go over the thing again—I mean the case for murder as against accident? It's so much more satisfactory than a telephone conversation."

Travers forthwith went over the events and arguments of the day. The story was more than once interrupted by the telephone or the arrival of papers, but by the time it was finished it was clear that the other was practically in agreement.

"There's only one possible thing to ask," he said, "and that is, you're quoting Major Wrentham as an absolutely reliable authority?"

"Absolutely! You've met him, Sir Francis, and it's quite probable you've formed the opinion that he's merely pleasantly bright and breezy. I admit it's an impression he does his best to create. But really he's a remarkably shrewd observer. And as far as timber felling goes, he's always up to his eyes in it at Hainton. If he's wrong, Sir Francis, I'll give a hundred pounds to any hospital you like to nominate."

The other laughed. "Let me see; you were at Cambridge together?"

"Practically brought up together."

"That's all right then. Now as to what I've been doing. The real problem seemed to me how Franklin was to get a footing on the premises, so to speak, without arousing suspicion. Brotherston, Hall and Brotherston are the Revere solicitors and you'll be interested to know I've just got back from seeing Sir Henry Brotherston personally. The heir is an American citizen—Cosmo Hubert Grant—living at the moment in New York. Perhaps you'd like to see the family tree as far as it concerns us. I'll let you have a copy for Franklin."

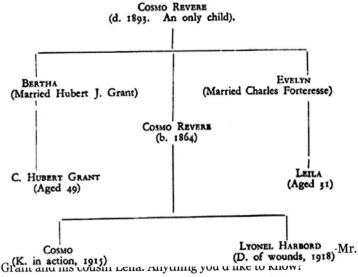

Grant and his cousin Leila. Anything you'd like to know?

"Everything you can possibly tell me, Sir Francis."

"Well, Grant's a wealthy man—president of the Grant Dental Corporation—and a very delightful fellow I understand. The doubtful proposition seems to be the niece about whom I thought Franklin seemed rather anxious.

"From what I can gather, Evelyn Revere took the Victorian road to perdition by eloping with her music master; an event which is said to have killed her father. Before he died, however, he seems to have closed his doors on the couple in the approved manner and made them an allowance of a hundred a year or so to keep them from actual want. Apparently they descended from the genteel to the shabby genteel and finally landed in Paris where Charles Forteresse got a job in an orchestra. He died about four years ago and his widow two years later. Then it appears Cosmo Revere sent immediately for his niece, who's been at Fenwold ever since."

"Is she provided for under the will?"

"Ah, that I can't say. We shall know as much as everybody else in a day or two. But I should say that, judging from the tone of Sir Henry's comments, his firm were considerably surprised, and even possibly remonstrated, at their client's action in admitting her to Fenwold."

"Rather an impertinence, wasn't it?"

"That's the very point. That's the mystery we've got to get hold of. She's certainly worth looking up—indeed Franklin requested me to take the necessary steps. And now what about yourself? Are you averse to giving up your valuable time to—er—lending a hand?"

Travers was a bit agitated. "I hardly see—I mean—well, what can I do, Sir Francis?"

"Franklin thinks you can do a lot. He asked me himself to induce you to stay down there for a bit. The thing is, are you keen yourself?"

"It sounds fascinating."

Sir Francis smiled. "It does, or I shouldn't be here at this moment. Now tell me. What was Franklin proposing to do?"

"Stay at the inn in the village and pose as a visitor who preferred it to Branford. He ought to hear a lot of gossip that way."

"I guessed somehow he'd do that. But I've been thinking and this is what I've worked out. Of course it's Franklin's job and it's entirely up to him to agree. But I did think perhaps he had to make a hurried decision so I took the risk of telling him to wait for a bit till he'd seen you again. Also he'll be waiting for you on the phone from two o'clock onwards to-morrow.

"This is the scheme. Sir Henry didn't tell me so but I'm perfectly sure he knows something—and something mighty curious. What he would like is for you to be temporarily associated with his firm and to act as Mr. Grant's accredited representative until his arrival. That will give you an entrée to the Hall itself. Franklin might go as your personal servant and take up his quarters there too. That'd give him heaps of leisure to look round. How's it strike you?"

"I think it's splendid! I suppose I'm to call on Sir Henry for the exact details."

"Quite so. Your name was, of course, *persona grata* when I put the matter to him. He's desperately anxious to avoid the least breath of scandal. This Cosmo Revere seems to have been a fabulously wealthy and most important person and to put it in one way—people like that don't *have* to get murdered."

"Enquiries have to be extraordinarily confidential and only what's absolutely essential must ever get out."

"That's it exactly. Everything that *can* be hushed up has got to be. The great thing, I think, is this. If Sir Henry wasn't alarmed; if he hadn't had suspicions himself that everything wasn't all it should be, he'd never have consented to our making an enquiry—because that's what it amounts to. To put it more bluntly, he's glad you and Franklin are going down there only because he fears anybody else would have stood on far less ceremony about all this Fenwold tradition business."

"How long do you expect it to take?"

"Well, that's more for you to say. There *may* turn out to be nothing in it. But you'll both be down there and in a position to judge. That's all to the good. No possible harm can be done in any case. Naturally of course one of the partners—Sir Henry himself probably—will be down a good deal."

"What's he like, Sir Francis?"

Sir Francis screwed up his features into an expression that told a good deal. "Oh—er—not a bad fellow. I've known him for years."

That was how it was left. By the following morning matters were definitely settled. The lawyers had succeeded in getting into telephonic communication with Grant and had apparently been left to carry on at their own discretion. At least a fortnight would elapse before the heir to the estate could leave for any extended stay in Europe. Ludovic Travers, as Sir Francis had hinted, could proceed at once to Fenwold Hall where his arrival that night would be expected. Moreover, on the Saturday he would attend the funeral as the representative of Mr. Grant himself. Sir Henry would also be present.

And finally, when Travers had completed all his jobs of work and started out, it was not in the Isotta. Through Leeke that would definitely establish connection with Geoffrey Wrentham. It was an inconspicuous blue saloon therefore, driven by a picked man from

Franklin's own department, that dropped him shortly before 6 p.m. at the door of the "Angel."

CHAPTER VI
"EVENING NEWS"—LATE EDITION

NO SOONER HAD Travers left for London that Wednesday afternoon than Franklin made a beginning. But a contemplation of the notes he had written produced absolutely nothing—nor could Wrentham help him. What for instance was the connection between Miss Forteresse and Leeke? Who was the Castleton—if that was the name—that Leeke had threatened her with? What was the truth about the absence of Cosmo Revere from the Hall the previous night and his failure to return? What was behind that clearing away of all evidence from the site of the tragedy? And what was that about the miniature Stonehenge and moonlight?

There was just a precautionary word before the major went to look for Westfield.

"It's your show really," he said. "I shall have to hare off like blazes as soon as he's gone. You'll have to do all the talking."

Franklin couldn't help smiling and Wrentham saw the joke.

"Perhaps you think I can't sit tight and that's where you're wrong. There's not a tighter oyster in the bed than your Uncle Geoffrey when he feels like it."

"I'll bet there isn't," said Franklin. "Still, you start and I'll carry on."

The bottles of beer and the glasses stood handy and Westfield, looking decidedly ill at ease on his entry, was soon made to feel more at home.

"First of all," began Wrentham, "before you tell us whatever it was you had to tell us, there's something I've got to say. It's like this, Westfield, and I'm going to be absolutely straight with you. Both Mr. Franklin here and myself are far from satisfied that Mr. Revere met his death as the result of an accident. We've got certain information but the trouble is how to fit it in. And of course we're both strangers here and that doesn't make it any easier. What we shall want you to do is give us all the information you can. Mr. Franklin will put certain questions to you and it's up to you to answer them. But you've got to remember one thing. If you mention a single word of this visit or anything we tell you to a single soul—You married, by the way?"

"Wife's dead, sir."

"H'm! Well, if you do let anything get out, you'll do yourself and us an enormous amount of harm. Can we absolutely trust you?"

"You can that, sir."

"Good! Then I'll add something else. The new master of Fenwold won't forget what you're going to do. It will be the first duty of Mr. Franklin here—and I can assure you that he has considerable influence—to bring your record to his attention and to let him know he has on his estate one man who can be trusted."

Franklin liked the way the man took it. He liked too the cut of his face, his steady eyes and quiet bearing and decided that Wrentham had done a good thing.

"Now what was it you wanted to tell us?"

The answer he got was a dramatic one, to say the least of it. It is given too without most of the Breckland dialect which Franklin was only able to follow with difficulty.

"A very funny thing happened to me last night, sir. About eight, old George Carter met me in the village and said as how he'd seen a man in Branford who wanted to see me about nine—most particular, at the Cock, and if he wasn't there I was to wait till he turned up. I said who was it? and he said he didn't know but the man said I'd know all right and Carter said he was a keeper. I thought it was funny at the time, sir, but I got on my bike and come to Branford and waited till closing time and after but nobody didn't turn up and then when I got home I began to think a bit."

"You thought somebody'd been playing a trick on you."

"That's it, sir. I sort of put two and two together like and wondered if I'd been got out of the way deliberate so that somebody could net a few rabbits on my ground—"

"Ground?"

"His beat," explained Wrentham. "The part of the estate he's responsible for as a keeper. By the way, Westfield, where do you live?"

"First cottage past the Lodge, sir. It's got a lot of hollyhocks in front."

"But isn't that a long way from Lammas Wood? That's in your beat, isn't it?"

"Well, when my wife was alive, sir, we used to live in the keeper's cottage on the Branford road. A young keeper who's got a family live there now as Captain Leeke thought the small one'd be big enough for me. I soon slip down there on my bike."

"You live all alone?"

"Except for the dog, sir. A woman come in and do for me in the mornings."

"It just struck me, that's all. Carry on with your story."

"Well, I didn't do nothing about it that night, sir, then early this morning I thought I'd have a good look round and as I was that way, sir, I thought I'd cut through the wood. Mr. Revere don't allow nobody in the woods where his hut is, sir, but I reckoned he wouldn't be about that time of day so I got as far as the gate and as soon as I looked down the path, sir, blowed if I didn't catch sight of a man about a hundred yards down. I didn't really catch sight of him, sir—I just sort of knew I'd seen a man. So he slipped out of sight and I gave a holler and nipped along to see who it was but when I got level where I'd seen him he wasn't nowhere in sight."

"You've not the faintest idea who he was?"

"I don't know who he was, sir. I had an idea he was a sort of suspicious person, if you know what I mean, sir."

"See any more of him?"

Westfield shook his head.

"And what time would this be?"

"About half past five, sir. Then I went along the path a good way and kept looking and listening and then I went in to breakfast. Then later on I thought I'd go back there again and that's how I came to find—what you saw, sir."

"That's a remarkable story," said Franklin. "And you haven't said a word to a soul about it?"

"No, sir. I wasn't supposed to go into that wood for one thing. Captain Leeke asked me how I happened to—to find him, sir, and I said my old dog was acting suspicious."

"And who's this George Carter?"

"He's a curious old fellow, sir; been in the village about eighteen months. He live in a cottage near the green. It's Mr. Castleton's cottage."

"And who's *he?*"

"Mr. Castleton, sir? He's the old vicar's son who used to be here before this one come. When his father died he went to Oak Cottage and he live there alone, sir, except that a woman come in the daytime and clear up and so on."

"What's Carter do for a living?"

"He go round the villages buying antiques. He used to hire the cart from the 'Coach and Horses'. Then he's got a big shed Mr. Castleton put up for him at the bottom of his garden where he keep things in. Mr. Castleton used to buy nearly all of 'em, sir."

"And what's Mr. Castleton do for a living? Got plenty of money of his own?"

"Not him, sir. His old father—rare old gentleman he was, sir—never had a penny to help himself with. This Mr. Castleton went to Cambridge and a pretty penny that cost so they say, sir, and now he don't do nothing and also he buy up antiques."

"He and Carter used to work in together."

"Well I reckon that's about it, sir. They say Mr. Castleton used to get Carter to show him everything he bought and I've often heard him boast how much money he was making out of Mr. Castleton. Then lately Carter's been saying nasty things about him as how he ain't paid him near enough what he ought and how he wasn't going to let him have any more except at his own price. Last week they say Carter had a dealer down from the city and he bought up everything he'd got."

"Where does Carter generally do his talking?"

"In the 'Coach and Horses', sir. There's two pubs in the village but only farmers and so on go to the 'Stag.'."

"I suppose you were annoyed with Carter about spinning you that yarn? Or did you know it wasn't he who made it up?"

"I didn't reckon *he* made it up, sir, because he don't do anything in the poaching line. His eyes are too bad for that, sir."

"A local man is he?"

"I can't say that, sir. He always spoke like all of us do about here. He don't come from the shires where they talk different."

"I suppose you haven't seen him since?"

"I went to see him after breakfast this morning, sir, and he weren't in so I asked over the road and they said as how he'd gone off in his motor van about seven."

"But I thought you said he drove a horse and cart?"

"Ah! so he used to. That was when he first come. Then he got hold of a motor van and Mr. Castleton he taught him to drive it."

"Curious! Mr. Castleton taught him you say?"

"Yes, sir. Carter said he was going to ask him to, and I've seen them practising at night on the road."

"Mr. Castleton sort of associates with everybody then."

"Not he, sir. He keep himself very much to himself. He's very superior like."

"Who looks after Carter?"

"Nobody, only himself. He's nearly always away, sir, at auctions and so on. He fetch his own milk if he want any and sometimes he have a meal at the 'Coach and Horses.'"

"Hm! Now about this Mr. Castleton. Does he visit much at the Hall?"

Westfield looked surprised at the question; possibly because it showed the questioner knew more than had been admitted.

"There's been a lot of talk about him and Miss Leila, sir. They've been seen meeting in the woods and then people put a lot more to it and that's how it grows."

"Has he been visiting at the Hall recently?"

"That I can't say, sir. There was some talk about Mr. Revere not having anything to do with him because of his turning Socialist. The master was a very particular man, sir; very particular."

What that all meant Franklin didn't quite gather, but he risked a further long shot.

"But isn't Miss Forteresse engaged to Captain Leeke?"

"There's been a lot of talk about that, sir. They say as how they've been seen out together at Branford but how much there is in it, sir, I don't know. They say too as how she's been carrying on with Mr. Haddowe—been in the vestry with him alone."

"Phew!" went Franklin, and, "Who's he? The vicar?"

"That's right, sir. The Reverend Haddowe. He took Mr. Castleton's place. He look old enough to be her father."

"A decent sort of chap is he?'"

"Oh, he's all right, sir. Don't treat you like dirt like most on 'em do. They say he likes his glass and his joke."

"Good for him! And what about Colonel Warren?" Westfield actually gave a snort. "Him! He's a pig, sir. Don't treat men like human beings. Nobody don't speak a good word for him. They said as how he was going to marry Miss Leila only the master he put his foot down about it."

Franklin gave a click of annoyance. Wrentham was highly amused.

"If Mr. Franklin's going to track down village scandal, West-field, he's got a job. In my village they've had me engaged twenty times in the last ten years."

"It wasn't the scandal so much," smiled Franklin. "The trouble is separating the smoke from the fire. By the way, Westfield, did you hear anything about Mr. Revere being away from the Hall last night?"

"I did hear something, sir, what didn't amount to much. The people in the Hall, sir, don't talk to us outside. Mr. Revere was very particular about that."

"The Hall kept itself strictly to itself, so to speak?"

"That's it, sir. You can talk better than I can, sir, but they were sort of up there and we're down here."

"A sound illustration," put in Wrentham. "But Mr. Re-vere *was* often absent all night, wasn't he, Westfield?"

"Oh yes, sir! Mr. Hood—he's the head woodman—know more about that. He used to be at the Devil's Fingers."

Wrentham was used to that sort of infernal nomenclature.

"That'd be those old stones he used to spend a lot of time at. Where are they exactly, Westfield?"

That led to the final job of work. Wrentham produced a large-scale map and with the keeper as guide they drew another of the village on a still larger scale. By the time that was finished it was getting late.

"Just one more question before we go," said Franklin. "If this Mr. Castleton was as poor as you say, how did he have the impertinence to consider himself as a possible husband for Mr. Revere's niece?"

"Well, he belong to a fine old family, sir. They say his grandfa-ther was a bishop and his mother was a relation of Lord Melcomb's, sir, because I used to live out that way before I come here. I remember her getting married at Melcomb Hall. She died in the 'sylum, poor thing."

Franklin and Wrentham exchanged glances. "Madness in the family, was there?"

"I don't know about that, sir; but they was a rum lot."

A final word of caution to Westfield and a hint to expect a visit from Franklin any evening after dark, and the interview was over. An hour later and Geoffrey Wrentham—needless to say to his great regret—was moving as fast away from the Cosmo Revere case as the Morris could carry him, with his only consolation the assurance that whatever happened should be reported.

As for Franklin, he sat up late into the night writing up the day's doings and then trying to get inspiration from a contemplation of his ultimate synopsis.

LEILA FORTERESSE—queen of the vamps.
COLONEL WARREN—blood, brag and bluster.
CASTLETON—local lounge-lizard with philanthropic tendencies.
CAPTAIN LEEKE—little man in a big job.
GEORGE CARTER—the man who had a lot done for him.
HADDOWE—the amorous vicar with a medieval mind.

As for the value of those first impressions, they were much nearer the mark than he could ever have anticipated.

CHAPTER VII
FENWOLD HALL—BELOW STAIRS

THE TRANSFORMATION of Franklin to Francis took best part of half an hour. There were clothes to be tried on and certain facial alterations to be made. For the latter, simplicity seemed to be best. A modification in the hair parting and a perfectly clean shave—leaving a small amount of side whisker accentuated by a temporary artificial addition—proved quite enough to give Franklin the appearance of a valet, though perhaps for a man of his presence, butler was nearer the mark. A black overcoat—in spite of the weather—and a bowler, added a definite restraint and when he took his seat in the car Travers had to confess that the effort was subdued but masterly.

"Nothing else happened at your end?" asked Franklin.

"I don't think there was anything else, except that Sir Francis rather wondered whether he ought to ask you to inform Scotland Yard of your suspicions. Then we got in a muddle. We didn't know if the Yard could act over the heads of the county authorities or whether they'd have to argue the matter out between them. That would have meant loss of time. Also I ventured to point out that as the whole of our evidence had been removed, nobody would be likely to pay much attention, especially if the inquest—And that reminds me. What happened?"

"What we expected. Verdict of accidental death."

"And what about his absence from the Hall on the Tuesday night?"

"Oh, they explained that all right. To tell you the truth I was quite satisfied about that myself. I told you all about those dolmens and how Cosmo Revere had certain theories about moon-worship. From what I gathered there's a group of three—like three archways—somewhere on the outskirts of the park and when it was moonlight he used to spend the whole night there making observations. The butler—Royce his name was—gave evidence that his master left the Hall at about 9.0 p.m. dressed in the walking suit he always wore on such occasions. He said nothing particular to Royce who naturally imagined he was going where he always went. He tapped on the bedroom door at 11.0 and as there was no answer he was sure. In any case the side door by the library was always left open so he could get in when he liked."

"And what about when he didn't arrive for breakfast?"

"That again was nothing unusual. Royce said Mr. Revere had often kept out till lunch. He had all the facilities for making tea and so on and the old chap seems to have really liked roughing it a bit. In any case he was getting rather crotchety and would resent the least interference. Royce was a splendid witness—remarkably dignified, well-spoken old fellow. A Mrs. Lacy, the housekeeper, gave the same evidence."

"It doesn't sound any too satisfactory."

"Ah, that's because of the way I'm telling it. If you'd been there—everything solemn and subdued—you'd have seen it in a different way. Everybody seemed to take it for granted that Cosmo Revere wasn't a man like other men; I don't mean any form of eccentricity, but the name he had, the great estate he owned and his lofty personal character. You could feel everybody mention him with bated breath. I expected Royce and the housekeeper to bob every time they said his name."

"That's the very view Sir Henry seemed to take. It'd have been sacrilege to have mentioned anything so vulgar as murder."

"That's just it. The verdict was what I said. It was assumed—and this is the weak spot—that he went out intending to go to the dolmens, but as it was a remarkably fine night, changed his mind and strolled through Lammas Wood. Then he caught sight of the hut and was attracted by the idea of felling that tree. That was all there was to it. Didn't take more than an hour."

"What did you do the rest of the afternoon?"

"Made a few local enquiries about Colonel Warren. He's all we heard he was. And he's certainly had hopes of the lady. I'm rather anxious to have a look at her, aren't you?"

Travers smiled tentatively. "Professionally—yes."

"Oh, and here's something else," said Franklin, producing a paper from his pocket.

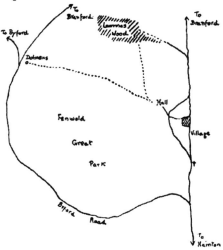

"You can keep that. I've got a copy of my own."

"Do you know, I think we're getting rather close," said Travers. "What about those duties of yours? Any idea how to carry on?"

"Just the vaguest," laughed Franklin. "I thought of using all the common-sense I had and putting down all the howlers to your eccentricity."

"A perfectly good sheet-anchor! If it'll help at all I'll give you a rough idea of what my man Palmer does for me. What we'd better do is have a good talk every night when you tuck me up. But to get along with, as soon as we arrive, hop down and stand by the door. Their people'll see to the luggage. I'm going to make out that you're a cut above the ordinary man. Report to the butler and I'll have put in a word for you. I shall call you John, but for God's sake don't forget that you're Francis!"

"How long have I been with you?"

"What do you say? Twenty years? This looks like the Lodge. Better hop out and sit with the chauffeur."

The wrought-iron gates were opened by an old man and as the car swept along the drive they saw Fenwold Hall for the first time. There was an evening sun that mellowed the grass almost to gold and the distant trees were a deep blue. In the south avenue deer were browsing and sheep, like monstrous daisies, dotted the parkland. On the lawn before the cold front of the building two peacocks were strutting. In that immensity of green the Hall looked monastic, inaccessible and frigidly remote.

As the car drew in to the stone steps that led to the semi-circular portico, a footman in brown and yellow livery appeared—and then a second. Before Franklin could whisk open the door of the car he was anticipated. And as Travers—no mean figure in his topper and professional get-up—stepped from the everyday into the historic, the figure of the butler—tall, perfectly poised and supremely competent—came to meet him.

"Mr. Travers, sir?"

"That's right. You were expecting me?"

"They rang you up from the Lodge, sir. This way, sir, if you please."

The entrance hall was a superb affair. Travers glanced round quickly with the eye of a connoisseur and what he saw made his collector's mouth water. In the middle distance was an early refectory table, legs thick as a man's thigh, and flanking it two great chests with intricate carving. Below the stair gallery on the panelling that rose to it from the floor hung pieces of armour and at the foot stood two period chairs. Along the east wall were two settles with monogrammed C.R. and the date 1602. But before he could do more than glance at the pictures Royce was taking his hat and gloves and handing them to a footman.

"May I show you to your room, sir?"

"Do, please. What's your name, by the way?"

"Royce, sir."

"Then I've a favour to ask of you, Royce. Look after my man if you don't mind. You'll find him different from the ordinary run. He's more of a confidential servant."

"Certainly, sir. I shall be very pleased indeed, sir. If I may say so, sir, we rarely get that sort of company nowadays."

The bedroom was charming and its furniture delightful. There was a Queen Anne tallboy that should have been in a museum, and a tiered walnut mirror that should have been used only by a duchess. The cheerful carpet and the bowl of roses gave a note of gaiety and the windows overlooked moreover the rose-beds that sprinkled the southwest lawns. Finally Royce had a message to deliver.

"Miss Forteresse's compliments, sir, and she begs you to excuse her as she has a severe headache."

"I'm sorry to hear that," began Travers—

"As Miss Forteresse ventured to think, sir, that you would like company to dinner, Mr. Haddowe will be dining with you to-night, sir."

"Who's he, Royce?"

"The vicar, sir. Dinner is at 7.30, sir. Walters will bring the wine list for your selection, sir."

Left to himself, Travers surveyed the room and the view from the window. "If Geoffrey were here," he thought, "there'd be some asinine remark about being born in the purple. But my God! what magnificence!"

* * * * *

As for Franklin he was escorted from his bedroom by a footman and down a staircase which led direct to the servants' hall. Royce made the most casual of introductions, but it was plain that among the underlings of Fenwold Hall the newcomer was to be definitely above the salt.

"Mr. Francis will take all meals with me, Parker. Anything he wants you will attend to."

The footman's "Very good, sir!" showed that discipline was sound. Close by at the end of a short passage was the butler's parlour; large and airy but cosy, with easy chairs and book shelves. Mrs. Lacy—a quiet-spoken, white-haired but still active woman in customary solemn black—rose and was introduced.

"This will be your home, Mr. Francis," said Royce. "Mrs. Lacy— or Mrs. Royce as she really is—and myself are both pleased to welcome you. Dinner for us is at 8.15. What will you take now? A glass of sherry or a whisky?"

"If you'll be so good as to join me," said Francis, "I think I'd prefer the sherry."

The healths were drunk and Royce hurried off to supervise what he considered his most important function of the day. The newcomer and the housekeeper sat chatting and things were mentioned that no outsider would ever have heard. The presence of Francis in that house and in that room was enough to place him as *of* the house; ready to serve its interests, to acknowledge its greatness, but to admit to himself and those of his standing, its mischances and even weaknesses.

There were, he learned, eleven maids in the house, including the cook. The Reveres had always been conspicuously conservative among the conservative. There had never been a chef at Fenwold Hall. There was a car for the meeting of guests arriving by rail and there was Miss Forteresse's two-seater, but when Cosmo Revere had gone about it was in a carriage and pair such as his father had used. Moreover he never had a personal servant or secretary. There were four footmen in addition to the butler; in the gardens a dozen men and lads and about the garages and stables a dozen more. Then there were the agent's staff, tradesmen, woodmen, keepers, stewards and farm-workers. Except for two farms let to tenants, the village of Fenwold had moved, lived and had its being round the person of Cosmo Revere.

"It must cost a colossal amount to keep up," remarked Francis.

"The estate of the old master was nearly a million," said Mrs. Lacy. "The late master lived much more quietly than his father, too. Of course when the young masters were alive, especially Master Cosmo, there used to be a lot of entertaining, but things have altered since the war."

"The arrival of Miss Forteresse must have been a godsend."

Mrs. Lacy shook her head. "Not to me. Her ways weren't our ways. I think she expected to be the lady of the house—and so she is in a way—but the late master must have told her the housekeeping was my province because she never speaks to me unless she's forced."

"That makes things awkward," suggested Francis sympathetically.

Mrs. Lacy gave the merest suspicion of a smile. "Everybody in Fenwold knows their place. If Miss Leila gives me instructions about things that are her province, I see they're carried out." She stopped for a moment to thread her needle. "When she first came the master started to entertain again. He soon stopped that. Her ways and his didn't agree. You know, Mr. Francis—the women of to-day, what they must seem to a gentleman like Mr. Revere. As Royce insists, class will tell."

Franklin nodded in agreement. "Her father, wasn't it?"

"Yes. The music master. He's had dinner many a time in this room." Francis felt the comment defined with sufficient accuracy the great gulf fixed.

"She'll be getting married one of these days," he ventured.

The housekeeper lowered her voice almost to a whisper. "The sort of husband she seems likely to get, won't be able to keep servants at all so she'll be able to do what she likes without gossip. Fenwold and scandal don't go together, Mr. Francis."

Enigmatical that, to one not in the know; but with volumes of insinuation. The conversation would certainly have to be kept alive.

"Very regrettable that sort of thing," he said. "It's not connected with any local person, I hope?"

She closed the subject as suddenly as she had opened it. "Unfortunately—yes. And with more than one. Are *you* married, Mr. Francis?"

The conversation took a new turn; then later a footman came in to prepare the table and Francis went up to his own room to unpack his belongings. It was dark when they finally settled down after dinner—Mrs. Lacy with her sewing and the men with their pipes and whisky.

"This must have been a terrible affair for you both," put in Francis at a propitious moment.

Royce slowly shook his head. "The master was getting old; very old, Mr. Francis. Only a bit younger than me, but he never got over the war."

"But he was robust enough," began the other—

"The body perhaps; the mind—no! More than once I've wondered whether he put himself under that tree."

"Royce, don't say such things!" said his wife quickly.

The butler shook his head again and for a minute nothing was said. Then Francis turned the old man's thought into pleasanter paths.

"I should think no man could wish for a better master."

The butler roused himself. "There wasn't one, Mr. Francis! He was a Revere of Fenwold and that's something these days. I was with him as a boy, sir. I was chosen by his father to accompany him when he made the tour as his ancestors did; the grand tour they called it—a year in France and a year in Italy. He moved among the best, sir, because he belonged there. When he succeeded, many's the great family that came here; the Duke of Breckland, the Calverlyes, the Montourelles. . . . Then the young masters were killed. . . . His Grace came personally to offer his condolences. . . . The eldest, Cosmo, was his father over again."

There it all was—the pride of family and the same sense of loss. Royce might have been speaking of his own son, rather than of an employer—the man who paid so much for labour; the market price or maybe more.

"Do you know Mr. Grant, the new master?"

"A fine gentleman, Mr. Francis. He came over at Mr. Revere's request after the war. His grandfather didn't take kindly to his daughter's marriage; thought she ought to have married into an English family. She's dead now; died two years after the boy was born. His uncle took very kindly to him. He wanted him to come to Fenwold, but of course that couldn't be done."

"Well, he succeeds to a magnificent property and a fine old name. And what sort of a gentleman is the vicar who's dining here to-night?"

Mrs. Lacy gave a snort and Royce looked round patiently.

"Now, my dear, you know you're set against Mr. Haddowe!"

"And why shouldn't I be set? I've said it and I say it again; he's not the kind of man we want here."

Royce abandoned the argument. "His predecessor, Mr. Castleton, was very low church; very!"

"What they call the evangelical school," suggested Francis.

"You know it's not that!" broke in Mrs. Lacy again. "I don't care if he's high church or low. I know what I've seen, and under the master's nose—"

"Come! Come!" protested Royce sharply. "Mr. Francis doesn't want to know about that sort of thing." He leaned forward again to the newcomer. "He's one of the old school is Mr. Haddowe; knows what makes up a good cellar and how to carry himself like a gentleman. He comes of good stock. You and I can tell a gentleman as soon as we see him, Mr. Francis. Your master's a gentleman. You don't need to look at him twice,"

"And what about having no maids at the vicarage?" came the voice, with maddening precision.

Royce remained unruffled. "He has two men to do his work, Mr. Francis. And why shouldn't he? I've heard he used to belong to some religious order which forbade marriage—and so on."

"Then will you tell Mr. Francis why he carries on with—"

Royce held up a restraining hand. "Now, my dear; we mustn't talk like this. Wait at least till he's out of the house." He smiled at Francis. "The vicar I was referring to. And how do you get along in life, Mr. Francis?"

Francis gave an account of his employer's virtues and eccentricities and the conversation became more general. As he realised, there would be plenty of time to get into the heart of Fenwold Hall. There was nothing to be gained by rushing matters; to gain the confidence of Royce and his wife was the main thing. When he rose to pay a visit to Travers' room he was already feeling at home in what he had dreaded would be impossible surroundings. He liked Royce. There was about him a natural dignity and kindliness that rang true.

"What time is breakfast, Mr. Royce?" he asked.

"Usually eight-thirty. Would that suit Mr. Travers?"

Francis was sure it would.

"You like an early cup of tea? Then Parker shall bring your tea and hot water at seven. We have breakfast at half past."

It was difficult for Franklin to keep back a smile. That he as a servant should have a menial of his own, reminded him of those fleas that had others on their backs to bite 'em and so on to infinity. But just then the bell rang and the indicator showed the small drawing-room. Royce made an inspection of his clothes and left the room. A moment or two later a footman appeared at the door.

"Mr. Francis? You're wanted in the hall, sir." Francis adjusted his own jacket and moved off. What he was to see was probably the last thing on earth that he expected.

CHAPTER VIII
FENWOLD HALL—ABOVE STAIRS

IT MUST BE confessed that Travers' feelings before that dinner were uncommonly mixed. True he had an appetite and a sub-conscious curiosity, but the prospects of an evening with the village parson were quite a different affair. There were, as he knew only too well, vicars *and* vicars, and what the odds were that he should draw a winner out of the lucky bag he didn't care to estimate. Still, if the man weren't parochial he might be supportable. If on the other hand he should turn out to be one of the unctuous variety—well, there could always be pressure of work to plead after the postprandial half hour.

His first impression of Augustine Haddowe, as he stood with legs apart in front of the fire-screen in the small dining-room, hands tucked under the back of his dinner jacket, was a pleasant one. The padre looked a man of the world for one thing and a man's man for another. There were laughing wrinkles at the corners of his eyes and the hand that shook that of Travers felt like a vice. But he

wasn't boisterous; his was rather a natural joviality and general benevolence. The whole sixteen stone of him seemed glad to be alive;
glad of the meal that was at hand; glad of the short drink that stood
behind him on the mantelpiece, and glad most of all to see Ludovic
Travers. You could see that there would be no obtrusion of religion
with *him*. Travers thought of an old Irish priest he once knew in
Galway and classed him as his spiritual brother.

"Royce has put us in here," he explained. "The dining-room's
an Inigo Jones affair. Much more comfortable here. What will you
take before dinner?"

"I think I'll have what you're taking, padre," said Travers. "One
can't go far wrong in following the Church."

"I wouldn't be too sure of that, my boy. Mr. Travers will have a
gin and bitters, Royce. You down here for long?"

"Some days probably. It's difficult to say exactly."

"Naturally, naturally. It's bound to be an intricate business."

Travers took his short drink with a certain solemnity. "This
must have come as a great shock to you, padre?"

Haddowe assumed an expression of due gravity. "Not only to
me—to everybody. So unexpected. If it had been myself now," and
he shrugged his shoulders. "In some ways I think the finest man I
ever met. Certainly one of the most interesting personalities."

"But the Fenwold traditions will go on."

"I hope so. We all hope so. What a wonderful family! And what
continuity! Centuries of growth and roots down deep in the soil.
Then one clap of wind and the last oak goes." He paused for a
moment and then went on without the least trace of affectation—
the words came so naturally. "*Urbes constituit œtas; hora dis-
solvit,*" then shook his head solemnly.

Travers, in the act of making the same melancholy gesture,
thought of an apposite question. "That curious carving in your
church, padre. What was its origin? Do you know?"

"Well—er—Mr. Revere told me it was something in connection
with the building of the original family vault. I believe the oak or
tree referred to was a famous one—"

The voice of Royce came in quietly. "At your pleasure, sir," and
they moved to the table. There was much to be said for the choice
of the smaller room. Across the five feet of table the diners were in

friendly contact. Through the open french window the gardens were spread out. Round the panelled walls were quiet landscapes. The Chippendale armchairs, the carpet soft as an old lawn, the twinkle of glass and silver, the inaudible but watchful movements of butler and footman in the background; everything was exquisitely set and comfortably perfect. The vicar, too, steered the conversation into the safe channel of generalities and it was not until Royce was placing the port on the table that there was any further reference to the man who lay in the great tithe barn, watched over day and night by men from the estate.

"Have you last Sunday's *Observer* handy, Royce?"

"I think so, sir."

"Let me have it, will you? There's something I'd like you to see—if you haven't already seen it," he explained when the butler had gone. "A letter Mr. Revere wrote on his pet obsession."

"Really! What was it?"

"A very unusual one. He had the idea that dolmens were used in England, or perhaps I should say 'Britain,' in much the same way as the Egyptians are said to have used the Pyramids—for astronomical calculations. Only he was trying to prove that with primitive priests it was connected with moon-worship at the same time."

"It sounds very fascinating."

Royce produced the paper and spoke to Haddowe. "Would you like a table set outside, sir, or would you prefer the small drawing-room?"

The vicar glanced at Travers. "Indoors, I think, don't you? Mosquitoes are apt to be troublesome."

With the stem of his pipe he indicated the position of the letter. Travers gave his glasses a polish.

Dear Sir,

I much regret that I must disagree with your correspondent who finds that moon-worship was confined to those peoples dwelling in tents. Without being too emphatic, moreover, I would give it as my definite opinion that there is an appreciable motion among stars that are generally regarded as fixed.

May I add that I hope to communicate in the near future in a letter to the "Journal of the Archæological Society" the results of researches and experiments which I have made personally and which throw considerable light on the whole question.

I have the honour to be, Sir,

Yours, etc.,

Fenwold.   *Cosmo Revere.*

"And what had he discovered?"

"Don't ask me," laughed Haddowe. "We had some really tortuous arguments on the subject, but frankly it was over my head."

"Do you know, there's a lot of truth in that question of the movement of fixed stars," observed Travers. "I'd love to see his papers. I suppose he kept very careful records?"

"Undoubtedly. I expect you'll find them easily enough—unless of course there's a special proviso in the will?"

Travers avoided that wily opening. "Curious that a man who owned Fenwold should need another hobby. I suppose this was the show place of the district?"

"Oh no! It was never opened for charity. Strangers were never allowed in the house or grounds. Of course he was a munificent contributor to all sorts of deserving things, but any sort of publicity was abhorrent to him."

"You must have known him very intimately?"

"I think perhaps I did. It was hard to say. He was a simple man and yet curiously complex in some ways. He hated everything modern. Even in the last twelve months he seemed to shrink more and more into himself."

"The loss of his sons?"

"I wouldn't like to say. Probably, yes. I was with the youngest son when he died of wounds in hospital near Rouen and when his father arrived too late. The quietness with which he took it was the most tragical thing I ever saw. Repression like that was bound to find an outlet one of these days."

Travers suddenly felt what he had not felt before—what that great house meant in which they were sitting. The feeling came in a flash and was gone before it could become anything more than a moment's sadness at the passing of beauty and then—he found himself looking into the eyes of his companion. They might have been sympathetic or questioning or watchful, but whatever they were it was something discordant—at least with that one moment.

"Life's a funny thing, padre," he said.

The padre smiled. "It's a theme—with ironical variations." He got up. "Shall we go into the other room?"

The small drawing-room was rosy with the screened light from the shaded lamp and in the air was a faint scent like lavender. Somehow it was altogether different from what he'd expected.

"This is Miss Forteresse's own room," explained the padre. "You've not met her yet?"

"I haven't had that pleasure," said Travers. "I was sorry to hear from Royce that she was indisposed."

"A very sensitive soul," said the other. "She feels the loss very deeply. All the impulsiveness, the—what shall I call it?—the insouciance of a continental upbringing, but a heart of gold. At this very moment, whom do you think she has in the house?"

Travers prepared to be suitably surprised.

"Her old nurse! Found out a year ago that she was crippled with rheumatism and in low financial water and promptly got her uncle to have her brought here. Looks after her like a daughter; has her in the bedroom next to her own and a French maid to see to her!"

Travers nodded. He hardly knew what to say unless he pronounced a benediction.

"We who are older find difficulty in seeing eye to eye with modern youth," went on the padre. "Are you a modernist, Mr. Travers?"

"I'm afraid you've got me," smiled Travers. "I'm averse from change, but that's probably laziness. You travelled much, padre?"

"Only in Canada. I lived there for some years. I still go over occasionally for a short visit."

"You never feel like going back?"

"To settle down? I'm afraid not. Life out there makes too many demands."

"But gives its recompenses? You people are making new worlds."

"That may be—only I don't mind reading history, but I've no hankering after making it. What I want nowadays is the quiet life—country, trees, hedges, fine weather, friends and books."

"*Mecum tantum ct cum libellis loquor*" quoted Travers archly.

"A sound hit!" laughed the padre. "But I can cap it. *Voluptates commendat rarior usus.* How's that for you?"

"I'm afraid I asked for that, padre, and served me right—trying to meet you on your own ground. I dabble in mathematics but, by jove! I'd rather have your Latinity."

"Every man to his trade. But talking of hobbies reminds me of something. Do you act at all?"

Travers almost blushed at the unconscious irony. "If you mean, 'Do you go in for amateur theatricals?' I'm afraid I don't."

"That's a pity. Miss Forteresse is awfully keen. We did *The School for Scandal* last March. Quite a good show. We *were* going to do *The Rivals.*"

"You can't get a full company?"

"Well, not exactly that. There's the question of Mr. Revere's death for one thing. The hospital at Branford is badly in need of money and the last show we did raised three hundred pounds. Personally I'm sure that Mr. Revere would approve, if he could only show that approval. What's your opinion?"

"Where do you hold your show?"

"In the village hall—quite a large place."

Travers thought for a moment. "My opinion, padre, is that I should be impertinent if I expressed any. You know the feelings of everybody better than I. There seems to be no connection with the Hall except in the case of Miss Forteresse."

"Then I think we ought to get on with it," said Haddowe with evident relief. "We can make it a week later—say for a month's time. Will Mr. Grant be down then?"

"That I can't say," said Travers warily. "I should rather think he will."

"Good! But it's a pity you're not keen. You'd have made a good Captain Absolute."

"What's wrong? Your leading man dropped out?"

"Hardly that. It's rather confidential. Do you know Gilbert Castleton—the son of my predecessor?"

"I don't know a soul!"

"If you did, you'd soon discover he's got a most peculiar temperament. Miss Forteresse—or Leila, as an old man and a friend of the family is privileged to call her—finds his acting a little too—er—vivid. Of course he's frightfully good. Member of the University Dramatic Club and so on—but temperamental?"—and a shrug of the shoulders expressed it.

"Sorry, padre," said Travers. "I'd like to help but I'm the world's worst actor. And I'm as blind as a bat without my glasses. But I *am* interested in Canada."

On that subject the padre was most interesting. He had spent years among the outlying homesteads of the foothills of the Rockies. In the war he had come over with a Canadian division and it was during a rest spell behind the line that he had met Cosmo Revere at the bedside of his son. The two seemed to have taken to each other and after the armistice the padre had spent a week or two at Fenwold Hall. Later, on the death of the then incumbent, he had been offered the living.

Then naturally they got to the war and the places they knew. The padre spun a good yarn or two and Travers settled deeper and deeper into his chair till his body threatened to escape to the floor, while the other sat, legs crossed and hands tightly together, giving a shrewd commentary on war from the point of view of an opportunist. Finally it was the tinkle of the Dresden clock that roused them.

"Good Lor'!" said Travers, sitting up in the chair. "No idea it was half so late."

The padre peeped through the window. "A wonderful night! Almost like day. Look at those flagged paths. Like drifted sand."

He pushed the bell and they went out together to the entrance hall.

"Will you ask my man to come here a moment." Travers said to Royce, and by the time Francis appeared the padre was ready for the walk.

"Your coat, sir?" asked Francis.

"No, thank you, John. I'm only going a short way with Mr. Haddowe."

"Your man?" asked the padre, surprised possibly at the humanity of the answer.

Travers nodded; then the padre did an unexpected thing—nothing less than thrusting out a hand to the surprised valet and making a speech of welcome. "I hope you'll be comfortable here. If Mr. Royce is looking after you, you won't have very much to complain of."

"I'm sure of that," remarked Travers, surveying with an inward amusement the startled Royce, the decidedly self-conscious Francis and the well-meaning vicar. Francis bowed stiltedly, then put his question.

"You wanted me, sir?"

"Oh, yes, John. Lay out those papers, please. I shan't want you more than half an hour."

Twenty minutes later Travers opened the door of his bedroom to find Franklin in it.

"I thought you'd see my remark about the papers. What I wanted really was that you should have a good look at Haddowe."

"Good!" said Franklin. "I had a look at him all right. Get anything out of him?"

"As a matter of fact, I oughtn't to say it, but I got him to tell quite a lot of local news. I shouldn't be surprised if he's rather useful."

"What was he like personally?"

"Oh, most charming. I now believe in the statesman who believed the best reason for the survival of the Church was that there'd be at least one gentleman in every parish."

"And you told him nothing."

"What was there to tell?"

"Well, I just wondered. He might have put some awkward questions as to why you were here. Still I'm glad you had a jolly time," and now Travers definitely caught the irony in the tone. "As soon as I saw him in that half light with the little scar over his forehead, I guessed you'd had a highbrow evening."

Travers looked at him soberly, like a man who is thinking; then his expression altered.

"That's right," said Franklin. "I knew you'd guess. And now what do you think of my old friend the Marquis?"

CHAPTER IX
MUCH ADO ABOUT A VICAR

WHEN TRAVERS AWOKE the following morning the first thing that came to his mind was the argument he had had the previous night with Franklin. Even now he wasn't altogether convinced. That Haddowe should be the picturesque and blasphemous hero of Franklin's story was really too improbable.

He slipped into a dressing gown, lighted a cigarette and tried to pick up the threads of the conversation—not only with Franklin but what had passed between him and Haddowe. He tried to recall the very gestures, but try as he might, remembered nothing false. Even those half-wistful utterances about the English countryside, its trees and hedges; well, take the view from that window. The mist hung in the elms and gave promise of a perfect day. Away beyond the lawns was the wide stretch of cool, morning green. Was a man a fool for wanting to end his days among that?

And yet he wasn't satisfied. Franklin would never have been so confident or allowed himself that ironical moment if he hadn't been sure beyond question. Then there came a tap at the door and Francis, tray in hand, entered.

"Your tea, sir."

Travers grinned—but he moved away from the window.

"Nice sort of problem you set last night. You're still perfectly sure?"

"Absolutely! But why problem? Doesn't it simplify matters? We've found one man who's likely to be mixed up in anything shady. We wanted somewhere to start from—and we've got it."

Travers sipped his tea thoughtfully. "Why did it seem necessary to Miss Forteresse for me to have company last night? Even if she *were* ill, I might—indeed, considering the circumstances and the proprieties, I feel I ought to have dined alone or without any ceremony whatever. It wasn't good form, John. It wasn't good form!"

"Did Haddowe invite himself?"

"Or was he asked specially, to form opinions of me? to see if I were harmless or not?"

"Then she asked him. You remember all the gossip about the pair of them."

Travers shook his head. "It's a queer business. We haven't got to the fringes yet. Take last night. I can't find a real flaw in what happened. He was a perfectly delightful companion. He was scholarly but didn't obtrude his scholarship. The things he talked about he could enliven with genuine humour. He admitted having spent a good many years in Canada but his accent never once showed it. And why should it? I'm pretty certain I should have to spend more than a few years in Canada before I acquired the accent."

"He mentioned Miss Forteresse?"

"He praised her excessively. Again, why shouldn't he? She may be all he claims for her. If he's in love with the woman the praise is natural. He did speak most disparagingly about Castleton. That, of course, may have been jealousy."

"That name 'Castleton 'is cropping up a good deal," observed Franklin. "It's time one of us cast an eye over that young man."

"That's just what I was saying. It's difficult to know where to start first. But about Haddowe—there was one thing that did strike me as rather peculiar. He seemed to me to be playing up to Royce. There again, he may have a genuine affection for him. Also he seemed rather anxious about holding some amateur theatricals in spite of Mr. Revere's death. He either wanted to rope me in or else to make sure I shouldn't take part. I'm not sure which."

"One thing I will do," said Franklin. "If there's collusion between him and her, one of them will report to the other at the earliest possible moment. He'll probably come here and if so I'll try to overhear what's said. In case she goes to him, I'll put Parry on the watch."

"Who's he?"

"You mean to say you don't know your own chauffeur! He's the chap who drove you down."

Travers breakfasted alone in the room where he had dined the previous night, a room which without the presence of Augustine Haddowe seemed far less friendly than before. His morning constitutional he took round the gardens—maze-like and almost endless what with lawns and ornamental beds, pergolas and herbaceous walks, quiet green corners with their stone or lead figures, rock gardens and pools that led down to the tiny river, and wild gardens sprinkled with bloom.

It was the loneliness there that attracted him and lured him to more than one pipe, and it was well past ten when he made his way back to the house. But he was not to reach the library without adventure. Coming through that same archway of clipped yew where Wrentham had caught sight of Leeke and Leila Forteresse, was a small procession. In a bath-chair pushed by a footman, was the closely wrapped figure of a woman. By her side, carrying a fawn Pekinese, was another woman, in black; some sort of silk it seemed to him, and round her neck a string of white beads.

There was no time to escape, but he stepped off the flagged path and tried to preserve an air of detachment. The voice of the younger woman floated across.

"Are you Mr. Travers?"

Travers gave his best smile, a sort of geniality that spread over his face and which—had he known it—made him look partly forlorn and partly attractive.

"Er—yes. You Miss Forteresse?"

She laughed. Quite a jolly laugh but not without affectation.

"Really too unconventional of us! Do leave your horrid work for a moment and come and speak to Angéle."

The footman withdrew as Travers came forward. In the chair was an elderly woman with, it seemed to him, hard, suspicious eyes. The hair was greying, but the face was scarcely what he expected—that of an old servant to whom the thoughts of a mistress would turn so warmly as to repay with gratitude remembered kindnesses. This woman looked to him keenly critical and even suspicious; one whose business in life it was to do things, to form quick judgments and make decisions. But an old French woman of the peasant class?—well, if she were her voice would prove it.

"This is your old nurse Mr. Haddowe was telling me about last night?"

"Yes. This is Angéle. She speaks hardly any English, unfortunately, do you darling?"

The invalid shook her head and Travers essayed a tentative, "Very glad to see you out this morning."

She gave a prim sort of smile.

"Réponds done Angéle!" said her mistress quickly.

Travers suddenly felt antagonised and in the mood to be obstinate. He broke into his best French. He was glad madame had so fine a morning for her promenade and sorry his French was not good enough for an extended conversation.

There was no doubt whatever about the surprise that gave her. Curiously enough her reply was none too gracious.

"Monsieur speaks French very well!"

The voice had character in it and in spite of its harshness, a certain charm. Travers shrugged deprecatingly.

"The words, madame, that's all. What's lacking is the Gallic background, don't you think so, with all of us?"

She started to speak, then stopped suddenly. For all that the answer had been there.

"And what do you think of our English gardens?" Travers went on.

The conversation dragged along in snatches. Madame thought them very beautiful. Every morning she spent an hour there; sometimes, too, in the cool of the evening. But when one is ill one must not make too much work for others. Travers, glancing at the face of Leila Forteresse, saw a woman on tenterhooks; an expression tense and watchful. Then she broke in suddenly:

"Angéle, darling; you mustn't tire yourself. You know it makes you ill. Mr. Travers, you must come and see us sometimes and have tea with Angéle. And you *must* speak to Kiki or he'll be cross; won't you, darling?"

Geoffrey Wrentham would have enjoyed that. A kittenish woman is at any time an embarrassing thing, but with Ludovic Travers as the definite object the sight was almost tragic. Not that she wasn't an attractive woman—she was all that. Just a touch of the plaintive for effect, but otherwise a certain fascination for a man who liked that sort of thing.

"I was sorry to hear about your indisposition. You feeling quite better?" said Travers, going off at a desperate tangent.

"Oh heaps!" Again that laugh. "Just the *teeniest* bit exhausted. Now shake hands with Kiki and you may run away to your horrid papers."

Travers wondered afterwards whether he looked or felt the bigger fool, but he took the paw sheepishly, bowed and sidled away. It was not until in the security of the next yew hedge he had lighted his pipe and sworn quietly, that he felt reasonably normal. And as for Madame Angéle, well, he didn't like it the least bit. If that woman had ever been a nurse, then he'd been a footman. That question about English and a Gallic background. True she hadn't spoken a word, but the answer had been in her eyes as plainly as if she had bellowed it.

* * * * *

The next hour he spent in the library. Cosmo Revere had evidently been a man of meticulous neatness. In long rows of files whose leather backs bore the titles of ingeniously named works of erudition, were household accounts and summarised statements of the estate's financial affairs. Each volume had its index, but the writing was not that of Cosmo Revere. In other files—disguised as imaginary novels—personal correspondence was chronologically arranged. This time the writing of the index pages was chiefly that of Revere.

Those letters immediately suggested one thing. Among them would certainly be those that had passed between Haddowe and his patron. He started his examination therefore at the year 1918. More than once the index showed a reference to a likely letter, but not till the following year was the name "Haddowe" actually mentioned. Two letters had been received but the title—"Haddowe, Rev. A."—gave no indication as to their contents. And when he turned to the letters themselves they were missing. Somebody had removed them from the files!

That was annoying. He pushed the bell for Francis and explained the situation. The curtain was drawn across the large window and the pair of them got to work. Things grew more and more interesting. Not only had every letter received from Haddowe been removed; everything concerning Leila Forteresse had also been abstracted from the files!

"When was it done?" said Travers. "Must have been yesterday or the Wednesday afternoon."

"Damnably suspicious," said Franklin. "Somebody's in a desperate way. Let's send for Royce and find out whose the other hand is."

Royce knew very well. At the beginning of every month, Waterlow, the village schoolmaster, spent his evenings at the Hall as a sort of private secretary. He generally filed and indexed business papers and only occasionally lent a hand at the private indexing. Royce was fully conversant with what was done since Waterlow, on the nights of his visits generally dined in the butler's parlour.

"Any point in seeing him personally?" asked Travers when the butler had gone.

"He can't know anything—except that the letters *were* in the files and we know that well enough. Also dare we risk taking him into confidence and making him suspicious? Suppose he said anything to Haddowe?"

"That's right enough. Let's have a look at Crockford."

The clerical directory was short and eloquently reticent.

HADDOWE, AUGUSTINE, Fenwold Vicarage, Breckland. Univ. of Oxford. B.A. 1894.M.A. 1898. d. 1895. 1896 London, f.c, St. Jerome's, Stepney, 1896-1901. Pine Springs, Alberta, 1902-1908, Monterret Nova Scotia, 1908-1914. Canadian Imperial Forces, 1914-1920. v. of Fenwold 1930. P. Cosmo Revere of Fenwold. (av. 300 l. and house. Pop. 628.)

"Now what about it?" said Franklin, indicating the gap after the war. "Tell you what I'll do. I'll put on a man at once to work back at St. Jerome's, Stepney. It's not so long ago as all that."

"And something else," suggested Travers. "Hadn't I better say something to Sir Henry before he arrives to-night? I think he'd better know we've other grounds for suspicion than those concerned with the actual death. Get Parry to run you into Branford as soon as he's finished and get hold of Brotherston, Hall and Brotherston from there."

When he had gone Travers resumed his inspection of the library papers. A further series produced the "dolmen "notes—piles of clippings from journals and books and mathematical formulae and graphs that conveyed nothing to an uninformed reader. Half an hour of that was enough. The best change that suggested itself was an inspection of Captain Leeke.

Travers found him at the office and in a few minutes the two were talking away in the agent's inner room. He seemed a restless sort of chap, all wires and whipcord. Perhaps the strain of the funeral arrangements was getting on his nerves, though nerves and a young man in the early thirties should have been strangers. There was something of a younger Geoffrey Wrentham about Leeke, thought Travers, with that tanned face of his and the lean, aristocratic air.

"This is a busy time for you," said Travers.

"Damn glad when it's over," grunted Leeke. "When's Sir Henry coming?"

Travers told him.

"He'll be able to run things. Best of those portly old boys; they look the part. It's a rotten sort of business."

"The sudden death, you mean?"

"Yes—in a way. And all this fuss. The Revere tradition's the blazing limit. Old Hewin, my predecessor's coming along this afternoon. He was in charge of the last Revere funeral. By the way, I suppose you fellows'll be wanting my accounts pretty soon:'" For the first time Leeke seemed to be really serious.

"No special hurry," Travers assured him. "When you're ready. Say the beginning of the week. Got plenty of staff in the office?"

"Heaps, thanks."

"By the way, Mr. Revere must have worked hard to have kept his records in such order."

Leeke gave a quick start, rubbed his hands together nervously and gave a hesitating sort of answer. "Chap called Waterlow used to help him. Mr. Revere hated secretaries like hell."

"Pity he hadn't more company," went on Travers. "Not much in a place like this. Who'd there be? His niece, yourself, and—oh, yes!—Haddowe. I was forgetting him."

Leeke smiled ironically. "Don't forget Haddowe. He's a perfectly indispensable sort of person. What was he like with you last night? Try to run the show?"

Travers made a wry face. "Well, I'd hardly like to go so far as that. But he's rattling good company."

"Absolutely delightful!"

This chap's got something on his nerves, thought Travers, and made no reply to the sneer. Then he pulled out his watch and got up.

"Must be running along now. As soon as this business is over you must come in and have dinner."

Leeke got up, too. "Thanks. I'd love to. I'm going your way if you're going to the Hall. This way. It's shorter and private."

Behind the first clump of trees the narrow path wound by a rambling, timbered cottage with jutting windows and quaint gables and twisted chimneys and a garden bordered by a lavender hedge.

"That's a charming place!" said Travers, having a squint over the gate. "Who lives there?"

"Nobody—at the moment. Miss Forteresse'll probably move into it shortly. Fenwold Cottage it's called."

"You may think me a fool," went on Travers, "but I'd rather settle down there than in Fenwold Hall."

"Don't blame you. That damn great barracks of a place terrifies me. Now that little show—and fifteen hundred a year; not bad, what?"

"Bit too near the Hall perhaps. Living at the rich man's gate."

"I don't know." Leeke didn't quite get the hang of the allusion. "Well, I go this way. See you later probably," and he disappeared round by the cedar.

Franklin was waiting. "I'm just off to Branford. Also Parry's seen something."

"Really!"

"And I can't quite make it out. About half past ten, Miss Forteresse came round the front of the Hall as if she was going to the Lodge and then she suddenly turned to the east towards the village. When she got out on the open park—lend me that map of yours a minute—she made for a bit of a hill, just here, in front of a big tree and had a look round and, as far as Parry could see, started signalling with a handkerchief. All the time she was looking towards the village green, so he thought. When she'd gone back the way she came, he had a look round and couldn't see a thing—not a cottage or a chimney or anything from where she stood."

"She couldn't have been signalling Haddowe?"

"Lord no! The vicarage is in the opposite direction. Has Haddowe been in this morning?"

"If so I haven't seen him."

Franklin grunted. "Quite possible I shan't see you again for a bit if Sir Henry's here. To-morrow, too, I hadn't better make myself too conspicuous or Royce might think things. This afternoon I'm having a look at those dolmens."

"Good!" said Travers. "Wish I was coming with you. Do you know, this place is absolutely humming with something. Everybody's got the jumps."

"The funeral probably?"

Travers shook his head.

CHAPTER X
VIRGIN SOIL

As soon as Francis had suggested a walk round by the dolmens, Royce had confirmed Westfield's information—that the man to get hold of if you wanted to hear all about them was Hood. When Francis knocked at the door of the cottage on the back road the head woodman wasn't in, but his wife knew where he was to be found and gave a route to the place where he was working. When he was found he was engaged in the not over robust task of cutting bean sticks for the Hall gardens. Information simply rolled in.

"I'm very interested in those dolmens where Mr. Revere used to work," began Francis. "Mr. Royce told me you'd only be too pleased to tell me all about them and I've got permission for you to show them to me. Are they far away?"

"Best part of a mile, sir," said Hood. "I'll put on my coat right away."

"I'm staying at the Hall," Francis explained as they walked along through the wood. "You're not tree felling now. Waiting for the spring?"

"In a way, sir. But we only fell if they want timber for the estate."

"Do you do much?"

"All depend what's wanted, sir."

"What about Mr. Revere? What time of the year did he like best?"

"Winter and spring, sir, though I *have* known him fell one in the summer."

"What sort of clothes did he wear usually?"

"Much like you and me would, sir. Shirt open and everything nice and easy like. Every now and again I used to give 'em an airing—or my missis did, though *he* didn't know it."

"The hut was kept locked?"

"Oh yes, sir. I had one key and Eagling—the head keeper—had the other. He had to see to the hut when it was moved and keep plenty of fresh water in it and so on."

"Mr. Revere intended to fell a big tree where he was—er—found dead, do you think?"

"I know he did, sir. He reckoned that oak that stood there was the best tree on the estate."

"What happened to his tools and clothes and things?"

"Captain Leeke's got them—the tools that is. Mr. Royce took over all the clothes, so they say."

"You must have been extraordinarily surprised that Mr. Revere was killed by a little tree like that. He was a good feller?"

"He was that, sir—a real good feller; he could handle an axe what you call proper. But it's like this, sir. We're all got to make a mistake sometime at our game and the master he made his—when he tried to clear that tree out of the way by moonlight. Then they say, sir, he was clear flying in the face of Providence, going against that prophecy that's in the church."

"*Who* say so?"

"Everyone in the village, sir. Some reckon as how that ain't a prophecy, sir, but I reckon it is."

Francis passed over his cigarette case and watched the woodman light up before he put his next question. "Where was the last felling you did?"

"Where we're going, sir—last spring. Them dolmens stood on the edge of the wood and the master had all the trees taken down round 'em so as to leave a clear space. Then we had to put up a split pale fence and a gate."

"Mr. Revere do any felling himself?"

"He felled one, sir, and a rare good hand he made on't. He weren't there much, sir—only came and had a look now and again. Captain Leeke he felled one, too—over a bet with Mr. Castleton." He smiled as if there were something funny in the recollection.

"Did he really! I didn't know that was one of his accomplishments. And over a bet?"

"That's right, sir. Them dolmens stand right against the back road to Byford and if nobody in particular weren't about, a lot of people used to stop and have a look when we were felling, and one morning Mr. Castleton came drawing along when Captain Leeke was there. We was just felling an awkward one and the captain he turn to Mr. Castleton when we got it down and say, 'Look easy enough—when you know how' sort of kidding him on. Then Mr. Castleton say it was like a lot of things, not so hard as it looked, and then the captain took him up quick and reckoned he'd fell a tree quicker than what *he* would. So I picked out a couple of smallish trees that had got to come down and lent them the axes and they tossed up for trees and got their coats off and went at it and Captain Leeke he just won—half a quid it was. Then Mr. Castleton wanted another go, but Captain Leeke wasn't having any. 'No you don't!' he say. 'You hand over that half quid!' and as soon as he got it he sent for a couple of gallons for us woodmen to drink his health."

"Captain Leeke and Mr. Castleton don't like each other very much."

"What, them two, sir! I thought they was going to have a scrap and that's a fact. You know what the captain is, sir, all sort of sneering; and Mr. Castleton he went all white."

"What sort of a job did they make of it—felling the trees?"

"Not so bad, sir, for a couple of raw hands. You could see they'd both swung an axe before. Colonel Warren came along later when Mr. Castleton had gone and the captain tried to have him on at felling one, too, but the colonel he wasn't having any."

"Knew he'd get beaten, eh?"

"Beaten, sir! Fancy him with an axe!" The prospect was too funny.

When Franklin saw those dolmens for the first time he was surprised at the size of them. Each was of the normal type—two uprights topped into an archway by an immense slab of stone. From each to each was about forty yards and the equilateral triangle they made appeared to be perfect. The traces of the trees that had been cleared could easily be seen and the wood was now a hundred yards away. A circular fence of split oak enclosed the whole area, and the entrance gate was locked.

Franklin raised himself to the top and dropped over. Hood followed him. The grass had been mown with a scythe and in places the earth had been disturbed.

"Looks as if someone's been digging."

"That'd be Mr. Revere, sir. He used to do a lot of digging about here. I might have brought my key, sir, if I'd known I was coming."

"What was he digging for?"

"That I can't say, sir, and it weren't my place to ask. The master thought a lot of these old stones, sir. He reckoned as how there wasn't three other sets like 'em in the world. Do you know, sir, that them three there made a dead pointer for the midsummer moon at twelve o'clock at night!"

"Really!" He tried to be impressed but hardly saw how the statement helped very much.

"Yes, sir," went on Hood, drawing back to let the other walk through one of the huge doorways. "Mr. Revere thought a lot of them stones. 'If them stones could speak, Hood,' he says to me one day, 'they'd have some funny stories to tell.' "

"I expect they would," agreed Franklin. "And what's that building over there?"

Hood explained that it was a shed, built against the fence and that Mr. Revere had kept there, under lock and key, everything he wanted. Moreover it was a handy place in case of a shower. The woodman had more than once been called on to help with measurements and, according to him, it contained digging tools, measuring lines, tinned foods, water and a tiny oil stove with apparatus for making a hot drink. Franklin wandered round, generally interested in the masses of weather-beaten rock and more so in the evidences of digging that seemed to have gone on promiscuously inside the enclosure. Then, out of a casual remark, came something really thrilling.

"Do you know, Hood, I think that fence is rather a pity. It spoils the view. Also it wouldn't stop a man who wanted to get in."

The woodman stopped dead in his tracks. "Now that's a funny thing you should say that, sir." He cogitated for a moment. "Mr.

Revere told me not to say a word about it, sir, but now he's gone I don't see how it matters. There *was* a man in here one night, sir!"

"Really! When was that?"

"A month ago, sir. Last full moon. The rummest thing you ever heard on. The master he undid the gate and was walking across to that dolmen there, sir, when he saw something. There wasn't no chance of deceiving *him*—he'd a' known if there was a fly on one o' them stones. And what do you think he saw, sir? There was a man lying flat on one o' them stretchers, right on top of the arch!"

"What was he? A lunatic?"

"Blowed if I know, sir. The master he hollered out, sort of sharp like he sometimes used to speak, 'What are you doing up there, my man?' and then this man, whoever he was, scrambled down and bolted for all he was worth and hopped over the fence before the master could see who he was. He told me it was as much as my place was worth if I said anything about it, but I was to keep my eyes and ears open."

"Hadn't Mr. Revere any idea who it was?"

"I don't think so, sir. Least he didn't say anything to me."

"And did you find out anything?"

"Not a thing, sir. Only he never come there again or, if he did, the master didn't say anything to me."

*   *   *   *   *

As Franklin walked back to the Hall he felt a curious elation; not at the quantity of eliminating evidence he had heard—he had expected that. Hood was virgin soil and was bound in the very nature of things to have had plenty of information. But that news about a man on top of the dolmen seemed to bring the case to the very verge of solution. A month ago—full moon. Surely an attempt then at what had definitely succeeded on the Tuesday night. In other words, find the man on the dolmen and you had the murderer of Cosmo Revere. And what were the essential qualifications according to Hood's story?

Above all—agility. And nerve to have got up there. And speed to have got away so quickly. And that seemed to let out Haddowe and certainly Warren and possibly Carter.

Then more reflection found the flaws. The theory assumed that Cosmo Revere had been killed at the dolmens by a blow from some weapon or something dropped on his head. But—

> *(a)* After his first experience he would have looked even more carefully at the dolmens and have seen anybody on top.
> *(b)* Where did the yellow sand come in? All the digging in the enclosure showed the sand to be white—or silver.
> *(c)* How was the body transported over half a mile away? Cosmo Revere weighed about ten stone.

Then, after tea he had another brain wave and Travers heard all about it the last thing that night.

"Now I want to put to you something absolutely preposterous," Franklin said. "Suppose that man on the dolmen was not there for the purpose of killing him. Suppose he was there as a spy to see what Revere was doing."

"And what *was* he doing?"

"Here's where you'll laugh. Digging for something valuable. Call it treasure or valuables."

"Then why was he killed?"

"Because the murderer thought he had on him a clue of some sort. I know it sounds like a penny dreadful."

Travers didn't laugh. "If you ask my opinion I should say there's a lot in it. He was almost certainly digging for something of value— to him. Something of archaeological interest. And he did have that enclosure erected. But that might have been to keep people from making a mess of his property."

"There's still plenty of time to laugh," said Franklin. "What about this. Could there have been a clue of any sort in that carved motto in the Revere pew?"

Travers grimaced. "Ah, now you're going on ahead. That sounds rather fantastic. From what I can gather, the Reveres never had any need to bury anything– at least they've got plenty of money without it. Also—to be perfectly brutal—detectives are like criminals who repeat their crimes and methods. You've had a case with a crypto-gram and you're on the look out for another."

"You're probably right," admitted Franklin. "But what was he digging for?"

"We can find out like a shot. Sir Henry was telling me to-night that Mr. Revere collaborated in the mathematical part of his work with Professor Merritt of Cambridge. I know Merritt very well. I'll drop him a line."

"Won't he be here for the funeral?"

"I rather think he'd be away at this time of the year. Also I haven't touched those stacks of letters that have come. Sir Henry's man has been at them ever since they arrived this evening. I take over all correspondence after the funeral's over."

"Well, as things stand, it seems to lie between Leeke and Castleton. Everything Hood told me points that way. The trouble is it doesn't explain Haddowe."

"Oh, he's converted! This is a sort of country monastery."

Franklin grunted.

"We'd better both keep on the spot to-morrow, don't you think?" said Travers. "I'm absolutely sure Sir Henry's got something he wants to divulge—perfectly discreetly, of course!—and whatever he tells me I'll take jolly good care you're there to hear. And what about trying to arrange for you to overhear the reading of the will?"

CHAPTER XI
WE WILL HEAR CÆSAR'S WILL

THE LAST WORDS of condolence had been said and the last car had carried the last county magnate from the place of final tribute. The last of the Reveres had indeed returned to his fathers and the grave was hidden under banks of flowers that were already wilting in the sun. In the Hall itself tradition still had something to exact.

As Travers sat in the great dining-room he felt more poetically minded than he realised. In his ears were still the cadences of that sonorous funeral liturgy and in the room there still seemed to be the deathly smell of lilies. The room itself, too, with its ancient furnishings, was as evocative of the past as the cloisters of a cathedral and as full of references to the brevity of mere mortality.

Standing at the table behind which Travers sat, Sir Henry was reading slowly. He was a short man, rather portly but with an excellent presence. His voice—cold and clear-cut—seemed to Travers—apt at the moment for similes—like the ticking of a clock that had recorded centuries and would record still more.

At the far end of the room, four people were seated, Leila Forteresse was heavily veiled and dressed as she had been at the funeral. On her right was Leeke and beyond him the vicar, looking a very dignitary of the church; a figure apostolic and benevolent. "What a cardinal he'd make!" thought Travers, while the voice of the lawyer ticked on. In the last chair was a director of Lawe's Bank, the firm with which the Reveres had done business since its foundation.

Behind them was a smaller group—Royce, Mrs. Lacy, the head gardener, the senior farm bailiff and Waterlow the schoolmaster. The room with its lofty roof gave back the echoes of the lawyer's voice like a clerk prolonging the responses and at every pause the silence was oppressive. When a man coughed or moved his feet the sound was magnified and unnatural. That room was no place for a person with nerves.

The voice ticked on. Travers fumbled at his handkerchief and then replaced it. All movement seemed out of place; an offence against the decencies. Then his ear caught a subtle change in the voice—

"... and to such other charities as he may determine."

Then a break. The reader would indicate beyond doubt that a pause was necessary. He picked up the glass of water, sipped it, put it down, then wiped his lips. He rummaged among the papers in his case and the actions and deliberation seemed to Travers symbolic. The last of the Reveres had assigned his main estate. Cosmo was dead, but Cosmo Hubert Grant reigned in his stead. In his hands were the traditions and the bodies and almost the souls of Fenwold village. What remained was merely non-essentials—the trimming of rough edges, the apportioning of crumbs that must reasonably fall from the table. Sir Henry picked up his papers, cleared his throat and resumed the ticking.

"To William and Agatha Royce as a mark of my appreciation of loving and ready service I bequeath the sum of three thousand pounds jointly; to Lionel Waterlow as a mark of recognition of his efficient and generous help at all times, the sum of five hundred pounds; and to every person in my employ, other than the aforesaid, at the time of my death a sum amounting to one week's wages for each completed year of service; all this with a full confidence that they will continue to serve the Fenwold Estate with the same loyalty as I have always observed in them."

The voice stopped ticking. Sir Henry took another exasperating sip of water. Travers wondered several things. What about Leila Forteresse? And Leeke? And Haddowe?

"It is my earnest wish that my successor will confirm in their several appointments all employees whatever of the Fenwold Estate, except where it may seem to him expedient to make changes, in which case he will award such compensation or allowances as may seem to him to be just and equitable."

What was that for? Travers shot a glance at Leeke, sitting rigid as a ramrod; eyes looking out beyond the room and lips set tightly.

"To my niece Leila, daughter of Charles and Evelyn Forteresse, I leave an annuity of five hundred pounds and the use for life of the furnished house known as 'Troytown' and situated in the village of Densham in the County of Sussex; the said annuity and house to be wholly under the control of my executors aforesaid, who shall constitute the trustees.

"Finally I commend my soul to my Maker, the Impartial Judge who alone knoweth men's hearts, whether they be good or evil."

"COSMO REVERE."

The last words had barely died away when Leila Forteresse swayed in her chair. Leeke and Haddowe sprang up—then, just as suddenly she seemed to pull herself together. She said something in a low voice—Travers couldn't catch it—and appeared to be shaking off, if not resenting, the attentions of the two men. The lawyer watched over the rims of his glasses, making no move. The clock ticked again.

"That terminates the reading of the last will and testament of Cosmo Revere, made on the twentieth of June of this present year. I am further to hand to Cosmo Hubert Grant and to Leila Forteresse, at the request of their late uncle, letters containing certain private wishes which have not been and will not be communicated either to his legal representatives or the executors of the Fenwold Estate."

Possibly Royce had received his instructions previously. As the lawyer came forward and handed over the letter on which the red splash of sealing-wax was plainly seen, the butler opened the door and stood by it. The letter was almost snatched and without word or glance she left the room. Leeke stood scowling. Haddowe moved off quickly in the wake of the vanishing woman, oblivious of the company behind him. Then the others moved and in half a minute the room was empty.

Travers polished his glasses nervously, but Sir Henry appeared wholly unperturbed. He replaced the documents in the case and took yet another sip of the water before he spoke.

"Where can I talk to you alone, Mr. Travers?"

"Up in my room," said Travers quickly. He pushed the bell. "I think we shall be perfectly private there."

Royce came in and Travers gave the order. "Sir Henry will have tea at once up in my room, Royce. And you might tell Francis I shall want him there."

"Oh, Royce," said Sir Henry. "It's possible that Mr. Travers will request you to give him certain information from time to time. You will do anything you can. And may I congratulate you on your good—I should say well-deserved fortune."

Travers also shook the butler's hand. The more he saw of Royce the more he felt attracted by the kindly dignity of the old servant. Royce, too, as he left the room, was plainly feeling an emotion that up to then he had kept rigidly under control.

"An excellent character that!" commented the lawyer. "You might do much worse than take him into confidence."

Francis was waiting with the tea and the three of them gathered round the table. It was some minutes before the lawyer came to the point, and when he did so it was rather abruptly.

"What was there you didn't understand?"

Travers looked at Franklin. The directness of the attack was disconcerting. "Well—er—quite a lot of things. Why was Captain Leeke omitted?"

"He has a thousand a year," said the lawyer dryly. "What was the meaning of the allusion to possible changes in staffing?"

"The death duties will be enormous. Why not reduce expenditure, especially if the owner is not in residence?"

Beyond the merest suggestion of a smile Travers gave no sign of disagreement. "Quite so. And why was Miss Forteresse's name tacked on the end?"

Sir Henry shrugged his shoulders. "Surely that's irrelevant?"

"Possibly, but it's decidedly curious," retorted Travers bluntly. "And why that exile to Sussex? Leeke seemed to take it for granted, and therefore I imagined Mr. Revere had mentioned it to him, that she'd have Fenwold Cottage?"

"We'll leave that for a bit. Was there anything else?"

"Well, nothing in substance. The handing over of that letter rather invited everybody to draw his own conclusions."

"Lawyers," observed Sir Henry inscrutably, "are only mouthpieces or Greek messengers. They neither set the stage nor control the emotions of the actors."

With his usual deliberation he set down the empty cup and lighted a cigarette. "What I'm going to tell you now is implicitly confidential. I expected you to ask about the date of the will. If you had, this is what I should have told you.

"Three days before the date of that will we got a letter from Cosmo Revere requesting that I should meet him at Cambridge. We arranged the details by phone, but no preliminary reason was given. I've known from Royce, for instance, that Mr. Revere was in the habit of going to Cambridge, as I told you, to see a man called Merritt, or something like that, who was working with him on some outlandish theory of stars, so I concluded naturally he wanted to kill two birds with one stone, Cambridge being much handier for us than Fenwold. As a matter of fact he did spend the night at Cambridge.

"What he really wanted was the complete recasting of the concluding portion of his will. Not only that. He produced the actual wording he wished to be employed. I ventured to point out that the discrepancy in the phraseology of the two parts would be apparent to any professional man and that the innuendoes in the final paragraphs would be difficult to explain. His attitude was a take-it-or-leave-it one. I don't know if you have heard so from any other quarter, but as he grew older he had become somewhat arbitrary and during the last year it had been very noticeable in the dealings he and I had together. In short, he rapped me over the knuckles. He submitted to a minor alteration or two and the following day the new document was brought to Cambridge for signature."

"You're not prepared to tell us the clauses revoked?"

"I fear not. That would answer those questions you put to me. I will say that we were instructed to attend to the house in Sussex. Also you mustn't imagine I let all this happen without some questioning, direct or otherwise. I'd known Cosmo Revere for forty years and that gave me some authority other than a professional one. I asked if the doctors had given him any warning. He laughed at the idea! I asked about the disposal of his scientific notes and papers and that made him rather annoyed. He insisted he had no immediate apprehension of death.

"But you've noticed the secrecy? Nothing was to be known at Fenwold Hall. He wouldn't even risk my coming there for fear it might cause comment. Above all, the new document was not witnessed there." He stopped with an air of cold finality and glanced at his watch. "I suppose I've plenty of time for my train?"

"Over an hour," said Franklin. "I'd like to say, Sir Henry, that the information you've given us will be of enormous help. But might I ask if you had any idea at all of the contents of the letter you handed to Miss Forteresse?"

"None whatever. I'm in the same position as yourselves."

"About the people actually present at the reading of the will. I noticed Mr. Haddowe there."

"That was merely custom. He represented the church; Leeke the whole estate; Royce and his wife the Hall staff, and so on. The same procedure was always followed."

"One thing I forgot to ask you," said Travers. "If the living was so small, Haddowe must have had private means. Why did the Reveres allow such a state of affairs?"

"You mean—a church insufficiently endowed? But it isn't. There's a standing charge of five hundred. Didn't you hear the penultimate clause of the first part of the will?"

"Oh yes," said Travers, lying brazenly.

"And just one other thing too before I forget it. I suspect that in the letter to his niece her uncle assured her that she could remain at the Hall until such time as the new house was ready. Cosmo Grant was probably informed of that in the letter we sent to New York. If you want a line of approach when dealing with Miss Forteresse there's one ready for you."

Travers thanked him as he rose to go.

"A further thought," he went on. "About this man Haddowe. I've been thinking a good deal since you mentioned the matter yesterday. You've realised of course that when he went to Canada he would have to apply to the Bishop of Alberta for a license and satisfy him as to the reasons why he left England? His character then must have been all it should be."

Travers nodded. Franklin's eyes never left the lawyer's face.

"Very well, then. We come to the time when Cosmo Revere offered him the living. The Bishop of Breckland would then make the most stringent enquiries into his record and we can be absolutely sure he would be satisfied with what Haddowe was doing after the war. Not only that. The precise term escapes me at the moment, but a Notice of Institution we'll call it, was placed on the church door for some time before the event and on it was written virtually that extract from Crockford. Moreover, Cosmo Revere himself must have made enquiries."

"He was biased," suggested Travers. "He was grateful to Haddowe because of his son. And since he was a munificent supporter of the charities of the whole diocese, it's likely—I trust I'm not libelling him—that the bishop would have taken a good deal for granted on the word of Mr. Revere."

"You mean, if there was any hoodwinking done, Cosmo Revere was the only one necessary to deceive?"

"Well, to be blunt, Sir Henry, *you* certainly took Mr. Revere's estimate of Haddowe for granted yourself."

The lawyer made a wry face. "I'm afraid we mustn't discuss that." He consulted his watch. "Just one last word. And I can't be too insistent. There *must* not be any scandal. I really can't insist on that too strongly. Miss Forteresse will soon be gone. If anything definite can be fastened on Haddowe, he must go too. But I do ask you to be circumspect. Trust Royce and nobody else. If you have news of any sort let us know at once. Older heads and counsels may avert regrettable occurrences."

"I quite understand, Sir Henry," said Franklin. "You shall certainly be kept informed. But you recognise that murder's a thing that can't be hushed up."

"We should create no precedent if it were," replied the other gravely. "The guilty have often suffered without the knowledge of the law," and he left Franklin to make what he liked of that final ambiguity.

In a quarter of an hour Travers was back. "I hadn't better stay any longer now," said Franklin. "It might cause comment. But what about taking Royce into your confidence at once? I can remain as I am."

"Sorry. You're too late. I ventured to do it just now—at least I asked him to come up here after dinner. You don't mind?"

"Mind? I wish he were here now. The sooner all the talking's over the better I'll be pleased. I feel I want to be *doing* something."

"Red Indian stuff?"

"If you like. I've heard quite enough about some people; what I want to do is look 'em over."

CHAPTER XII
ACCORDING TO ROYCE

LEILA FORTERESSE again dined in her own room and Travers, armed with Franklin's list of questions, compared them with his own and made a summary. It was just before nine when the butler appeared in the upstair room.

"Come in, Royce," said Travers. "Take this chair and make yourself comfortable. John! see Mr. Royce has his favourite drink."

The butler was obviously wondering what was wanted. He wondered still more when Travers put his first question.

"The rooms on each side of this; are they absolutely closed up?"

"Yes, sir—at least they're not in use."

"Keys in the doors?"

"Mrs. Lacy has them, sir."

"John! go and get them. Have a look through each, lock it and bring the keys back here." Then he explained.

"As you possibly gathered, Sir Henry advised me to take you into confidence, Royce. I should probably have done so in any case, but that's why I asked you to come up here. It means, of course, that we regard you as absolutely to be trusted; what I don't know is, how many other people can be, and until I do know I must make sure we're not overheard. What it all amounts to is this. From certain information we've obtained, both Sir Henry and myself are assured that various things that have happened recently at Fenwold Hall aren't all they appear to be on the surface. Some of these happenings may even be connected with the manner in which Mr. Revere met his death."

"You mean . . . it was not an accident, sir?"

"To be perfectly frank, we very much doubt if it was."

The butler's face suddenly seemed older and more strained. "You don't mean, sir . . ."

"Never mind what I mean," said Travers gravely. "I may even have to add that it wasn't suicide—and still not answer your question. We don't know what killed him, Royce, but I'm trying to find out."

Royce was distressed beyond words. One could see there were doubts that were troubling him. Was he himself to be involved? Had his estimate of Travers been correct? One felt too that he was indignant and vaguely disturbed that the Hall should even be called in question or be a matter of vulgar contact.

"It's a bad business," Travers went on. "Still, there's going to be no scandal. We're resolved on that. That's why we want your help. Can we rely on you to help us—and keep everything implicitly to yourself?"

Royce was still flustered and rather on edge. The day had been a trying one for him and its emotional experiences more exacting than the responsibility that had been thrown upon him. It was Travers himself that really set him at ease, with his quiet, unexaggerated statements, deference and unassuming personality.

"I'm afraid I shan't be able to do very much, sir, but I'll do what I can."

"That's splendid," said Travers warmly. "Now don't let Francis disturb you with those notes he'll be taking. You can trust his discretion as much as my own. And don't be surprised if it so happens that I know more than you've given me credit for. And now for your help. First of all, who was the man who, as Colonel Warren knew, called to see Mr. Revere on Tuesday?"

"A man called Carter, sir."

"When was it exactly? Tell me all about it."

Royce's story was this. About six o'clock on the Tuesday evening a man rang the bell at the entrance-hall door. The footman on duty answered immediately and recognised the caller as Carter. He thought it better however to pass on to Royce the request to see Mr. Revere, whereupon the butler came himself and, very indignant at his ringing the *front* bell, asked what his precise business was. The man refused to state it but insisted that it was something of extreme urgency. Royce thereupon reported to Mr. Revere, who was in the library, and was instructed to bring Carter in. He was there half an hour.

Mr. Revere had dinner in the small dining-room and went up to his room about a quarter past eight. At about nine Royce happened to be in the hall when he reappeared, dressed for walking and wearing the clothes that had been found in the hut. All he said was, "Don't know when I shall be in, Royce."

The scene at the Hall the following morning when Leeke rushed in was a tense one. Royce had first been told and had gone in search of Leila Forteresse. He found her in the small drawing-room with Haddowe, studying some papers which the vicar had spread out on the Sheraton table. Royce broke the news as gently as he could. "Do you mean he's dead!" shouted Haddowe, looking frightened out of his wits. At the same time he was gathering up the papers and thrusting them anyhow into his pocket. Royce thought the look that passed between them was an alarmed one. Then she went white, put her hand to her lips and, as Haddowe rushed to support her, collapsed into a chair. "Water! Quick!" exclaimed Haddowe. "And fetch her maid!"

When Royce got back with the water the maid was already there. He heard some words spoken in a foreign language as he entered, but Haddowe came forward at once and took the glass from him.

When the body of Cosmo Revere arrived in the Hall yard, the butler came once more into the picture. He had followed on the heels of Haddowe in case there should be any orders for him. Leeke asked if there were any precedent to govern the lying-in-state, whereupon Royce had recalled that the dead man's grandfather, who was killed in the hunting field, had been placed in the tithe barn. He also added, embellishing the story as garrulous old men will, that the horse had at once been shot. "That's what they ought to do to that tree," exclaimed Warren. "Cut it down and burn the lot!"

"We can't do that!" protested Leeke. "It wouldn't be legal till after the inquest. They might want to look at the site."

"Legal! What do you mean 'legal'?" retorted Warren. "I say you can remove the tree."

"Not only that," put in Haddowe. "If it's left there, all the people in the district will come and look at it. The place'll be like a circus."

Leeke gave in at once. Royce received some preliminary instructions, had the clothes taken from the hut and went back to the Hall. *But his idea was that he left behind him three badly flustered men.*

With regard to Colonel Warren, Royce was emphatic. He had taken to calling a good deal at the Hall, but had considerably outstayed his welcome. Cosmo Revere had a distinct aversion for him and had not scrupled to tell his butler so. The last time he called he asked to see not Cosmo Revere but his niece, and had taken her out in his car. Where they went Royce didn't know but Miss Forteresse was absent from three o'clock till ten. On her return she was sent for and spent some time in the library.

With regard to the remaining information that Royce was able to give, one important thing must be taken into account. The butler was a privileged person and was admitted to a degree of intimacy that is rarely accorded. For this there were several reasons. Royce had graduated from the service of the young Cosmo Revere to his present position. He was not one to take a liberty, abuse a privilege or betray a secret. Revere must have experienced all that and more than once have been glad to leave for a moment his isolation to find company or take advice from the man who had grown old with him and whose sterling character he knew.

The most interesting of these revelations concerned the coming of Leila Forteresse to Fenwold Hall. Haddowe had dined there overnight and the following morning Revere had mentioned the possibility of her arrival and in such a way that there seemed a definite connection. The words used were, "What would you say, Royce, if Miss Evelyn's daughter came to Fenwold?" The butler was much affected at the question. The next words were even more to the point. "Old men like you and me, Royce, can't afford to imperil our own forgiveness."

Nothing was said for some days. Then one morning in the beginning of January there was a further statement. "I have heard from Mr. Haddowe and he tells me Miss Leila will be here to-morrow."

Now Haddowe, although only two months in the parish, had been absent from his pulpit the previous Sunday. It seemed reasonable to conclude therefore that he had been despatched as Cosmo Revere's agent, not only to see the niece and report, but to conclude, if he thought so fit, final arrangements for her coming to Fenwold.

"Make an urgent note to see what D. House has to report," he said to Franklin, then told Royce about the missing letters. "You see, Royce," he added, "what we're up against. And that reminds me. Just before Mr. Haddowe's induction, did he spend any time here?"

"A week-end, sir."

"Did the bishop by any chance happen to be here at the same time?"

"Now you mention it, sir, he was. He usually came once a year, sir, the bishop did."

"That explains a lot then. Now, Royce; would you mind telling me all you can about Miss Forteresse's stay here, particularly her relationships with her uncle?"

Royce's story split itself perfectly cleanly into three parts. There was the period when she was new to the Hall and to life as lived by and expected of an English county family. Then had come a transition period when she was finding her feet and was more or less in conflict with her uncle. Lastly had come the time when she went her own way, subject only to occasional reprimands or expostulations. What the end would have been there is no telling.

At first there had seemed nothing too good for the newcomer. A man of such generous character as Cosmo Revere would have no halfway line. Leila Forteresse, except in matters of administration, was the mistress of Fenwold. A special reception was immediately arranged for her—the first the Hall had seen since the war. There was considerable entertaining. When Cosmo Revere attended any county function the name of his niece appeared with his own. There was talk of a town house for the season. A well-mannered hunter was purchased for her use in the park and a couple of holes were laid out under the supervision of the Branford professional so that her golf lessons could be given on the spot.

The reasons for the subtle changes that slowly evolved were not hard to seek. To transplant a woman, temperamentally hostile, from heaven knows what Bohemian upbringing into the austerity of the Fenwold tradition was asking for trouble. To expect such a woman to acquire the nice graces and social suavity that should be at the head of Cosmo Revere's table; to expect her to shed the speech, habits and mannerisms of a lifetime and acquire a wholly new series, was surely asking too much. Add that Leila Forteresse had no reason for respect, that the Fenwold tradition had done little for her mother, that she was calculating by nature and knew how far she could go, and there you are. But whatever the causes it is unquestioned that she abandoned her attempts to acquire the Fenwold colour and, slightly more glorified and better financed, reverted to her natural self.

Cosmo Revere must often have winced during the period of his niece's social education. On one occasion—when Montagu Mason's Mousmé Club band was imported for a garden party—he was shocked. The revel of saxophones among the Fenwold elms and the cacophonies of the negro experts must have been for him a pretty violent contact with modern ideas of merrymaking. The riding too, and the golf, had been abandoned. Then there had been the hushed-up scandal of the introduction of a roulette board at a bridge party when the tearful wife of a certain celebrity admitted to her husband I.O.U.'s amounting to hundreds. Worst of all was the huge charity gala at Branford when, with a partner imported from town, Leila Forteresse did a series of dances that ravished certain beholders and scandalised infinitely more.

The third period therefore is easily accounted for. It might be wondered why her uncle didn't present an ultimatum. Perhaps he saw the uselessness. Her allowance was a check but not a very effective one to handle. What really mattered to Cosmo Revere was the dread of scandal. Should she leave the Hall, tongues would wag. More than once however sharp warnings had been given, as in the case of Colonel Warren.

Haddowe throughout had been of enormous support to his patron. Royce had often heard expressions like, "We must hear what Haddowe thinks about it," or, "I'll get Haddowe to see what he can do." The vicar indeed, had become indispensable. His manner to Royce had always been perfect—a blend of courtesy and geniality—and whenever he took upon himself to give orders or make suggestions it was with such charm and tact that notice had not been unduly drawn to the assumption of authority.

As for village gossip about him and Miss Forteresse, the reasons were obvious. Gossip is no respecter of persons. Male and female are the only ingredients necessary for an unsavoury titbit. Mrs. Lacy—as her husband admitted—was prejudiced and had probably misconstrued some paternal gesture. Yet Franklin made one pertinent note. *Why had not Cosmo Revere remembered in his will this paragon of vicars?*

About Leeke, Travers asked little. He did gather that the agent came from an old, impoverished family; that he dined and lunched frequently at the Hall; that he had his own establishment near the estate office and that he had been first favourite for the hand of Cosmo Revere's niece. The couple had been seen embracing in the seclusion of the wild garden and once Mrs. Lacy had blundered into an amorous passage in the small drawing-room. He was a great racing man. He never missed Newmarket or the local meetings and had often distributed a tip round the servant's hall.

Castleton was a much more interesting character. He had visited frequently at the Hall and at one time Cosmo Revere had appeared to take very warmly to the son of the late vicar. Then Castleton had also become entoiled in the charms of Leila Forteresse and had worn his heart very much on his sleeve. After a time he probably realised that her nature was essentially shallow and had indulged in fits of sulks and adoration alternately. There were other complications. One night at dinner he had expressed himself too freely on matters to which his host could not possibly fail to take exception and had generally behaved so badly that the other's opinion had undergone a decided change. Then Castleton did two foolish things, at least in his capacity of suitor. He made a very communistic speech at a Labour meeting and later, when Cosmo Revere refused to receive him at the Hall, sent to the local press a letter—extremely able and witty—discoursing on feudalistic survivals and the Fenwold pretensions in particular. After that his name was no longer mentioned at the Hall. In spite of this Leila Forteresse had been seen leaving Oak Cottage unchaperoned and unattended; a proceeding natural enough in Bohemia but devastatingly self-explanatory in Fenwold village.

That virtually concluded Royce's revelations. He was actually in the act of leaving the room when he hesitated and turned back.

"There is something else I think I ought to tell you, sir. I believe, sir, Mr. Revere had been receiving anonymous letters."

"Really! And when was that?"

The butler considered for a moment. "I can't say to a day, sir, but when he spoke to me first it would be about six weeks ago. It was like this, sir. The master rang for me and when I came into the library he had a letter in his hand. 'Royce,' he said, 'the writer of an anonymous letter is the worst kind of scoundrel' or words like that. 'But' he said, 'do you think a man may be entitled to profit by information he may suspect to be correct?' Of course that didn't give me much time to answer, sir, but I ventured to make the following observation: 'Well, sir,' I said, 'of course it all depends; but if I received a letter telling me I was going to be poisoned, I should take good care what I ate.' I don't know why, sir, but the master seemed very pleased with that. 'Bravo, Royce!' he said, sir, and laughed; that's all. Then about a week later the same thing happened again. He had a letter in his hand when he happened to be giving me some orders and just as I was leaving the room he said, 'Not poisoned yet, Royce!' just like that, sir. And that was the last I ever heard about them."

"A curious business!" remarked Travers. "By the way, I suppose Mr. Revere never told you at any time that he'd seen a man hiding among those dolmens when he was down there at night?"

"No, sir. I never heard about anything of that sort."

* * * * *

It was midnight when Travers and Franklin had finished.

"There you are," said Franklin bitterly, gathering up his notes. "You pay your money and you take your choice."

"I think the whole situation's clarified," said Travers. "If, for instance, I could have believed Cosmo Revere capable of taking advantage of an anonymous letter, I should have said he changed his will because of what was in 'em. Also we have a shrewd idea of the people affected by those changes—the Forteresse woman, Leeke and Haddowe. I certainly think Leeke's your best card at the moment. At any rate, why worry? We came down more or less on a gamble and now we know we're in for a longish job."

"Progress is slow," objected the other.

"I don't know. One thing *does* please me, and that is that I'm really beginning to get the Fenwold atmosphere into my system. I mayn't know much about people but I'm learning the backgrounds."

"That's more than I am," said Franklin gloomily. "This palace of a place haunts me. Take that corridor outside—or gallery or whatever they call it. A hundred yards of opulence. Three hundred feet of furniture and pictures! I'm out of my depth. I know something about the butler's parlour and that's all. Tomorrow I'm going to look at some more—first hand."

"As, for instance?"

"Carter. The man who sent Westfield on a fool's errand, the man who brought that urgent message to Revere. That's the chap I want to have a few homely words with."

"And what's to be your method of approach?"

"The night brings counsel," said Franklin mysteriously. "But what about you. Aren't you keen on looking somebody else over?"

"Well, to tell you the truth, I rather thought of another heart to heart talk with Haddowe," said Travers airily.

"And *your* method of approach?"

"The night brings counsel," smiled Travers. "But in case it doesn't, I rather thought of going to church."

CHAPTER XIII
THIS PIOUS MORN

As Franklin set off, the bell was sending out its last minute appeal for morning church. According to Royce there was a short cut to the village—marked, as a matter of fact, on Franklin's private map—a path leading over the park to the boundary wall, and the butler had provided a key for the door which opened on the village green.

What Franklin had in mind was to pose to Carter as a collector of genuine cottage and farmhouse furniture; the sort of stuff in fact which the dealer would be likely to acquire in the locality. As for the rest, he would trust to luck. Unless forced by circumstances he would not divulge any connection with Fenwold Hall. Anything he had to buy should be sent straight to London. That was the reason he changed his black and put on a tweed suit and soft hat.

He chose the long way, round by the lodge. The little he had noticed of the village on the Wednesday morning had left no definite impression on his mind and this second visit should improve his local colour. What struck him at once was the quantity of woodland. Each cottage with its garden looked as if packed round with green cotton wool and the road itself was a perfect avenue. He recognised Westfield's cottage, then on the right came the first break—a track that led away between high thorn hedges. On its direction post were the words "Gravel Pit." The track was dry but deeply scored and seemed to cut a hundred yard tunnel whose sides were the steep banks and hedges. A sharp turn and the pit was in sight, its bottom overgrown with weeds and here and there heaps of yellow sand or flints or sifted gravel, but the five minutes he spent there taught him nothing.

It was noteworthy, too, that up till then he had seen not a living soul during the walk. By the village green moreover not more than a couple of people were in sight. The ground sloped lop-sidedly and just visible through the trees was the thatched roof of what would be Oak Cottage. Carter's house, set clean on the corner, was a tiny affair of probably four rooms at most and round it the hedges were high enough to obstruct all view except through the small gate that led to the front door. A few yards further on, towards Branford, a gate marked "Private" opened on a gravelled road overgrown with weeds and almost covered in by trees. Prepared to plead ignorance if challenged, he took this private road. A few yards on was another gate on which was painted "Oak Cottage."

As he stood there by the gate, he had an excellent view. Above his head were the dense branches of a magnificent oak, and beyond him the road, now fairly clean, led to a garage at the side of the Cottage. This was a delightful looking place with its grey thatch, deep-set windows and lawn bordered with flowers. Away to his left was Carter's untidy garden, his wooden garage and his shed.

But it was the sight of Oak Cottage that made him change his mind. Why not ask if Carter lived there? Surely a sound excuse and a chance to see Castleton in person!

As he walked up the slight incline that led to the front door, he noticed about Oak Cottage that air of loneliness that announces the absence of inmates. He pulled the bell chain that hung by the door of the porch and heard it ringing somewhere inside—and that was all he did hear. He moved to the back door and knocked and, as he waited, looked round the open space that lay between the house and the park. Occupying most of it was another lawn, but at the far end some sort of a rockery seemed to be in course of construction, while to the right he could see through a gap in the privet hedge a small kitchen garden.

Everything extraordinarily neat! thought Franklin. And how tree-encircled the place was! Precious little fear of being over-looked. Of Carter's cottage only the chimney top was visible.

But it wouldn't do to stop there long, so he made his way out by the narrow drive that led to the village green. Then over the gate he had a further peep and tried to memorise the lie of the land. And as he came down the incline towards Carter's cottage he noticed the high banks and hedges that shut off everything.

He was really thinking of that as he knocked at the back door. A second knock produced no answer. Almost without knowing it he tried the latch. To his surprise the door opened! That was curious—unless of course Carter should be in the shed or garage. But the shed was empty except for a worm-eaten table and some wrecks of chairs, and the empty garage was locked. Rather puzzled he stuck

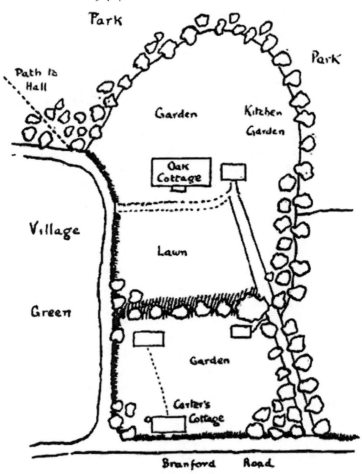

his head inside the kitchen door and listened. Then he stepped in and hollered. "Hallo! . . . Anybody there?"

It was clear there wasn't. For a moment he stood there wondering what to do. Then the kitchen table caught his eye, with its open drawer and contents strewn on the brick floor. In the corner too was a dilapidated bureau, its drawers open and its contents scattered everywhere. In another couple of seconds he was looking into the front room. Here there was more disorder. On the floor lay an overturned chair and a broken cup and saucer. On the deal table was its drawer as if it had been ransacked. The one sign of life or order was the thud-thudding of a dirty-looking grandfather clock. The weights nearly touched the ground. If that were any sign, it was best part of a week since it had been wound up.

He tip-toed up the wooden stairs. At the top was an unfurnished cubby-hole of a bedroom. Leading from it was another and here the disorder was repeated. One drawer of a deal chest was on the ground. Bedclothes were tossed on the floor and the home-made rug thrown in a heap. On the wall by the side of a cheap wash-stand, with dirty water still in its basin, hung a mirror, and the sudden sight of his face gave him a start.

Back in the kitchen and with one hand on the latch of the door, he had another look round. On the table was a dirty plate and the crumbs of a meal. The floor seemed fairly clean; at least there wasn't the sign of a footprint. Then he nipped across quickly and lifted the top of the bureau. One thing alone seemed of interest—a crumpled piece of blotting paper. A search through the litter of the floor discovered another—more used and dirtier still. Above the sink was a small mirror, used by Carter for his shaving, judging by the pot with brush still in it, and stooping down to this he took a quick look at the reflections of the sheets. Then he frowned and looked again—this time at himself. Then he made as if to return to the upstair rooms.

That was when he caught sight of the piece of silk—ends still hanging from the door across which they had been fastened. Somebody then had expected visitors—and wanted to know if they'd turned up. A couple of seconds after that discovery he was outside the cottage. Behind the shed and garage was the dense undergrowth of the shrubbery and the trees that hid Oak Cottage from sight. Then again something happened!

As his eyes lifted to the branches of the oaks he saw a flash like the sun's rays on glass. With leisurely steps he made his way round to the front of Carter's cottage, then turned like lightning and crawled round the corner to the water-butt and watched the branches of the trees through the slit of light that separated it from the wall. The flash was more than once repeated but the owner of the field-glasses made no move among the trees. High up, he seemed to be, in that big oak that overhung the private gate.

Once more Franklin thought delay was a bit risky and started to crawl back again over the newly-cindered path. Then his fingers touched something peculiar—charred pieces of tough paper, some black, some pink and some a vivid red. As he moved along, close in to the wall, he picked up half a dozen of the charred pieces. Round the corner he straightened himself and out by the front gate kept well under the hedge till he reached the door that led to the private path.

* * * * *

It was nearly one o'clock when he had finished with those two sheets of blotting paper and changed to his usual black. After lunch he made his way round by the gardens to the main drive. A hundred yards short of the Lodge he turned off suddenly into the fringe of trees that bordered the road and, as the coast was clear, slipped through a gap and round to Westfield's back door. The dog—a curly-coated retriever—began to bark furiously and the keeper opened the door. It took him a second or two to recognise his visitor and show him inside.

"One or two things I want to see you about, Westfield," he began. "Have you seen Carter?"

"Yes, sir. Least I didn't see him; he see me. He came round here Friday night about half-past nine and said someone'd told him I wanted to see him."

"Get any satisfaction out of him?"

"I did, sir—and I didn't. He didn't know the man he saw in Branford, but he give me the description and I'm blowed if I could recognise him either. He was a bit riled when I sort of hinted he was responsible for me going a fool's errand."

"Nothing else?"

"No, sir. He wasn't here five minutes. But now I come to think of it, he bid me five pounds for that chair you're sitting on, sir."

"Did he, by jove!" exclaimed Franklin, hopping up to see the fine, old fiddleback with its perfect, cabriole legs. "He's evidently a shrewd judge. What's he like to look at?"

The substance of Westfield's description was this. Carter was an oldish man, but still very active. His complexion showed he knew the shortest way to the bottom of a glass. He wore an old-fashioned pair of spectacles stuck on the end of his nose and his eyebrows stuck straight out. His few teeth were stained and he had a habit of promiscuous spitting. His hair was white at the temples and he stooped a good deal. In height he was the same as Westfield—about five foot six. His speech was grumpy and generally lurid. He was the sort of man who'd be a bad enemy and yet he was known to be a man of his word. His clothes were none too good, but he always sported a collar and tie.

"Had he any enemies?" asked Franklin.

"Not that I know on, sir. He said some nasty things about Mr. Castleton, as I told you, and the other gentlemen, and they say as how he'd said he know a thing or two about Captain Leeke if he wanted to open his mouth. Also he's one of them Communists, sir. I haven't half heard him say some things in the 'Coach and Horses' I shouldn't have wondered if they'd turned him out!"

"Things about the estate and Mr. Revere?"

"That's it, sir. Rare hot and strong he was." Franklin thought he knew where he'd imbibed those doctrines and the thought brought another question.

"How long's he had that motor van?"

"Last winter time, sir. He said in the 'Coach and Horses' as how he was going to have one and Mr. Castleton was going to learn him how to drive."

"Where'd he learn?"

"Down the Branford road, sir. I see them there one night about dusk, and later on, as I was going by Carter's corner, Mr. Castleton he come round by the green and say, 'Have you seen anything of Carter, Westfield?' 'No, sir' I say, 'only when I see him just now with you.' 'Tell him there's a woman want to see him, if you run across him,' he says, and so I . . ."

Franklin cut that story short. "I saw Hood the other day and he gave me to understand the head-keeper—a Mr. Eagling—had a key to Mr. Revere's hut. Where does Eagling live?"

"Single cottage right against the gravel pit, sir. Only Mr. Eagling ain't head-keeper now, sir. He got the sack last Saturday—a week ago, sir."

"Did he! Do you know why?"

"They say, sir, Mr. Revere found out he'd been feathering his own nest and Captain Leeke had orders to sack him. They reckon as how Captain Leeke told him if he owned up he wouldn't be prosecuted, and they say he owned up, sir."

"Hm! Well, now; this is what I want you to do, Westfield. Don't make yourself conspicuous, but try to find out all you can about Carter's movements since he got back after going away with his van on the Wednesday morning. If you discover anything important, come straight to the Hall."

* * * * *

"That's an amazing day you've had," said Travers when he heard all about it. "What's the idea of the man in the tree? And who was he?"

"I've worked it out like this. Suppose it was Carter. His cottage has been gone over with a small-tooth comb. He may have something which somebody's anxious to get hold of. Carter knows it and is scared stiff. He put the silk across the door and then perched up the tree with his field-glasses to watch in case they came back."

"But why up the tree? He's got to sleep *in* the cottage to-night!"

"Not necessarily. I wouldn't mind sleeping out of doors myself. Plenty of haycocks about. However, take the other theory and say it was Castleton. That's more likely, because Carter's car wasn't in the garage. If it was Castleton, then Carter's bolted and he made all that mess himself, getting away in a hurry. And if so, why the hurry?"

"And what's Castleton doing up the tree?"

"I thought of that this afternoon. Remember Parry watching the Forteresse woman? Well, Castleton and she probably signal to each other. As I work it out you can get a clear view from up that tree right across the park to where she was standing. Castleton was up the tree preparing to look out for the lady. Just then I strolled right into his grounds and round to his back door. Then I went to the back of Carter's cottage and inside it. Castleton wondered what the blazes I was up to and that's why he switched the glasses on to me. He wouldn't come down because he doesn't want it known that he uses the tree for that purpose."

Travers clicked his tongue in annoyance. "To think I couldn't see that! Hm! And why's Carter bolted?"

"Ah! that I can't say—yet. Still, here's what was on the blotting-paper."

agle has sold his
ke been robbing you, sir
in glove with Mr. Castleton
who's to know
how can he spend money
laughing at you, sir
ain Leeke can't deny

"Of course they weren't quite like that," he explained. "I had to fit in obvious gaps. You see how clumsy the writing is on this original and what a devil of a quantity of ink he used."

"To be absolutely obvious, Carter wrote the anonymous letters."

"It looks like it. The first extract is about Eagling and if Westfield's story is right—and I don't see why it shouldn't be—then Mr. Revere acted on it by making enquiries, as a result of which Eagling got the sack. Only, what grudge had Carter against Eagling?"

"Might have had an argument in the pub."

"And how did he know anything about Eagling? Or Leeke? Or about anybody being hand in glove with Castleton?"

"Lord knows!"

Then Franklin's face lit up. "Oh, before I forget it! What about that treasure theory now? Suppose somebody else *did* search Carter's house for the clue which Carter took from the pocket of Revere!"

"And that reminds *me*" said Travers. "Your theory of that carved motto being a cryptogram has had the bottom knocked out of it."

"Who by?"

"Haddowe. I'll show you the chit. He sent it along this morning. If you remember I told you I asked him about it last Thursday night. It's the real and veritable reason for the carving. Mind you, I don't regard it as a complete explanation, but it's interesting all the same. It's an extract from a printed sermon by Littlebury, an early Puritan divine."

"And concerning this same speaking by the Divine Will against the vaine assumptiones and pretensions of men, my grandfather, himself a man of some learning acquainted me with a notable happening that came within his owne knoledge he being a native of those parts where the thing took place and was commonlie knowne and reported that a gentleman of great house and some notabilitie was of the mind to make for himself and his family a greate burriall vaulte the like of which had not been knowne aforetime, this vaulte being builded benethe the Greate Oake that grew in the church-yarde and the same was cutte in the pew which he and his children did commonlie use to his greater honour and to the intent to magnifye the work of his hands. But shortly after even when the masons had not as yet sette hande to the work there arose a prodigious storm of wind which cast down that great tree and made the work of none availe and shortly after the said Cosmo Revere did die whereat the work whooly ceased and was accounted a judgment of God which indeed it was and so accepted of all men."

"Hm!" went Franklin, handing back the paper. "Well, it won't be the last theory that goes phut in this case. All the same I wonder if the bloke who wanted the last word in vaults ever guessed he'd be responsible for the way a jury gave its verdict. Funny how the rank and file accepted that motto as a prophecy."

"They! They'll accept anything. What about those pieces of charred material you were going to show me?"

Franklin took the envelope rather gingerly from his breast pocket. "You'll have to mind how you handle them. What do you make of 'em?"

"Rather small, aren't they? Makes it a bit difficult. Are they papier maché?"

"That's what I thought. And they hadn't been there long. The last rain here was a fortnight ago and a rain'd have taken all the stiffness out of 'em. *And* the colour. I should say Carter had a spring clean and burnt up all his papers before bolting. There was a thundering good pailful of paper ash on that path. More than one good fire, I should say. And what *were* they?"

Travers handed back the envelope. "Might have been some rubbish he picked up with a lot he bought at a sale. Anything else did you notice?"

"One other thing. Did you notice how carefully I told you about those mirrors? Notice anything curious?"

"Can't say I did."

"The one upstairs I didn't have to stoop to, but the one downstairs I did."

Travers didn't see it. "Give it up. What's the answer?"

"That's the trouble," said Franklin. "There isn't one. I was just putting up a bluff, hoping you'd suggest something. And hadn't you better be getting ready for church?"

CHAPTER XIV
THE CHURCH HOSPITABLE

TRAVERS WAS SURVEYING the set of his black tie when the usual double tap announced Franklin.

"Just thought of this," he said, handing over a letter. The paper had evidently been borrowed from the servants' hall.

Dear Sir I thought you ought to know theres been a burglery at Mr Carters house. I was going by there last night and I saw a light and a man came sneaking out with a sack but I didn't know who he was as it was too dark but he acted very suspitious and when heed gone I knocked at the door and couldn't get no answer and the back door wasn't fastened and I thought you ought to know about it.

from a Friend.

The envelope was addressed—

Mr Turner
Poliseman
Fenwold
Breckland.

"What's the idea?" asked Travers, laughing in spite of himself. "Trying to draw Carter into the open?"

"Exactly! When the policeman gets this he'll simply have to take notice, and once a policeman goes to a cottage in a village everybody'll start gossiping. Parry's slipping off to Branford to catch the last post. You really think it's a good idea?"

"Extraordinarily good! Are *you* going to be in the neighbourhood when Turner delivers it?"

"Daren't risk it. Parry'll be about. Later on he'll probably go to the local pubs and stir up questions. May be at church myself to-night by the way," and he hurried off to see to the despatch of his anonymous effusion.

Travers, with half an hour still on his hands before the service began, strolled down to the hall. Then he peeped into the small drawing-room and, nobody being there, sent for Royce.

"Is Miss Forteresse upstairs?"

"I believe so, sir."

"Give her my compliments, Royce, please, and if she should have thought of going to church I should be very grateful for her company."

In three minutes the butler was back. "Miss Leila regrets, sir, she will be unable. Madame Angéle is very unwell to-night, sir, and she doesn't like to leave her."

"I'm sorry to hear that. And by the way, Royce, I may be a bit late to-night. Tell Francis I'll have something quite simple in my room."

Travers found plenty to occupy his thoughts during his short walk to the village church. He wondered, for instance, how Haddowe would shape. Even if that incident which Franklin had witnessed in the fog could be satisfactorily explained away, there still remained the affair of the missing letters. He hoped somehow the man wouldn't be emotional. Roguery was one thing; hypocrisy another. And whatever else he did, he should certainly reveal the relationship between himself and the souls committed to his charge. What would he be? The discerning shepherd or the outpost of gentility in that particular parish?

Once inside the Revere pew—or compound as it might have been aptly called—he was in a world of his own and segregated as it were from the rest of his species. The church seemed very full; perhaps the events of the week had given the village a certain notoriety. Then the bell ceased, the organ rumbled down in its bass and as Travers heard the steps of the vicar as he came from the vestry, he rose with the congregation to his feet. The organ played sentimental nothings for a moment or two, then died away.

"Enter not into judgment with thy servant. . . ."

The service had begun.

It may have been the influence of those grey walls that made Travers so poetically philosophic, but more than once as he listened to the perfect economy, the sonorous magnificence of that voice, he found himself weaving his fancies around it. Not a syllable seemed wrongly placed or over-emphasised. Such a voice, he thought, should never be allowed to descend to the mouthing of mere commonplaces; it should be reserved for the declamation of tragic verse or the melancholy rhetoric of old Thomas Browne. When, too, he surveyed the figure of the vicar in his vestments—the scarlet of the hood against the white linen, the gracious benevolence of his face, the eyes that looked clear and kindly over the congregation—that particular illusion passed and another took its place. What a judge was lost in Haddowe! What mercy seasoning justice, what majestic exposition of the inevitability of the law, what dread condemnations and what noble clemencies!

The text was announced— "We spend our years as a tale that is told." Then he wondered how the simplicity of that stark simile would stand expansion and what Haddowe would make of it. As to that, never once during those twenty minutes did his thoughts wander far from the voice and rarely could the speaker's mind be anticipated. It was a memorial service in which Cosmo Revere was not singled out from our common mortality. It was Villon in terms of the Book of Common Prayer; a requiem for all lives that are lovely and pleasant and an exhortation to the acceptance of the inscrutable purpose. Then it ended triumphantly with the promise of recompense and the certainty of resurrection.

When the last word was spoken and the last simple gesture made, Travers was sorry. He could have sat there a good many more minutes. And yet, before the service ended and he had had time to analyse his feelings, he knew how insincere the whole thing had been. The driving force had been the head rather than the heart. There had been no passion for the well-being of men's souls, but rather something academic and scholarly. It had been the gentleman of the parish expressing his gentility. Haddowe had revealed not so much the will of God to man as the elegy which Augustine

Haddowe thought fit for the stage setting in which he had delivered it. The final benediction too—recalling the flaunting of crimson robes, the gemmed fingers of a white hand and the hushed silence of the multitude in a papal square.

Although the organ had ceased and the only sound to be heard was the shuffling of the verger's feet as he moved along the pews, Travers stayed on, reading the inscriptions on the mural tablets and listening for the sound of the vestry door. When the vicar did come, it appeared that Travers had nearly missed him.

"Do you know," he said, "I had an idea you'd be here. Usually I go out by the vestry."

Travers hardly liked to mention mundane things in that place, but when they were out in the porch he offered his congratulations. "That was a magnificent sermon you gave us, padre."

Haddowe looked distinctly pleased. "I'm glad you liked it. It's not too easy to find the exact medium of expression for a country audience."

"And that note about the carving. Extraordinarily good of you."

"A pleasure, my dear fellow; a pleasure. I knew I had it somewhere. Curious how that comparatively harmless piece of bravado should have grown into a species of village superstition."

Travers hoped it wasn't being done too blatantly, but he tried to appear unconscious of the fact that his footsteps were being directed along the path to the vicarage and not to the main road. It was only when they reached the door of the creeper-covered, Georgian building that he appeared to realise his whereabouts.

"I mustn't keep you like this, padre. When will you be coming to dinner again?"

"If I were diplomatic," said Haddowe, "I shouldn't say what I *am* going to say, and that's whenever you ask me. I hope that's not too flagrant?"

"Just what I wanted to hear. Let me see now. What about Wednesday?"

The vicar thought for a second or two. "Ah! that's unfortunate. And that reminds me, too. I knew there was something I wanted to say. Are you very busy? Why not have supper with me?"

"I wouldn't dream of it," said Travers. "Why should I foist myself on you at short notice?"

"Nothing of the sort," retorted Haddowe, almost hustling him through the door. "You'll get a plain meal; a cold one, but . . ."

"There's many a worse thing than that," smiled Travers, passing over his hat and gloves.

"Just come in here a minute," said Haddowe, showing his visitor into the study. "If you'll excuse me a moment I'll fix things up. Shall I send a man along to the Lodge to let Royce know you're feeding here?"

"That's very thoughtful of you," said Travers, and then gave a glance round the room. There was little enough to be learned from it. The books that packed the walls seemed all on matters of pure divinity and a most uninteresting lot. He pulled out one with a promising title—*New Wine in Old Bottles*—and found it a collection of sermons, though on the fly-leaf in writing so faded as to be almost illegible, was the name "Henry Castleton." Others were the same and the inference clearly seemed to be that Haddowe had purchased *en bloc* the library of his predecessor.

The room in which they had supper was a gloomy one with the usual vicarage laurels brushing against the windows and its furnishings so meagre as to look comfortless without a fire.

"You must take everything as you find it," apologised Haddowe. "I'm sure you don't mind. Also we'll look after ourselves."

"It looks quite palatial," prevaricated Travers. "If I never get a worse meal than this—or worse company—I shall be a fortunate feller."

"Help yourself to the ale. It's perfectly harmless," said Haddowe. "Have you heard about my domestic arrangements, by the way? They caused quite a sensation in the village when I first arrived."

Travers expressed polite ignorance.

"There are no women in the house. I have a couple of men—perfectly competent and so on—who do all the housework and garden between them. One can drive my small car at a pinch."

"You mustn't mind my asking," said Travers, "but is this a Tolstoyan sort of theory by any chance?"

"Dear, dear, no!" laughed Haddowe. "You see I've spent all my life with men—Canada, France and so on. I simply couldn't imagine life with women in the house."

"You find them function quite adequately?"

"Absolutely. The house is clean—or it looks so to me—and one of them's a good cook. To be perfectly candid, I get the service I want and without fear of village scandal. Of course I can't very well entertain, but that's hardly expected of a bachelor!"

Travers agreed. All the same he felt an extraordinary curiosity to clap eyes on those two men. What sort of polish would they have and what would be the footing on which they stood? But it was much later in the evening, when they had returned to the comparative comfort of the study, that he thought he saw his chance.

"Sorry, padre, but there's something I've forgotten. Might one of your people take a message to the Hall?"

Haddowe got up at once. "I'll find one of them. Will you write it—or phone?"

"'Fraid I must write."

"You'll find everything you want there," and he indicated the desk as he left the room. Hardly what Travers wanted, but he scribbled hastily—

"Forgot to tell you to have all papers ready by 9.30.
"L. T."

addressed it to "J. Francis," and sealed up the envelope. Somewhere outside was the faintest sound of feet and as he opened the door cautiously he caught a glimpse of Haddowe at the end of the passage, and with him another man—a thin, pale-looking sort of fellow with a mop of untidy hair. His sleeves were rolled up and as he listened to the whispered voice he nodded from time to time as if he understood.

Travers opened the door with unnecessary noise and came out to the passage. The man must have shot off like a streak, because the vicar was alone.

"Here's the chit, vicar. Ask your man to hand it over to Francis personally. It's frightfully important. And give him this, will you?"

The vicar protested; Travers insisted, and the half-crown was taken. The vicar disappeared with the note and in a minute or two the pair of them were once more pulling at their pipes and yarning away. Then Travers found an opening.

"What did you do with yourself after the war, padre?"

Haddowe knocked out his pipe, pulled out his pouch and began refilling with curious deliberation before he answered.

"It was rather strange really. Like so many more, I felt the excitement of the war and of course I got into a rut. Also I'd made quite a lot of friends out there, so I didn't feel like going back—not at once. Then a friend of mine, a wealthy American, put up a proposition. You're not letting me bore you?"

"Good lord, no! I'm most interested."

"The proposition was this. He knew I'd been working in Canada and that's why he approached me. His idea was that every year after the war heaps of Americans and Canadians would come back to see the battle-fields; and also there'd be a good few men who'd stayed on in France. What he suggested therefore was a kind of home-plus-hotel where visitors and their families could be entertained and kept out of the hands of the sharks. Well, we opened up in Cherbourg and had another place in Paris. Afterwards we extended our amenities to all American and Canadian sailors using the port."

"A pretty big thing!"

"It was. The other chap didn't do anything but put up the original capital and act as life president and, between you and me, I was secretary and chaplain and conductor of tours and most other things." He paused to light his pipe. "I think we did an enormous amount of good, particularly among the seamen."

"What's happened to it now?"

Haddowe smiled. "You insist on my being vainglorious. I believe the man they got after me didn't make himself one of the people with whom he had to deal. I may be doing him an injustice, but the fact remains that the Anglo-American Rest Home, as we called it, was closed shortly after."

"Must have been a responsible job."

"It was. We used to circularise the branches of the British Legion and the American and Canadian societies, and you'd be surprised at the number of people we had to accommodate. As a matter of fact the place is now a hotel—The Anglo-American—and run on the usual lines. I'm sorry really. The sailors would miss it so much."

The conversation veered round to the sea and submarines and modern warfare, and when Travers pulled out his watch he was amazed at the lateness of the hour.

"'Fraid I must be going, padre. My man expected me a quarter of an hour ago. You've given me a great evening. When can you come to the Hall? What about lunch on Wednesday?"

"That's very nice of you," said Haddowe. "I shall be only too pleased. And what I was going to tell you about the Wednesday evening was this. You know that performance of *The Rivals* we're going to give? Well, I got a letter from the hospital a day or so ago. It seems they're in urgent need of money, so I thought we'd get on with our show as soon as possible. We ought to raise even more than our last year's three hundred pounds."

"When did you think of having it?"

"Well—er—in a fortnight. Wednesday and Thursday week to be exact," said Haddowe, rather apologetically it seemed. "You see rehearsals are already well advanced. Also Miss Forteresse is liable to be leaving us at any moment now and we really must avail ourselves of her excellent—I might almost say unique—services. Moreover," he went on, "we don't depend for an audience on Fenwold itself. All the county people in the district come on the second night. Similarly with our company. Except Leeke, Castleton and myself, our talent is drawn from outside the village."

"So you're in it, padre?" laughed Travers. "Who are you? Sir Anthony?"

The vicar smiled deprecatingly. "As a matter of fact I am. A curious role for a man of peace like myself. Goodbye! I shall probably see you before, but if not—lunch on Wednesday."

Once more Travers' thoughts were mixed as he strolled back to the Hall. Haddowe had really explained things very well. Mention of the seamen had brought that episode at Camden Town a bit nearer but, even then, surely there might be some explanation of the "man of peace" and the negro and the torrent of blasphemy in the fog? True there were the missing letters—and that frowsty servant. It was all very puzzling—and very intriguing.

Once more that Camden Town affair. What about this for an explanation. One of his seamen had been victimised and Haddowe had promised to help. He'd followed the rogues as far as London and with certain holds over 'em had forced that meeting in the fog. He'd got the money back and was insisting on the return of the passport. When he saw he was in for trouble he used a language which his assailants would understand as a sort of protective colouring.

Franklin was waiting up in his room.

"Well, what did you think of the sermon?"

"Rather over my head," said Franklin. "When I go to church I like to feel my conscience gnawing. Give me the Salvation Army, not that autograph album stuff."

"Everyone to his taste," smiled Travers. "And what about the fighting parson?"

"The voice was right enough. And wasn't I right? He ought to be an ambassador—or a viceroy."

"I thought a judge—or a cardinal. What did you think of his man?"

"Can't place him. He looked like anything on earth but a professional servant; accent pure cockney; nails filthy—and he smelt most abominably of turpentine."

"Rubbing himself for a sprain," suggested Travers.

"Maybe. And talking of those servants of Haddowe's, do you know I'm told they never hardly go out? The most unsociable set of blokes you ever met. Royce says they were asked up here for the servants' hall Christmas party and didn't come. Very occasionally one goes to a pub and then bolts out again. People in the village are actually saying they're foreigners!"

"Really! Perhaps Haddowe's pretty strict or else they're amazingly shy. Still it's funny."

"Anything happen to-night?"

"One very curious thing. Haddowe wants that dramatic show I was telling you about put forward a bit. He's really very anxious about it and I'm damned if I can see why. First place it's the wrong time of year. And—say what he likes—it's bad form after Revere's death. He says Miss Forteresse might be going away, but then—can't the woman come here again if they want her? There's something wrong somewhere."

"But how can that be connected with the murder?"

"It isn't—at least I don't see how it could be. It just intrigues me, that's all. Oh, and by the way, I thought of a rather neat explanation of that little scrap Haddowe had in the fog. . . . "

"Just one minute before you explain that away," said Franklin quietly. "Would you mind telling me if this is your writing on this envelope Hallowe's man brought?"

As soon as Travers had got his glasses polished it didn't take him a second to answer. "It isn't! It's the same sort of envelope. The writing's an excellent imitation, but it isn't mine."

"Do you know, I don't know why I had that suspicion? Now, who opened that letter—Haddowe or his man? And why? . . . I wonder if you'd mind telling me everything that did happen this evening?"

CHAPTER XV
A LION AMONG LADIES

"WHAT'S THE PROGRAMME to-day?" asked Travers a trifle anxiously as he took his morning cup of tea.

"I think it'll be a bit mixed," said Franklin. "Parry's just off to Carter's cottage to see what happens with the policeman, and I must wait and hear what he's got to report; then I ought to keep indoors a bit or Mrs. Lacy'll be wondering what's up. This afternoon I rather thought of making a start on an alibi test. It's like this. Royce says Mr. Revere left the Hall at 9.0. Even if he'd gone straight there he couldn't have got to Lammas Wood before a quarter past. Now Westfield was lured away to Branford till closing time, which is 10.0, but he *might* have got back to his beat at 10.15. Anybody therefore who has an alibi for the hour 9.15 to 10.15 ought to be out of it."

"But if Westfield *was* lured away, you haven't to look any further than Carter."

"Why? Mightn't Carter's story be true?"

"Certainly it might be true. I'd believe it with a great deal more confidence however if he'd say what he wanted to see Mr. Revere about earlier in the evening. And how're you going to apply the tests?"

"To be frank, I don't know," said Franklin perfectly optimistically. "There are ways and means. All I *do* know is that if I had the authority of the Yard behind me I'd clean up this case in a week, or bust."

"God forbid!" said Travers piously. "And what people are you going to apply the test to? Haddowe's out of it. His men would never talk—that is if you got the chance of asking 'em."

"Leeke, Castleton and Carter are my three hopes. There's just the chance that chap Eagling might have been mixed up in it—not as a principal; he hasn't got the brains for that. Still, his alibi ought to be easy. The others—well, you never know. They say you can't move in a village without everybody knowing it."

"The trouble is there's such a devil of a lot of space to move in. I expect you and I could go all round that village if we wanted to do so, furtively, without being seen or heard."

"True enough. Still we can't grumble. To-morrow we ought to have enough evidence to start eliminating definitely. What are you doing this morning? Anything special?"

"Correspondence first. Must keep up some reason for being here. Why? Did you want me?"

"No, I just wondered, that's all."

"There was just one thing I did want to do," confessed Travers, "and that's to run an eye over Angéle again. There's something queer about *that* woman or I'm a damn bad judge. Nothing to do with the main case of course. And what about those pieces of papier maché? Thought of anything else?"

Franklin shook his head. "Not unless they're part of a burnt lamp-shade. They're not heavy enough for trays or ornaments. Something else I am going to do by-the-by, and that's put Parry watching L. F. We might get a possible connection through her to Castleton or Leeke—or Haddowe for the matter of that. Parry's a good man, but he'll have to be extraordinarily tactful."

*   *   *   *   *

It was just after ten when Royce, as previously instructed, reported that Madame Angéle had gone by the sunk garden on her morning constitutional, whereupon Travers slipped out by the back of the dining-room, cut across the west lawn and once more ran clean into the party. Of the footman there was no sign. Angéle was in the middle of a speech, delivered with much more animation than could have been expected of an invalid. The change in her at the astoundingly unexpected appearance of Travers through the clipped archway was really uncanny. She broke off in the middle of a gesture and seemed to shrivel up. Her eyes closed languidly and her hands drooped over the rug that covered her skirts. Leila Forteresse too seemed to close up and the smile she gave Travers was a wintry and watchful one.

"Good morning!" was his greeting. "And how's the invalid this morning?"

"Not at all well. I shall be so relieved when she leaves Fenwold. I don't think it suits her."

"I'm sorry to hear that," said Travers sympathetically, and before he could be stopped, spoke to the invalid direct. "You find our English weather very trying, madame?"

The eyes opened and there was something in the look that was not all exhaustion at the effort. It was too peering, too suspicious, and the lips seemed to tighten themselves as if guarding against too incautious a reply. But that reply never came. Leila Forteresse laid her hand on Travers' arm and the pleading wistfulness of her tone was only too apparent.

"Please don't talk to Angéle this morning! She had such a harassing night. Didn't you, darling?"

The footman came up from nowhere and Travers drew back. "I say; I'm awfully sorry. I didn't realise." Then he looked up again. "I wonder if I—if you could spare me a moment. I don't think it will take more."

This time her look was nervous. Then she coloured slightly. She was wondering—but just what would be hard to say. Then, "Go on with the chair, Brown," she told the footman. "If I don't catch you up, wait by the lily pond."

"It's really nothing important," explained Travers as they went along towards the breakfast-room. "And I was extremely sorry to hear about your old nurse. Which part of France does she come from?"

He watched her face and noticed the hesitation. "Oh—er—somewhere near Toulouse—I think."

"How very curious. I happen to know that part particularly well. I wonder if I know the very spot?" He changed his tone to one of pleasant anticipation. "I must ask her when I see her again."

"Do you know France well?"

"Some of it. Round Toulouse, for instance. And the Riviera. And the Somme area—the rest, not very well." He drew back for her to enter, then pushed forward a chair.

"Won't you sit down? What I really wanted to see you about was this. I don't know what your intentions are, but I'm instructed to inform you that there's no necessity whatever for you to hurry on or be disturbed about any plans for leaving the Hall. Mr. Grant insists that you stay here just as long as you consider it convenient."

There was certainly relief in her face, though precisely why was not evident. "That's very good of Mr. Grant and—and you, Mr. Travers. Only, I heard from Sir Henry Brotherston this morning. The house in Sussex is quite ready. Angéle is going at the end of the week."

"I hope the change will be helpful," said Travers kindly. "Difference in climate, however small, often works miracles. But," and here he gave his best smile, "we're not losing *you* yet, Miss Forteresse?"

She was obviously feeling much more at home. The laugh she gave was quite a flirtatious one. "What things you dear men do say! No; I'm staying on for the dramatic show we're giving. Then I'm going down the next day."

Travers thought suddenly there might be no harm in being kittenish too. "That's splendid! I mean about your not going yet. Do you know I don't think you and I see half enough of each other."

She looked at him very coyly. "And whose fault is that?"

Travers actually blushed. "Well—er—I really don't know. You see—well—you're a young and remarkably attractive woman and I—er—well," and he shrugged humorously.

She balanced her chin on her knuckles and smiled again—a smile perfectly inscrutable. Whether it was maternal or mysterious Travers didn't know; moreover he was hopelessly inexperienced. But he did know it was decidedly alarming.

"You shall take me out to tea—at Branford—this afternoon. Do you drive?"

"Oh rather!" exclaimed Travers. "I say, that's awfully decent of you."

She rose quickly. "Now I must hurry back to Angéle."

But she didn't hurry. She stood there looking at him with all the allure in the world, lips deliciously pouted. Through Travers' mind there flashed like lightning the hackneyed thought of the Mona Lisa and then the plaintive seduction of that woman he once saw in *Vaudeville*. He too rose nervously as she came nearer; her look now provocative, now amused. A yard from him she stopped short and held out her hand in a languid sort of droop. Travers didn't quite know what was expected of him but he took it, felt its cool softness, then kissed the fingers. He heard her whispered, "You *dear* man!" and felt the fingers withdraw, but when he looked up she was already through the door.

He gave a dismal whistle and mopped his face with his handkerchief. That's what came of trying to be ingratiating; attempting to get the lady into a fine opinion of herself and her charms so that she might be the more accessible for conversational purposes. How was he to know she'd take him for as big a fool as the rest of them? But of course that sudden warmth on her part had been wholly insincere!

Then, as if he couldn't trust himself any longer in that room, he made his way to the library. Even there he still felt something of the alarm that had run through him as she made her slow approach. He could still smell that sleepy scent that he caught as she brushed his ear with her lips. And then he whistled again. So subtle had been his approach and so warm the response that he had forgotten the chief reason for which he had sought that private interview!

But that could be done in the afternoon and as he thought of what that ride might have in store he shook his head perplexedly. Then he began work on the unfiled accounts and correspondence, but half an hour of that was enough and drove him in search of relaxation—this time in the office of Captain Leeke.

Leeke wasn't there. A couple of clerks were hard at it and a nice-looking youngster, scarcely out of his teens, did all the explaining.

"Captain Leeke is out at the moment, sir. Did you want him particularly?"

"Not very," said Travers. "You're his—er—understudy?"

"That's right," smiled the other. "At least, I'm learning the job."

Travers nodded pleasantly and stepped out again to the road. The understudy came out too.

"You like it here? The work and so on?"

"Oh rather! Of course I haven't got the hang of everything yet. Captain Leeke is awfully decent."

"I'm sure he is. And how's the work going?"

"Oh, frightfully well. You see we got a good start this time."

"Really! How was that?"

"Well, I don't know exactly, but about a fortnight ago Mr. Revere asked for the accounts to be made up just as they are quarterly; you know, complete vouchers and all that."

"That was lucky," said Travers thoughtfully, "and—horribly prophetic. I expect you were surprised."

"Captain Leeke was jolly annoyed!"

Quite a nicely mannered boy, thought Travers, but it won't do to let him think there's any sort of inquisition.

"You must come and have lunch with me some time," he said. "And don't work too hard!"

That, he thought as he began again in the library, was what could arise out the most unmeaning of words. If that special audit meant anything, it was that Cosmo Revere had acted on the accusations of the anonymous letters. A strange and furtive thing for a man of the intellectual fibre and spiritual calibre of Cosmo Revere to descend to. Yet there the facts were. He preferred to think that something must have been known beforehand; that the letters had merely made certain what had already become more than suspicions.

Still, there it was. Eagling had gone and Leeke had been given the strongest of hints that his house would have to be proved in order. And had Cosmo Revere been so sure that he had revoked a legacy? And had Leeke feared the result of that audit? Travers didn't know. He tried to recall the face of the agent as he had sat that afternoon listening to the ticking of Sir Henry's voice, but nothing came to him that answered either of those questions.

* * * * *

Franklin was given a much-edited account of the morning's doings. There was no mention of vamping, and the afternoon drive became a casual acceptance of an invitation.

"There's still one mystery in this house," he concluded, "and that's the French maid. Have you seen anything of her?"

Franklin shook his head. "No luck at all. A footman—Brown—hands over all meals at the door. Sometimes she goes out with L. F. in her car, but from what I've gathered she's as much a jailer as maid."

"We shall have to think of a scheme," said Travers. "How did Parry get on this morning?"

"Oh, he saw Turner go in. He's now off to have a drink in the pubs and ask awkward questions and spread the news generally. To-night I'm going the round myself."

"Reaping where another's strewn!"

"That's the idea. And I may be late."

Travers grinned. "Well, if I don't see you before you start, don't forget the old adage and go mixing your drinks."

"Not much fear of that," retorted Franklin. "There'll be damn little moaning at the bar to-night. And, by the way, what about an advance on account of wages?"

CHAPTER XVI
TRAVERS TAKES TEA

IT HAD BEEN doubly tactful of Travers to refuse the driving seat. For one thing the hands that held the wheel could scarcely be otherwise employed and for another he could settle well out of the way in his corner of the two-seater. Not that there seemed any immediate danger of philandering. From what could be judged of his companion's expression she had long since forgotten that brief *rapprochement* in the breakfast-room, and he might have been no more than what he was supposed to be—the dignified representative of two of the executors; perfectly charming and all that, but my dear, *too* professional!

"We'll go round by Toftwold," she announced, turning into a side road. "No use going straight to Branford. Isn't the weather too magnificent?"

The conversation became informal. Once they pulled up to greet a kindred spirit—an Eton-cropped flapper with a couple of Sealyhams—and once they drew in at the drive of a house while she paid a call. Half an hour after the start they arrived in Branford and before Travers knew what he was in for, the car was again careering along a drive.

Travers smiled forbearingly. "Where this time?"

"Only the teeniest call," he was told. "I really must see Colonel Warren. That's the house. You simply must come in and chaperone!"

Travers' summing-up of the situation—that he was to be on show before the gallant colonel as the victim of the charmer's bow and spear—was probably near the mark. Colonel Warren was in and a maid showed them into the drawing-room. Before Travers had time to run his collector's eye over the china, the colonel came in; full of bluster and the joy of living in a world which included himself.

"Hallo, colonel!" was the greeting he got. "They gave you my message?"

The colonel bowed over the drooping hand. "Oh yes. And you're very early." Then he had another look at Travers. "May I introduce Mr. Travers. A very dear friend."

Travers nodded, smiled and took the hand the colonel let escape. "You down here for long?" fired the host.

"Some days," said Travers slowly. "It depends on developments."

The colonel grunted. "This sort of thing doesn't do you lawyer fellows any harm. Have a whisky and soda?"

"Thanks. But I really won't. Doesn't do you old campaigners any harm, but it's a bit too early for me."

Warren missed the retort. "I'll see about some tea," and started for the bell.

"Please don't," said Leila Forteresse. "We're really not staying a minute. Too bad of us to give you all this trouble. What I really wanted to know was, are you all right for Wednesday's rehearsal?"

"What time?"

She gave Travers a glance as much as to say. "Isn't he too impossible!" then, "Seven—we thought. Poor man! You'll miss your dinner."

"Can't be helped," said the colonel. "Can't do too much for charity." Then he frowned. "My man won't be able to stay. Could you drive me back in your car? Come to supper. You come, too, Mr.—"

"Travers," put in the owner of the name. "Sorry, but I shall be frightfully busy. But I hope that won't stop Miss Forteresse."

She laughed. "Well, we'll get you home somehow, colonel. Do you know your part?"

"Every word. Absolutely perfect. Tried it over with my housekeeper."

"Naughty man! But it was splendid of you really! You and Captain Leeke, you know, ought to have rehearsed together. How did you get on at your big killing on Tuesday? Make pots and pots of money?"

The colonel smiled complacently. "We made 'em think a bit. Good man, Leeke. Bit excitable of course. Wants an older head to steady him."

"Bridge," she explained. "The colonel and Captain Leeke are simply wonderful." She held out her hand with the same old languid droop. "We'll see you on Wednesday then," and made for the door, the colonel cutting in before Travers and fussing till the very last moment.

"Too antiquated for words!" was her comment as the car shot out into the main road. "Simply beastly wealthy of course."

"What was the idea of the big killing? Some challenge or other?"

"The colonel fancies himself enormously," she explained. "I think it started at the club. He challenged two really wonderful people if he might bring his own partner." She laughed merrily. "You see Captain Leeke told me his side of it all. He said he had to drag the colonel out of every call. Simply daren't leave him in with the bid!"

"Must have been rather funny," said Travers. "When was this big match?"

"Last Tuesday." She made the statement with no modifying regret. "A week to-morrow. I wanted to come but—I didn't know the other men very well. And people will talk so dreadfully!"

"Did they have an all-night sitting?"

"Oh no! Only dinner and bridge. I rang them up at about ten—too anxious of me! They were ten pounds in then. Captain Leeke said they'd the most marvellous hands. He made over fifty."

"Did he, by jove! And what's this?"

"This" was the yard of the Golden Fleece—a wonderful old place; all rafters and irregular passages and funny little windows.

The drawing-room was practically empty and he found a seat for tea overlooking the river.

"Who's the colonel going to be?" he asked. "Sir Anthony?"

"Wouldn't it suit him too perfectly? But Mr. Haddowe's taking that. He's frightfully good. Colonel Warren's Sir Lucius. Captain Leeke is Bob Acres."

"It ought to be a rattling good show. I really must book my seat. Does one book?" and so on though the usual series of trivialities. And, try how he might, Travers gathered very little. Her life at the Hall, for instance, she avoided neatly and the one question he did put as to her life before then was so adroitly turned aside that he abandoned any further attempt at extorting a biography.

When the final cigarette was smoked and the reckoning paid, she suggested a drive over the heaths by Westlake. That meant another hour, and Travers all the while putting his horns out of his shell, then dodging them in again. He seemed to be puzzled, intrigued, scared and flustered in turns, and yet the fact remains that he didn't find too obtrusive her eternal talking in superlatives and the buoyancy of her fluttering personality. But then, as Wrentham had warned him and as he apparently recognised, Leila Forteresse was an unusually fascinating woman.

One thing gave him matter for thought—a reference to Angéle.

"Oh, I asked Angéle about her home and I was all wrong. It wasn't Toulouse—it was Toulon. Wasn't that too perfectly ridiculous of me!"

"Quite a natural mistake," said Travers. "I know that part a little but not much. It's the sort of place one always goes through—like Grantham."

"Poor Angéle! She's really quite a dear, you know. And absolutely alone in the world. That's why I simply had to take her in."

"It was an extraordinarily charitable thing to do," said Travers. The opening had been given but he left the conversation where it was till they were back in the Hall.

"I can't tell you how I enjoyed this afternoon," he said, with an expression of deliberate earnestness. "I wonder if you'd let me do something for you in return?"

She smiled, all anticipation.

"It's about Angéle. A friend of mine—a famous authority on rheumatic complaints—is meeting me at Branford this week on a purely business matter. I think I might say he's the authority. He's done some perfectly marvellous things. May I bring him to see Angéle?"

He saw the apprehension in her face. Even before he put the question he could see she was preparing to say what she did.

"Oh, I can't! I mean—she's dreadfully nervous. You've no idea! She wouldn't hear of it."

Travers remonstrated gently. "But he's a perfectly delightful person! His clientéle is mostly feminine. I'm sure she'd be charmed with him—and he speaks French admirably."

This time she was feeling more sure of herself. "No, really! It's awfully good of you, but you don't know Angéle. Her case is so dreadfully complicated and she positively loathes a doctor looking at her," and she turned to go.

"It's an awful pity," went on Travers. "Don't you think you ought to put it to her?"

She shook her head and then hurried away up the stairs that led to the far gallery. At the top she turned and waved her hand; then at the absolute corner—blew a kiss!

Travers in his own room wondered if the new footing on which he stood would mean her occasional resumption of meals downstairs. He wondered too how he could get back to his original isolation or whether it would be better, now he'd been admitted to the inner circle of her acquaintance, to profit by the admission. The question there was how? Six months in the company of people like Haddowe and herself would leave him in all probability just as ignorant of what they had to do with the under-currents that he knew existed below the Fenwold surface.

One simple thing could be done however—to ask Royce his opinion of the invalid. Part of the answer turned out to be illuminating. A doctor—a stranger—had twice been called in to see Angéle. He had been met by her mistress and taken straight upstairs, where the interviews had lasted about half an hour. The doctor—Royce had forgotten the name even if he had ever heard it—had spoken to nobody downstairs, but had left at once, ostensibly for Branford. According to Brown the footman, the report he left was that Madame Angéle was in no pain and nothing more could be done for her than was being done at the moment. All she needed was rest and absolute seclusion.

On the whole Travers was decidedly pleased with his afternoon. Leeke and Warren had been cleared away at one swoop and Angéle and her illness looked more and more worth study. The thing was, were she and her mistress and Haddowe in agreement? If so, they'd had nothing to do with the murder. Murder would surely be the last thing in the world that Haddowe wanted. With Cosmo Revere he knew where he was. With a new patron he'd have to start his hood-winking all over again. Then what on earth were the three up to?

The first idea he had about that was this, made into the very speech he got ready to recite to Franklin.

"I know Haddowe hadn't anything to do with the murder. All the same he's got to be watched—in other words, he's a side-line. Now you haven't got time for side-lines. Why not let me get on with the Angéle-Forteresse-Haddowe group on my own account, seeing my position here gives me opportunities you haven't got?"

Then he thought of an illustration which seemed rather apt and rehearsed it for the absent Franklin.

"You and I are both waiting for a murderer whom we expect to turn up at a certain time and place and while we're there, all at once I see an urchin tying a squib on the tail of an old gentleman's coat. I tell you about it. 'Damn it all!' you say. 'Have you no sense of proportion? It's a murderer we're looking for.' Then very humbly and very politely I say, 'Well, would you mind if I go on looking— with you—but keeping an eye on the boy with the squib to pass the time away?'"

Then last of all he did think of something concrete. The idea that came was so preposterous that he discarded it half a dozen times before deciding to give it a chance. Even then it was all very vague—just a thought arising out of the meal at the Branford Inn. Franklin would certainly never hear about it. And when he did write the letter addressed to Durango House, it was chiefly because the idea was so tenuous that delay would have meant it would never have been written at all.

* * * * *

By the last post came the letter from Cambridge.

Lanfranc College,
Cambridge.

My Dear Travers,

I think I can help you over the digging operations you mentioned. This was a hobby of the late Mr. Revere and consisted merely in the search for what might be called prehistoric kitchens. I was not interested myself but, as far as I recall Mr. Revere's explanation, these consisted of clay-lined holes filled with water into which was dropped a stone previously made white hot. The heat thereby imparted to the water facilitated a boiling process—a method of cooking unknown by means of vessels as we know it today. The stones themselves appear to be highly prized by collectors.

The mistakes in this are due to my untrustworthy memory. I was concerned, as you may know, with the mathematical side of Mr. Reverey's researches only.

Come and see me when you are in Cambridge. I regret that a severe cold kept me from the funeral, but I am relying on your good offices to let me have the editing of any of the papers which may be suitable for publication.

Yours sincerely,

HERBERT MERRITT.

As for the arguments which the letter would provoke, Travers deliberately avoided them. After all, things might have happened to Franklin that would make any argument unnecessary.

CHAPTER XVII
AND FRANKLIN HAS A BITTER

WHEN FRANKLIN RETURNED that night, shortly after ten-thirty, he reported an evening that had been moist but not exhilarating. At the "Stag" he had been inveigled into a game of bowls—all very well in its way but, as far as his visit was concerned, perfectly useless.

The players had been so intent on the game that there was opportunity for only the smallest of small talk, and as the evening began to draw in and the dew fell he made his excuses and tried a change. The sum total of his information was that Mr. Castleton was spoken of with considerable respect. On very rare occasions he had had a drink at the "Stag," but generally he kept himself very much to himself. Captain Leeke, he gathered, was reasonably popular on the estate; one who knew his job and who had the reputation of being a bit of a flyer, especially among the petticoats.

But before proceeding to the "Coach and Horses," Franklin took a walk round the village green. The smoke was coming from the chimney of Carter's cottage but the occasion was scarcely convenient for a visit, and he passed on up the slope.

At the gateway of Oak Cottage he turned his head and caught sight of a figure in flannels lounging in a deck chair half-way down the lawn. That opportunity seemed too good to miss.

"Excuse me, sir," he called out, "but does Mr. Carter live here?"

The figure slewed round in the chair and Franklin saw a tanned, attractive face; slightly superior perhaps but clever and rather likeable. The voice, as far as he could judge, was a cultured one.

"I'm afraid not. The next cottage, at the foot of the hill."

Franklin still held his ground.

"Do you think he's likely to be in?"

Castleton got to his feet and stretched his arms; then he had another look at the stranger and smiled. The white of his teeth showed up clear against the brick-red of his skin.

"Why not go and see?"

A perfectly good answer, thought Franklin ruefully, and turned back down the slope. Behind the screen of trees that hid him from Oak Cottage he hurried back to the main road. Inside the door of the "Coach and Horses" he looked back towards the gate, but there was no sign of Castleton, who doubtless by that time had forgotten the pertinaceous questioner. Inside the private bar the oil-lamp was already lit, and a couple of men, one a farmer by the look of him and the other a postman in uniform, were yarning over two mugs of beer.

Franklin gave them good-evening, called for his bitter, then politically made it three, and a minute later was joining in the conversation. Neither seemed to have the least idea who he was or where he had come from—a peculiar thing for a village and certainly adding colour to Westfield's implication that the Hall kept itself very much aloof from the commoner herd.

Another round was called for. Then the conversation gradually petered out and the farmer, seizing his chance, resumed what Franklin's entry had interrupted.

"So you took the letter, Fred?"

The postman nodded affirmatively. "I thought to myself, 'This is a rum 'un,' when I read the address. Course you mustn't say a word to a soul, but Turner opened it and showed it to me; then he got his helmet and off he went."

The other chuckled to himself. "Regular April fool they made of him!" He had a pull at his mug. "I 'spose you ain't seen anything of Carter since, Fred?"

"Nothin' at all. I'll bet he weren't half riled!"

"Carter?" put in Franklin. "Is that the old chap who lives at the corner cottage? Antique dealer or something?"

"That's him," said Fred. "He's a rum 'un. Don't care what he says, do he, John?"

The farmer chuckled again. "He give my missis ten bob for an old chair all fallin' to pieces." Then he assumed a more judicial expression. "Still, no doubt he get a livin' at it. We can't all be the same trade."

"I came over to see him specially last Tuesday night," said Franklin. "I suppose he didn't come in here?"

"I didn't see him; did you, Fred?"

"Not that I remember. Tuesday? No; I didn't see him Tuesday. Last night he was in though, cause I had a pint with him. He weren't half riled! Had that old motor van of his break down at Norwich and had to leave it where it were and come home by train."

"I had bad luck that night," went on Franklin. "I came to see two people and both were out. Carter was one, and when I went to Oak Cottage Mr. Castleton wasn't in either."

The farmer paused in the act of lighting his pipe. "Mr. Castleton? I saw *him* on Tuesday. You know, Fred, after that Flower Show meeting, just after I left you. He came by the farm and pulled up to ask me what lighting-up time was."

"Then he'd be going the opposite direction to Branford?"

"Course he was! Looked to me as if he was goin' to Westlake."

"Then I probably passed him," said Franklin with a gesture of annoyance. "Would it be about ten?"

"Quarter to it was, 'cause I pulled my old turnip out," and he gave an illustration by producing a monstrous silver watch from his fob pocket.

"You didn't hear him come home?"

"My missis reckon she did. That little toot-toot he have instead of a horn, she reckon she heard that just as she was gettin' into bed, and that'd be just gone ten. Evenin', Arthur!"

The newcomer was a keeper by the look of him, and then for a good twenty minutes the conversation passed out of Franklin's control; indeed he was once more preparing to move on when the farmer cocked his ear. In the tap-room could be heard a voice. There was a dramatic hush.

"That's old Carter!" whispered the postman. "Let's go and hear what he's got to say about the burglary."

"What burglary?" asked the keeper.

"Never you mind that. Come you on in before he go," he was told, and the party got on its legs, finished the drinks and moved out, Franklin at their heels.

With its plain benches and deal tables the tap-room was a much less comfortable place than the private bar. An oil-lamp hung from a rafter and the air was foul with the smell of stale beer and tobacco. In a corner, half-pint mug in hand, sat Carter, looking surly and saying nothing. At the other end of the long table were a couple of labourers enjoying some sort of a joke.

The farmer took up his position at the bar, the others round him.

"What are you having, gentlemen?"

The orders were given and then came a special invitation for Carter.

"And what are *you* going to have, Mr. Carter?" Carter's was a deliberate sort of voice; pugnacious and even churlish.

"Nothin' at all, thankee. When I've finished this I'm a-goin' home."

Westfield's had been a good description as far as Franklin could judge in that light, but after the statement that Carter was a man he'd been looking for a week ago, he kept himself well in the background. Luckily, too, the curiosity of the company was directed to other things than himself. The farmer, by virtue of position or his own assessment, seemed to be spokesman and set the ball rolling.

"What's this they're sayin' about a burglary at your place, Mr. Carter?"

Carter looked at them from under his shaggy eyebrows.

"They? Who's they? That what beat me. Anything happen and it's allust *they* say this and *they* say that," and he grunted.

The farmer was considerably taken aback. The unexpected retort had caught him clean in the wind. He hemmed and hawed.

"Well—er—well, come now, Mr. Carter. You know how it is. If anything happen, people want to hear about it? Ain't it natural now?" and he appealed to the company. Then, possibly emboldened, "The thing is, did you have a burglary or did you not?"

It looked at first as if Carter wasn't going to answer. He picked up his mug, gave it a swish, then emptied it slowly. Then, with every eye watching him, he set the pot down on the table.

"There might be something in my house that people want to lay their fingers on—and then again there might not."

He got to his feet.

"One thing I have got that you can all come and put your fingers on if you like."

He opened the door with his left hand.

"You may get a lot more out o' that than you can out o' me; and that's—my old pump."

Then the door closed after him. Whatever else Carter knew, he certainly had a good idea of what constituted a good exit.

"There you are, gentlemen; what d'you think o' that?" asked the farmer, looking very much of a fool. That was all Franklin heard as he slipped into the passage and out by the front door. Then he sauntered round to the back, but Carter had disappeared. For a minute he stood there irresolutely, wondering what to do, then made off quickly for Westfield's cottage.

Westfield let him in at the first bark of the dog.

"Thought you might have been in bed, Westfield," said Franklin. "Everybody in a village seems to turn in as soon as it's dark."

"About half past ten's my time, sir," said the keeper. "I generally like to have a good look at the paper."

"Have you found out anything about Carter?"

"Can't get hold of a word nowhere, sir. Nobody seem to have seen him on the Tuesday night."

"Well, keep on with it. Only for the Lord's sake be careful. If you get a chance to speak to him direct, put it to him sort of casually. What about Eagling? You don't happen to know where *he* was on the Tuesday?"

"Eagling? He was at Branford, sir. Just as I come out of the 'Cock' I saw him with his son-in-law what live at Branford."

"Splendid!" said Franklin. "Well, you carry on as I told you. If anything happens, let me know. Don't trouble to come out," and he slipped out of the back door. The crepe-soled shoes made no sound and yet the dog gave a growl.

Outside the gate he could have sworn he almost ran into a man; at least at one moment there seemed to be a shape in the dusk and then it disappeared on the far side of the road He stopped for a moment and listened. In the hedge that fronted the belt of trees was a quick rustling—or was it the wind that caught it from the open park?

Travers told his own story, then listened to Franklin's long recital.

"Rather looks as if we're getting on too fast. If everybody's out of it, where's your man to come from? Leeke, Warren, Castleton, Eagling; all with perfectly sound alibis, though Eagling never was a strong candidate in any case."

"I shall concentrate on Carter," said Franklin. "He always was a likely one. That dolmen theory's out too."

"What's puzzling you?" asked Travers, watching the frown on his face.

"If there's nothing at all to that treasure theory, why was everything turned topsy-turvy in Carter's cottage? He didn't bolt—because he turned up on the Sunday night. And there was good reason for his being away, if his car broke down."

Travers took off his glasses. "I don't know. Can't make head or tail of it. Still, I think you'll agree with what I was saying about the

Haddowe trio. And in that context, did you ever want a garden of your own when you were a small boy?"

Franklin wondered what was coming.

"I know *I* did. I pestered the gardener till he let me have a plot of my own—which I made the most damnable mess of! Now I've just the faintest idea of a theory of what Haddowe may be doing in Fenwold, though I don't know where the women come in. I know—at least I'd lay a hundred to one against it being connected with the murder." And then followed the fable of the squib on the old gentleman's tail.

Franklin was immensely amused. "I know what it is. You've got a hunch of some sort."

Travers was very apologetic. "Well, perhaps I have, but it's diametrically opposed to the murder. Also as soon as the least thing turns up I'll tell you like a shot. Now what have you got for me to-morrow?"

"What you like in the morning. In the afternoon—a call on Castleton."

"Castleton! What on earth for?"

"He can give us an introduction to his protégé, Carter."

"Yes—but what excuse can I give?" Franklin told him.

CHAPTER XVIII
THINGS BEGIN TO HAPPEN

TRAVERS MADE a really interesting deduction the following morning. It was all very involved and came as the result of a good hour's reasoning while waiting for sleep the previous night.

The point was this. Assume that Haddowe was engaged in some underhand and almost certainly remunerative occupation and that the two women were with him. Then what of the maid? What was she—purely servant or partly jailer? From that point something else suggested itself. Since Leila Forteresse had no connection with the servants' hall, from what quarter did all these conspirators get their information; information which would be desperately important, since all conspiracy must needs be on its guard? Was the maid this connecting link? But she couldn't be. Franklin's information was that only on the rarest occasions had she gone downstairs.

That gave the answer. The real link must be the footman, Brown—the only one who was a member of the morning constitutional procession of Angéle and the one who handed over the meals at the door of the upstair room. Was Brown a purveyor of information or was he merely a polite answerer of questions and sufficiently obtuse to be ignorant of the fact that he was being questioned? In any case the idea was one which it might be profitable to explore.

As for the exploration, a good many ideas were discarded before he decided on the best of a bad lot. The help of Royce had to be enlisted—a difficult thing since the butler was almost incapable of visualising a situation in which a Fenwold servant should allow himself to be tampered with as Brown was supposed to have done. Still, it was settled. The footman was to be given a job of work where it was impossible to miss a conversation between Travers and the butler, and the essentials were these.

"How is Angéle, Royce? Have you heard this morning?"

"No sir. But she was very unwell yesterday."

"So I believe. I wish I could do something. I'd rather like to have a word with her myself. Will you let me know as soon as she comes out this morning?"

"Very good, sir."

"And by the way, Royce; I shall be out definitely this afternoon and evening. I may get back to dinner, but I'll let you know."

All that remained after that was to await developments. The results ought to be the missing of the morning constitutional and the taking of an afternoon one instead. If the scheme were successful, Brown should prove a useful decoy.

At breakfast he found a letter announcing the arrival of Sir Henry the following afternoon. Then, before he forgot it, he wrote a chit for Castleton, thought of asking Royce to see it delivered, then changed his mind and consulted Franklin, who suggested Parry and took the business over himself.

It was getting along towards the end of the morning, after a couple of hours over what seemed endless and boring affairs of other people, that he gave a stretch and a yawn and thought a turn in the gardens would be at least a bit of a change. Under the cedar on the north lawn he was putting a match to his pipe when he caught sight of Leeke coming through the kitchen garden door and felt his spirits rise at once at the sight of a conversational fellow creature. As he was careful afterwards to explain to Franklin, there was no manufactured desire to be pleasant or any forced amiability—the greeting was quite the ordinary one to a man of Leeke's standing and special circumstances.

"Morning, Leeke! Weather still holding good?"

"Yes," remarked Leeke with a peculiar sort of drawl. "Not so bad. There was something I wanted to see you about, by the way."

Travers could sense the hostility and was frantically puzzling his brains to find out the reason. But he gave his very best smile.

"Well—here I am!"

"It's like this," said Leeke with a scowl on his face like a thundercloud. "If you want to know anything about my office I should be glad if you'd come to me and not go questioning young Hatton."

"I'm afraid I don't understand you," said Travers, who'd forgotten the incident. "If Hatton's your deputy, all I did do, now I come to think of it, was in a purely impersonal way—asked him if he was comfortable so to speak. In any case," and his voice took on a bit of an edge, "I can't say I like very much your method of approach to me now!"

That was enough to set Leeke off altogether. "Impersonal or not, it was damned interference—and whether you like being told about it—"

"Just a moment!" interrupted the other, beginning to feel more and more injured every minute. "I tell you you're absolutely mistaken, and what's more I expect you to believe it. If inadvertently I've offended against any professional etiquette by having a perfectly friendly talk with—"

"Friendly talk! If you were anxious to know about those accounts, they'll be in at the earliest available moment." Then, as a sort of vitriolic afterthought, "We've no use for your detective work here at Fenwold."

Travers made an effort to keep his poise and made a deplorably bad hand of it. "Who are you to speak of Fenwold? And what do you mean exactly by detective work?"

Leeke thrust out his chin pugnaciously and flourished a news-paper under the other's nose. "Do you think we're all fools? Or can't read the papers?"

"What I do think is that you're making an unnecessary and ex-ceedingly vulgar scene—and a fool of yourself at the same time. You realise of course that I'm here as Mr. Grant's representative?"

"I don't give a damn whose representative you are. Nor how you managed to push yourself into the Hall—"

Travers was furious. "You recognise that I shall have to take ac-tion on this—"

"Action be damned. You're too late! My resignation goes in to Sir Henry as soon as the accounts are in and that's to-morrow—and it'll take a cleverer fellow than you to find a flaw in 'em."

Before Travers could splutter a reply, he was off towards the door, looking as if with a stick in his hand, he'd have slashed at everything in reach. Travers watched the door smashed to, glared, then bit at the end of his pipe. What the devil was the matter with the fellow? Absolutely inexplicable the whole thing—and it hadn't taken a couple of minutes! Then his own grievance rose up at him—all that brawling for no conceivable cause—and that damnable re-mark about detective work. And what on earth was in that paper he'd been waving about like a madman?

What Travers couldn't see at the moment was the funny side of the matter—himself like an infuriated secretary-bird and Leeke like a game-cock. As for himself, by the time he'd got back to the library, he'd never been so angry in his life. Damn the fellow—and his impertinence! Perfectly disgraceful and so uncalled for! Then gradually he cooled down. The anger smouldered, He began to feel himself a very ill-used person. And finally he got sufficiently near normal to think it all out.

In a way he *had* been wrong to speak to Hatton at all. But Leeke was badly on edge about those accounts. Somehow or other he must have got himself into the very devil of a muddle. That paper too. Where had he got hold of it? Parry would have to go into Bran-ford and buy a copy of every newspaper he could find there. And if Leeke's implication were correct, what was any mention of detec-tive work doing in the press? He couldn't for the life of him think of anything even remotely connected with himself which the papers would trouble to print.

Then of course before he'd spent another ten minutes on those infernal accounts he started thinking of everything all over again. Perfectly preposterous the whole affair! Ridiculous situation for a man to be trapped into and so on, till in the middle of it all a footman brought in a note. Travers must have scowled at him without knowing it, then he slit it open.

Dear Travers,

I'm sorry about just now. I'm afraid I lost my temper and perhaps you will accept this explanation and apology.

As I told you, I shall be handing in my resignation to Sir Henry to-morrow. I don't think I'm doing much good in Fenwold.

Yours sincerely,

P. R. LEEKE.

Travers hadn't recovered sufficiently to be any too generous. He read the note again, snorted, and laid it aside. The fellow was now becoming pathetic. And what the devil had Sir Henry got to do with it? Merely adding insult to injury! And of course Franklin needn't be told about that exceedingly absurd affair except in the merest outline. Nothing whatever to do with the case, but purely a personal matter between himself and Leeke.

* * * * *

Strange to say, at almost that identical moment, Franklin was also thinking of doing a small amount of editing. Parry had returned from Oak Cottage full of news. In his own words his story was this.

"I took the note, sir, from Mr. Travers and Mr. Castleton was in. He told me to wait for an answer and in about ten minutes he gave me this—and a bob for myself.

"Then he started talking about the village, sir, what a pretty place it was and which way had I come. Of course I wasn't saying a word, sir, about that key of the private door you'd let me have, so I told him round by the village. Then he put it on a bit too thick. 'It's a nice walk to the Hall round the back way,' he says and starts telling me all about it, so as soon as I got a little way along the road I nipped over into the park and went back among the bushes as far as a few yards off the private door and waited to see what happened.

"About ten minutes after that I saw Miss Forteresse coming across the park towards the gate and she stopped behind a big thorn bush and then Mr. Castleton, he comes along—I didn't see how he got over the wall—and they stood there talking. I got as near as I could, sir, but I couldn't hear very much so I crawled to the side where I could see what they were doing. He seemed to be making up to her and she wasn't going to have anything to do with it. Then he got sort of sulky and they started to walk towards where I was and just as I was getting ready to bolt she caught hold of his arm and I heard her say, 'Was it all right? Did he really die of an accident?'

"'Of course he did,' says he. 'What do you want to know for?'

"'Oh, I don't know,' she says, 'only everything seems peculiar. Why's that man Travers really at the Hall?'

"'You told me he was acting for Sir Henry,' he says, and, 'If you're not satisfied, why don't you find out?'

"'Hm!' she says. 'Don't worry about that. I can twist him round my little finger.'

"'You would,' he says, sort of sneering. Then he got hold of *her* arm. 'Look here, Leila,' he says. 'I'm not going to stand it any longer. You said it'd be all right if we got your uncle's consent. Let's get away out of this! Let's go now! Oh, very well then—after the show.'

"Then he got hold of her round the waist and she started pushing him away. Then she stopped that and the last I saw of them, she had her arms round his neck like one of those film scenes, so I slipped away into the bushes and over the wall and went right round by the Lodge with this letter, and all the time, sir, I kept repeating what I'd heard in case I'd forget it."

"I hope it's all right, sir?" said Parry anxiously.

"It's right enough, Parry. Lucky, of course, but you made a good job of it. Slip off now to Westlake, will you, and try to do that alibi before lunch. Try the garage first."

As Franklin analysed the statement, however, there seemed far less in it than had appeared at first hearing. The comparative intimacy between Leila Forteresse and Castleton certainly gave a definite motive for the murder. Those vague questionings however as to the exact position of Travers at the Hall, proved nothing;—unless of course Haddowe had prompted them and had had therefore his own suspicions as to the manner of Cosmo Revere's death. Franklin was pleased with that last bit; it explained so easily the vicar's enthusiasm for the rapid cleaning up of the site.

One thing was certain—Travers needn't be told the lady's opinion of his powers of resistance! Then he remembered the letter from Castleton and hurried off to the library. Travers' face was unusually solemn.

"Hallo!" he said. "What've you been doing?"

"Oh, I don't know," smiled Franklin. "Usual impersonation. Walking to and fro in the earth. Seeking information and finding none."

"You're very scriptural."

"What can you expect—after Haddowe on Sunday. And you're looking none too pleased. Anything up?"

"I just had to speak rather sharply to Leeke," explained the other. "I'm afraid he's got into a mess with his accounts. And he was very impertinent."

"Not surprised at that."

"Well I was," said Travers bluntly. "Something very curious came out, too, in the course of the argument," and he related the episode of the paper and Leeke's allusion. "Do you think we'd better send Parry off to Branford to get hold of as many of to-day's papers as possible, to see just what's there?"

Franklin was completely puzzled. "Why on earth have they got anything about you in the paper?"

Travers shrugged his shoulders. "Lord knows—unless somebody's left me a fortune. There was nothing in the *Telegraph"*

"Nor in the *Mail.* And the allusion was about detective work."

Travers smiled—the first time for an hour. "Perhaps it was *Punch!*"

Franklin laughed, then, "You're not very anxious about Castleton's chit. What about seeing what's in it?"

"Why not," said Travers and opened it.

Dear Mr. Travers,

I shall be very pleased to see you this afternoon and shall most certainly be in from 3.0 onwards. The chance of entertaining a literary lion of any magnitude is too good a one to be missed. 'That sound's ambiguous but it isn't meant to be so, and I should be delighted to see you in any case. And of course you'll stay to tea.

Yours sincerely,

G. E. R. CASTLETON.

Travers forbore to blush, though that first Fenwold recognition was far from unpleasing. Economics too weren't every man's meat. Then Franklin's voice came in.

"Another one apparently who's seen the papers!"

"How do you mean?"

"Well, I know your writing for one thing. All he'd know was that it came from a certain Mr. Travers at the Hall—Parry would tell him that much. I'm damn sure he'd never have been able to read it himself. Not only that. The world must be full of Traverses and as he couldn't possibly have deciphered that scrawled 'Ludovic 'of yours—well, he must have got his information elsewhere."

Travers frowned, then laughed. "You must have thought me a very conceited person!"

"You literary people want taking down a peg," retorted the other, then told him what had happened with Parry.

"Just what I assured you!" said Travers triumphantly. "Leila Forteresse and the Hall group know nothing about the murder!"

"Don't be too sure. If Haddowe knew anything he wouldn't be such a fool as to tell it to that feather-headed baggage. And if he didn't, he'd say still less. Her name's Leila—not Delilah."

Travers coloured slightly, then shook his head and looked thoughtful. "I don't know so much. She's an extremely clever woman." There seemed to be the faintest suggestion of a grunt, then he changed the subject.

"What are you going to do about it?"

"Nothing at all. Just go on as we've made up our minds to. No use abandoning anything till it's exhausted."

"Yes, but you're sure—"

"To tell you the truth, I'm not sure of anything. You'd say, for instance, that this morning proves that Castleton and the Forteresse woman communicate and it was Castleton who must have been up that tree. I'm not so sure it wasn't Carter after all."

"Why?"

"What about that cryptic remark of his in the pub, about there being something in his cottage which people might like to lay their hands on?"

"You've got a hunch!"

"Not in the least. The only thing I *have* been thinking is this. Carter's our main plank. But the chap you're going to visit this afternoon is also decidedly suspicious, in spite of his alibi. We shall know more about that by the time you get back. In any case, why shouldn't he and Carter have been confederates? We heard an awful lot about their squabbles from Westfield—that reminds me I must see him after lunch. When people make a song about a thing they're like the lady who protested too much. Why shouldn't all those squabbles of Carter and Castleton have been a fake?"

"Too much for me," confessed Travers. "Next thing you'll do is to say you're not sure I didn't do the damn thing myself!"

CHAPTER XIX
TRAVERS GOES VISITING

THE BIG SALOON deposited Travers by Carter's cottage where Parry was instructed to keep an eye open for the appearance of its owner. There was nothing conspicuous about that. The road to Oak Cottage was far too fretted with gullies from the winter's rains.

Travers had dressed himself with particular care. His soft hat was of the palest grey and his suit slightly darker, with the connecting link of a jet-black tie; the whole effect being to his mind that a literary man who could afford to unbend a bit but had no desire to caper.

Castleton was reading in a deck chair on his front lawn and seemed obviously flattered and immensely pleased. From his record Travers was expecting to find a mixture of puppy and crank. Castleton was neither. His manner was perfect—a nice blend of gratification and natural courtesy. He was about five foot ten, on the thin side, but wiry looking, and his face, Travers thought, was one of the most attractive he had ever seen. His voice, his intonation and his mannerisms unconsciously told his breeding. Altogether he seemed rather shy; quite jolly company and thoroughly English. His age would be about thirty.

"It's very nice of you to let me come and see you," said Travers.

"It was good of you to come. Shall we go inside?" and he showed the way into the small entrance hall, furnished with a couple of country Chippendale chairs, a Stuart hutch and a fine Sheraton barometer. A bunch of marigolds in a copper jug made a delightful contrast with the grey of the walls.

"Shall we go into my room?" asked Castleton. "Or would you rather sit outside?"

"Oh, indoors I think," said Travers and ducked his head to avoid the low rafter that formed the top of the drawing-room door. "You've a lovely place here, Mr. Castleton I"

"I'm glad you like it. I'm afraid I haven't enough money to keep it up properly. But I *am* trying to do something to the rock garden."

"I wasn't thinking of the outside so much," said Travers. "The situation of course is splendid, on the top of this rise of ground. I really meant these lovely old rooms and the perfect things I'm sure you have in them."

"Even that might be better," remarked Castleton modestly. "You see, the house dates from 1760, so I try to keep everything in it round about that date. It's rather difficult at times—and not always possible, as you see."

"That was one of the reasons for my asking to see you," explained Travers, taking a cigarette from the box the other passed across. "I'm a collector of sorts and you know what people we are. As soon as we hear about anybody else's collection we make any shameless excuse to see it. Have you any special line, by the way?"

"Only in pictures. I like the best of the Norwich School, only naturally they're beyond my pocket. That Cotman water-colour I got from a local dealer who didn't know what it was."

"A lucky find!"

"Wasn't it? You collect Ralph Wood figures don't you?"

"Who on earth told you that?"

"You did," smiled the other. "It's in your book."

Travers thought for a moment, then laughed heartily. "An excellent example of the mystification of common-sense! I suppose you haven't picked up any figures in your travels?"

"I think perhaps I have one," and he went to the corner Chippendale cupboard and selected a figure from the centre shelf. It was a beautifully modelled group; a shepherd with a lamb slung round his neck and a dog at his side.

"What's your opinion of it?" he asked with all the anxiety of the partial expert.

"Of course, it's of less value being unsigned," said Travers, running his long, sensitive fingers over it. "I should say it's perfectly right. At any rate I'm prepared to back my opinion to the tune of twenty pounds."

Its owner was delighted. He took it over to the window and examined it again himself.

"I'd almost like to take your offer. Would you mind if I kept it for a day or two? It's rather an experience to live with a piece one has risked good money on—and found to be worth it."

"Do, please," said Travers. "Of course I'd never dream of depriving you of it unless you let me have it as a favour. If I find it's worth more than twenty pounds we can always adjust that later. You've nothing else in my line?"

Castleton showed him round the cottage, bedrooms and all. There were heaps of things that Travers envied him; that miniature Queen Anne bureau, for instance, that early dresser and a most exquisite Bow figure. By the time they had gone the round it was four o'clock; indeed it was the chiming of the lacquer grandfather in the dining-room that recalled to Travers his waiting chauffeur.

"You're sure you won't have some tea?" asked Castleton.

"I'd love to, but I've got an appointment in Branford. I'd much rather stay and have another look over those delightful things of yours. And now will you do me a favour? It's a most unusual one."

"Only too pleased."

"It's this. I understand you know more than anybody about a man named Carter. Now my man, Francis—he's more of a confidential servant really—has an idea this man's his uncle. He's always understood he'd an uncle of that exact name in these parts, but when he called Carter was out. I wonder if you could help him in any way?"

"That's frightfully curious," said Castleton. "I'll tell you what I know about him. I ran across him in a London antique shop one day, and he told me when I chipped him about his accent he'd like to get back to the county again, provided he could supplement his savings with some kind of employment, especially in his own line. At that time the cottage where he lives was vacant so I offered it to him. The idea was that he should set up as a dealer and offer me first choice of anything he picked up. So he did—at first. Then I found out he was double-crossing me in a way dealers have. He'd see something in a house and the people wouldn't sell. 'Don't blame you,' he'd say. 'And if you *do* let it go, don't take less than so-and-so,' naming twice its value. You see, often people used to come to me with things, knowing me and my father and that I collected them, but when they brought these things to me that Carter had told them about and I had to refuse, it looked rather queer—sort of gave me a bad name."

"He was playing the dog in the manger."

"Exactly. Not only that, he started abusing me, I've been told, in the local pubs. About a week ago he said something particularly poisonous and I haven't had the chance to get hold of him since. When I do, he'll have to listen to a few home truths. Also he owes me for a half year's rent."

"Why don't you kick him out?"

"Just what he'd like. He'd get me committed to the expense and then he'd pay up and put his fingers to his nose. Also, between ourselves, I'm not very well acquainted with these Rent Acts."

"Neither am I," laughed Travers. "You think he's keeping out of your way."

"I'm sure of it. Also—I wouldn't like to say this to anybody—I have an idea he's going mad!"

Travers whistled.

"Yes, really. I have an idea he's been perching up those trees there at the bottom of the garden. What he wants there, heaven knows. However, send your man along by all means, if Carter doesn't turn up, and I'll tell him everything I can. What about going down to see if he's there now? I'd rather like a witness. Oh, I forgot. I hardly expect he'll be in. There's a two-day sale on at Capston, near Norwich. He's almost bound to be there."

"Does it really pay those little fellows—a big sale like that?"

"Oh, rather. That's the very place to pick up the comparative rubbish the big men won't handle. Shall we go and have a look?"

"Splendid! You sure it isn't troubling you?"

"Not in the least. But there's one thing I wish you *would* do," and he produced Travers' best known volume. "Would you mind signing this?"

Travers flicked the pages over and smiled "Your father's copy I see."

"Yes. He was awfully fond of it."

"You've got a bad investment here from a collector's point of view," said Travers as he wrote his name and the date. "Still, I'm not so cocksure as to deny that you've given me extraordinary pleasure." He moved out to the hall and picked up his hat and gloves. "I'll have another look at that figure some time. My eyes are rather bad and play me tricks at times."

"The war?"

"Well—er—yes. A gas-attack to be prosaically exact."

"Do you know," said Castleton as they moved down the hill, "that's the one great envy of my life, missing all that. I don't think any of us of this later generation can ever call ourselves full men. Nobody's life could ever be called complete without that terrific experience."

Travers shook his head. "I don't know. I see your point, but—well, isn't it a romantic one? Here we are then. You go first."

The first glimpse of the back door settled it, with its tacked-on notice—a piece of cardboard clumsily scrawled.

Back Thursday.

G. CARTER.

Castleton scowled in annoyance.

"Nobody's fault," said Travers. "He'll probably come home to roost on Thursday night." Then suddenly changing the subject. "When will you have dinner with me?"

Castleton flushed with pleasure. "Well—er—that's very good of you."

"The pleasure'll be mine. The Hall's a pretty lonely place nowadays. Of course there's Miss Forteresse. I expect you two know each other very well."

"Well—er—we act a lot together. The local dramatic show, you know."

Travers nodded. "Now what about Friday? How'd that suit you?"

"Splendidly, thanks. About seven?" and the last Travers saw of him was a wave of the hand from Carter's corner as the car turned into the bend of the Branford road. Half a mile on, he tapped on the window and changed his seat to alongside Parry.

"Sorry to have kept you waiting about like that, Parry. And what's your opinion of Mr. Castleton from what you saw of him this morning?"

"Him, sir? I think he's a slippery one, sir."

"Well, you may be right. Do you know the best bookseller's shop in Branford? Then pull up at it, will you?"

The rest of the journey Travers was thoughtful. In spite of the reasonable impression that Castleton had made on his mind, he was far too wily a bird to trust wholly to appearances. The Castleton of the afternoon was not the man of Royce's description. Something was wrong somewhere. Had Cosmo Revere taken umbrage at some trivial remark? And was Royce seeing with the jaundiced eye of a blindly loyal servant? Yet there was that little question of the book! After that, too, the local paper might clear the air.

There were two booksellers' shops in the small town and the first gave him what he wanted.

"Do you happen to have a copy of *The Economics of a Spendthrift*"? he asked the girl at the counter.

"Who's it by?"

"Man called Travers."

The girl had a consultation with what looked like the proprietor, who came forward himself. "We haven't it at the moment, sir, but we can get it for you."

"I'm afraid that'll be too late for me. I was hoping you had a copy in stock."

"Well, sir, that's funny, because we did have one, but we sold it as soon as we opened this morning. We'd had it in a long while too."

"Perhaps the chap I wanted it for is the one who bought it. What sort of a fellow was he?"

"Gentleman from Fenwold. A Mr. Castleton. Do you know him?"

"Castleton? No. That wasn't the man I was buying it for."

"The offices of the *Branford Herald,* Parry," said Travers when he came out, feeling remarkably pleased with himself. Castleton's copy had certainly been stretched a bit and dirtied generally, but there was no disguising the newness. As for the signature, it had been far more recent than those in Haddowe's books with the elder Castleton's name.

The editor of the local paper was in and proved to be only too anxious for the visitor to consult the files. They were perfectly indexed, and Travers had no trouble in finding what he wanted—the speech made by Castleton at the Labour Demonstration and the letter written by him on the subject of the survival of feudalism.

The former surprised him by its importance. A former Cabinet Minister was the show speaker, but it was noteworthy that at the final rally in the Town Hall, with its audience of two thousand, Castleton should not only have been considered of sufficient importance to move a resolution, but should have made a thundering good job of it into the bargain. As for the letter Travers rather enjoyed it. Of course it had a certain amount of parade and some declamation of the obvious, but its caustic irony was undeniable.

But putting aside any perfectly formal political gestures or presentation of personal grievances, however refreshingly set down, there was much in those two outpourings of Castleton for Travers to ponder over. Take the extracts he made—

"There is no more mischievous delusion than that which blindly accepts Time as the cure for everything. The War, as a war, belongs to the past, but to a past discredited and even shameful. (Hear, hear.) To invest that war or its individual episodes with romance is simply the glorification of butchery and the canonisation of the bestial. (Loud cheers.)

"Shall I tell you why a wealthy man—shall we call him Lucullus?—views with a perfectly even mind a tax on the food of the people—on the bread which is the essential of their existence? The reason is this. Bread for him is a symbol or a table decoration. For us it is three quarters of a meal. We carve it, bite it, masticate it, and to be blunt, fill our bellies with it. (Laughter.) But what does Lucullus do? The third footman—or is it the fourth?—puts a little roll of it by his fingers. To be eaten? Heavens, no! Lucullus feels for it, breaks it idly with his fingers and as far as he's concerned, that's the end of it. (Laughter and applause.)

"In this twentieth century it is incredible that the State should admit of any landlord but itself. No man is so conscientious, so impartial, so impervious to the tongues of slander and scandal, so filled with the fervour of serving others, as to be trusted with the absolute control of either the food of another or the roof that covers his head."

There was heaps more in the same vein. Hardly in keeping, thought Travers, with the man who grumbled about Carter not paying his rent, who accepted eagerly an invitation to the Hall—and for dinner at that—and who spoke with quiet sorrow of the war as the one thing that had made those who took part in it men in the completest sense! Which then was the real Castleton and which had been playing a part? If the Castleton of the afternoon had been the actor, why had he thought it necessary to act? And why that perfectly abominable lie about the book?

Travers shook his head. Franklin should have a very detailed account of the afternoon's happenings and impressions and thereafter must find the answers for himself. And whether those answers would have anything to do with the killing of Cosmo Revere was a matter more problematic still.

As for the newspapers, Parry bought copies of everything available in the day's issue and never a one had in it any mention of himself. Too big an order, thought Travers, to get hold of every paper since the date of his arrival at Fenwold. Perhaps if he ran across

Leeke again he'd bottle up his pride and ask him point-blank what it was and where he'd got it.

CHAPTER XX
FRANKLIN FINDS A THEORY

IN SPITE OF Franklin's prophecy that it would once more be a case of labour lost, Travers' first enquiry on his return to the Hall was about Angéle's constitutional. She had had it—from half-past five to a quarter to six. All that remained apparently was to reverse the process and announce in the footman's hearing that the next morning he would be out. But he couldn't very well do that since he would *not* be out; Haddowe, he suddenly remembered, was due for lunch. Still, there would be plenty of time to test Brown further.

Franklin listened with extraordinary interest to the long account of Castleton—and Travers' deductions.

"I know what I'd do if I had my way," he said. "I'd see that woman who cleans up his house and pump her for all I was worth. But there you are. That's the devil of it! You daren't ask a question. Damn that lawyer and his secrecy! When's he coming down did you say?"

"Sir Henry?" asked Travers suavely. "Just after lunch to-morrow. He may be able to get away again on Thursday afternoon. Depends on the work he proposes doing."

"Precious little I shall see of you then. And hadn't you better send a letter to Castleton saying I shall be round to-morrow at four? And when's he coming to dinner?"

"Friday at seven."

"Hm! And you really do think he's a highly suspicious character?"

"Well, I wouldn't go so far as that—not at the moment. I know he's a *poseur*. Attribute it to my overwhelming personality if you like, but he certainly rubbed down his socialistic edges for the purpose of making an impression on me. I'd even go so far as to say his socialism is all pose, otherwise he wouldn't have been ashamed of his principles in front of a purely private individual who, for all he knew, might have been of the same persuasion. As to the book— well, there he was simply a liar. He sprinted off to Branford, bought a lucky copy, swatted it up, bent it about a bit and dirtied it, faked his father's name—then started to pose."

"Yes, but he bought your book *before* he got your letter asking if you might call."

"Good lord! So he did! But you and I were the only ones who knew I intended to call!"

"He must have anticipated damn shrewdly," said Franklin. "And did *he* see anything in the papers?"

"But there wasn't anything in the papers!"

"There might have been—yesterday or the day before." All the same, Franklin looked worried. "The great thing is he *did* anticipate meeting you at some time or other and therefore he's got something to be anxious about."

"Just what I told you," repeated Travers. "The whole place is undermined. It's like an ant-heap only you can't see the ants. Leeke's all upset; Haddowe's scheming his eyes out; Angéle's a fake; the Forteresse is all nerves—and suspicion; Castleton's lying like hell, and Carter's—well, Carter's said to be mad. He's certainly behaving in an extraordinary manner."

Franklin nodded, then suddenly thought of something. "I knew there was something on my mind. Westfield's missing. Can't find him anywhere."

Travers dropped his philosophic pose and looked up quickly.

"I told you I was going to see him after lunch, so I went along to the office and they referred me to a chap called Morris who's acting as head keeper. I found him all right but he hadn't seen anything of Westfield, but he thought he'd be down on his beat where some young birds had to be fed. When he got there this chap, Morris—don't know how he knew—said the birds *hadn't* been fed, so we went along to Westfield's cottage, and when we got there his dog was barking like mad and the door was locked. Then off we went to see the woman who usually clears up the place in the morning, and she said she'd been along and couldn't get in. Usually, I should have said, Westfield let her in himself. Of course, after that all there was to do was to get Morris to slide a knife along the catch and open the window on the plea that Westfield had had a fit or something. Morris got inside all right but Westfield wasn't there. And his bed hadn't been slept in."

"You been down since?"

"I did the next best thing—told Morris I'd meet him at the 'Angel' round about nine. He took Westfield's dog home, by the way."

"You think something serious has happened?"

"Don't you? His dog was ravenously hungry and thirsty as hell. A man doesn't go away all that time without attending to his dog." He had a sudden idea. "I think I'll get Royce to give me some sandwiches and push off early and have a good look over his beat."

There was a tap at the door and a footman entered with the evening's letters.

"One registered package, sir, which Mr. Royce signed for personally."

Travers opened it, smiled and passed it over.

"The report at last. They seem to have made a good job of it."

Durango House had certainly taken considerable trouble, spurred on no doubt by Sir Francis' personal interest. There were newspaper cuttings, sub-office reports, agents' reports and, best of all, two brief synopses prepared from the bulky volume of oddments.

"LEILA FORTERESSE.—Father kept a music and dancing academy in the Rue Maillot and at night played in the orchestra of the Hôtel de Londres in the Avenue de l'Opéra. Daughter attended the English High School kept by the Misses Roberts in the Rue Guichart. In 1922 she first did a dancing turn in the select Cabaret Corlette in the Rue Daumont off the Avenue des Princes, with a partner, André Bourgues. Considerable success, then a contract with the Gaston Bros., who control a chain of super-cinemas in the principal French cities, including Cherbourg. Three years ago she suddenly abandoned this highly remunerative career. The Gastons brought an action for breach of contract (Enclosure F.) and recovered total damages of 27,500 fr. No trace after that until the death of Mrs. Forteresse, when she reappeared in the Rue Maillot.

"General information is that her name was connected at various times prior to her retirement, with Maurice Gaston, her partner André Bourgues, Pierre Ernestin the millionaire car manufacturer, and Georges Grosange the author. She had the reputation of being an expensive hobby and her style of living was certainly beyond her actual income. She gave as her reason for retirement that she was entering a sisterhood. (Enclosure R.)."

"Hm!" grunted Franklin. "Cherbourg, eh? And what about Haddowe?"

"AUGUSTINE HADDOWE.—At St. Giles, Oxford, had the reputation of a brilliant classical scholar but inclined to kick over the traces. There was much comment when he took orders.

"He left St. Jerome's, Stepney, ostensibly because of the death of his father in Winnipeg. At Stepney he shared rooms with a Canadian named Garner, who left England at the same time. Report from Winnipeg states no death of the name of Haddowe occurred at the time, but may have been step-father. Haddowe not traceable in Winnipeg or district.

"Licensed by the Bishop of Alberta, but was concerned at Ford's Crossing on the border with a curious fur-smuggling affray, in which Garner was killed and Haddowe himself wounded in the shoulder. He left the district immediately.

"Next heard of in Nova Scotia where he applied for a license from the Bishop but accepted no cure. He assisted occasionally however at Monterre, from which place he was often absent, but where is not known.

"In the war, served with the 3rd Canadian Division; was popular with all ranks and was awarded the M.C. for conspicuous gallantry.

"After the war was a well-known figure in Cherbourg where he was known as a man's parson of the robust type. The Seamen's Annexe to the Rest House was an immense place and, in the opinion of those qualified to judge, was of enormous service to the men. Again there were absences which cannot be traced or accounted for. (Special refs. T—W.)."

"Probably be more to come," said Travers. "You'd better take over the lot, don't you think. Won't do to trust anything to my room. And when'll you be in?"

Franklin stowed them away in his breast pocket. "Sorry, old chap, but I really can't say. Might have to hang about a lot. By the way, why doesn't the lady dine down here occasionally now?"

"Angéle supposed to be very ill—comes on at night usually! The other keeps her company."

* * * * *

As Franklin approached that spot in Lammas Wood it was with feelings vastly different from those of a week before. Then there had been mild interest tinged with respect, and a certain impatience at an accident which looked like spoiling the last days of a holiday.

Now there was a vague apprehension, a sense of the unreal and a recalling with almost painful vividness of the first sight of the dead man. For one thing, he now knew more or less intimately, if not the actors in the drama, at least those whose fortunes were most affected by it. He knew the village, and most of all he knew the Hall—that centre from which the small community radiated—and could feel something of its brooding and inherited magnificence. But above all, he felt at the moment, more than ever he had done, the presence of the sinister; of something working patiently, relentlessly, mole-like; something which could be sensed everywhere but which eluded all definite contact.

The body of the keeper was *not* lying where his master had been found. The idea had been far-fetched; perhaps even a symbolic one, since Cosmo Revere had also gone out at night and had been found in the woods which Westfield alone had frequented. But, as Franklin could see, the earth of the bare circle had not been disturbed. Nature alone had taken the first steps to change its surface, with curled tips of bracken protruding timidly or the fragile growths of young nettles.

As he walked back to the village he asked himself many questions. If Westfield's absence was a legitimate one, why had he left no word? If he had been made away with, how had it been done? Had he let out an inadvertent word or made a veiled suggestion? Had he questioned Carter too closely and given him—and therefore Castleton—cause for action? And surely those visits to the cottage had been secret enough and unobserved? True there had been that half-seen movement in the hedge and that rustling sound—but that again was far from certain. But if those visits *had* been watched, then every movement of his own might have been watched also. Somebody knew who John Francis really was. Somebody at that very moment might be watching from behind that very hedge! Melodramatic perhaps—but the fact remained that one murder had been committed and a second seemed more than likely.

And then of course he realised something else. If Westfield had been removed, then somebody was fighting for his life like a rat in a corner, and that somebody was the murderer of Cosmo Revere. Instead of one obscure trail to follow there would be a choice of two. Work from Westfield and you arrived at Lammas Wood; start paradoxically from the previous night and you came to last Wednesday morning. The situation was clearer—or might have been were things different. Once more Franklin longed for the authority of the law, for the hue and cry to be sounded and the body of Westfield recovered. If only—Then he smiled. Ifs and ands and pots and pans and all the rest of the jingle!

When Morris entered the private room at the "Stag" he was accompanied by Turner. Neither had any news. All the constable had decided was that if Westfield hadn't turned up by the morning he was going straight off to Branford to report the matter to his superintendent.

Franklin walked back with the constable as far as the private door to the park.

"Wasn't there a burglary there the other night?" he asked as they passed Carter's cottage.

"Someone playin' a joke, sir. Carter weren't in when I got there, but the door what they reckoned was open weren't open at all. Somebody must a'told Carter I'd been round 'cause he come along to see me about it later in the mornin'. He didn't half kick up a row!"

"What sort of a chap is he, this man Carter?"

"Oh, he ain't so bad, sir, take him all round."

"Used to work with Mr. Castleton at Oak Cottage there, didn't he?"

"When he first come here, sir, he did. They're been havin' a few words lately so I'm told."

"And how do you find Mr. Castleton?"

"Him? Oh, he's all right, sir. Bit queer livin' all alone like that. Still, he do some rum things sometimes?"

"Such as what?"

"Well, takin' up with that Carter. He ain't the sort o' man for a gentleman like Mr. Castleton to 'sociate with. Hallo! There's my wife wavin' to me, sir. 'Spect she want somethin'. Women allust do. Yes, sir. I'll let you know in the mornin' if he turn up."

*   *   *   *   *

Franklin worked till late that night putting his suspects through the sieve of available evidence. First of all, Leeke and Warren were definitely out of it, except in the incredible circumstance that they, with Leila Forteresse had conspired to manufacture the alibi. That left Haddowe, Castleton and Carter.

And what of Castleton's supposed alibi? The murder was done between the times 9.15 and 10.15. At 9.45, however, Castleton had been seen by the farmer and at just after ten he had called at the Westlake garage where the proprietor was doing a job of work, and had asked for a couple of gallons. Further, "just after ten" the farmer's wife had recognised the toot-toot of his horn, though that of course was poor evidence.

Was Castleton's alibi good? Could Cosmo Revere have been killed and his body disposed of as it had been, before 9.45? Franklin thought not. Everything depended on where he had gone after leaving the Hall. And where he *had* gone was on the face of it pretty obvious—to see Carter at his cottage. But he couldn't have done that. As soon as he passed through the private door he must have been recognised by somebody on the village green. And he wouldn't have entered Carter's garden by way of Oak Cottage since that was the last place on earth he'd desire to be seen in. Then how could he have got to Carter's cottage in the semi-dusk? All round the boundary was a split oak fence!

Let's be logical or perish, thought Franklin at that stage of the argument. He didn't go to Carter's cottage and therefore he was killed somewhere else—in the wood for example. But he wasn't killed there. On that part of the estate there was no yellow sand. And yet, if Castleton killed him, it must have been there or else the murder couldn't have been completed and the accident staged by, say, 9.30. Also there was no reason for Cosmo Revere to have met *Castleton* at all! Carter was the person he ought to have met, after that mysterious visit of the earlier evening.

Franklin tried a new method of approach. What about motives? Leeke had the best, but he was out of it. Take the Forteresse motive—that the death of the uncle would remove any obstacle to a marriage with the niece. There Castleton stood alone. Carter was absolutely unaffected and there seemed every reason why Cosmo Revere should have welcomed a marriage between his niece and the sobering Haddowe—unless of course he had found something out about Haddowe. Still, leaving that for a moment, as Travers had said, there seemed to be little to be gained by Haddowe if he killed his patron.

What of the affair at the dolmen? There again Castleton fitted in. He knew the locality. He could have scaled the side stones and mounted to the top, and that Carter most decidedly couldn't have done. And he was of the sort of indeterminate build which Cosmo Revere couldn't have recognised at a glance, as he would have done with Haddowe or Carter. Moreover, Carter couldn't have sprinted from the dolmen to the fence.

And the felling of the tree? Castleton again—with just the right amount of knowledge to make a fool of himself. And he knew that district like the back of his hand.

After that of course it was reasonably plain sailing. Castleton at the moment was acting suspiciously, but he simply *couldn't* have known the whereabouts of Cosmo Revere on that particular night. *Then it must have been he who employed Carter to do the luring!* Castleton was the master spirit and the other the dupe. Carter was in hiding of some sort because he knew his own life wasn't worth tuppence! He'd thought perhaps he was doing something suspicious in luring Cosmo Revere to the particular spot, but he hadn't counted on murder. It was Carter whom Westfield had seen in the wood the following morning! Carter who'd gone to see what had really happened, and Carter who'd bolted from the village as if the devil were after him! Once Castleton could get rid of *him,* he would be absolutely safe himself. And Carter had come back the one day and night to see just what was happening. That yarn of Castleton's about Carter's rent was moonshine. Rents were due at the end of a quarter, or at Michaelmas, and Castleton would never have waited for weeks like that without taking action.

Franklin leaned back in his chair and stoked up a final pipe with a glow of satisfaction. Carter was the key. Carter was desperately afraid. It was Carter who'd been in the tree taking good care Castleton shouldn't get at him. Carter was the man and Carter would have to be got hold of at the earliest moment, whatever the risks.

As for Leila Forteresse, Angéle and Haddowe, it was Travers' job of work to see what they were up to. In his own words, it was up to him to find out just what sort of squib was being attached to the old gentleman's tail.

CHAPTER XXI
HADDOWE COMES TO LUNCH

"You're looking remarkably cheerful," said Travers as Franklin came in with the morning cup of tea.

"Why not? It's a glorious morning; I've got a kind master, and I'm going out visiting this afternoon. What more do you want?"

Travers smiled. "Well, I want you to do a job of work for me for one thing. Have a good look over the vicarage."

Franklin raised his eyebrows. "Why not the Bank of England while you're about it?"

"Because it's much easier," said Travers, perfectly seriously. "I'll ask Haddowe to dinner and we'll try to lure those two men of his away."

"And how're you going to do that?"

"Use Brown the footman. Still, we can think that out later. And what's the programme for to-day?"

"The programme's half over. I've seen Turner and Westfield hasn't rolled up. We're just going to give the morning post a chance, then Turner's going to Branford."

More than once during breakfast Travers wondered just how Franklin was getting on with the case. Nobody could call him a talkative colleague. There had been that affair of the two mirrors; then those pieces of charred papier maché, and neither mentioned since. But whatever Franklin was thinking, there must be a remarkably good reason for his keeping it to himself. And with regard to his own problem of the squib and the coat-tail, there was something he had thought of the previous night.

"Royce," he said, after breakfast, "could you possibly send me in by Francis a small piece of linen with a few drops of methylated spirits on it? Only don't let him see you put it on or know what it is."

"I wonder if you got that smell right," said Travers when his man came in. "You know, the one you noticed about that man of Haddowe's. Have a sniff at this. What do you think it is?"

"Turpentine!" said Franklin promptly. "Not very strong, but it's there."

"That's all right then," said Travers and went clean off at a tangent. "Anything particular happen last night?"

"Nothing—except that Westfield wasn't found."

"You mustn't mind my worrying you like this. The fact is I'm so damnably impatient. I keep on wanting things to happen."

"They'll happen all right!" smiled Franklin. "You're like a boy at a firework show—don't want to wait between the rockets. And how's your own squib going?"

"Going—but not going off," laughed Travers. "Honestly, what Haddowe's up to in Fenwold I can't fathom. I keep having faint ideas but that's as far as I get. I do know he didn't kill Revere, and that's all I do know. You going to see Turner now?"

"Going! My dear chap, it's half an hour since I saw you. In five minutes I'm going in to Branford by your orders to see Turner's superintendent. The post's in and no word from Westfield. Now listen to this carefully. What time do you expect Haddowe?"

"Round about 12.30."

"Well, I'll arrange things so that the superintendent or detective-sergeant comes here to see you during lunch. Ask him in while Haddowe's here and watch his face. It's a pretty forlorn hope I admit. Then make an excuse and call me in too."

*   *   *   *   *

In accordance with his overnight confidential arrangements with Royce, Travers slipped out by the side door and took his work to the summer house in the wild garden, where he spent a couple of laborious hours. Then just after noon he went back to the library. Angéle, so Royce informed him, had had her constitutional. Travers rubbed his hands together. Brown was getting quite a reliable person! Then a footman informed him that Haddowe had arrived and he hurried out to the entrance hall.

"Good morning, padre," said Travers, his face beaming. "You're quite a stranger."

"Work, my boy, work!" and Travers almost felt his bones crunch with the handshake.

"Well, someone's got to do it. Let's have a walk round. You're not too tired?"

"Tired! I could walk you young fellows off your legs," and he took Travers' arm with such a boyish gesture that even the footman had to smile.

"A wonderful morning," said Travers. "Look at that clump of delphiniums. Did you ever see such a blue?"

"There's a finer one," said the padre with a twinkle in his eye and a wave of a plump forefinger at the sky. "And what about that chap?" as a peacock came flaunting across the lawn.

"Bit too gorgeous for me. Oh—something I wanted to ask you. Are you an authority on dolmens, by any chance?"

"*Sutor ne supra crepidem judicaret*" said Haddowe with a sideways tilt of the head.

"Now, padre! It's too fine a day for that sort of thing! Still, say it again."

"Alas for lost Latinity!" sighed Haddowe and repeated the tag.

"I've got it," smiled Travers. "But mightn't the cobbler have a hobby? He might know for instance where the stone came from out of which those dolmens were hewn. I always imagined there wasn't any rock in this part of the world."

"Ah! there I can help you. There's a deep cutting about a mile away on the other side of the Byford road. Mr. Revere always said the stones came from there. Some sort of out-crop I imagine."

"I thought it must be something of the sort. Curious sort of mind I'm cursed with, padre. Always want to explain things. Loose ends terrify me."

"A very useful obsession too—the itch to find things out. Well," and he sighed heavily, "when you get as old as I, you'll be glad to leave some things unexplained." Then he gave a dramatic start. "My dear fellow! I'm forgetting the very thing I meant to say as soon as

I arrived. Do you realise I didn't know till this morning who you really were?"

Travers did his best to look puzzled.

"I didn't know you were *the* Travers—the author. *The Economics of a Spendthrift* now! Upon my soul, I ought to be reprimanded."

"You've given me one consolation," smiled Travers. "I know I've been loved for myself alone! But how did you like the chapter on parsons?"

"Don't ask me!" said Haddowe with a look indescribably arch. "Remember Gil Bias and the Archbishop of Salamanca. But there," and he waved a white hand, "you mustn't take me too seriously. I enjoyed it immensely."

The gong sounded and they retraced their steps. At the morning's lunch the padre excelled himself. There might have been better company but where to find it Travers wouldn't have known. There was quick repartee, a deft turn of phrase, an apposite quotation, shrewd observation and personal anecdotes. And as far as pure information was concerned, one or two interesting things emerged.

The padre, for instance, took a folded newspaper from his pocket and showed a picture to Travers.

"That's how I remembered you," he said. "I knew I'd seen you somewhere before."

Travers gave a glance, then made a wry face. "Who on earth troubled to put me in the papers, padre?"

Haddowe lowered his voice to a humorous whisper. "This is an old copy, probably when you published your last book. I always save up my newspapers because of the serials. If they're good I read 'em twice!"

Travers laughed. Haddowe was so obviously apologetic. And then another piece of information.

"Talking of those dolmens. I don't mind confessing I did everything I could to keep Mr. Revere at it. I agreed with most of his theories, and if I couldn't I said something that made him ten times more eager to get on with the job. You see why. It kept him away from himself. When he was out there, especially in the moonlight, he was happy."

"That was kindly done of you, padre," said Travers, with a private admiration for the ingenuity that had kept Cosmo Revere out of the way.

Haddowe shook his head deprecatingly. Then came something in the nature of a request.

"I wonder if you'd do something for me?" he asked, leaning across the table in a fatherly sort of way. "I ventured to ask because Mr. Revere agreed on a previous occasion and, I believe, enjoyed the visit immensely. Could you put up Jerome Paull on Friday night?"

"Jerome Paull? The producer?"

Haddowe assented modestly. "I wouldn't ask you only my own place is hardly suitable. He happens to be a great friend of mine and can spare only the one night. He supervised *The School for Scandal* for us last March."

"I say, you're frightfully palatial, aren't you, padre? Why he's a fellow of international reputation. What's he charge you?"

"Nothing at all! Pure kindness of heart. You'll put him up then?"

"Oh rather! When's he coming?"

"He should be here by tea on Friday. I'll meet him and bring him along if I may."

"Do, please. And of course you'll come to dinner on the Friday. I'll make a note to tell Royce. Oh, here he is!"

When Travers had given his orders, the butler had a message. "Superintendent Burton wishes to see you, sir."

"Who's he, Royce?"

"The superintendent at Branford police station, sir."

"What's he want?"

"He didn't say, sir—except that it was urgent."

Travers gave the padre a sideways glance, "You may well look," said Haddowe. "What's your crime?"

"Just trying to think. Let me see. I haven't exceeded the speed limit."

"*De minimis non curat lex*" remarked Haddowe with humorous gravity. "At least superintendents don't."

"Ask him to come in here," said Travers, and, "You don't mind, padre?"

Haddowe smiled and waved his hand. But he drew back his chair, crossed his legs and sat facing the door with finger tips tightly together. Travers got up to greet the superintendent as the butler ushered him in. There was nothing unusual about him; he could hardly have been mistaken for other than he was.

"What's your trouble, superintendent?"

"It's about this man, Westfield, sir. I've been into the case and I don't like the look of it. I wondered if we might search the woods in case he's had an accident."

"That sounds an excellent idea," and he turned to Haddowe. "You know Westfield, padre. It appears he's missing."

Haddowe was genuinely surprised or Travers was vastly mistaken. "No, I didn't know anything about it. When did it happen?"

Travers explained and added a plausible account of the way in which he himself was interested. "He'd been recommended to me as likely to take Eagling's place as head keeper, so I thought I'd like to run my eye over him." He turned to the other. "I think, if you don't mind, superintendent, you'd better let the keepers search the woods. They're full of young birds. You go with them of course. They'll know every inch of the ground. And just a minute, Royce. Will you send Francis in?"

In came Francis, head at the exact deferential angle.

"Did you make that enquiry for me, John, about Westfield's relations?"

"He has none, sir. The superintendent here—"

Superintendent Burton took up his cue. "I've made very close enquiries, sir, and as far as can be ascertained, he hasn't a relation anywhere."

Travers thought that out. From his pocket Haddowe took the newspaper which had been folded to show the photograph of Travers, turned back one of its folds, gave a quick glance at Franklin and quickly replaced it.

"I'll make a suggestion if I may," said Travers. "Wait till to-morrow so that the woods may be all beaten, and then see if the broadcasting authorities will send out an S.O.S." Once more he turned to Haddowe.

"An excellent suggestion!" was the padre's comment. Burton agreed.

Travers rose. "I'll take you round to Captain Leeke myself. John! See the Hall chauffeur goes to the station. I'll explain to Sir Henry."

Haddowe rose too. "Don't you move, padre," said Travers. "I shall be back in five minutes."

"I'm afraid I must," said Haddowe. "I should have had to go in any case. Some big authority or other has written me that he wants to look over the church this afternoon."

* * * * *

Half an hour later every available man had moved off to the Lammas Wood beat and Travers and Franklin were comparing notes in the privacy of the upstair room.

"Why did you want me to call you in?" asked Travers when he'd gone over the conversation at the table.

"To have a good look at Haddowe myself for one thing," said Franklin. "I'm tired of peeping behind curtains."

"He's dining here on Friday. Won't that change your plans?"

"You mean about Castleton? The thing is, do you want him and Castleton here at the same time? If not it'd suit me all the better if you'd write a chit and ask Castleton to come to dinner to-morrow instead."

"I'll write it at once and you can take it with you now."

"And what happened to Haddowe when Royce announced the policeman?"

"Nothing much," said Travers. "He seemed more amused than anything. Also he took up a bit of an attitude in the chair—sort of judicially clerical. Personally, I thought he carried it off magnificently. Do you know, I rather like Haddowe!"

"He's a cheerful rogue; I'll say that for him," was Franklin's comment. "He's got what they call the grand manner. And he's also got an exceedingly dirty look in his eye."

When Franklin had gone, Travers sat with his documents in readiness, killing time and waiting for the arrival of the lawyer's party. Once he smiled to himself as he recalled Haddowe's reference to the book and a chapter on parsons which didn't exist. The padre must have got hold of a *Who's Who* or some other book of reference and if so he knew practically all there was to know about Ludovic Travers—that the connection with Brotherston, Hall and Brotherston, for instance, was at its best a kind of sub-letting or lending from Durangos Limited.

Royce's voice came in.

"Captain Leeke would like to see you a moment, sir."

"Funny!" thought Travers, "I've only just spoken to him," but when Leeke came in he gave him his most disarming smile.

"Hallo, Leeke! What's all your trouble?"

Leeke's was a small difficulty that might become a big one—a question of overlapping between the Hall and Estate accounts. He seemed friendly enough and far less on edge; at least, after a quarter of an hour's chat, Travers thought the moment not unfavourable for a question about that newspaper.

"Fact of the matter is," said Leeke frankly, "I don't know where the damn thing came from. Somebody sent it to me by post."

"Anonymously?"

"That's right."

"Good Lord! You don't happen to have it with you by any chance?"

"I think I know where to put my hands on it. If you'll wait a couple of seconds I'll fetch it."

Exactly one moment after Leeke had returned—and gone again, Travers was startled out of his wits. He made a move for the door to send for Franklin—then suddenly remembered. Franklin was already with Castleton!

CHAPTER XXII
FRANKLIN GOES VISITING

IT IS NOT at all a bad feeling if a resplendent neighbour passes when you are wearing an old suit, to know that you have an even better one than his if you care to wear it. That was something of the assurance that formed the background of Franklin's thoughts as he strolled across the park in the direction of Oak Cottage. Ostensibly he was a gentleman's servant—sufficiently servile, perfectly unpolished and one from whom much gratitude would be expected for favours bestowed. There would be Castleton too—probably very "nice," unbending ever so slightly, charmingly courteous and unconsciously patronising. Lastly would be himself—John Francis, who was really John Franklin, with all sorts of things in the wardrobe drawers.

Castleton was in his favourite deck chair on the front lawn. He showed no particular enthusiasm at his visitor's arrival and his greeting was business-like and matter-of-fact.

"Good afternoon, Mr. Francis. You want to see me about Carter?"

"Yes, sir. If you can tell me anything about him I shall be very grateful."

"I don't know that I can help very much. However, come along in. Let me take your hat."

The room they entered was the one he already knew from Travers' description. The first thing to do was to hand over the note.

"This is rather lucky," said Castleton smiling. "Do you know what's in it?"

"I'm afraid not, sir."

"Well, will you explain to Mr. Travers that I shall be very pleased to come to-morrow night instead of Friday. I couldn't have come in any case. There's a big rehearsal on. Now you want to know about Carter. What exactly is it you want to know?"

"It's like this, sir," began Franklin. "My mother's maiden name was Carter and she always said her brother lived in Breckland only she'd lost sight of him for some years. I know we always used to—to sort of think of him as Uncle George. Then this happened to be the first time I was down this way and somebody mentioned his name, so I wondered if he was the one. You see, sir, he was mother's only brother and younger, so the ages would be about right."

"Well now, I'll tell you what I know about him," said Castleton, squinting sideways out of the window. "I was in a small antique shop—very cheap affair just off Wardour Street—trying to strike a deal over some china and the proprietor happened to be out. The man who was attending to me must have noticed some slip in my accent, because he asked if I came from Breckland. He said he'd lived there all his early life—somewhere north of the county I think—and wouldn't mind getting back again. He had a bit of money saved and if he could get hold of a small cottage he could pick up a living as a dealer. I don't know if Mr. Travers told you, but I offered him the cottage he now occupies. To be perfectly frank, I thought I should be doing myself a good turn at the same time, because he could collect things for me or give me the first offers. Well, he came down the following week-end and had a look round. The rent was to be twelve pounds without rates and he took the cottage at that. He was a bit of a rough diamond of course, but I must say the first few months he was here, he was a capital chap to get on with. That's all I know: at least it's all I care to tell you—if he's your uncle."

"I haven't heard much good about him myself, sir," confessed Franklin. "He doesn't seem to have treated you at all well. But is he often away like this, sir? I don't seem to be able to get hold of him."

"You mean absent from the cottage? Very frequently. It's his living and he has to be. He's exhausted most of the villages round here and naturally—I don't know if you are conversant with the antique trade?—he has to depend on auctions or go farther afield. Also if he goes to an auction he makes a good living by standing in with the ring. I know that according to Act of Parliament there isn't supposed to be any ring nowadays, but there you are. A little dealer, if he's in the swim, can pay his expenses and get hold of a fiver." He laughed. "I hope he does to-day. Perhaps he'll pay me the rent he owes."

"Perhaps he will, sir," said Franklin lamely.

"Do you know I did everything I could for that chap," went on Castleton, obviously very annoyed. "I took him round with me to sales and introduced him to people. Go to any auctioneer you like— Peekes of Branford, Wilier of Littlewood, any of 'em—and they'll tell you how I vouched for him personally. I went with him more than once to have a look at something he didn't feel competent to handle. I bought his stuff, even when it was rubbish. I had a way cut in my private road so he shouldn't have to go round. I got his van for him and taught him to drive it." He broke off suddenly "I'm sorry. I shouldn't have let you hear me talk like that."

"That's all right, sir. If he *is* an uncle of mine I don't know I'm as keen as I was on making his acquaintance. But do you happen to know, sir, if he was at home last Tuesday night—a week ago?"

The question was a risky one, as he knew, and he had his answer ready to explain it, but Castleton seemed to see nothing peculiar in it.

"Last Tuesday night? Yes; of course he was! I went out to West-lake with my car and got back about ten-fifteen. I saw a light in his bedroom. I remember now because I thought I'd see him the following morning and come to an understanding of some sort."

Franklin found no comment and his purpose apparently accomplished, rose to go. He did appear however to be struck with the beauty of the room. "It must be very nice to have all these fine things, sir. There's nothing like the good old stuff. Beats all the modern, sir."

Castleton smiled tolerantly. "You may be right. But hasn't Mr. Travers a fine collection?"

Franklin shook his head enthusiastically as they came out to the lawn. "Wonderful, sir—especially the china. Do you know, sir, he's got some figures you wouldn't think it possible to make them by hand?"

"Really!"

Franklin waved his hand towards the north lawn. "That's more in my line, sir. You see that rock garden you"—(he almost said, "You're building," but pulled up in time)—"you've built there, sir? As soon as I saw how your lawn sloped I said to myself if this was mine I'd have it all one big rock garden; you know, sir—terraced right down to the back door."

"It might be rather jolly," agreed Castleton, but decidedly impatiently.

The caller moved a yard or two off the path and surveyed Castleton's attempt. "Mr. Haddowe was telling Mr. Travers, sir, that there's an old quarry where you might get some rock."

Castleton moved on to the gate.

"So you know Mr. Haddowe, do you?"

"Well, not know him, sir. He's been to the Hall once or twice. He's a very nice gentleman, don't you think so, sir? He shook hands with me the first time he saw me."

"Did he really!" Castleton seemed highly amused. Then he opened the gate.

"Not a bit like a clergyman, is he, sir?"

Castleton's eyes narrowed. "Just a question of taste. You can't be sure of everybody you run across, you know? Nowadays one never knows who's who. Very glad you came. Hope you find your uncle. *Good*bye!"

Franklin hardly knew what to think as he went down the slope. That was a curious remark about not knowing who was who! Anything behind it, he wondered. Still, things had gone off quite well; no awkward situations, and he was sure he hadn't given himself away.

He turned into Carter's path, tried the front door and looked into the windows. On the back door was the notice Travers had seen. Still, why worry? Carter could be drawn out into the open—the visit had told him that. It might need a little diplomacy, but if human nature were what one expected it to be, then Carter would be at hand when wanted.

As he strolled through the village he was still ruminating. Almost a brick he'd dropped over that rock garden. It was at Travers' visit it had been *almost* finished. Castleton must have been frightfully keen to have pushed the work on from the stage at which Travers had seen it. What was the idea of the hurry? Expecting visitors?

Then the posing which Travers had noticed. Precious little of that with him. Castleton had been almost rude at times. And all that humbug about not caring to say anything against an uncle and then going on and letting everything out just as he'd probably intended to do from the outset.

And that partial alibi which he'd given Carter. What real good was it? If the two had been in a conspiracy together, then he could do no less than prove Carter to be innocent. As for the light in the bedroom, even if the story were true it proved neither that Carter was in the room or out of it. The whole problem lay in the place of the killing—and the whereabouts of that yellow sand.

The thought seemed to direct his steps and he took the sharp left-hand turn and picked his way along the narrow lane. A pity no rain had fallen for all those days; as it was there could be no mark of the vehicle that might have removed the body. Then he heard the tapping of a hammer and round the bend came in sight of the pit. In the bottom, as on the stage of an amphitheatre, sat a roadman straddle-legged over a heap of stones.

"Fine afternoon!" said Franklin.

"Aye. Rare good harvest weather."

He moved on round the base of the sheer wall, dotted with stones and fretted with small holes round which the martens fluttered. Then he came back to the man.

"You been here all the week?"

"Started yesterday, sir. Surveyor he come and took me off the road. They're goin' to do that bad bit along to Byford."

"Those are fine stones you've got over there. I don't know that I ever saw bigger."

The roadman shook his head knowingly. "Them, sir! I've seen 'em so big, two on 'em wouldn't go into that barrow."

"Really! And what do they do with them?"

"All sorts o' things, sir. Parish have 'em for borderin' the roads. Whiten 'em up so as you can see 'em in the dark when you're drivin'. Mr. Castleton have some for his garden and the reverend he had some for his drive."

"I saw Mr. Castleton's. And now I remember I've seen them all along by the green. Who's having those there?"

"Nobody yet, sir. They ain't ordered."

Franklin nodded, wished the man good-day and moved on towards the Lodge. Westfield's cottage looked peaceful and secluded with its hollyhocks reaching to the eaves and he wondered what the result of the search had been, though in his mind he felt he knew the answer. Then a few yards further on he saw a car drawn up outside the vicarage gate and as he turned into the park the vicar emerged from the church walk with another man—a visitor by the look of him and probably the owner of the car.

Franklin stepped out across the grass, cut back to the trees, then doubled for the shelter of the hedge. Haddowe was shaking hands with the stranger—a well-dressed, scholarly sort of person with a high-pitched voice, though the distance and the lie of the breeze made it impossible to catch a word of the actual conversation. But what did surprise Franklin was the stranger's face. Somewhere or other he'd seen it before. A visitor to the Hall on the day of the funeral? No, that wasn't it; he knew the face too well for that. The name wasn't on the tip of his tongue; it was a recollection hardly as vivid as that and yet he was certain he knew—and knew well—the man who was just stepping into the car.

That afternoon the park was full of sunshine, but it seemed to Franklin as he walked across the open grassland, to be even more full of curious associations. In the distance was the mass of the Hall, backed by clumps of elms—the view that Haddowe had seen when he first came to visit Cosmo Revere. Here Leila Forteresse had had her riding lessons and over there by the trees had sat the incongruous saxophonists who awoke in Fenwold strange and disordered echoes. In the far distance was the blue of Lammas Wood and to the right the chimneys of Leeke's house. To the left was the faint path that led to the dolmens and behind him, trying desperately as it were to peer at it all, the windows of the vicarage. There it was—the whole of a drama spread out under the heavens and each actor with a drama far more personal within.

The next couple of hours were tedious ones, and when the search party returned he felt more despondent still. Every yard of the Lammas beat had been hunted and as there were no ponds to drag it seemed certain that wherever Westfield was it was not on the estate. Superintendent Burton announced his intention of going at once to the county town to inform his superiors and that seemed all he could do. Then Travers rang and Franklin found him dressing for dinner—and extremely perturbed. Travers plunged into it straightway.

"Something most exasperating has happened. You remember that newspaper incident of Leeke's? Somebody sent him that paper anonymously! And what do you think it was? The *Daily Record* of last December!"

Franklin's thoughts could have been read on his face, from the bewilderment to the answer.

"You mean when they published your photograph with mine after the Perfect Murder Case?"

"Exactly! And there's more to follow. I told you Haddowe showed me at lunch a paper so folded as to show my photograph only. What I couldn't tell you, because I've only just got the hang of it, was that when you were in the room he folded back the paper quickly and had a peep at you. It must have been the same paper—he's identified you!"

"Yes, but suppose I hadn't come in?"

"He'd have sent for you on some excuse or other. Not only that. Don't you think Castleton hared off to Branford that morning because he'd received the same paper by the early post?"

Franklin made a gesture of annoyance, started to speak stopped—and frowned. When he did speak he seemed more worried than annoyed. "Castleton knew who I was this afternoon. I'm sure of that now—from something he let fall. Sort of sneering remark about not knowing who people were." He shook his head. "It's the very devil! Who sent the papers, do you think?"

"Haddowe of course!"

"Why so sure?"

"He's the only one who's told a deliberate lie about 'em. I'll bet he never read a serial in his life. He was exhibiting the paper as a direct hint that he might go a step further if necessary—if we interfered too closely with whatever he's up to."

"We mustn't be prejudiced," said Franklin. "I know it's very tantalising after asking Haddowe to lunch to look over *him*, to find out he's been the one to laugh up his sleeve. Still, that's not the point. Why did he send the papers?"

"To clear us out of the village—or the Hall. To make our position untenable."

Franklin grunted.

"What's worrying me," went on Travers, "is to know how I'm to behave with Castleton and him. How can I prevent them knowing I know they know?"

Franklin smiled grimly. "Sounds like Wilkie Bard! Still, if you don't mind taking advice you'll do as I do, and that's nothing. I've often had to do it—talk nothings to a man and know he saw my bluff. I don't give a damn what they think. After all we're here with full authority—you especially."

"True enough," said Travers more cheerfully. "For all that I'm afraid it'll freeze the genial current of *my* conversation. Hallo! There's the second gong. Pop up after ten if you can manage it. Leila Forteresse is dining downstairs to-night, by the way."

CHAPTER XXIII
FRANKLIN THINKS HE KNOWS

As he sat in the comparative cool of the butler's parlour after dinner that evening, Franklin's thoughts were a long way from the book he had on his knees. In spite of his assumption of indifference in the presence of Travers he was infinitely more worried than he cared to admit—even to himself. If Haddowe and Castleton knew the probable object for which he and Francis had come to Fenwold, all sorts of things might happen. As he had half tentatively let float through his mind in Lammas Wood, one murder had been committed and another seemed more than likely. The natural sequence must surely be a third and this time a double one.

This time too he was hardly disposed to think of the idea as a melodramatic one—what he did think of was the elementary precautions that might be taken. All that should be necessary was a sort of dissociation—that Travers should be in one place and himself in another. A murderer couldn't be omnipresent and dispose of two at the same time, and if two—say Carter and Castleton—tried it on, the synchronisation would have to be extraordinarily good. That was the defence, that *both* would have to be got rid of. Leave one alive, or delay the murder, and the killing would be fatal for the murderer.

"You're very serious to-night, Mr. Francis?" said Royce, putting down the *Morning Post.* "The weather, I think, is very distressing."

Franklin roused himself. "Very hot, sir; very hot indeed! But very good harvest weather."

"Earliest I've known for years. Now, my dear, you'll try your eyes."

Franklin looked round at the housekeeper, with pencil and dictionary, engrossed in a cross-word puzzle.

"Trying to make a fortune, Mrs. Lacy?"

She laughed. "Royce always grumbles at me doing these puzzles. What's the harm in them, I'd like to know."

Royce shook his head. "You can't get anything you don't earn. Just a modern craze, Mr. Francis."

"Well, I shan't get very rich out of this one," retorted his wife. "It's got to go in to-morrow morning and there's a whole corner not done yet. What are you like at them, Mr. Francis?"

"The world's worst!" admitted Franklin modestly.

She clicked her tongue humorously. "Do come and have a look. Here's the corner, I across—'If this can't come to I down.' And then I down is, 'This can go to I across.' I can't make head nor tail of it."

"There's a catch in everything of that sort," remarked Royce.

Franklin smiled. "Far too clever for me. Mr. Travers now—if you could get him to help you—"

"Oh, Mr. Francis, how could I?"

Franklin scratched his head. "Well—er—I don't see how we could. How many letters? Eight in each. If it's a corner they must begin with the same letter. I *have* got sense enough for that."

He started muttering away at the alphabet, "If this can't come to that, then that can go to this," and so on. Half way through, his face lit up.

"I think I've got it! Mahomet and the mountain! If the mountain can't come to Mahomet, then Mahomet can go to the mountain. No, that's not enough letters."

Mrs. Lacy's face fell again. "I knew there'd be a catch in it somewhere!"

"Wait a minute!" said Franklin. "Let's have a look at the dictionary. Mahomet . . . It *is* right! You can spell it Mahommed. Let me put it in for you—There! Now you see if it fits in with the others."

"Mr. Francis is a very clever man, my dear," Royce pronounced benignly. "And he doesn't admit it—which is an uncommon thing these days. Another whisky, Mr. Francis?"

"A very long one then—nearly all soda. Have you finished with the *Post?*"

It was really very amusing how pleased Franklin was over that little relaxation. Fancy himself as a cross-word solver! Rather neat too—the chap who made it up. If the mountain can't come to Mahomet, why shouldn't Mahomet go to the mountain? Why not indeed? Plenty of things in life like that. Often people made difficulties where there needn't be any, and so back to where the cross-word had interrupted him—the events of the afternoon. There was five minutes' silence.

"It's working out splendidly!" came the voice of the housekeeper. "'Oder' is a river in Germany, isn't it?"

Royce looked round over the top of his spectacles as Franklin got to his feet.

"Would you excuse me a moment. There's something most important I've forgotten to do."

Outside in the servants' hall, he found Parry, engaged in a game of cards.

"Sorry to trouble you, Parry, but could you spare me a minute?"

Half an hour later Parry was off for the night with a bottle of beer and a package of sandwiches, ready to mount guard at a spot in the park where he could overlook both gardens. At five o'clock he was to come off duty, but as soon as possible after breakfast Franklin would go to Branford to get through to London an urgent call for an extra man—ex-Sergeant Potter if possible. And as soon as Parry had gone, Franklin went up to Travers' room and waited.

What had caused all the commotion was that mountain and Mahomet business—and an odd association. If Cosmo Revere couldn't go where the sand was, why shouldn't the sand have come to him? Then the sequence—sand, the visit to the gravel pit, the huge stones, and the stones in Castleton's rock-garden. Franklin thought he saw it! Those great flints had had no rain on them for weeks and still held the sandy gravel just as they'd been delivered from the pit. Cosmo Revere had been killed as the man on the dolmen had intended—by a stone that had dropped on his head. But where had the murderer been? Not in the village; that had all been argued out before.

And what about that rock-garden? Why had Castleton finished it in such a hurry? Franklin thought he knew. Somewhere under its earth and stones was the body of Westfield—safe beyond hope of discovery! In the spring, plants and bulbs would make that garden look as if it had been there for centuries and who was to disturb it as long as Castleton owned the property? Fantastic perhaps as a theory—and as a theory that couldn't be tested, and yet—perhaps there was a chance. That afternoon for instance, he'd looked long and hard at that rock-garden. Would Castleton think he had suspicions? If so he'd shift the body again—always assuming it was there!—and he'd have to do it at night.

And who'd killed Westfield? Carter? If so, all that theory of Carter going in fear of his life was wide of the mark. But was it? Mightn't Carter be about to get his revenge? Had he killed Westfield and hidden his body under the rock-garden at night? And would he inform the police anonymously? After all, he had written the anonymous letters. That of course would mean that he'd have to bolt himself. Or had he bolted already?

Travers came in with a slight odour of cigar smoke about him and looking as if he'd inhabited Fenwold since his youth.

"Hallo! There you are then! We've had some excellent music to-night—a Beethoven sonata, some Chopin, and one or two of the moderns. That woman plays extraordinarily well. Bit slapdash, but marvellous execution!"

Franklin nodded.

"Sir Henry's got quite a good voice. By the way he's having Leeke on the carpet to-morrow. Don't know why exactly. Something must have happened before we got here." He peered at Franklin as if noticing his face for the first time. "You're looking worried?"

"Yes. It's about Westfield. I'm practically sure he's been done in."

"Good God! You don't mean murdered?"

Franklin told him all about it. Travers was positively spluttering with anger.

"I say, that's damnable! Quite a decent chap apparently and—er—really it makes one's blood boil! What are you going to do? Go for a warrant?"

Franklin shook his head. "Can't do that. It's all conjecture. Westfield may be miles off for all we really know. Pretty fools we'd look if we rushed off there with the police. And haven't we been told there's to be no scandal? We should only have to rake up all the Revere business. It's one and the same thing."

Travers clicked his tongue in annoyance.

"What you might do for me if you anyhow can is to find out just how deep Castleton was in with that woman. What Parry overheard can't really be taken as evidence and I'd like that motive to be as strong as possible. I'll try Mrs. Lacy myself—in her good books for the moment. Also there's something else we've got to realise. Suppose Carter does send an anonymous letter to the police and they dig up the rock-garden and find Westfield's body. As far as we're concerned the case'll be over. And if we don't want to be drawn in, the sooner we get out the better. If we have to give evidence of any kind—and I don't see how we can avoid it—the very scandal Sir Henry wants to avoid, and what Durangos are being paid to avoid, will simply be broadcast."

"Damn the scandal! You mean to say you and I are going to clear out and let whoever killed Revere get clean away with it?"

"Not at all. Whoever killed Westfield killed Revere. If he gets hanged for the one, why worry about the other?"

Travers muttered something to himself, then whipped off his glasses.

"If we do go away, I'm coming back here again next Wednesday! There's something extraordinary going on about this dramatic show of Haddowe's. I can't put my finger on it, but it's there. It started as soon as I got here. Now there's this Jerome Paull business and so on. What's it all about? Why's Haddowe so frightfully keen? Tell me that now."

"No use asking me. Just a minute though," and he mentioned Haddowe's visitor of the afternoon. "Very strange! Do you know I knew that chap's face as well as I know my own?"

Travers started to put his glasses on, then took them off again. "Look here. I'd better own up about all that. No wonder you knew his face. That was Charlton-Powers, the consulting expert of our own Fine Arts department."

"Good God! How'd *he* get down here?"

"I sent for him. You see I had an idea—simply that squib business—that Haddowe might be hanging about here so as to remove something valuable from the church; got the idea from a detective story—very good one—about a parson who collared a whole stained-glass window, so I asked him to come along and see just what there was there—glass, plate, furniture and so on. His report ought to be here first thing in the morning. Honestly I didn't think it important or I'd have told you," and he looked at Franklin very apologetically.

Franklin seemed already to have forgotten the explanation.

"I've got an idea on something of the same lines, about Carter. Will you do a little job for me? First thing in the morning look out for me a piece of furniture—quite good; sort of thing you might be lucky enough to run across in a farmhouse attic; kind of thing Carter'd give his eyebrows to get hold of."

Travers smiled. "What's the idea?"

"We'll plant it somewhere and let Carter know, and—"

"Yes, but how can you do that if he's bolted?"

"We don't know he *has* bolted. If he hasn't, he'll try to buy that piece of furniture, provided we can think out a decent scheme."

"Capital!" said Travers, then yawned. Franklin followed suit.

"I'll push off now. Got to work out to-morrow's programme. I'm most damnably tired. Do you realise what a hell of a day this has been? I seem to have been haring about since before breakfast." He yawned again. "Don't forget that piece of furniture. Not too ornate. Just neat, but not gaudy."

CHAPTER XXIV
ONE DAMN THING AFTER ANOTHER

THURSDAY WAS A curious sort of day, all odds and ends and things important mixed up with trifles. What Royce had been thinking those last few days is hard to say, what with the Westfield affair and mysterious conversations and Francis in and out at odd times and away for long stretches. The old butler must have shaken his head more than once. The lofty, the spacious times of Fenwold seemed to have departed, and Royce must have felt like a verger once employed in a cathedral, who now in the same building taken over by a cinema company, still served as usher.

Travers' first job was to lay a false trail, for Brown and Royce had instructions to send the footman to the library to fetch a paper from the desk. What was written on another paper—left glaringly in the foot-man's sight—Travers absolutely refused to divulge, on the plea that it was too silly. Franklin did gather, however, that it was about a supposed arrival from Scotland Yard, who would be dropped from the car at 9.30 p.m. at the junction of the Branford and Hall back roads the following evening.

Franklin had his new man Potter to meet at Branford and then bring him back in a hired car. The ex-sergeant was to put up at the "Stag" and snatch his sleep as best he could. The trouble was that he and Parry had to be on guard together. If the night was warm there was no need for both to keep awake, but at the first sign of movement in either of the gardens, certain things would at once have to be done, and these would require two pairs of legs and a couple of bicycles.

Travers had an exceptionally busy time till Sir Henry departed by the late afternoon train. There was the following letter that came by the first post.

Dear Travers,

I came down yesterday and visited the church as you suggested. It is a singularly uninteresting building, qua building. Its contents are not much better—windows very late, pulpit formal and the work of a local craftsman, and the oak of the general pews badly in need of restoration. I admit the Revere pew has a certain singularity on account of the carving.

The register begins at 1605 and is in three volumes, its contents being unrelieved by any happening of even local interest. The vestry has the usual iron-bound coffer and two early coffin-stools.

Two pieces of plate remain—a paten undated, but with conventional vernicle graving, and a communion cup, probably purchased at second-hand, since the date is 1589 and engraved "Fenwolde" above an excision mark of the original ownership.

Should anything arise out of my visit, ring me up at headquarters and I shall probably be able to get down again at fairly short notice.

Yours sincerely,

S. Charlton-Powers.

P.S.—Your parson wasn't at all well informed on church architectural matters.

That, of course, hit Travers' theory a very shrewd blow. What he retained after a worrying half hour was sufficient faith in the original theory to be sure that a modification might be near the mark. If Haddowe wasn't making something out of the church, why not the Hall? That produced an idea at once, and he hurried off to interview Royce.

"Tell me, Royce," he began. "Do you ever remember during the last few years anybody taking photographs of the Hall, particularly interiors?"

Royce had an answer at once. "Mr. Haddowe took some, sir, when he first came here."

"You mean the year of the armistice?"

"That's right, sir. If I remember right, sir, he said he'd particularly like some souvenirs of the Hall and he went in to Branford specially, sir, and got a very good camera."

"He took them himself?"

"Yes, sir. Quite a lot of them—inside and out."

"What I meant was, did he wander about unaccompanied?"

"I believe he did, sir."

Travers could see things sorting themselves out again.

"Am I right in saying he also took some later?"

"Well—er—yes he did, sir, now I come to think of it."

"But not by himself personally."

This uncanny knowledge seemed almost too much for the butler, as his face showed. "That's quite correct, sir. It would be about a year ago. He brought along a gentleman one day when the master was out—"

"At the dolmens—or Cambridge?"

"Cambridge I believe, sir, but I know the master was out, and they had permission to take some views of the Hall. Miss Leila was with them, sir."

"I see." Travers nodded to himself. "And what about later?"

"The same gentleman came again, sir. I think he was a foreigner, sir."

"Really! That's very interesting! And Mr. Revere was out again?"

"Yes, sir."

Travers thought furiously, then came to a decision. "Keep this strictly to yourself, Royce. Forget absolutely everything we've been talking about."

Royce bowed, then cleared his throat. "I think there's something I ought to tell you, sir. I don't know if you are aware of it, sir, but Captain Leeke is leaving."

"I thought it quite possible," said Travers.

Royce lowered his voice. "Just after lunch, sir, Captain Leeke came and asked if I'd do him a special favour. He seemed very upset, and wanted to know if Miss Leila would see him for a moment, so I gave the message personally, sir, and the answer was she was sorry she was unable. The captain was very disturbed, sir, but I think he'd been expecting it, because he gave me a letter and told me to take it myself and bring an answer. When I came down again, sir, I had to inform him there was no answer. He looked very angry, sir; very angry indeed. I never saw a man look like it. Then he turned on his heel as they say, sir, and then he stopped and spoke to me. 'Good-bye, Royce,' he said, sir. 'It's quite possible I shan't see you again,' and before I could say anything he went off round the shrubbery."

"Thank you, Royce," said Travers quietly. "You'll be sorry to lose Captain Leeke?"

"Well, I must say I shall, sir." Travers caught the regret in his voice. "They all seem to be going, sir; first the master, then Miss Leila, and now Captain Leeke."

Travers was sorry for the old man, clinging to the Fenwold of his youth and living in an age over which modernity had already thrown a shadow. Even the departure of Leila Forteresse had a tragic side, in spite of the uneasiness her presence had often given him.

She was with them at lunch that day, and when the visitors left, saw them off with Travers from the portico steps. During Sir Henry's visit she had seemed singularly restrained; there was nothing deliberately pathetic about the pose she assumed—it was more in the nature of a watchful repression; the fear of saying too much or trespassing beyond the delicate bounds of the late bereavement or the coming departure. There was anxiety also. More than once she sounded the lawyer as to his knowledge of what had been in that private letter, and Sir Henry, it seemed to Travers, had been rather curt in his disclaimers.

Those at least were the impressions Travers had formed, but he was a prejudiced observer. The look she gave him, however, as they watched the car disappear among the trees of the drive was distinctly provocative.

"What now, Mr. Travers?"

"As far as I'm concerned," he said, "work, unfortunately—and plenty of it."

She glanced at her wrist watch. "You won't take me to Branford? There's heaps of time?"

Travers countered her smile with an enigmatical one of his own. "No more play. How am I to go to that wonderful show of yours if the work isn't done? But I'll take you round the rose garden."

When he did get away, it was with a feeling of enormous relief. He pitied those unfortunates—Haddowe, for instance, and herself—who were always more or less under the strain of playing a part. What exactly had been behind all that fooling around of hers? Merely a too generous response to advances or a total inability to exist without some man on the end of the string? One person she wouldn't fool—and that was Haddowe. Whatever truth there'd been in village gossip, Travers was sure the man of peace would never have assumed the role of *ami complaisant*. Had his own original suspicions been correct? Was all that vamping business being done in order that Haddowe might be kept informed of how the land was lying in every possible direction? Travers didn't know, but he thought he knew the reason why she spent most of her time upstairs. Whatever Angéle was doing, and whatever she herself was doing up there with Angéle, at least in their bedrooms they had the chance to be natural.

At Franklin's pre-dinner visit came the inspection of the piece of furniture Travers had picked out—a small, carved Stuart hutch that stood under a window of the long gallery.

"How would you describe it?" asked Franklin.

Travers ran his long fingers over it lovingly and pointed out the original condition and metal-work.

"There's one in the Victoria and Albert almost the same, but not so good. I'd put this about 1620. Call it an elaborately carved Stuart chest. Value?—well, probably about fifty pounds."

Franklin told him the full scheme. Royce had a nephew-in-law, a farmer, at Byford, and the chest would be put in his attic. Carter would be quite unlikely to know of any connection between Fittleton—the farmer's name—and Fenwold Hall, and when he got a letter he ought to go and see the chest at once. If Carter didn't go, then it would practically prove he'd bolted. After that it was ten to one on the police turning up.

"I'll tell you what I should do if I were you," said Travers. "Get it to the garage—tell Parry all about it, of course—and wash it over with strong soda water to take off the natural polish. Don't overdo it. Then when it's nearly dry, throw a pail or two of greasy kitchen water over it. See it's dry before you put it in the attic, and smother it well with dust inside and out. When your man brings it down for Carter to see, let him wipe it a bit and say how dirty it was. If you don't think I'm butting in, I'd like to have a look at it before it goes."

"I wish you would. Looks to me as if I was just putting my foot clean in it."

Travers smiled. "I don't know about that, but we've got to remember Carter's sure to be a very wily bird. You'd better be going, hadn't you? Castleton's due at any minute."

"Don't forget what I told you about him," was Franklin's final word. "Pay no attention to all that paper business. For all we know, he mayn't have had an anonymous paper. He may know you for what you're supposed to be and me not at all. That's the risk I'm going to take if I run across him again. And keep him here till ten, won't you?"

*　*　*　*　*

What Franklin had in mind as he set out across the park was a complete survey of the whole of that corner situated between Castleton's private road and the village green. This time he made no use of the door, but circled round to his left, and making his way through the narrow belt of trees, came out at the fence overlooking the garden of Oak Cottage.

Since Mahomet and the mountain, the theory had moved on a bit. All those arguments about the place of the murder had been reviewed. For instance, if Cosmo Revere had been killed by the dropping of one of those flints on his head, why should the flint—anything up to three stone in weight—have been removed from the garden? Then the thought of dropping produced another idea. Dropping—the man on the dolmen—the man in the tree!

Yes, but exactly how? Too much, of course, to find out precisely on what plea Cosmo Revere, of all people, had been induced to go to a certain spot. And supposing he'd been killed in the garden after all. But he *couldn't*. The arguments still held good that he must have been seen by somebody as soon as he left the park. Ah! but did he leave the park? Did he come round exactly as he himself had done, to a spot overlooking the garden? Franklin thought that was it. Carter had lured him there, had held him in conversation, and Castleton up the tree had merely to let fall the flint. Between them they'd got the body into Carter's van, had gone off the back way to Lammas Wood—the same way Wrentham had first gone—and while Carter prepared the body, Castleton felled the tree. In fifteen minutes they could be back again.

What Franklin looked for was therefore obvious enough. First of all, was that tree easily scaled? then did its branches reach over the spot where Cosmo Revere must have stood? The questions were answered in a way he wasn't expecting. The branches of the oak did *not* reach out beyond the boundary fence, *but,* on the other side of the private road stood another oak, smaller, but with branches even sturdier. Its trunk was so near the fence that when he raised himself he could see round it. And there, plain enough on the far side, was the bruised bark where the heads of the massive nails—still visible themselves—had been put in to give hand and foot hold—a sort of rough-and-ready ladder—and had since been driven home. The tree had certainly been climbed, and what would have to be done, therefore, was to return at dusk and mount it himself, to see how things looked from that massive lower bough, for example. If he stood on the fence he could just about swing himself up.

Then came another discovery, just as important. Right against the trunk of the tree, four of the pales of the split oak fence—room enough for a man to get through—had been removed and replaced. There were the additional nail-marks—and a split in one of the rails—and a different sort of nail—and still a shine on the nail where the hammer had recently hit it. That was the way the body of Cosmo Revere had been got through to the garden, and so into Carter's van.

Franklin made his way to the hedge, slipped through to the Branford road, and then along to the "Angel" to kill time for a couple of hours, first with a game of bowls and then over a glass in the private bar. There were just half a dozen or so of them chatting away about nothing in particular when Franklin made his unobtrusive exit by the back door.

Five minutes later, he was up that tree and finding things safer than he thought. The branch on which he stood was thicker than a man's body, and parallel to it above his head ran another, by which he could steady himself and on which the flint might have rested. The top of Revere's head wouldn't have been ten feet away. The dropping of the stone might have unbalanced the holder—but not till it had actually fallen, and then it wouldn't matter. Would it be any use trying to get Castleton away by daylight, so as to have a look at that upper bough for traces of the sand where the flint had rested? No! that wouldn't do. Carter might be there, even if the other had been got out of the way. Then he suddenly realised something. Carter might be up the other tree at that very moment!

Like a flash he swung himself down and moved off along the shelter of the fence. Carter up the tree or not, something still had to be done. The hard ground would leave no footmarks, so it wouldn't matter about taking off one's shoes. Again he raised himself by the fence-top and slid over, and this time moved more quickly. What he did seemed more like childish mischief than serious work—the deliberate displacement of several of the stones of the rock-garden and the wanton pulling up and scattering on the grass of some of its plants. And just in the middle of that something really happened!

Away by the gate he heard the sound of heavy steps, and without any concern as to the order of his going, slipped off back to the fence. Then came Turner's voice and the flash of his lantern.

"Hi! Come out o' there! I can see you! It ain't no good runnin' away!"

"That remains to be seen," thought Franklin, and nipped like a streak towards the Branford road. Twenty seconds later he was re-entering the private bar of the "Stag" and resuming his place in the conversation. A quarter of an hour—or two rounds of drinks later—he gave a ceremonial good-night, and left the others to it. Along the village green he felt so cheerful that he whistled *Annie Laurie*. Outside the gate of Oak Cottage he stopped to tie up his bootlace, and there Turner accosted him.

"Hallo! What are you doing here this time of night?"

"What am I doing? What do you mean, 'What am I doing?' "

"Oh, I'm sorry, sir, I thought you was someone else. Mr. Francis, isn't it?" and he flashed his light.

"Here! Stop this!" exclaimed Franklin. "What the devil are you supposed to be doing?"

Turner explained. That burglary at Carter's had rather put the wind up Mr. Castleton, and as he was going to be out he asked the constable if he'd mind keeping an eye on his place after dusk. Then came a description of the mysterious movements and the hair-breadth escape.

"Pity I wasn't here," said Franklin regretfully. "We might have had some fun. I've been in the 'Stag' all the evening. You any idea who it was?"

"I've got my eye on a certain party," said Turner darkly. "I had him up once before."

"Well, I hope you get him. It's a nice state of affairs if people can't leave their houses for an hour without this kind of thing happening. Any news about Westfield, by the way?"

"No, sir; none at all. There's another rum thing now!" and a further five minutes elapsed before Franklin could get away. He was only just in time to have a word with Parry and Potter when he saw the lights of Castleton's car moving up the private road.

* * * * *

Back at the Hall, Travers had some news.

"I had to give Royce a certain amount of explanation, after what he told us about Castleton, for having him here to-night, also I told him not to come on duty. But he's just told me something. If it's absolutely necessary, one of the gardeners could be induced to say what he saw with Castleton and the Forteresse in that stone summer-house by the lily-pond one night rather late."

"Good!" said Franklin. "That may come in handy. No sign of her down here to-night?"

"Lord, no! Castleton dragged her name in unnecessarily on one occasion. He also hinted he might be leaving Fenwold in the very near future. Do you know I can't understand that fellow. I'm really awfully disappointed—and rather hurt, in a way."

"It's that blasted woman! The whole of this place she's set by the ears." He tossed his head in annoyance. "By the way, I deliberately put myself in Turner's way to-night. I hope he tells Castleton he saw me. If he does, and he suggests inquiries, he'll be more at sea than ever, because I can be proved to have been in the 'Stag.' Still, after what I told you, he ought to move the body—if it ever was there."

"The chest we got down as soon as you'd gone," said Travers. "It ought to be ready for planting to-morrow. One thing, by the way, I didn't quite get the hang of. What exactly is happening if Carter turns up to buy it?"

"Well, Fittleton'll let him have it for whatever he offers—in reason—and then we could bring a case against him for unlawful receiving. Then he'd have to talk."

"But my dear old chap," expostulated Travers. "Isn't that very elaborate machinery to set in motion?"

"I don't know. It'll be an excuse to hold him. Oh, and something I want you to do for me. I've got a letter to send off to-night with some money in it, and I haven't got my chequebook. Will you write me out a cheque if I give you the notes?"

"Of course I will. How much for?"

"Twenty-five pounds, if you don't mind. And payable to bearer. And would you mind having small notes? I hate carrying fivers about. Always afraid of losing the damn things."

That small transaction ended the day, as far as investigations were concerned. Franklin felt tired, and treated himself to his first reasonably early night. Travers wrote a letter to Geoffrey Wrentham, then turned in, too. And as he lay waiting for sleep he failed entirely to put two and two together. If he had, he must have noticed that Franklin was carrying his theories still further—and what was more important still, had said nothing about it.

CHAPTER XXV
ENTER A REALLY BIG LION

IT WAS NEARLY seven when Haddowe brought his lion to the Hall. He was full of apologies and explanations. Preliminaries had had to be arranged at the church hall and one or two settings looked over; also as dinner was to be earlier, he thought it better to get business out of the way beforehand. In other words, there they were, with nothing to worry about till the hour of rehearsal.

Jerome Paull was a much smaller man than Travers expected. The face he recognised at once—more like that of a Russian revolutionary than the greatest Shakespearian authority and master of stagecraft of his time—with the Semitic nose, thick lips, sallow complexion, sleepy eyes and dark, damp hair that drooped over his forehead. But he could talk! Travers had the short drinks brought out to the lawn, and before he'd been there five minutes, knew that if he kept his ears open during the short stay of the guest, he'd know ten times more about play production than he'd otherwise have picked up in a lifetime.

Leila Forteresse joined them at dinner—the most cheerful party that had dined at Fenwold for a good many years. The vicar was in his usual form; Paull was volubly fascinating, and Leila Forteresse chattered away—perhaps a bit too feverishly, but probably feeling the need of a little relaxation after so many meals alone. Travers hardly put in a word, the conversation fluttering between English and French, and himself rather like a sober old setter in the middle of a heath full of starting rabbits far too elusive to chase. Royce, too, was looking cheerful, and moved about the room as if things were back again in the days before the war.

Paull and the vicar were apparently old friends. The former had been in charge of official concert parties during the war, and had first met Haddowe at a show he had given to the Canadian Division. A prodigious unbending that, thought Travers, for the great Jerome Paull, and looked at him with increased respect. After the war Paull, of course, had made Paris his headquarters. Leila Forteresse, too, seemed a friend of much older standing than the performance of the previous March. Travers wondered again what Paull was thinking as he looked at her from under those heavy-lidded eyes of his.

"You're coming to the rehearsal to-night, Mr. Travers?" he suddenly asked.

"I'm afraid not. Really I'm frightfully busy, and you'd probably find me very much in the way. Of course, I shall be at the show; bang in the front row."

"But we must have an audience!" And he appealed to the others.

Travers shook his head. "Sorry! Don't mind lending a general hand and all that, but—er—well, I don't know how to put it. Sheridan seems too remote from the modern to hold me." He saw the brick he'd dropped. "Of course, I don't claim to be modern in the intellectual sense," he hastened to add. "What I meant was, attracted too much by the noisily obvious."

"Mr. Travers simply adores jazz," explained Leila Forteresse.

"Sheer heresy!" exclaimed Haddowe. "Look at him! I refuse to believe it."

"Thank you, padre," said Travers, laconically. "But speaking seriously, I'd love to come along some time late, but I must get back. What about your company? Everybody turning up?"

Everybody apparently was expected to, and a formidable lot they sounded. The Julia, for instance, was Lady Withertree, better known as Kathleen Carey, of the *Proscenium,* whose Peggy Prude in the *Ugly Duckling* is still remembered. Castleton, too, and Leila Forteresse, and for Mrs. Malaprop, no other than Susan Fletcher, whose husband had taken Byford Hall. Then there was the decidedly useful loan of scenery and costumes from the county repertory theatre, and one of their best men in charge of the lighting sets.

"You'd really describe your last show as up to the best touring company standard?" asked Travers.

"Oh, easily. Don't you think so?" Haddowe put it to Leila Forteresse.

"It was awfully good. I think this will be better, don't you, M. Paull?"

Royce suddenly produced a letter for Travers. "This is very urgent, sir."

It turned out to be an old envelope resealed, and in it a note from Franklin.

"Sorry," said Travers. "It was rather important. Still, it's good news, in a way. The man who was coming to see me can't turn up, so if you'll put up with me, I'll come along towards the end and fetch you all home."

"Splendid!" said Haddowe. "We'll see if we can convert the heretic. And just a second, Royce! If you people don't mind my being serious for a moment, I'd like to say we do want this performance on Wednesday—and Thursday especially—to be an extraordinarily good one. I know Mr. Travers will do all he can because he's just said so. But he's a very busy man, and—well, without any more words, I'm sure he'll help us exactly as Mr. Revere did last time."

Travers nodded and smiled.

"I shall be only too delighted. Carry on just as you've always done. Royce will see to that. He knows more about it than I." Haddowe looked remarkably pleased.

"I knew you'd say that. What about it, Jerome? Shall we let him off the rehearsal?"

"If you'll pardon me, sir," broke in Royce, "I take it you'll require refreshments as last time?"

"That's right, Royce, except that this is summer and then it was spring, and a very cold one, too. However, Miss Leila will see Mrs. Lacy about that." He turned to Travers. "If you don't mind, I'll see Leeke personally about the stage hands, and so on."

Travers waved an airy hand. Paull watched the butler as he left the room.

"Give me that old chap for a month, and I'll find you a better Duncan than Charles Selby. About that seat of yours, Travers. I should sit at the side if I were you."

"Sorry. I thought it was time I dropped a brick!"

Paull explained. Since Michaeloff's theory, the balance of design had shifted. The stage was no longer to be regarded as a focussed point, but as the meeting of two lateral rays. The stage should be split to its wings and not massed to its centre. Travers was nodding his head mechanically and wondering what on earth it all meant, when Haddowe discovered the time. Then there was a quick pushing back of chairs, and in five minutes Travers had Fenwold Hall more or less to himself.

When Franklin came in a moment or two later he couldn't resist a little leg-pulling.

"Well, Peeping Tom? Which keyhole were you at?"

"That one—but it was my ear. That chap Paull seems an extraordinarily long-winded sort! You don't mind going as I suggested? If you're with Haddowe while I'm on that expedition of yours, I shall feel safer."

"Good idea!"

"By the way, what exactly do you expect me to look for?"

"Honestly I don't know. I told you my original idea and what I found out from Royce, and you've seen Charlton-Power's letter. If I interpret that photographing business correctly Haddowe's got his eye on something valuable inside the Hall. If it weren't too farfetched, I should say it was furniture. You remember that piece of linen you smelt the other morning? That was methylated spirits—the thing they use for french polishing."

"Yes, but Haddowe can't fill his pockets with furniture and walk out of the place as if it were a collection of church plate!"

"My dear chap, I know that. That's what I'm worried about. All I said was it was a theory!"

"Just a minute, then. Let's get right down to it. If he did take furniture, would it pay him?"

"Pay him! This house has individual pieces—and I haven't seen half of it—that are worth thousands. There's a rare Chippendale settee that's worth three thousand if it's worth a bean."

Franklin gave his usual grunt. "Well, I don't see how he stands the faintest chance of walking off with things like that. We might know more after to-night. After that I must leave it to you. You never know when my hands'll be full."

"Well, jolly good luck!" said Travers. "You ought to have a clearish field. One of Haddowe's men, if not both, will go along to the back road junction. Has Parry taken the chest yet? It looked a remarkably good job to me."

"We both went this afternoon. Fittleton posted the letter straightaway. Here's a copy."

Dear Mr. Carter,

My wife was cleaning up in our attic this week and we came across an old chest which was a bit dirty, but we know you've bought some things round here, so will you come and look at it. It's all over-carving, and my wife says her grandfather was offered a lot of money for it. A neighbour of ours says you gave her five pounds for one, and this is a lot better than hers.

If you don't come for it at once I shall write to that man who advertises in the newspaper.

Yours respectfully,

W. Fittleton.

Travers handed it back. "You may think me a bit of a fool," he said, "but I can't quite get the hang of this chest affair. Do I take it you're going to camp out for a day or two at this man Fittleton's house so as to catch Carter *in flagranti delicto?*"

Franklin shook his head.

"Now why are you worrying your head about that? I'm not going there. All I want him to do is to buy it."

"Exactly. And if he's not a fool, as soon as he's bought it he'll slip it up to London and show it to one of the big dealers. Whatever happens, I look like losing fifty pounds—until or unless you recover through the chap who buys it from Carter, and that'll be the devil of a long job."

"Don't you believe it. It'll be far easier than that," Franklin assured him, and that was all the explanation he gave—an explanation which, as far as Travers was concerned, left him just as much in the dark.

* * * * *

It was just before half-past nine when Travers arrived at the church hall, and the half-dozen cars drawn up outside showed that the company had arrived in full force. What surprised him was the size of the building. Cosmo Revere must have built with an eye on posterity rather than the present. It was lofty, too, well lighted with a modern plant, and at the back ran a kind of minstrel's gallery. Jerome Paull had apparently been putting his ideas into execution—the chairs were already arranged with a wedge-shaped aisle or gangway. The great man himself was perched on top of a tall chair in the orchestra, and on the stage some sort of argument was taking place. Everybody was talking at once. One lady was flopping despairingly into an easy chair and Leila Forteresse was shaking her fan at Haddowe, who, with sleeves rolled up, was still looking decidedly warm. On a bentwood chair sat Colonel Warren conning his part in the middle of the hubbub, while Leeke was leaning over to Paull and pointing to the wings. Travers settled into his corner feeling much like a butterfly which has alighted on a buzz-saw, and waited for things to sort themselves out.

Peace came more quickly than he had hoped, and a new scene was begun. Castleton entered, ogling the imaginary pictures, and Lydia Forteresse, having informed the empty hall in one of those impossible asides what a terrible person he was, approached the unwanted lover.

> *Absolute.* [Going towards her] Ma'am!
> *Lydia.* Oh, heavens! Beverly!
> *Absolute.* Hush! Hush! Be not surprised!

Remarkably well done, thought Travers, in spite of the stilted dialogue. And nothing gauche or nervous about it. There they were, going at it with the slickness of professionals; Lydia flirting behind her fan, and Absolute debonair and then impassioned, and finally Mrs. Malaprop showing herself in the wings. What Travers felt was the sureness of the touch. The modern clothes were no particular incongruity; they were merely unnoticed. All that one saw and heard was a pair of not too sincere but perfectly flesh-and-blood lovers. Then the broader comedy business.

> *Mrs. Malaprop.* Hold! Hold! Assurance! You shall not be so rude.
>
> *Absolute.* Nay, pray, Mrs. Malaprop, don't stop the young lady's speech; she's very welcome to talk thus; it doesn't hurt *me* in the least, I assure you.
>
> *Mrs. Malaprop.* You are too good, captain—too amiably patient; but come with me, minx. Let us see you again soon, captain; remember what we have fixed.

And so on with a bit of stage play till the imaginary curtain fell. Travers risked a tentative clap in the comparative silence, and it seemed to roar among the echoes.

"How's it going?" called Haddowe.

"Magnificently!" said Travers, then came up and was introduced all round. He stayed with Jerome Paull during one short scene, then wandered back to his corner, and before the night was out had had quite enough of it. There were oases of acting in deserts of lighting experiments and grouping and posturing, and it was midnight when it was all over.

Colonel Warren had apparently been consigned to the mercies of another member of the cast. Paull and Travers strolled back together, and behind them came Leila Forteresse and Castleton, both in good spirits, judging by the occasional laughter. On the portico steps the four of them stood chatting for a minute before saying good-night.

"You'll have a long walk back," Travers remarked to Castleton.

Castleton gave her a quick look. "Oh, I'll slip across the private path. You can easily hop over that wall."

"Well, don't break your neck," said Travers. "If you do, make sure you've left me that figure in your will."

"When are you fetching it?"

"Whenever you ask me," said Travers shamelessly.

"Come to-morrow," exclaimed the other eagerly. "Come to tea! And bring Miss Forteresse with you!" He turned to her. "I say, do come!"

"How very exciting!" was all the answer he got, but apparently he found that sufficient, for he gave a sort of: "Cheerio, everybody!" and left it at that. A few yards away the walk became a double, then the sound was lost.

* * * * *

"Sorry I'm so late," said Travers, "but I simply couldn't get away. What happened?"

"Nothing at all. Haddowe's two men didn't stir an inch. By the way, what excuse did you give Haddowe after you'd got that dud note I sent you at dinner?"

"I said a man I was going to see wasn't turning up."

"Splendid!" said Franklin, quite amused, in a way. "In other words, you cancelled out that comic message you left for Brown to see."

Travers was flabbergasted. "Good Lord! So I did. But didn't anything happen at all?"

Franklin shrugged his shoulders and made a grimace. "Not a thing, except that whichever way I went round that damned house I kept on hearing voices. Finally, I got up a tree and trained my glasses on a window where I'd seen a sort of flickering light as if a fire was in the room. So there was—and a very funny thing for a hot summer night. I couldn't even see all the fire because some sort of a table was in the way."

"What sort of a table?"

"Here! What do you think my name is? It was a table—that's all I know. Small, and rather like a table one has drinks on."

"Great pity! All your trouble for nothing. I've had a pretty dud evening, too. Everything down there open and above board, as far as I could judge. People all very charming, and so on, and that's all there was to it. Oh yes; and I'm going to tea with Castleton tomorrow—"

"Not alone!"

"Oh, Lord, no! The lady's going with me."

"Well, it's to-day you're going," said Franklin, looking at his watch. "And that reminds me. If you're buying that Ralph Wood figure will you try and buy something for me, if Castleton'll sell it?—that figure of the Parson and Clerk he's got on the top of that bureau. I rather took a fancy to it."

"It's only early Staffordshire. You ought to get it for a couple of pounds."

"Right-ho! You get it. And have you forgotten that Angéle goes to-mor—to-day?"

"I haven't. But what can I do? I've tried all I can to find out what that woman's been up to."

"Never mind," said Franklin soothingly. "I've arranged to have her met at Liverpool Street and followed right down to Sussex, and when she gets there she'll still be watched because I've got a maid planted in the house!"

Travers was delighted. "Good work! Do you know I rather thought of calling when we get back to town. That house is not so far from my sister's place."

"You haven't got back from that tea-party tomorrow yet. And don't forget to buy that figure. The parson looks rather like Haddowe!"

CHAPTER XXVI
AND EXIT ANGÉLE

TRAVERS WAS HAVING his after-breakfast cigarette with Jerome Paull on one of the seats in the rose-garden when a footman informed him that he was wanted on the phone. It was Brotherston, Hall and Brotherston ringing up, and their senior clerk speaking. Would Mr. Travers and his colleague meet Sir Henry that morning at Cambridge, as he had certain extremely confidential matters to discuss. Sir Henry would not be at the office, but was proceeding straight to Cambridge, where he would arrive shortly before eleven at the "Trensham Arms."

Travers hurried back to make his excuses to the guest, then sent for Franklin.

"It's now 9.15. Say we leave at 9.30, how long will it take Parry to get us to Cambridge?"

"He can't go," said Franklin. "He's been up all night, and must have some sleep."

"It might excite comment if I drove the car myself. How're the trains?"

They seemed to be excellent. There was a slow from Branford at 9.50, which would land them in Cambridge well before 11 o'clock. The Hall chauffeur could take them to the station. So Travers got together the papers he thought he might want, Franklin made his own preparations, and the train was caught.

"Rather interesting to think Angéle will actually be coming through Cambridge while we're there," said Travers.

"Isn't it? If the times had fitted in, I'd have been inclined to have had a peep into the carriage to see how the rheumatics were coming along. That maid's going, too—for good. Mrs. Lacy's going to let Leila Forteresse have one of the household staff as a temporary maid till she goes away herself."

"I'd like to travel down to town with the pair of 'em," said Travers. "You know, all disguised in the real detective fashion—whiskers and all."

"And I wouldn't mind going through the luggage. Wonder if Royce has checked up on the family silver?"

At the "Trensham Arms" they were dead on time. Travers inquired at the desk whether a private room had been engaged for that morning, and finding that none had, decided to save time by booking one himself and ordering lunch for three, to be served privately.

At 11.30 there was still no sign of Sir Henry, and Travers' having skimmed the cream off the morning papers, was beginning to get restless. A quarter of an hour later he made a further inquiry at the desk.

"Have you a time-table handy? I want to see the arrival trains from London."

"They're all here, sir," said the clerk, handing over a printed card. "Slow at 11, express 11.30, and slow again at 12.15."

"Ring up the station, will you? and find out if the 11.30 is in."

It *was* in, and at 12 o'clock, moreover, there was still no sign of the lawyer.

"What on earth's happened?" asked Travers anxiously. "Do you think he's come by road and met with an accident?"

"We'll soon find that out," said Franklin. "I'll try to get a trunk call through."

In five minutes he was through to Brotherston, Hall and Brotherston, and the senior clerk was called to the phone.

"Has Sir Henry started for Cambridge?"

"Cambridge, sir? We know nothing about it here."

"But didn't you call up Fenwold Hall this morning and ask Mr. Travers and myself to meet Sir Henry here?"

"No, sir. There must be some mistake. Sir Henry came to the office at ten this morning, as usual, and left a few minutes ago; but he's not going to Cambridge."

Franklin's face told Travers what was up, and the two looked at each other with expressions that were decidedly sheepish.

"Damn clever!" said Franklin.

"But if we've been lured away—"

"If! We *have I* We've been sold a pup."

"Yes, but why?"

"Just a minute. We'll look at the time-table. Here we are. Branford to Liverpool Street 9.50. That's the one we came by. 11.15; that's the one Angéle was to take. Then there's another a quarter of an hour later."

"Very short interval, surely?"

"Both call at Ely. The last one connects with trains for the north—and the Harwich boat. But I'm damned if I see the point. Why should we be lured to Cambridge?"

"May I suggest something? She travelled by her proper train—the earlier one—but changed at Ely; altered her appearance in the waiting-room—all that rheumatism was humbug—and went on to town by the second one."

"You settle the bill and cancel the lunch!" ordered Franklin, and Travers left him turning over the pages of the time-table. When he returned, Franklin had a definite plan.

"We'll go to the station first. There's a train back for you in forty minutes, and one for me to town in half an hour."

When they got hold of Ely on the phone, Travers' theory seemed to be confirmed. A youngish lady had had a bath-chair deposited in the cloak-room. She had been alone, and the description given was so vague that it seemed hopeless to try to make anything out of it. There was no information whatever about general luggage.

"Take half a day to go there and find out," said Franklin in exasperation. "They've split up for a fiver, and where they've gone, heaven knows."

"You'll know whether they get to Densham or not," suggested Travers.

Franklin treated that as it deserved. "I shall go straight to town. It won't do for both of us to be away any longer in case they've got us here for another reason, so you get back to Fenwold at once. I shall be along early in the morning—by road, probably. You might warn Royce." He glanced at the station clock. "Five minutes left. I'll try to get through to Durango House." And off he rushed again.

Whether he got through or not, Travers didn't know. He did see him sprint from the telephone-box as the guard's whistle went, and caught the wave of his hand as the train drew out. Then he went along to the refreshment-room and ordered a luncheon basket for his own train, and by the time he had settled to his corner seat in the first-class smoker, he was pretty glad of a rest.

There was a good deal to think about, too. Just why was Franklin so perturbed at losing the trail of the nurse and the French maid? After all, if both were eliminated, the general position seemed unaffected. Neither could have murdered Cosmo Revere. Both might be connected with Haddowe, but then, hadn't Franklin distinctly laid it down that he'd no time for Haddowe and his schemes, and must confine himself to the major problem? Then Travers thought he'd found the answer to that. After all, Franklin hadn't come to Cambridge of his own accord. Once he was there he was naturally interested in the seller of the pup, and why the animal had been sold. His anxiety about Angèle was simply a desire to get his own back—and a perfectly understandable exasperation at having planned out—and to no purpose—to have her watched across London and into her new home.

Then came a short attack of despondency. All that time spent over that woman and very little really done. It was an extraordinarily anomalous and hampered position that he and Franklin occupied, and Franklin was affected more than himself. Nobody could be openly questioned; nobody could be given the least suspicion that anything was wrong, and the law could never be called in for assistance. At all costs and whatever the other side knew, their own isolation—a futile isolation—had to be maintained.

Suppose that as soon as he got back he could confront the Forteresse woman? But then, what would be the good of that? Why let her know that he had the faintest suspicion? Then he fell to wondering what Angèle could have been doing in the Hall those long months. What remunerative and certainly crooked work of the kind he'd suspected of Haddowe? Was she really crippled and levying a sort of blackmail in comfortable convalescence? Impossible! The woman was a fraud if ever there was one. Then how could she have spent her time? What could *any* woman do with herself? Knit? Sew? Certainly unremunerative and hardly surreptitious. Write? Then what about? Draw? Sketch? Paint? . . . And just then the train ran into Ely, and Travers had his head out of the window and was beckoning frantically to a porter.

He got a sheet of paper out of his case and wrote a telegram. The man's eyes opened at the size of the tip, and so important did the telegram seem that he watched the porter into the office before resuming his seat—and his lunch.

Even then it wasn't long before he started wondering again. What exactly was Franklin up to with that chest? Why was he being so contradictory in his explanations—and even enigmatical? If he wasn't at Byford, how could he get hold of Carter and make him talk? That was as far as he got, and the only thing to do was to possess his soul in patience till Franklin's return. But one thing he did know. Whichever way one looked for the rumblings of thunder that echoed all round Fenwold, always in the distance there seemed to be the formidable figure of Haddowe.

It was half-past three when he got back to the Hall. As he recognised, his attitude towards Leila Forteresse would have to be unaltered—merely a courteous and possibly enamoured blandness. There was, of course, the outside chance that she was far from fully informed. Haddowe might have acted behind her back. But his first greeting was designed to parry her own attack.

"You're looking extraordinarily fit!"

She smiled. "Am I really? Not one of those robust women? Don't tell me that!"

"Why not—if it's true? How's Angéle getting along these days, by the way?"

"But she's gone! She went this morning!"

"How perfectly unpardonable of me! So she did. And I didn't see her before she went."

Informed or not, she carried it off remarkably well, and her voice had the exact shades of solicitude and patronage.

"Poor darling! She was dreadfully distressed. One does get so attached to places! I do hope she has a comfortable journey. There ought to be a telegram to-night." Then very abruptly: "Shall we take my car—or walk?"

"Walk, I think, don't you?" And for his own malicious amusement: "One can't be too careful to avoid scandal!"

The tea itself, very dainty and most informal, doesn't matter. Castleton laid himself out to be his fascinating best, and Travers amused himself by interpreting innuendoes, tracking down allusions and following the direction of glances. With himself his host was effusive and even ingratiating, and there was much mention of books, particularly his own—a most uncomfortable business for one so modest as their author. Outside in the garden it was difficult for him to maintain his fatherly air. Was the body of Westfield really lying under those plants and stones? And didn't it look as if there'd been more alterations?

"Rock-garden not finished yet?" he asked.

"It's the fault of that man of yours," explained Castleton. "He put the idea into my head of bringing it right down here, practically to the door; you know—all terraced."

"He's a keen gardener is Francis. But why don't you put it off till September? Isn't that supposed to be the month for all that sort of thing?"

"You see the trouble is, I shall probably be away then. I may have to go visiting," and he flashed a glance at Leila Forteresse.

Travers was glad when they'd got away from that rock-garden. At any moment he felt likely to betray himself. Indoors again, he bought his Ralph Wood figure, a pair of Spode plates and Franklin's Parson and Clerk; all the business, of course, very off-hand and mildly apologetic and quite in the nature of favours mutually conferred—at least, that is how it must have appeared to the third party.

And lastly, there were two other things Travers thought he might with confidence report. At some time there had certainly been a very definite understanding between the couple, and at the moment it was infinitely more ardent on Castleton's side than on hers.

* * * * *

One most important thing did, however, arise out of that visit to Oak Cottage, since all that talk about books gave Travers an idea, and determined, indeed, the manner in which he spent the remainder of the evening. The allusion was to the buying of first editions as an investment, and that was why Travers shut himself up in the library, and told Royce to see he was on no account to be disturbed.

The trouble was, of course, that if Haddowe had removed any books of value from the library, why hadn't they been missed, and how were the losses to be traced? The indexes he found were lamentably out of date, and the last one seemed to have been compiled in the 'nineties. Still, he wrestled with the available material before dinner and got little satisfaction out of it.

Then he tried another line of approach. It was hopeless to tackle thousands of volumes. Why not have a general look round among what was still left to see what might have been purloined? An hour of that produced results which even the grubby and laborious search could scarcely have merited.

What he had found were ten volumes in all. Of these seven were discarded as affording no real clue. The remaining three told a story that could be plainly read. Take their names and bindings: *Tom Jones*, 1783, leather; *Hudibras*, 1709, leather; *Pilgrim's*

Progress, 1706, original cloth. Their value was a matter of shillings; their value as clues was enormous. In all three were traces of labels that had been removed with just that infinitesimal amount of slovenliness that made all the difference; in two a red tab, in the other a green; and all three shrieking with most audible voice to so keen a collector as Travers that they had been purchased in Charing Cross Road—two from Messrs. X. and the other from Messrs. Y.

As Travers lay in bed that night he was not at all displeased with himself, and life once more had its compensations. What seemed definitely to have emerged was this. In the library had been a few first editions, whose value ran into thousands of pounds. Haddowe had taken them and substituted for them early editions whose bindings and appearance generally would attract no attention. And Haddowe had been as safe as houses. Even if Cosmo Revere had once been a reader or a browser among books of that kind, his last hobby—sedulously fostered, moreover, by Haddowe — had absorbed his interests and used his available leisure. Then, too, strangers or casual sightseers had never been tolerated in the Hall, and no dealer, however princely or disguised, had ever set eyes on its contents.

*   *   *   *   *

He was awakened by Franklin's tap on the door, and surprised at the lateness of the hour—well past eight.

"Hallo! Where did you spring from?"

"Left town before five," said Franklin. "My God! What a day!"

"I expect it was. How'd you get on?"

"Get on!" He tossed his head. "We tried Sussex and Harwich and later trains—and, of course, nothing happened. Why should it? All the time I knew we had no chance. For all we know, that woman's looking at the moment like a flapper and hopping about like a two-year-old. I ask you; what a hope!"

Travers agreed. A needle in a haystack was nothing to it.

"One thing we did find out. I sent along a man hotfoot to Ely and he traced the luggage. It went away with two ladies by private car from there. Of course, the damn fool of a porter didn't remember the number of the car—or its make. And that's all we know about the elusive Angéle. My God! didn't I curse that woman!"

"I hate to ask it," said Travers, "but why exactly are you so anxious to find the lady? I mean, how is she so frightfully important? Nobody seemed to care tuppence-about her while she was here—except perhaps my kindly-disposed self—and now she's gone she's an absolute furore!"

In spite of the banter in the reply, Travers could sense a certain closing-up; a desire to beg the question.

"Am I an octopus? Did I have time to worry about her? But if you do want to know, I don't care a cuss where she's gone. But if she was perfectly normal in her going, then that wasn't the reason we were decoyed away. For all we know, her method of going away may have been arranged beforehand: after all, we didn't need to be lured to Cambridge for that. Perhaps I'm a bit involved. The crux of the matter is this. If Haddowe lured us away, then it was probably for a reason to do with the Haddowe-Forteresse-Angéle group. If he didn't, then it's much more serious. Instead of being squib business for you, it's murder business for me."

Travers nodded. "I take it, then, you've definitely dissociated Haddowe from the murder?"

"Who says so?"

"Well, you've just implied it. Also, you said everything depends on whether Carter buys that chest!"

Franklin smiled forbearingly.

"Let's get this perfectly clear. All I've *guaranteed* to you and myself is that Carter and Castleton are, or have been, allies. But why should that stop Haddowe being an additional ally? You suspect Haddowe of removing what we might call antiques. Who else could handle them—and dispose of them—like Castleton or Carter? Haddowe maligned Castleton to you—isn't that suspicious in itself? He didn't know Carter; all the more reason to assume he did know him—and only too well."

"Give it up!" said Travers, with mock despair, and began his own account of the previous afternoon.

"And there's a job for you this morning," he concluded. "I wired Charlton-Powers from Ely, and he's coming along during church service. I'd like you to be here if you can manage it."

"Suit me all right."

"What's worrying me is how the Forteresse woman can be got out of the way. Royce can fix up Brown."

"I'll try to think of something," said Franklin; "but I must slip off now and see Potter. That further alteration to the rock-garden looks very bad. What time's your man due?"

"Just before eleven—by the back road." And as Franklin was opening the door: "Oh, just a moment. I knew there was something else. I have an idea Brown or somebody's been in this room. I've lost my chequebook!"

Franklin raised his eyebrows.

"You don't say so! Anything else gone? And if you remember, you had it last night."

"I know I did. That's the annoying part. I don't seem to have lost anything else."

Franklin raised a dramatic hand. "Hold hard a minute. You're a casual sort of bloke. Didn't I see you stuff it in this drawer?"

He rummaged for a moment.

"Here it is all the time! You know, you're the sort of chap who'll get mislaid for his own funeral."

"That's funny! How the devil did it get there?"

Franklin shrugged his shoulders.

CHAPTER XXVII
ANOTHER OF THE FINE ARTS

BY A WONDERFUL stroke of luck Leila Forteresse solved her own problem that morning by going to church. As she explained to Travers, not without a certain wistfulness, it was her last Sunday in Fenwold.

"I wish I'd known half an hour ago," said Travers unblushingly. "I might have arranged to go, too. It's *my* last Sunday, you know."

"How exciting! Don't say, you dear man, that you're going to town with me!"

"Unfortunately no," sighed Travers. "That is if you still adhere to going on Friday. Mr. Grant should arrive then, and naturally I must see him before handing over things. How did Angéle stand the journey?"

The question was sufficiently sudden to cause some hesitation.

"Oh, very exhausted, poor darling, when she got to town; so Elise—I trust her enormously; so nice, don't you think, to have people like that?—made her stay with friends over the week-end. Now I must simply fly! Don't forget we're lunching together!"

*   *   *   *   *

Charlton-Powers was met by Franklin and escorted upstairs by way of the side door.

"Sorry to be so mysterious," said Travers, "but it all has to be so desperately secret. All I'm afraid is that I've dragged you down on a fool's errand. The mad idea is that certain objects of value—pictures in particular—have been removed from the Hall, and what we want you to do is make a rapid examination. It's possible some furniture has been taken, though I don't see how for the moment."

"Theft or substitution?"

"To tell you the truth, I don't know. We're hoping you'll find out."

Few things in life are more fascinating than watching a man who is master of his job; there is in it, too, an amazing levelling of classes, as the navvy finds when he swings his hammer in Mayfair. Of course, if you are partially informed, all the greater the admiration; at least, that is how Travers felt in the presence of Charlton-Powers. All Franklin could do was listen and try to understand.

Imagine the long galleries of Fenwold Hall, like an E that has lost its middle prong; the line of three hundred feet or so running east and west and the shorter galleries cutting back from each end. Imagine the walls crammed with pictures, and furniture everywhere between the windows or beneath them; at the western end the rooms occupied by Travers, and at the other those of Leila Forteresse; each with its separate and subsidiary staircase.

Imagine, too, Charlton-Powers in yellowish tweeds; an inconspicuous, paterfamilias sort of man, bald-headed and with a straggly moustache, becoming more and more excited every minute. He would screw his eye-glass in with such facial contortion that the effort appeared more in the nature of an operation; then he would glare, then down the glass would flop and remain dangling until it had to be brought into play again. As for expecting him to limit himself to pictures—as well turn a hungry horse into a clover-field and request him to confine himself to plants with four leaves.

The running commentary was something like this:

"Both James the First. . . . Pity those brasses are new. . . . No, I should call it Queen Anne. I don't think it's a transition piece. . . . William and Mary. Notice the gate supports. . . . Curious to find a French piece here! . . . No use for Pembroke tables, have you? . . . Don't like that fluting on the legs. Wonder where the urns and pedestals of that sideboard are? . . . Why *did* they put those heavy tops on walnut bureaux?"

Travers soon learned to answer no questions and make no suggestions, and that was after his allusion to a pair of seventeenth-century pewter alms-dishes as "plates" and his failure to recognise a prune-blossom vase as Ming. Even allowing for the fact that such work had been Charlton-Powers' bread and butter for a lifetime, and that he had an enormous flair for it, still the exhibition was an amazing one. In would go the eye-glass and up would come a porcelain bowl. "Mark of Hsun Te," and a grunt. Or it might be a pair of vases. "K'ang Hsi, but rather uncommon," or, "Remarkably fine Bristol, that. Any family connection at all?"

His most joyful discovery and biggest disappointment came together, and that was when he caught sight of the Chippendale knee-hole writing-desk. He made a bee-line for it, halted, and let the monocle drop. Then he frowned and ran the tips of his fingers over it. "What a pity! So distressing to see reproductions here."

But time was going on, and Travers induced him to concentrate on the pictures. The monocle was now more or less permanent and the commentary thus.

"I suppose there are more portraits in the downstairs rooms? . . . Can't mistake those bulbous women. . . . H'm' Reynolds, but much too simpering. . . . A very early Hogarth, don't you think? . . . Francis Cotes. Worth an awful lot of money one of these days. . . . Wardour Street stuff! . . . Look at that magnificent fore-shortening—but the design! . . . Richard Wilson. . . . Wonder what that is?" This last a very refreshing remark.

The interesting disappointment was before a quiet Dutch interior—a woman surveying herself in a bed-room mirror.

"I'd have sworn that was Vermeer! Would you mind if I twisted the frame?"

This time the monocle was not enough; a powerful glass came out of his breast pocket. Ten seconds were enough.

"There's one of your copies," and he waved his hand contemptuously. "What about these? . . . Canaletto. H'm! . . . Lely again. Curious mixture those Reveres must have been! . . . Crome, and the Yare by moon-light by the look of it." Then again the pause. "But is it?"

To bring the matter to an end, there seemed to be in that gallery alone, and of easily accessible pictures alone, extraordinarily good copies of a Piero di Cosimo, two Cromes, a Vermeer, a Hobbema, a small Rembrandt of the exterior of a tavern, and an Antonio Mori.

"Anything in the bedrooms?"

"Heaps," said Travers. "But there's only time for a quick look."

The bedrooms, one of which had been used as a spare drawing-room, gave even more evidence. Four Chippendale chairs were reproductions, as were a bureau and a side-table.

"What I can't understand," said the expert, "is why there *are* reproductions. You see the monogram—T.C.—just below that scroll? Chippendale signed like that is, as far as my experience goes, quite unique. The value of the originals must have been enormous—and there must have been originals here some time or other."

"A fire, perhaps. Some of the originals destroyed and the reproductions made to replace them."

"That's an excellent idea. What I rather thought of was that a daughter took some on her marriage, and these reproductions were made to keep the sets complete. Surely there must have been in the Hall at some time or other a complete signed set of that Chippendale?"

"Just a minute," said Travers, consulting his watch anxiously. "John, you take that parcel of books down to the garage and tell Royce on the way that we've been called away to lunch. We'll push off to Branford and continue the inquest there. I'll tell you what I want you to do about those books on the way."

Half an hour later over a lunch for three at the "Angel," the conversation was resumed.

"What was your idea of the place generally?" asked Travers.

"Stupendous! It's a museum. Badly lighted and disgracefully arranged, but still—a museum."

"What's a rough valuation?"

"My dear fellow, I saw nothing—not a single downstair room. Say half a million pounds worth. In any case, figures are fantastic; prices depend on so many things."

Travers went over the whole story and the picture he painted was a romantic one; Angéle, crippled for the purposes of her airing, then coming to life and painting away day in and day out—a twentieth century Lady of Shalott. Then the smuggling in of canvas and panels and materials and the smuggling out by the pseudo-doctor—or perhaps the great smuggling out that had taken place the day before at Angéle's departure. No risk of course of immediate discovery, and if the discovery were one day made that Fenwold Hall possessed a considerable number of what looked like copies, who was to know that it ever possessed the originals?

"Would you call the forgeries well done?" he asked.

"Excellently! Whoever this woman was she knew her job. I don't know if you read any reports of that exhibition of fakes Sir Robert Witt had at the Burlington, but he definitely stated that cracks and abrasures could be so skilfully imitated that differences were actually made between say, fifteenth and seventeenth century wear-marks. This woman of yours certainly did the painting, but most of the seasoning must have been done outside. If you like I can take one away and find out exactly when and how it was done!"

"That's good of you," said Travers, "but I'm afraid Mr. Grant will have to inherit that investigation along with the rest of the property. What would the value of those Chippendale pieces be, supposing there were a full set?"

"Heaven knows! Thousands and thousands."

"What would be a perfect set?"

Charlton-Powers smiled. "Impossible to say. Purely a matter for the taste of the man who had them made. By the way, where on earth did the Revere family make all their money?"

"I don't know exactly. You must remember they've had the devil of a time to do it in. I believe one of them got out of the South Sea Bubble before it burst. Also there've been some remarkably good marriages—and they've all been quiet livers; no squandermania or anything like that. They say the world's a small place, but here's an instance of England's being a large one, because I never heard the name mentioned in any—what we might call munificent connection till the eve of the day we came here. All I do know is, we mustn't have the least suspicion of scandal. That's why the whole thing's such a nightmare."

"Only one nightmare for me," sighed the other, "and that's not being able to spend a week there."

"Why shouldn't you? I'll speak to Mr. Grant when he comes, and he'll jump at calling you in for investigation."

That, of course, sent Charlton-Powers on his way rejoicing. But just as his car was moving off, Travers had a last question to ask.

"I suppose there'd be no difficulty about a market for those things we discussed?"

"Market! My dear chap; not a thing is catalogued. I only wish I'd nobbled them myself!"

Travers laughed. "Well, you'll get your chance next week. Don't forget those books."

* * * * *

"There we are," said Travers as the car started back for Fenwold. "The squib looks like going off. Those books ought to be reported on by Tuesday, and the picture question's settled up to the necessary point. The furniture I'm not so sure about. If Haddowe was responsible for those reproductions, how did he get them smuggled into the Hall—or the originals out?"

"Just what I've been wondering," said Franklin. "Haddowe might have enticed Cosmo Revere away—to the dolmens for instance—but Royce was there all the time, and he's incorruptible. And what about the gaps in the walls while the originals were absent? If the abstraction and the substitution took place at the same time, that makes it twice as difficult."

"It's beyond me," said Travers. "Best thing we can do is report it to Grant as soon as he arrives and let him make his own decisions. In any case my side looks like being finished—if he's getting here on Friday."

"I'll still keep on the look-out for Angéle. If we get hold of a single picture it'll be evidence enough. Also if that Forteresse woman leaves the Hall, I'll take good care *she* doesn't vanish."

"Don't think you need worry about her," Travers assured him. "She'll hang on for that show of theirs. And how about you? Any chance of anything definite by Friday?"

Franklin suddenly looked extraordinarily serious. He hesitated so long over his answer that it almost looked as if he was afraid of committing himself.

"I can't say. If the chest is sold—perhaps yes."

"You and that chest—"

Franklin nodded his head rather wearily. "Yes, I know. But many a small worm has landed a devilish big fish." He rubbed his hands together nervously. "If I wanted to boast I should say that if human nature is what we've always supposed it to be, then this time next week you and I will be back in town."

Travers polished his glasses and thought it all over.

"Why's Parry driving us?" he suddenly asked.

"His job's over—and Potter went back to town to-day."

"You mean to say—Westfield's been found!"

"That's it. Your suspicion about that rock-garden was right. The body was removed early this morning."

"Good God! . . . I say, how perfectly bloody!" Neither said a word for a good minute. Franklin sat with a queer frown on his face, squinting out of the window. Travers was moistening his lips nervously. The car slowed down.

"Here we are," said Franklin. "If you don't mind going in on your own, Parry and I will go round with the car. I've got a—er—man I must go and see."

*　*　*　*　*

"Look up Long Fordham, Parry, while I go and telephone," said Franklin. "When we do start, I want you to slip her along."

They slipped along to such purpose that the twenty miles were done in half an hour—and country lanes at that. Long Fordham Hall was a modern and unpretentious building, well back from the road. Franklin was evidently expected. At the first mention of his name he was shown into a kind of library-workroom, where an alert looking man with snow-white moustache rose at his entrance and held out his hand. Franklin began his introduction, but found it unnecessary.

"We're not so benighted that we don't read the papers," smiled Major Iddesdon. "Let me get you a drink. I hope it's nothing serious you want to see me about?"

"I'm afraid it is, sir. And if you'll pardon the expression it's the Chief Constable of the County I have to see and not the owner of Long Fordham Hall. Also I can tell you only part of a story, and I'd like you to listen to that from my point of view."

The other frowned. "I'm afraid I don't altogether understand you, but do I gather that you want to see me officially and wish to lay down conditions?"

Franklin smiled. "Not at all. I just want you to put yourself in my place. If you do that, I'm sure you'll agree to the rest. Now; do you remember a day or two ago a man named Westfield being missing from the village of Fenwold? And being applied to for an application to be made to London for an S.O.S.?"

"Yes."

"I was behind that application. I now know that Westfield has been murdered. Outside in my car is the man who knows where the body is."

"And where is that?"

"Under two feet of earth in a dried-up pool on the heath that lies between the Byford and Branford roads, going out of Fenwold. Here's a map and here's the spot."

"Hm! And who's watching it?"

"Nobody. That's the last thing in the world I want done That's why I want you to put yourself in my place If you like I'll tell you the whole story."

CHAPTER XXVIII
FRANKLIN IS FRIGHTENED

FRANKLIN WAS UP very early the following morning and before he saw Travers—well over three hours later—no less than three things had to be done. Of those three things, two were mentioned but not explained; the third Franklin kept to himself. One was a clue that suggested itself in the car the previous evening, and which became on the Monday a very spasmodic affair in its following up, since it was chronologically mixed with the other two.

How it arose was like this. Parry had been instructed to take his time on the homeward journey and Franklin sat with the landscape in the back of his mind and the case in the front of it. As he thought things over, he came to those pieces of charred papier-mâché—puzzled over an explanation, then dismissed them from his mind. Then when his review was over he smiled to himself at the thought of Travers and his squib. The sequence then was completed in a matter of seconds and of its own accord. Squib—bonfire—rockets—Guy Fawkes—and, "Good Lord! I wonder. Surely not!" In other words, had those pieces of charred paper once been masks? the sort of thing urchins amused themselves with on November the Fifth?

That was why, after events that have not yet been related, Franklin delayed his stay in Branford till the shops were open. Unfortunately for his brand new theory, he might as well have returned to Fenwold. Neither of the toy-shops could give him the slightest information. All the same he certainly knew the charred fragments *had* once been masks. When he'd examined them before he had had no theory to which to attach them, whereas after the morning's examination he wondered how on earth he hadn't thought of it at once.

But why should they have been bought it in Branford? After all there was no particular secrecy needed. Why not try the general stores at Fenwold?

"Something rather silly I want to buy if you have it," he told the old lady in the cluttered-up shop as he took the packet of tobacco. "It's for my young nephew. I suppose you haven't got a mask? The sort of thing boys like to wear on Guy Fawkes' Day?"

"I did have some," she said, "but I sold all I had out. Young Willie Mews bought all the lot I'd left." She gave a call to the back of the shop. "Polly! How many of them masks did you sell to young Willie Mews?"

Her daughter poked her head round the back room door.

"Five, mother. You know there were five 'cause we let him have them cheap."

Franklin smiled. "That'd be *after* November the Fifth."

"Nearly Christmas, wasn't it, mother?"

"I say, don't worry. I just promised my young nephew I'd get him one if I could. You know what boys are!"

"That I do, sir. I've had six of my own."

"Have you really! Well, thank you very much. If I happen to run across this boy Mews, he might have one he hasn't destroyed."

"He ain't likely to do that, sir!"

Franklin agreed. All the same he stopped round the corner where a dozen urchins were squabbling over cricket.

"Can you tell me where Willie Mews is?"

"This is him, sir!" came a couple of voices at once.

There was no point in talking to the boy privately; that would have made him nervous and added a mystery which he wanted to avoid. All he did was to produce a sixpence and state a case, and with a remarkably friendly face. Once more there was nothing doing.

"Well, you may as well have the sixpence all the same. It's for the whole lot of you mind you, so you'll have to share out. Is that why you bought all those masks? Some for all these chaps here?"

Another boy vouchsafed the information.

"Mr. Carter give him the money, sir, and he had 'em. He give Willie twopence for hisself."

"That was very good of him," said Franklin. "Well, don't squabble over that sixpence. Have a committee meeting and make up your minds what you're going to buy."

*   *   *   *   *   *

To go back to the hour of seven the same morning, when the Chief Constable arrived at Branford and a doctor with him.

"Parry knows just where to go," said Franklin as they changed cars. "It's rather a tricky road."

On that August morning the heath was at its best. The bracken stood in clumps like an immense fernery six feet and more in height and breaking up the green were patches of heather or sunken pools, overhung with silver birches. In the distance were darker masses of pine woods and in the far distance mists that announced a day of intense heat.

Parry turned the car abruptly into a grass flat between two stretches of bracken and slowed down behind a straggly larch hedge where the car would be invisible from the road.

"Keep well out of the bracken, Parry," admonished Franklin. "We don't want to get wet to the knees."

A wide detour, keeping well under cover, and they halted on the edge of a hollow whose sides were a vivid green and bottom a dry, drab brown.

"Leave the spade, Parry, and go on ahead to the road. Give a whistle if you think anybody's coming."

He glanced at his companions, then moved down slowly to the bottom of the dried pool. The bank made a sudden and unusual shelving and the soil had been disturbed in the shade of the tall bracken that grew to its very edge.

"That's where he is, major," said Franklin quietly. "Do you see what a spot it is? A good day's rain and the pool's half full again. No rabbit digger would ever be likely to have to disturb the soil here. If Parry hadn't chanced his arm and cut through the park on his bicycle, Westfield might have slept till judgment day."

"The soil hasn't been moved since?" asked the doctor.

"Look at it. Last night's gossamers everywhere." He shook his head. "I don't think the man responsible for this'll want to come here again. Of course, if you'd prefer somebody on guard at night, major?"

"I think there'd better be somebody. The body will have to be produced, even if we don't want it produced prematurely. We're doing something that's highly irregular, so we hadn't better take any more risks."

"Irregular or not, we know it's necessary. Produce that body a moment too soon and I can guarantee nothing."

Franklin turned the earth back and the doctor made his brief examination. There was merely a slight turning over of the body and then he got to his feet again and brushed his knees.

"What was it, doctor? Skull smashed?"

"Knife—probably—in the back." He glanced at Iddesdon.

"I don't think I'd better say any more. He's certainly dead enough."

"You identify him all right?" asked Iddesdon. Franklin nodded.

"Then we'd better get him covered up again before we're found here. You're sure the disturbance won't be noticed?"

"The sun'll dry up everything in an hour," said Franklin. "Just let me smooth down that top."

"I'm exceedingly grateful to you, sir," were his last words at Branford. "As I told you, I want no public recognition in this case. If I have to give evidence at the inquest—well, I have to, but I tell you frankly, I'd rather not. You have the body officially exhumed at 7.30 on Thursday evening, and I'll have the parties in your hands before midnight. If anything goes wrong I'll let you know."

Franklin's last journey was to Byford, where the car was left just short of the village. As soon as Fittleton showed him into the parlour he knew something had happened.

"I see you've sold the chest!"

"That's right, sir; Mr. Carter come along last night."

"Sunday, eh? Tell me all about it."

"Well sir, he come along—the missis was out as it happened—and asked me if he could see it, so I took him upstairs on the landing. 'It ain't much good,' he says, and has a look at it. 'What do you want for it?' he says. 'What'll you give me?' I says, and he says, 'Five pounds, and it ain't worth that. Look at the state it's in.' 'State or not,' I says, 'I want fifteen quid for it.' And then we argues and argues and then we bargained at eight pound ten."

"Jolly good business! And he took it away?"

"Took it away at once, sir. He got me to put my old mare in the cart and I drove him right home with it. We was just a-gettin' it inside the gate round to the back when—do you know, sir, I'd allust heerd old Carter was a rum sort of chap, but if you ask me I should say he's dotty!"

"Dotty! Why?"

"Well, we'd just got it sort of half round the corner when all at once he grabs hold of me, sir, and pulls me down behind the hedge. 'Don't make a sound!' he says. 'That's Castleton's goin' by and I don't want him to know I'm about,' and he clutched hold o' me sir as if we was two boys inside an orchard. Then Mr. Castleton he stopped a minute and had a look at the mare and cart, and when he'd gone on again, old Carter he didn't half let rip." The old farmer's voice became hoarsely confidential. "He swore he'd do him in!"

"Did he! He'll have to be careful what he's saying. Did you tell Mr. Castleton?"

"Not I, sir. It weren't my place."

"Then take my tip and don't. Keep everything to yourself. If you get into any trouble—which you certainly won't do—I'll be responsible. Forget the chest was ever in your house—and don't let your wife know too much. Did Carter pay you all right?"

Fittleton handed over the money—eight pound ten in notes. Franklin insisted on leaving behind a substantial tip, and made his gratitude perfectly clear, though once more he was careful to urge implicit secrecy. He carried the affair moreover to a logical conclusion by looking in at Carter's cottage on his way to the village shop. It was shut up. Travers' gloomy prophecy looked like being true. Carter had apparently had on hand a ready customer for his purchase and had gone off to conclude the deal. But for the previous day being Sunday, he'd probably have gone then.

*　*　*　*　*　*

When Franklin left the gang of boys—already quarrelling over the spending of the sixpence—he strolled on towards the Lodge, then cut through the hedge and found a shady spot under a tree on the edge of the park. As he stoked his pipe and sat stolidly puffing away, it was hard to believe he was alone. All sorts of expressions ran across his face. Every now and then he would frown or nod his head or pucker up his eyes as if trying to hear a speaker who was laboriously stating a case in the invisible background.

Had his thoughts been audible, some might have seemed ironical. The masks presumably—he hadn't dared press the question—had been still exposed for sale in the shop. Suppose then Carter were asked why he'd bought them. What might his answer be? Probably this. Weren't there politicians who won the favour of voters by kissing their offspring? Why then shouldn't he try to get a potential seller into a coming-on disposition by offering a timely gift to a small son of the house? Nothing unusual about that except the shrewdness of the foresight. And if Carter had found his bribery of no particular use, and had had the masks left on his hands, why shouldn't he have burnt the trumpery bribes when he got rid of the rest of his cottage rubbish?

What else he was thinking was not apparent from his expression, but when he got up to go he had smoked more matches than tobacco, and as soon as he got back to the Hall he hunted up Travers.

"We uncovered the body this morning. The Chief Constable was there, but we're not acting for a bit till I'm sure."

"Poor chap!" said Travers. "The same damnable trick?"

"Knife in the back. Once they got him there it wouldn't be necessary to go through all that performance in the tree. Fittleton's sold the hutch, by the way. We've got Carter just where we want him."

"But suppose he bolts?"

"He won't bolt. Carter isn't different from any other man. It's all a question of human nature."

Travers asked no more questions. What Franklin had to say he'd say in his own time, and if he said nothing, there'd be good reason for the reticence.

"Now I want you to do something extraordinarily important. It may seem to you foolish—personally I don't think so. You remember what I told you the other day. You and I are the only ones who know how Revere was killed. Westfield let out that he knew something and he's paid for it, and while you and I keep together we're running the same risk. Honestly I'm scared. I know—I can feel it— that things are coming to a crisis and it's going to be touch and go with the pair of us unless we separate. What I propose is this. Send for Royce and arrange with him that you're supposed to be away. If you don't like that, stay in and don't see anybody from outside. Do all your work in your own room."

"Right-ho! If you think it's necessary it's good enough for me. But I don't see how I'm to go away altogether."

"I've been thinking," said Franklin. "There's no real necessity for that. I must be here myself for at least to-day and if I get away to-morrow that'll set you free again."

"Something important on?"

"Very! Got to see if Carter was at that sale last week—and where his van is. And heaps of other things. You sure you don't mind being cooped up for a bit?"

Travers laughed. "Good Lord, no! I've got heaps to do I suppose,; by the way, and talking perfectly seriously, we're in no danger of being poisoned?"

Franklin smiled. "Don't think so—unless Carter's a friend of the cook."

Half an hour later, Franklin was in his favourite chair in the butler's parlour, drawing away at his pipe and occasionally at a tankard that stood at his elbow. After lunch he would have to be off again, and where exactly would be the best place to start he was in the act of considering when Royce came in.

"Oh, here you are then. Mr. Castleton's asking to see Mr. Travers. I said he was away. Would you like to see him yourself?"

"Where is he, Mr. Royce?"

"In the library."

Franklin pondered for a moment or two, then, "Perhaps I'd better," and followed the butler out.

"Good morning," said Castleton. "Royce tells me Mr. Travers is away. Can you tell me when he'll be back?"

"He certainly can't be back before to-morrow morning, sir."

Castleton gave a click of annoyance.

"I say; how very exasperating! Where is he, do you know? Can I get hold of him?"

"I very much doubt if you can, sir. But he's returning definitely to-morrow."

Castleton picked up his gloves and moved slowly towards the door like a man in deep thought. Franklin was in the act of ushering him out, when he appeared to make up his mind.

"Look here. Could you see me yourself for a moment or two to-night?" He pulled out a letter and glanced at it. "Say eight-thirty sharp. Do you know the back room at the 'Stag'?"

"Yes, sir."

"Can you meet me there?"

"Yes, sir. I'll be there. At half-past eight you said, sir," and he drew back to let the other pass.

CHAPTER XXIX
FRANKLIN IS TENDER-HEARTED

As FRANKLIN SAT in the back room of the "Stag," waiting for Castleton to put in an appearance, there was more than one thing that was worrying him, and worrying him pretty seriously. Why exactly had Castleton wanted so urgently to see Travers? Merely to spy out the land? And what had been his object in asking himself to come down to the village? Surely there couldn't be any thought of an attempt against his life? The "Stag" was far too public a place for that. And what would be the use of killing one and leaving the other? Now if Travers had been in and Castleton had asked *both* of them to come and see him at Oak Cottage, then there'd have been something to be suspicious of.

Whatever answers he found, he was very wide of the mark, as he discovered within two minutes of Castleton's entering the room.

"Will you have a drink, sir?" he asked, picking up his own glass of bitter.

"No really, thanks. I'm in a desperate hurry. Been gardening all the evening and keeping an eye out for that uncle of yours."

The grey flannel trousers and white cricket shirt looked delightfully cool, but the shoes were decidedly dirty.

"What's he been up to now, sir?"

"To tell you the truth," said Castleton, his voice lowered to a whisper, "I think he's really gone mad!"

"Good lord, sir! You don't say so!"

"What do you think he's doing?"

"No idea, sir."

"Up in the trees at the bottom of my garden. He's been there two nights running. He's watching my house!"

"I say, that's a funny thing to do, sir."

"I know it is. And it's worse than you think. He's got a gun up there, waiting for a chance to shoot me. I saw the light shining on the barrel!"

"But why should he want to shoot *you*, sir?"

"I tell you the man's mad. I've given him notice—sent him a registered letter; also he thinks he's got a grievance against me. He's your uncle, isn't he? Come and see him. See if he'll listen to reason from you."

Franklin shook his head slowly. "I don't see that that'd do much good, sir—if he's mad."

"Then come along and lend me a hand to get hold of him! I'm almost sure he's up there now."

"Well, what can I do, sir?"

"Do! Plenty. Are you all alone?"

"I might get somebody from the Hall to help, sir."

"There's no time for that!" exclaimed Castleton impatiently. "And we don't want strangers butting in." He seemed to be thinking desperately. "You and I can do it. Earlier in the evening I put my car down the drive just in front of the middle gate. You know my garden, do you?"

Franklin nodded.

"If he bolts we can chase him. You come along in five minutes," he rose and looked at his watch, "and sneak up by the private road as far as that middle gate and then stop there. I'll slip along now up to my bedroom, and as soon as I make sure he's there, I'll flash a light three or four times. As soon as I do that, you wave a handkerchief, to let me know you're there. When he sees that light he'll be bound to bolt down from the tree. You stand fast and I'll come out in case he comes my way. If he drops near you, you collar him. Is that all right?"

"That's all right, sir."

"We must get this right, you know," said Castleton, earnestly. "Would you mind going over it yourself to make sure you've got it correctly?"

But as soon as Castleton had left the room, Franklin stood irresolute. He frowned, stared at the ceiling and waved his hands helplessly, like a man in the very devil of a hole. Then he pulled out an old envelope, ripped it up and wrote a hasty message. In the bar only one man was sitting.

"Evening, landlord. Give me an envelope, will you?"

"What sort, sir?"

"Any old sort," said Franklin hastily. "I'm in the devil of a hurry." The landlord looked at him, then fetched the envelope.

"Sorry I was a bit rude," said Franklin and hurried out. He put his message in the envelope, and addressed it and wrote on it "Urgent." The first person he met was a village youth.

"Do you want to earn five shillings? If so, run with this letter to the Hall and give it to Mr. Royce, the butler. Do you know him?"

"Yes, sir."

"Here's your money. Cut across the park and run like hell!"

"My God! What a gamble!" thought Franklin. But surely! surely they couldn't do anything, whoever they were. What point in killing him and leaving Travers? Then a sudden realisation sent a queer movement down his spine. Was *he* to be done in first and Travers—told some extraordinary lie or other about his absence—to be caught unawares?

All that was a matter of seconds, then the panicking was over. There might be a way out. But he'd have to go—there was no avoiding that.

Just short of the gate he took off his waistcoat under cover of the hedge. Then he took off his socks, did his shoes up again, cautiously climbed over the road gate, and moved along gingerly in the dark. He stretched out his hand till he touched the middle gate, knelt bolt upright by the post and squinted through the bars.

In front of him, not ten yards from the gate, he could see the car and beyond it the whitish mass of the cottage. Once he was sure he heard a movement above him, but it might have been only the leaves fluttering. His heart was going like a mill-race as he felt for his handkerchief and gripped it between his teeth, and as he leaned his head against the cool of the post he felt the perspiration trickle down his cheek. A mosquito buzzed somewhere. Then he heard a movement that couldn't have been the wind and with a suddenness that was startling a light flashed from a bedroom window; flashed again, again, again!

He got to his feet and waited; hands stretched curiously above his head, and body taut. With arms drawn rigidly to the side, he shook his head, but the handkerchief scarcely moved. Everywhere was as still as death. There was a thud! Franklin's body seemed to be on the ground, and he was moaning as if in desperate pain. A rapid movement among the trees and a second form dropped by the gate, and as it hit the ground Franklin came to life.

"Got you, Carter!"

But he hadn't! Carter seemed to leap back and that was all Franklin saw of him for a moment. Then apparently he came into sight, for he made a rush for the hedge. He cut left into Carter's garden, paused for a second, then ran madly to the front gate and the road. Then he stopped and listened again. Then he flopped down heavily on the bank panting like a dog and wiped his forehead with the back of his hand. In a minute he'd regained his breath and only then he appeared to notice that waistcoat and socks were still in his hand. He put them on again, tied his shoes and got to his feet. Then he went slowly along the road to the top of the slope.

In a minute Castleton's white shirt could be discerned, and as he caught sight of Franklin he came rushing up.

"Did you see him? Have you got him?"

"He got away, sir," said Franklin, wearily, leaning his arms on the top of the gate.

"Why the hell didn't you stand fast as I told you? I'd have had him if you'd kept still. Blast him!"

"Blast him is right, sir," said Franklin, mopping his head with his handkerchief.

"Hallo! Where's your hat?"

"Lost it, sir; chasing through that shrubbery—or else on the road."

"I'll have a look for it to-morrow. Come along in and have a drink."

"No thank you, sir, not if you was to pay me for it. I must get back to the Hall. I believe the master's back, sir. That was his car passed me as I was coming here just now."

Castleton hesitated for a moment—or was he startled?

"Was it really? Well, that won't stop you having a drink?"

"No, really sir, I won't, thank you. But one thing you might do for me if you will, sir, and that is, if I send you my address, will you let me know what happens to him? I'm going away to-morrow and I shan't be this way again."

"Why don't you come in and write it down? You look as if a drop of brandy would do you good."

Franklin moved ever so slightly away.

"No, I'll be all right, sir. Bit upset, that's all. Good night, sir!" and he drew slowly away towards the park.

"Good night!" came Castleton's voice. And had he moved from the gate?

No sooner was Franklin inside the door that led to the park than he took to his heels and ran as if ten thousand devils were after him. He risked the trees and the bad going, and when he slowed down it was in the lights from the kitchen window. Outside the door of the servants' hall he stopped to get his breath, and mopped his fore-head again. When he entered, Parry and one of the maids were the only occupants.

"I want to see you in my room in about ten minutes, Parry, please. Is Mr. Royce in, Aggie?"

"I think so, Mr. Francis."

Royce was in, and alone. As soon as he caught sight of Frank-lin's face he jumped up in alarm.

"Mr. Francis! What's the matter? You look very— Let me get you some brandy."

Franklin gulped it down.

"Heart a bit queer. And I did a silly thing—tried to chase a rab-bit. Mad things we do—if we don't stop and think."

Royce shook his head.

"That was what my own boy did, Mr. Francis. Ran, and got heat-ed—and got a chill. Some more brandy?"

"No more, Mr. Royce, thank you. It was very good of you. I think I'll just have a wash and that'll freshen me up." He turned at the door. "Mr. Travers had the note I sent?"

"It went up to him at once, Mr. Francis."

Franklin thanked him again and hurried off upstairs Travers looked extraordinarily relieved to see him.

"What on earth was the matter?" he asked anxiously.

"Castleton asked me round to see about Carter, and like a damn fool I went."

"Went round to Castleton's cottage!"

"Yes."

Travers waved his hands with an expression of utter incompre-hension. "You tell me to keep upstairs and then you deliberately go right into Castleton's house! Then I get a frantic chit—not a word mind you, about where you are!—saying I'm not to stir an inch or see a soul till you get back. The only clue I've got is 'Castleton is' and that you crossed out. Really now, is that being quite fair to me? I don't mean not telling me; what I mean is going off like that and running risks."

"I'm awfully sorry old chap; really I am. The fact of the matter is this. I was out all the afternoon and evening, and I didn't worry about Castleton. All I thought was he wanted to have a drink with me at the 'Stag 'and spin me some extraordinary yarn or other that wouldn't much matter. Then as soon as he asked me to go round to the cottage I panicked badly—and sent you the note. You see I'd told him earlier in the day that you were away—so had Royce—and that's why I didn't worry about myself. Then I realised that it didn't matter about you as far as Castleton was concerned. He could polish me off. Nobody'd know where I was. Then as soon as you got back—it didn't matter a hang to him when—you'd have been attended to. You see, both Royce and I told him you'd be back in the morning."

Travers didn't see it.

"I'll tell you the whole story," said Franklin, and did so; at least he told a great part of it. The first time Travers stopped him was at the removal of waistcoat and socks.

"What on earth was that for?"

"Because I didn't want to get killed. I knew there'd be an attempt to kill me just as Revere was killed—by dropping one of those flints on my head, so I wrapped my waistcoat and socks round my knuckles, and when I stood up I kept my arms stiff and my head well under. When Carter dropped the stone I was ready for it, and even then it knocked me over and nearly sprained my wrists. You can guess what it'd have done to my skull."

"Good God! And how'd he see to aim right?"

"I had instructions to wave my handkerchief, so I had it between my teeth. Carter dropped down to finish me off and I grabbed at him and missed him. Then I chased him and lost him—and that's all there is to it, except that Castleton missed him, too. He offered me a drink, but I wouldn't stop."

Travers looked at him queerly.

"And you knew all this was coming and you deliberately went under that tree!"

"That's right. Now we know—then we didn't. It might have been a bit of a risk—and I think I've exaggerated it—but the means justified the end. In five minutes I learned what it had taken me days to suspect."

"Hm! It's all very bewildering. Tell me; why did Castleton behave so decently afterwards?"

"Decently! After luring me there for Carter to polish off!"

Travers smiled. "That's told me something! What you've proved definitely then is that Carter and Castleton have been concerned with the business all through."

"My dear fellow; haven't I been telling you so all through? There is just the chance that Carter forced the other to do it. He may have had some hold over him. He knew a lot of curious things if those anonymous letters were correct."

Travers grunted. "It's a pity you didn't have the luck to catch hold of Carter red-handed. You'll never get him now—chest or not."

"I don't know," said Franklin, pausing in a peculiar way and shaking his head regretfully. "You see, I *could* have caught him if I'd liked. I could have grabbed him—but I let him go!"

"What! You let him go! Why, the man's a murderer!"

"I know he is," and his voice went dead tired. "Didn't you say we had to avoid scandal?"

"Scandal!" He almost shouted it out. "Scandal you say? My dear chap, there must be limits!"

"Perhaps I was too tender-hearted. I don't know. Would you mind if I push off now? I'm a bit done in."

"My dear old chap, do!" said Travers, hastily, at once all concern. "You must have had a hell of a time. Let me get you a brandy."

"No it's all right, thanks. A night's rest'll soon put me on my pins." As he opened the door he turned round. "Don't think I'm a fool, but lock your door to-night—and keep your window fastened. That's what I shall do to mine."

CHAPTER XXX
TRAVERS HAS A BREATHER

THE FOLLOWING MORNING Travers was awakened by the usual tapping on his door. By the time he had hollered, "Come in!" he remembered Franklin's injunction of the previous night and hopped out of bed to turn the key. By that time Franklin had reassured him with a double tap.

"Sorry to drag you out so early."

"What *is* the time?"

"Just gone five. I'm off now, only I wanted to have a word with you before I went."

Travers looked surprised. "I didn't think you were serious when you sort of hinted you might be going."

Franklin shook his head. "I was serious enough all right. The only thing is I find I've been handling the wrong end of the stick. If you don't mind my saying so, *I'm* the chap that matters. That's why they tried to get me last night —"

"That reminds *me*. As soon as you'd gone, I thought about it. Why didn't they knife you or rough-house you last night, instead of going through all that performance from the tree?"

Franklin smiled. "Well—er—have a look at me. Don't you think I could eat a couple like that if it came to a rough-house? And you bet they knew it. What I wanted to say was, Castleton knew I was a detective, and therefore presumably the more dangerous of the two. If I go away—and I've got to go in any case—and they don't know where I am, they simply daren't lay a finger on you. You'll be safe as houses."

"But I don't know that I want to be as safe as houses," remarked Travers with unusual bellicosity.

"Oh yes you do. I want you to be—I mean I don't want to be away on a job of work and worrying whether you're all right. Here's the address and telephone number where you can get hold of me—care of the Chief Constable. And here's a list of things I want you to do. If you don't mind I'll go over 'em. First of all, if any questions are asked, I've gone for good. My sister is ill and as you're going away yourself on Friday—be sure to spread *that* round, by the way—you thought there was no need for me to come back here."

"Where are you? In London?"

"That'll do all right. Then while you're here, just carry on normally, except for taking elementary precautions; don't go out alone with Castleton—or Haddowe—for instance, and if that fellow Carter has the damned impudence to call, refuse to have him in, or send him away with a flea in his ear. To-day you'll have to go— to Branford, where you'll see a plan of the hall for Thursday's show—not Wednesday's, that's when the *hoi polloi* like me roll up. Thursday's show then, and book yourself a seat on the end of a left-hand row as you go in, and well to the front. Book two more exactly in the same place, only a few seats behind, and send these to me at the address you've got there. I've written it all down; you can't go wrong."

"You really think everything'll be over by Friday?"

"It's got to be, hasn't it? if Grant's coming. And it can't be over before, because he'll have to make certain decisions for himself—your squib for instance. And that reminds me. You carry on with that job of yours, and if anything comes from Durangos act as you think fit."

Travers clicked his tongue. "Do you know, you're getting a very exasperating person? You're still begging the question."

"The question? You mean, will it be over by Friday? Well, you know what I told you. Human nature, that's what it is; love of money and the root of all evil." He changed the subject skilfully. "By the way, Harris is looking after you while I'm away. He knows everything there is to do."

He fairly pushed the papers into Travers' hand.

"Good-bye, old chap. Keep a weather eye open. I'll let you know all that's doing the first chance I get. You've done some thundering good work over this case and I'm damn grateful. You can't stop me saying that."

Before the other could start the least expostulation or get out a single one of the questions he was bursting to ask, Franklin was out of the door. Travers stood there for a moment, looked puzzled, then smiled and shook his head. Then he sniffed the close air of the room, opened a window, lit up a cigarette and settled down in an easy chair.

*   *   *   *   *   *

Most of the plans that Franklin had suggested, solved themselves. Castleton and Haddowe both called when Travers was actually out and neither repeated the visit. On the Tuesday evening Sir Henry arrived and Charlton-Powers came down by the late train. With Haddowe engaged on the dress rehearsal and the Wednesday's performance, there wasn't much risk of the expert running up against *him*.

With Charlton-Powers came the reports from the two booksellers. In one case the volume had been exposed for sale, but the *Hudibras* had been unearthed from elsewhere. In both cases there was a definite connection with Haddowe, the enquirer and purchaser being "a man of refined appearance and clerical voice; tall and very stoutly built." In both cases he took the volumes with him, and what was even more damning, enquired about other volumes, and firms likely to have early editions in stock.

As for the more leisurely examination of the pictures, Charlton-Powers was sure the copies were of very recent making. A later X-ray series of photographs ought to tell the whole story.

"Marvellous people they must have had at work!" he told Travers. "That woman Angéle for instance. Actual attempt to copy the brush-work of the originals—the way the particular master laid on his paint. Then the ageing processes, such as deterioration, mellowing of colour and cracking; really uncanny!"

"They'd do that outside?"

"I imagine so. Once the copy was made, the original could remain till the copy was definitely ready for substitution. Of course, the beauty of the whole proceeding was that if an expert had a look at 'em, he'd say, 'Such-and-such a picture in the style of So-and-So,' or, 'Pity these aren't originals!' and that'd be the end of the matter as far as he was concerned. Valuers for probate have to *value*; not enquire into the kind of thing a man's presumably collected."

"What's worrying me," said Travers, "is the furniture. How was the substitution done—if it was done?"

"Personally I'm of the opinion that you're suspecting too much," said Charlton-Powers. "You can't juggle with pieces of furniture or take 'em away rolled up in your pocket or in a suit-case. The books and pictures were quite another story. I'm sorry to disagree, but I really do think the theory I gave—about a married daughter—would fit the case. After all, it's a thing that often occurs, provided furniture and so on are not heirlooms."

"There'd have been enough without touching the furniture?"

"Enough! Think of Rosenbach, old boy—and first editions. Take a single Vermeer or Hobbema! If your man Haddowe was half what you imagine him, his eyes must have popped out of his head the first time he saw this place. He could have walked off with a couple of hundred thousand pounds' worth in a weekend bag—if there hadn't been the difficulty about replacing them."

On the whole, Travers was inclined to agree. One trouble had been Haddowe's reason for employing a male staff at the vicarage, but the turpentine smell and the men could both be explained if that were the scene of the ageing processes necessary for the faked pictures. Royce, when questioned, knew of no occasion when any furniture had been replaced or sent away for repair.

The most vital thing, however, that happened during Travers' short breather, was some news that arrived on the Thursday afternoon by special messenger from Durango House.

With regard to original enquiry and later request for urgent information from France only, hope to supply information to-morrow with regard to marriage of suspected parties. More detailed evidence follows.

Travers wasn't overwhelmingly surprised; indeed, putting together the evidence of Royce, the original report from Durangos, and what he had seen or deduced for himself, nothing else could satisfactorily explain the hold which Haddowe had willingly or unwillingly obtained. As for the letter which was due in the morning, it looked like being too late. Cosmo Grant would simply inherit a further small amount of trouble.

Then at the very last moment, between five and six o'clock, something else happened. Franklin sent a letter from Branford.

Dear Travers,

Still alive as you see, and flourishing, and glad to tell you the case will all be over to-night. Hope you haven't been having too dull a time, going easy as per recommendations.

There are one or two things we want you to do for us— Mr. Grant is here with me at Branford, where we have just arrived from London. He knows all there is to know at the moment, and agrees that the best action to take is this.

i. Inform Royce and Sir Henry confidentially that Mr. Grant arrives to-night at 8 p.m.

ii. See Haddowe, Castleton and L. F. at the show and tell them you are giving a small supper-party as soon as it's over, and for any reason that appeals to you. That is all you will do in the Haddowe business.

iii. *Take your car down to the show and then Parry will fetch Mr. Grant with it. Parry will then carry out instructions Mr. Grant will give him personally.*

Don't forget to look out for me as you enter. I shall touch you as you pass.

J. F.

It was very curious, perhaps, why Travers should have felt a very definite regret as he read that note for the second time. It *would* be rather jolly to *get* back to town—and yet the thought of leaving Fenwold brought a feeling that was difficult to analyse. It was not so much the loss of comfort and exalted ease—he could have afforded those any day if his tastes demanded them. It was not that. It was the recognition that for all the chilliness and hauteur that had struck him when he first saw it, Fenwold Hall was a lovely and lovable place. It was an evocation of the past; of the times when life was stately and men had time *to* pause and look on beauty. There was a kind of seclusion that brooded over it and harmonised with his own peculiar personality. Admit the truth and call it a feudal survival; admit its immensity—the breadth as it were of the canvas—and even then you had to admit a magnificence and glamour and a strange, holding sort of appeal.

While he was dressing, and over his dinner, he went again and again over those questions that had already gone through his mind a hundred times since Franklin went away, and even at the last moment when the car drew in at the gate of the church hall, he had found no satisfactory answer. All he did know was that the stage was set. What the curtain would finally fall on was quite another thing.

CHAPTER XXXI
TRAVERS HAS A FIELD-NIGHT

The Discovery

As Travers was moving along the left-hand wall in search of his seat, he felt a light touch on his coat, and there sure enough, was

Franklin. If it hadn't been for the touch and the position he occupied, he'd have been passed without the slightest risk of recognition. His hair was grey at the temples, a faint moustache just darkened his upper lip, and the glasses he wore put a good ten years on him. With him was a younger man with a back straight as a ramrod.

The seat Travers occupied was probably the most uncomfortable he had ever had in his life. Half a guinea for an armless, bentwood chair, a bare twenty inches of space on his right hand, and a circumscribed view from the extreme left of the hall, seemed a magnificent contribution to charity, whatever the performance put up by the company of all the talents. The building seemed crammed to capacity, and before he had been in his place a minute the orchestra—an imported quintette—struck up a Handelian air.

The lights were gradually lowered, the footlights flashed, and to the crackling of a tentative applause the heavy curtain drew back, disclosing the familiar back-cloth of a street in Bath. Fag and the coachman had their gossip while Travers polished his glasses and tried to accustom himself to the limited light. His seat appeared to be a good twenty feet back from the stage, and its sole advantage— with every deference to the opinion of Jerome Paull—seemed to be its inconspicuousness. There ought to be no trouble whatever about slipping away unnoticed.

It didn't take him long moreover to discover that his remembrances of the play were rather hazy, but in the semi-darkness he managed to discover from his programme what the next scene was—*Mrs. Malaprop's Lodgings in Bath*. That sounded more promising. When the curtain drew back again, he really thought he was going to be interested, if only in the quiet appreciation of Leila Forteresse—a lovely figure in powder and brocade, and her voice as fascinating as herself.

Of course all that other business would keep popping up into his mind. Little questions and doubts insinuated themselves. Why had Franklin wanted him just there, where he was sitting? And what was he proposing to do himself? Then he'd fix his eyes on the stage again; tell himself that everything was being done extraordinarily well and that the absence of self-consciousness and the sureness of the two women in their prattle was promising amazingly for the rest of the evening.

As for the new-fangled ideas of lighting, well, frankly he couldn't see any difference. Julia sat on a settee well to the right, and for the moment the action was all one-sided. One had to admit, of course, that that table, clean in the middle of the stage with the light focussed on it, did perhaps divide the setting into Paull's two parts. The room now—exceedingly well done; reproductions, of course, but quite effective; those silk pictures, for instance, and the miniatures and that Chippendale settee and the really superb table—a tiny, graceful sculpture in mahogany.

Then all at once things began to happen somewhere in the back of his mind. Confused ideas rose higgledy-piggledy and began to sort themselves out. He remembered a table—the very spit of that one on the stage—that he'd once wanted very badly. He recalled the very wording of the catalogue:

> "Chippendale tripod table with galleried top;
> claw feet and handsomely carved pedestal.
> A very remarkable piece."

Remarkable it was, and so had been the price! He had left a commission at a hundred and fifty guineas, and it was made eleven hundred! Curious, too, that whoever supplied the reproductions for those stage settings should have had a reproduction of a rare piece like that. Owners of unique things would hardly lend them to be copied. And hadn't Franklin seen a table of sorts in the bedroom of the vicarage, and with a fire going, on a sweltering summer night? Then those reproduction pieces at the Hall; surely Charlton-Powers' explanation was hardly a satisfactory one? *He* didn't know Fenwold Hall. Reproductions in a place like that! Of course, Haddowe's books were a kind of reproduction—so were Angéle's pictures. Then he saw it, or thought he did!

The annoying thing was, the very discovery put him in an awkward position. He glanced at his programme again. *Act. ii. Sc. i, Capt. Absolute's Lodgings in Bath.* He'd certainly have to wait for that if he wanted the faintest chance of confirmation before going to Royce, and the devil of it was the longer he waited, the bigger risk he ran. Was the furniture on the stage original or reproduction? If he went behind the scenes during the interval it was very doubtful if he'd be able to tell, especially in that artificial light. All very well for a chap like Charlton-Powers, who could smell 'em a mile off.

There was only one thing to do—sit tight. Then the scene seemed interminable. When Sir Anthony made his exit he half rose to go, but it proved a false alarm—Mrs. Malaprop called for Lucy; then when the mistress left, the maid had to talk to herself. What people saw amusing in it he didn't know, and then when the scene was over, the relief was enough to make him clap as vociferously as his neighbour. Then came ten minutes' wait; hall full of chatter; people forming groups or rushing about everywhere; lack of control that was positively indecent; and then, thank heaven, the bell!

Captain Absolute's lodgings were far from palatial, and yet you couldn't call the room a man's room. A back-cloth showed panelling and a picture or two. In the centre stage was an early gate-legged table, of no particular value whether genuine or not. But by the wall were two Chippendale chairs; one covered by a carelessly flung coat, the other with a back as delicately fragile as the ribbon it imitated. By the side wall stood a serpentine-fronted sideboard that made Travers screw up his eyes as he looked at it.

A titter of amusement ran round the hall at some remark of the gallant captain, and Travers slipped out under cover of the noise. The rest of that evening was a hectic affair. Five minutes later, for instance, he was in the Hall interviewing Royce and trying to avoid the new arrival. Then he slipped out by the side door, and his long legs going to some purpose, set off back to the show. Franklin was waiting inside the Lodge gates by the parking place.

"I saw you go," he said. "Anything up?"

Travers told him.

Franklin whistled. "I say, that makes things complicated! What's the best thing to do? Have the originals gone or are they there?"

"Lord knows! We'd better be prepared for either."

"Right-ho!" said Franklin. "No time to talk. You get back to your pew, and don't stir. If you're wanted I'll come along."

"Who's the chap with you?" asked Travers as they crossed the road.

"Detective - sergeant from county headquarters. Major Iddesdon's at the Hall with Mr. Grant. Too many people might recognise him here," and he slipped round to the back of the building.

Travers followed more leisurely. The second interval was at hand, and under cover of the applause that called the players a second time before the footlights, he regained his seat. But he sat with feelings with which the movements on the stage were not even remotely connected. He was gratified, of course; he could hardly help being that, but Lord! what a fool he'd been. Clue after clue stuck under his nose, and not a one seen. And he'd look a bigger fool if the discovery had come too late. If the originals had gone, Haddowe looked like getting away with it after all—and whose fault would that be but his own? Travers wriggled in his seat, and his neighbour must have thought him a remarkably restless person.

Another glance at his programme. He'd wait till the next scene—*Acres' Lodgings*—and go behind the stage. Some time or other that supper invitation had to be given, and that looked the likeliest opportunity.

Counter-Attack

The men's dressing-room was a spacious affair and well fitted, and as Travers stuck his head round the door he caught sight of Haddowe and Castleton yarning away over a cigarette. The latter was blowing rings into the air, and the vicar was right back in his chair with his legs crossed on top of a table. Neither looked startled at his sudden appearance. Possibly his extra-ordinarily enthusiastic smile set them at ease.

"Hallo, stranger!" exclaimed Haddowe, rolling his legs off the table. "Come along in. How's it going? And have a cigarette."

"Thanks," said Travers. "And I'll have some beer—if it's cold. No, don't trouble, Castleton! The show you say? Going magnificently. You people are simply wonderful!"

"You really mean it?" asked Castleton.

"Of course I mean it. You two fellers ought to be on the regular stage. Excellent beer this is!"

Haddowe turned to Castleton. "What else does he want?"

Travers smiled. "You may think I'm pulling your legs, but I'm not. Honestly, your show is absolutely topping. And now I'll return your beer. Will you and Castleton, padre, come straight to the Hall after the show? I'd like to give a little supper-party; going away to-morrow for one thing, and I think we ought to celebrate this show of yours for another. Will one of you tell Miss Forteresse?"

"I say, that's extremely handsome of you," said Haddowe, and Castleton mumbled a clerkly sort of echo to the parson's thanks. Horribly unreal they both looked; faces almost hideous with grease-paint and pencilling.

"You'll want to change, of course," said Travers. "Or why not clean up and come as you are?"

"Oh, I don't know. It won't take ten minutes. What about you, Gilbert?"

"I'll be all right. You don't mind a lounge suit, Mr. Travers?"

"My dear fellow; come in sack-cloth if you like—so long as you roll up. I'll wait for you all afterwards. Just the four of us, remember."

The fourth act went on its unhurrying way, with Travers about as happy as a housewife who suddenly remembers she left home with the gas full on. Franklin and the detective-sergeant had gone, and what was happening, heaven alone knew. If the furniture had gone, why shouldn't Haddowe make his get-away at any moment after the show? And Leila Forteresse, too, for that matter? And what was being done about Carter? Had Franklin arrested him already? Was the supper-party to make sure Haddowe didn't abscond? And why was the Chief Constable at the Hall?

The last interval arrived with still no sign of Franklin or his colleague. Travers strolled outside and restlessly spoilt a cigarette, and when the last act began he was finding it hard to keep his seat. Everything around him seemed banal and unnecessary—the titters of laughter, the applause, and even the presence of people on the stage. Ten minutes of that and a programme-seller tapped him on the shoulder. A gentleman wished to see him in the vestibule.

Franklin motioned him outside.

"Everything's going fine. Ford got three more men from Branford, and just before the interval a small motor-van took aboard a load at the vicarage back door. Ford's following it up, and we've got a message through to Branford to hold it there. As soon as you've got Haddowe away, we'll search the vicarage."

"Somebody still in?"

"One, at least. Not only that; the first van may have been only a blind. Now there's something absolutely vital that you've got to do. Come along with me and rehearse it."

Travers did his best, though he couldn't see rhyme nor reason in it. Franklin gave no explanation, and there wasn't time for questions.

"Now then, take it steady," was Franklin's final admonition. "Be as natural as you can, and everything'll go off like clockwork. Stay in your seat till the end and then look up your supper-party. Everything's arranged for. I've seen Grant and the Chief Constable, and if there should happen to be any hitch, you're to go straight to the library. Don't forget! There's your car, in front of the gate."

"What about Carter?"

"He's all right. We've got him where we want him," and off he hurried again, this time to the road. Travers sidled once more to his seat. What a night! Talk about a thistledown in a water-spout, it wasn't in it. He polished his glasses nervously, and made up his mind to concentrate on what was going on up there on the stage. All he was in time for was to see the whole company advance to the footlights. Sir Lucius, stilted and spasmodic, spoke his piece; Bob Acres chimed in, and Sir Anthony said the final word. A huge roar of applause. The performance was over.

Travers stood up with the rest while the company appeared again and again. He watched the flowers pile up on the stage and the presentation of the huge boxes of chocolates he had had sent down from town. Five minutes of that and the hall began slowly to empty. Outside could be heard a continual tooting and gurgling of horns as the cars moved out to the road from the parking place inside the lodge gates.

He stood there till the hall was practically empty, then made his way behind the stage. Everybody was there, laughing and chattering, and Leeke was pouring out champagne which a footman was taking round. Travers felt rather out of it. He did make what seemed to him at the time a feeble speech of congratulation. Another quarter of an hour and Leila Forteresse re-appeared, still in her costume, and her face flushed with excitement.

"Wasn't it all too wonderful! Where are the men?"

"They'll be here in a minute," said Travers. "May I help you with those flowers?"

"Brown will see to them in a moment. Aren't they simply too gorgeous?" She put her arms round the mass of long-stemmed buds and leaned her cheek against them, and Travers the poet and Travers the misogynist were for once in agreement. One thought he had never seen anything so bewitching—and the other felt his pulses stir. Then Brown appeared, and the flowers and the beribboned box were taken off. Then came Haddowe, in magnificent spirits, taking an arm of each.

"Well? Now we're ready for you. Bring out your supper!"

"Castleton ready?" asked Travers, and wondered if Haddowe had noticed the jerkiness in his voice.

"He will be in a minute. We might make a start. There's bound to be a bit of a crush."

The Hall car was found, and Leila Forteresse and Haddowe and the masses of flowers and the chocolates found their way in.

"I don't think you'll be able to get through for a minute or so," said Travers. "The gates seem to be blocked with cars. Everybody's coming out. You people push on while you can. I'll find Castleton and bring him along with me."

He met him, as a matter of fact, just coming out of the door, and explained the situation.

"I think we shall catch the others up. We might even get there first. I had my car put right against the church." He stopped for a moment—his heart was beating so rapidly that Castleton was bound to notice something. "What about cutting through the churchyard and avoiding the crush?"

Outside the lych-gate, in comparative blackness, Travers' car was waiting by the path. Parry sat at the wheel, and thrust out his right arm and leaned over to open the door.

"All right, Parry," said Travers, then drew back to let Castleton enter.

"No, after you," said Castleton.

"Not at all," insisted Travers. Castleton stepped inside.

Then something happened which Travers hadn't expected. The door was slammed to from the inside and the car shot off. Castleton must have been jerked clean off his pins. Before Travers could make a sound, the car had gone, and there he was, standing on the path and snapping his eyes in the uncertain light and looking an absolute fool.

"It's all right," said Franklin, stepping out from behind the hedge. "Here's your car—or another one."

"Yes, but what—"

"Hop in quick, old chap! You've got to catch the others up. They'll let you through the gates all right. And keep your pecker up!"

The devil seemed to be in the cars. As Travers stepped in, the driver must have let in the clutch with the engine racing. The car gave what seemed like a leap in the air.

Then something else happened. As he bounced in his seat and put out a hand to steady himself, he felt something warm! Another man was in the car!

"Good evening, Mr. Travers. Pleased to make your acquaintance!" came a voice.

Travers whipped round and drew back to his corner. What the devil else was going to happen?

"Who are you?" he said curtly.

"My name's Grant. Shake hands, Mr. Travers. I've been hearing quite a lot about *you!*"

The Show-down

As they swung round on the outside of the queue, Travers noticed the Hall car with its flowers protruding from the windows, still waiting for a chance to slip through. Their own car had been let pass as if by prearranged signal, and once they were clear, they fairly hurtled down the drive.

Everything still seemed unreal to him as he listened to Grant's thanks and laudatory remarks. He was not hazy so much about what had happened as what was going to happen. That business with Castleton had been too mysterious for words, but why had Grant taken the trouble to come and meet him in the car? As they came into the entrance hall he shot a quick glance at the new owner of Fenwold. He was certainly not unlike his uncle, though Cosmo Revere had been more of the spare type; taller perhaps and dynamic enough; all quick little movements, and with a face deceptively pleasant. The accent, too, was hardly noticeable, and the voice, though not too attractive, at least far from aggressive.

"This is the fellow who's been doing things," he said to the Chief Constable as they turned into the library. Sir Henry rose fussily from his seat and came forward, looking remarkably anxious and far from happy generally.

Travers and Iddesdon shook hands.

"I'd like to congratulate you, Mr. Travers, if—"

"You folks stay quiet for a minute!" broke in Grant. "As soon as those two come in major, you sit there, and Sir Henry, you stay right there. And when I give the word, Mr. Travers, you go right ahead with what you've got to say."

"I'm sorry," said Travers, "but I don't quite follow. Go right ahead with what?"

The other raised his hand. In the entrance hall a woman's voice was heard laughing quietly, then came the boom of Haddowe's bass. Royce's voice cut in coldly official.

"Mr. Grant has arrived unexpectedly, Miss Leila. He asked to see you and Mr. Haddowe as soon as you returned."

There was still the questioning look on Haddowe's face as the door was opened and the pair of them came in. Grant moved forward. The door closed.

Travers wondered who would do the introductions—a nerve-racking sort of business. One couldn't very well be friendly with people soon to be up before the beak, and it wouldn't do to alarm them by being distant. Grant's voice interrupted the soliloquy.

"So you're Cousin Leila! Do you know it's real good to see all the Reveres right here where they belong! And this is Mr. Haddowe. Well, well! And you all know who I am." He indicated the vacant chairs. "Let's sit down and have a family conference."

Haddowe's eyes narrowed slightly and a faint smile appeared at the corners of his mouth. Leila Forteresse gave him a quick, appraising sort of look; then smiled, too—the kind of smile one gives when the speaker of the evening rises or the bishop has just opened the bazaar. Both sat down; curiously enough, neither had said a word. Grant crossed his legs and leaned back in his swivel seat at the desk. Iddesdon sat bolt upright, Sir Henry looked magisterially forbidding, and Travers was watching nervously.

"Mr. Travers, I think you know," said Grant. "We also hope to know him better. This is Major Iddesdon, who's come to see me to-night on a mighty important business. Sir Henry we all know—but we don't know *him* as well as he knows the law; and the law's a very tricky thing to know."

He paused and looked round the room reflectively.

"This is a wonderful place I've come to. I thought so when I came here to see my uncle, just after the war. He was a fine old man. I don't think I ever met a man who made you feel as he did, what a man could be. If he were in this room, I'd like him to agree with—and endorse—what I'm going to do."

He leaned forward, and the change in his voice was startling.

"What are you folks going to say?"

Leila Forteresse had an air of embarrassment—and she was puzzled. She looked at Haddowe, but got no help. He was far too busy collecting his thoughts and assuming his favourite pose; head slightly forward and finger-tips together.

"Of course we're all delighted to welcome Mr. Grant to Fenwold. We hope, moreover—"

"Now isn't that real kind of Mr. Haddowe?" interrupted Grant, beaming upon the company generally. Then he nodded once or twice, and finally looked across at Travers.

"Do you know, I thought somehow Mr. Haddowe would say something like that. What do you think, Mr. Travers?"

Travers cleared his throat. All that cat and mouse business was getting on his nerves. He thought he knew what Grant expected him to say, and the sooner he said it and got out of that room, the better he'd be pleased.

"It's—er—rather awkward for me to say what—er—I've got to say. Perhaps, if you don't mind, I'll start at the very beginning for the benefit of the people concerned, although I have an idea that Mr. Haddowe has a shrewd notion already. Still, that's rather getting away from the point.

"Briefly, then, it was suspected by certain people most competent to judge, that for some time prior to Mr. Revere's death, things at Fenwold hadn't been all they should have been, and so—er—at Mr. Revere's death, Mr. Franklin—the extraordinarily able head of the detective department of Durangos, Limited—came down here as my supposed confidential servant. Mr. Haddowe, I rather fancy, knows all that. What we definitely found out is this.

"Haddowe, here, has abstracted from the library a number of quite valuable first editions and substituted for them editions very much inferior. Miss Forteresse—or should I say Mrs. Haddowe?—with an expert posing as her invalid nurse, is responsible for the removal of certain very valuable pictures."

Haddowe sprang to his feet.

"But my dear sir—"

"Let me finish," said Travers. "There'll be plenty of time for you to talk."

Haddowe waved his hands helplessly and turned to Leila Forteresse. She sat looking straight at Travers, lips pouted to an enigmatical sort of smile.

"I don't propose to go into details, because in some of them I might be wrong, and that would lead to—er—unnecessary argument. With regard to certain thefts of valuable furniture, however, I do want to be more explicit. It should have been foreseen and prevented days ago—only I happened to be such a fool that I couldn't see the obvious."

Grant waved his hand carelessly.

"Mr. Travers," he confided to the company, "is too modest!"

"I didn't see, for instance, why the county and village should twice be treated to an eighteenth-century comedy of manners rather than a far more popular modern comedy or farce. I saw no connection between Chippendale and Sheridan. I didn't realise why Haddowe sounded me as to my theatrical knowledge the first time he clapped eyes on me, or why immediately after the death of Mr. Revere he should be so keen on giving the performance by hook or crook. I didn't realise why, in the presence of an indisputable authority like Mr. Jerome Paull—and also in front of Royce—he should induce me to say that everything should be done as it had been done before at a previous performance when Mr. Revere was alive.

"Royce saw no reason, therefore, to inform me that Haddowe and Jerome Paull—the latter, of course, perfectly innocently—had selected for stage purposes and removed from the Hall certain articles of furniture; and I saw no reason to ask him. When Mr. Franklin and myself were lured away to Cambridge last Saturday morning, we suspected merely a—er—facilitation of the departure of Miss Forteresse's nurse, and possibly some pictures. Neither of us thought for a moment we'd been got out of the way so that articles of furniture might be removed from the Hall.

"You might be interested to know what Haddowe did. Months ago he photographed those pieces of furniture which he needed to put with those he took last March at the performance of *The School for Scandal,* so as to make up a complete, and probably unique, set of signed Chippendale. He had very careful measurements taken also. Then he made the reproductions. When the originals arrived at the church hall on Saturday, they were used for certain tests, and then removed to the vicarage for safety. There they were compared with the reproductions, which were modified and marked accordingly. To-night I saw those reproductions on the stage. At this moment they may be in the Hall. Where the originals are now—"

"The chief might say a word about that," broke in Grant.

Iddesdon turned to Haddowe. "Your van was held UD at Branford half an hour ago. I'm the Chief Constable of the county, by the way. The driver and one of your men are being held there, too. All the furniture is being placed in the large garage—both what was taken from the van and what was actually on the stage."

Grant got to his feet.

"Mr Travers the major and I are both indebted to you for what you've said—and done; and to Mr. Franklin as well. As to those antiques, I guess they'll look better right here where they belong than over in New York."

Haddowe got up slowly, his shoulders hunched and jaw set. He flashed a quick look round the room.

"Now I shouldn't get uneasy, if I were you," Grant remonstrated gently. "There's one of the major's friends outside each window and another or two outside the door."

Then Travers did something. As he owned up to Franklin afterwards, he hadn't the faintest idea why he did it, and every time he thought of it, it sent an uneasy feeling down his spine. All the same, he sprang up and advanced on Haddowe.

"Haddowe, you sit down and listen to me!"

The strange thing was that Haddowe lowered himself to his chair and watched him steadily. Travers glared down from his six foot something and wagged a monitory forefinger.

"Do you know that when you amused yourself with those anonymous newspapers, you killed Westfield as surely as if you'd cut his throat? That's what you and your—your roguery have got you into. And now you get up here and bluster! I tell you, you don't know half the information we've got. What about that night in Camden Town when Peters brought you that money? When he slugged you as the negro went down? The night you got that scar."

Haddowe sank back in the chair, his eyes staring. What story lay behind that night Travers never knew, but it must have been something so damning and the knowledge of it so unexpected that for a moment he went a ghastly white, then buried his face in his hands. And most unexpected of all, the woman sprang up, leaned with her arms across his shoulders, and glared at Travers like a tigress.

"That's better," drawled Grant. "Now, major, it all depends on what we're told in the next few minutes where these people spend their night. I certainly show a Christian charity. I very nearly called them a couple of crooks."

Sir Henry got up quickly.

"No scandal, Mr. Grant. I beg of you! Haddowe will tell us what he knows."

"I guess he will," said Grant, and Travers slipped out of the room.

* * * * *

In the entrance hall was a sight at which Fenwold Hall would once have shuddered—Franklin seated by the library door, small table in front of him, finishing off a cold supper. As Travers emerged from the door, wiping his forehead, he laid down the napkin.

"Everything all right in there?"

"I think so," said Travers. "At least, things look like sorting themselves out. But where's Castleton? Why didn't you have him in?"

"Castleton?" said Franklin slowly. "As soon as he got inside that car, two plain-clothes men collared him. He's now in Branford gaol, being held for murder."

"Murder! But Carter did the murder!"

"I know he did. So did Castleton. They were one and the same person!"

CHAPTER XXXII
FRANKLIN SUMS UP

"YOU'RE A bigger fool than I!" said Franklin. "Don't you believe it! You might have had your clues stuck under your nose, but I had mine presented on a silver salver.

"You see I exaggerated the difficulties. You had something to occupy your time; I had to kill a lot of mine, and when I started thinking, all I kept worrying about was the inability to cross-examine possible witnesses. As things turned out, that didn't matter a bit.

"Take the elementary evidence. Yellow sand—therefore Cosmo Revere killed on the east side of the Branford road; murderer knew the ground, could fell a tree, and must have had something in which to transport the body. Eliminate Leeke and Haddowe on account of alibis, and all that's left is Castleton!

"Then the most ridiculous mistake was made—with regard to Castleton's alibi. We both thought of Lammas Wood in terms of the way we went there the first time; along the Branford road and then to the left down that track. If, therefore, Castleton was seen going to Westlake at 9.45, he had a good alibi. That, of course, was very loose thinking. He hadn't the ghost of an alibi. The best road to Lammas Wood is round the other way. In any case, what did it matter? As soon as Cosmo Revere was killed—say, at 9.10—the body was in the dickey of his car and was taken to Lammas Wood. I should say he left it there concealed and then came back later after he'd returned from Westlake—disguised as Carter, of course—and finished off the job at his leisure. In the morning he went back again to make sure everything was right, and that's when Westfield saw him. Westfield's number was up from that moment because Castleton wouldn't know exactly how much he saw.

"You follow that all right? Then let's go back to the time when we agreed that Carter and Castleton had been working together. After this I didn't tell you what I was doing, and this is the reason. I didn't want you to meet Castleton and give him the slightest suspicion by alteration of voice or attitude. Also I hadn't a full case to put up to you till yesterday. However, there we are. I'm sorry, in a way, I didn't let you know, and yet—well, it's turned out all right; we'll leave it at that.

"When I went on with that theory, this is what I began to notice. Carter and Castleton were complementary persons; what one lacked the other had. Carter couldn't have run away or climbed the dolmen or felled the tree, but Castleton could! Castleton couldn't have lured Cosmo Revere away, but Carter did! They helped each other in business; their initials were the same and their houses were as good as the same. Then I began to wonder. First it was a sort of game I was playing with no particular hopes of result. At any rate, here are some of the things I thought of.

"There were two mirrors in Carter's cottage; one I stooped to and the other very much higher. If anybody saw Carter shaving, it would be downstairs where the mirror was his height. If he used one in secret, the mirror would be Castleton's height.

"Those anonymous letters helped Castleton by removing a possible rival in Leeke. Carter couldn't have profited by them. A small snag was the mention of Castleton, but that might have been put in to allay suspicion.

"Now a very important thing—the night in the 'Stag' when Carter made his famous exit. Irving couldn't have done it better. Every word and gesture perfectly synchronised till the curtain fell as he shut the door! And you'd told me your impression of Castleton was that he was always *acting*. Haddowe told you he was a very fine *actor*.

"Not only that. Carter didn't want me to see *him*. He came to the 'Stag' to see *me*. And he disappeared afterwards.

"And something else. After I'd once seen Carter I never got the chance again. You see, I might have compared *ears*. And Carter generally came out at night when the disguise was good. And he never had a woman in his cottage. And his initials, as I said, were G.C. Very handy in case of any confusion with clothes.

"Very well, then. I decided to take that as a further theory and work at it. If I'd been the law I could have finished it all up in a day or so, because Castleton would have had to give definite information about his meeting with Carter; also, I could have proved there were none of Carter's finger-prints in his cottage. But I couldn't do that. What I did do was this.

"Human nature is what it is, and we're told the love of money is the root of all evil. Castleton, with the collector's mania on him, wouldn't lose the chance of getting hold of that chest. He'd go as Carter and see it. Right-ho, then! You gave me a cheque and I gave you some notes. I hid your chequebook so that you'd have to pay Castleton cash. I also asked you to buy something for me so that you'd have to spend more money. Out of the notes Carter gave Fittleton no less than five were those I'd given you!

"Then I had a bit more luck. Those pieces of charred paper were burnt masks—sort of things boys decorate themselves with on Guy Fawkes' Day. Carter had bought several. Why? I'll tell you. When Castleton taught him to drive that van—you bet your life Castleton hated that horse and cart business like hell!—he did it in the dusk and had a dummy sitting beside him. He experimented with the masks for the face. He may have used one or he may have found they weren't any good, after all; at any rate, he burnt them when he cleaned up the cottage.

"Can't you see it all fitting in? Heaps of things aren't there when you look for 'em. But I'll tell you something that nearly upset me for a moment—the night when Castleton asked me to try to get my uncle down from the tree. He said he'd flash a light in the window. I knew he couldn't, but when the light *did* flash, I was terrified! How could the theory be right? How could Carter be in the tree and Castleton in the house? Had Castleton got a new ally?

"Do you know it took me five minutes to think that out? Castleton's car was drawn up just short of the tree where he was. The lights of the bedroom were worked from the battery of the car *from up the tree!*

"Mind you, as soon as Castleton dropped down I knew it was he. You can't drop from a height and keep your stoop. As I told you, I could have grabbed him, but I let him go. We weren't ready for him yet. I had to show him that I thought it was Carter, but I never worried about him bolting. If he still thought I'd got no suspicion of him, he'd certainly stay on for that show. Also—human nature! How could he bolt and leave behind him that house full of lovely things? things it had taken him years to collect. But it was touch and go. As I stood talking to him at the gate, I'm dead sure he had a revolver in his pocket.

"Of course, to go on ahead, when I went away on Tuesday morning, I soon got a case together. I went through the files of the local paper and found auctions and auctioneers and made inquiries. Just what I thought. The two had never been seen together. Fittleton, of course—haven't I told you about him?—Well, I'll tell you later. But you'll see that a casual passer-by as they were getting the chest round to Carter's back door, gave Castleton a chance for a bit more acting. Fittleton never *saw* that passer-by.

"Why did Castleton do it? Well, this is how I work it out. He was hard up. He had an annuity of a hundred a year and those two cottages only. The car he bought when the furniture and books of the vicarage were sold. He was a very fine actor, but hadn't the guts to start at the bottom of the ladder. He had a sound knowledge of antiques, but hadn't the pluck to go as assistant to a dealer, or the money to buy a partnership. He was 'county,' public school and Cambridge; on visiting terms at the Hall and in the general swim—therefore he couldn't go buying things round the villages. That's why he thought of Carter—jolly good fun, you know! and so on. The disguise was child's play—teeth out, stoop, glasses and voice. Dialect comes second nature to a man who's really a native of his county.

"Then he found it a paying game. Things rolled in, and what's more, he got in the swim with the dealers. Also it was exciting, as you collectors know. And it satisfied his actor's complex. Then came the Forteresse affair and the row with Revere. If he'd had any sense he'd have apologised handsomely and put things right, but no; he couldn't do that. He had to go on posing and acting and chattering till he found the door of the Hall bolted and barred. On him, mind you! Not a soul in the village to associate with. No freedom of the Hall and grounds and walks; and the news probably going all round the county.

"That's where Carter got to work. Carter was Castleton's second self. He abused the estate and Cosmo Revere. He talked Bolshevism and wrote the anonymous letters. He hinted at things Leeke had done, and threw dust in people's eyes by abusing Castleton. Fun. wasn't it?

"Motives? Well, if Revere was dead, there'd be a legacy for the niece—and Fenwold Cottage. He'd marry her—so she'd promised—and then to hell with the Revere tradition and Royce and everybody he had a grudge against. By his marriage he'd be a sort of Revere himself—and set up for life!

"Exactly how he worked it out is probably like this. That silly, damn carving on the Revere pew gave him the idea of felling the tree, and he tried the murder first from the top of the dolmen. Then Carter was useful again. He called to see Revere, and what he told him we shall never know, unless Castleton owns up, and he's never likely to do that. The fact remains that with Westfield out of the way, the coast was clear. Cosmo Revere came to the spot under the tree, and as he was fanning himself with his hat, down came the stone. Then out came the railings and in went the body.

"Carter's cottage, I think, comes in like this. Suppose, after all, the jury didn't return the right verdict; then Castleton had another card up his sleeve. Carter's cottage should look as if its owner—the man who called to see him that evening—had bolted after doing the murder. You might ask why Carter didn't go for good, since everything *was* all right. I think this is why.

"First we came to the Hall. The Forteresse woman told Castleton about it, and he got alarmed. Then on the Sunday he saw me snooping round the cottages and got more alarmed still. Carter had to return for the purposes of espionage on you and me; and, of course, on Westfield."

He banged his fist on the palm of his hand.

"That damn woman! She's the one who ought to pay. Did Haddowe know she was fooling about with Leeke and Castleton? Of course he did! She was his intelligence staff. Haddowe's a bigger man than all the rest put together."

Travers was smiling. "You've got a Camden Town complex!"

Franklin laughed.

"Well, he *is* a bigger man—but he didn't know what he was starting when he began that forgery business. No wonder he was petrified when Royce walked in with the news that Cosmo Revere was dead.

"Oh, and just one other thing. Yesterday morning Castleton saw a big dealer in Ipswich about buying the whole of his stuff. Iddesdon stepped in there and found out that the dealer was to come along to-day morning, as it were, so he arranged for Castleton to receive a telegram this morning postponing the visit for a day. That put Castleton up a gum-tree. He couldn't bolt. He *had* to hang on."

"Do you know I can't believe it about Castleton," said Travers, almost regretfully. "What a fool!"

"Remember what Westfield said about the family? 'They're a rum lot.' That's a very comprehensive remark in the country."

"What'll happen to him?"

"He'll hang for Westfield's murder. If the other gets brought in—and I don't see how it can help it—he'll be up on a double charge. As for your friends downstairs, I rather think there'll be very little doing—if the boodle's returned. What are you laughing at?"

"Well, I hardly like to tell you. It isn't funny, really—only the funny side happened to strike me. Just the thought of you and me sitting there talking to Castleton about your uncle! and he very sympathetic, and so on. Wonder what he was thinking?"

"I wonder," said Franklin quietly.

There was a tap at the door, and Royce entered. The old butler bowed respectfully.

"Mr. Grant's compliments, sir, and would you be so good as to see him in the library."

Travers glanced at his watch. "Good Lord! Two in the morning! Both of us, Royce?"

"I believe so, sir. But I'll inquire, sir."

Travers jumped up and took the old fellow's arm.

"No you don't, my boy! You'll come down with us."

Franklin smiled as he followed them out. Cosmo Revere was dead. Cosmo Grant was waiting in the library. And his butler was being escorted down the great staircase. Two o'clock, indeed; and as the bellman might have added: "Two o'clock—and a wonderful morning."

THE END

CPSIA information can be obtained
at www.ICGtesting.com
Printed in the USA
LVOW10s2247170118
563083LV00019B/889/P